LOST AND FOUND

Lost and Found

By Rachel Biale

© Copyright 2022 Rachel Biale

ISBN 978-1-0879-7551-1

All rights reserved. No part of this publication may be reproduced, stored in a retrieval system, or transmitted in any form or by any means—electronic, mechanical, photocopy, recording, or any other—except for brief quotations in printed reviews, without the prior written permission of the author.

Cover photo by Nathan Dumlao.

Cover and book design by Skyler Kratofil.

Published by
Wildcat Books

LOST AND FOUND

Rachel Biale

Wildcat Books

In memory of my parents, who were on the *Atlantic*:
Chaim Korati (Tramer) and Anina Korati (Vohryzek)

Table of Contents

December 1944 . . . . *3*

Part I: October 1940 . . . . *7*
Part II: 1941. . . . . *187*
Part III: November 25, 1940. . . . . *217*
Part IV: November 26, 1940. . . . . *255*
Part V: April 1, 1941. . . . . *285*
Part VI: June 10, 1941 . . . . *307*
Part VII: November 1944 . . . . *367*
Part VIII: November 1944 . . . . *439*

AFTERWORD. *485*
*Historical Facts about Events
in the Novel.* *489*
Photographs and Illustrations *493*
ACKNOWLEDGMENTS. *501*

DECEMBER 1944

Was that a knock on the door? *Nein*, just a loose hinge. This new place is certainly a step up, but so many things still need repair. And the neighbors—noisy all day long. I'll get used to it; after all, we moved in less than a month ago.

Back to the dishes. Better finish quickly, before this water gets as frigid as the air in the apartment. Only the three plates and mismatched cutlery from breakfast still to scrub—a minute or two. Back to the rest of the list: laundry, electric company to contest the bill, the boy to the doctor for his cough. He gets sick so much more often than the older one did... The Asiatic climate? The local hygiene? Or reacting to something he senses in me—a vulnerability—since that day?

No! Go back to the list. Better that way. And take a deep breath to smooth that tightness in the chest. On the way home buy half a loaf of bread, two onions and chicken feet for soup. Vegetables, too. Not much in season now—potatoes and turnips. Carrots, if I'm lucky. That'll make a presentable dinner with last night's leftover chicken thigh. It's still four days until the new ration card for poultry; for meat—another two weeks. If prices are good, buy an orange for the three of us to share and candy the rinds with the bit of sugar you managed to save.

The last plate now—the water is already cold; see the circles of grease floating on the surface? Careful, it's my favorite. As always, turn it over to say hello to the silver imprint: crossed staffs bisecting "Rosen" and "thal," a crown hovering in the middle.

"The best of the best." I can hear Oma's exact cadence.

"*Nein*," Grandma Schiff's turn, "Meissen is the best. Rosenthal is second, but a very good second."

They could never let that rest, those two. And now I must repeat it each time I glance at the back of the plate? *Ach* . . . still, I do love this plate, even though it's second hand, maybe third. It took months for the tin can on the shelf by the door to fill with enough coins to buy it. It's quality china . . . you barely see the hairline crack.

The feel of the cold porcelain is precious. And the dignified Rosenthal crest, the only Rosen-anything to still hold onto . . . The fate of all the others—Rosenberg, Rosenwasser, Rosenbaum—shrouded in the darkness over Europe.

Stop! You must stop! Can't. Here comes the parade of names and faces. Herr Rosenberg the dentist, teeth so white they seemed made of fine china. Fraulein Rosenwasser next door, her summer hats so crowded with flowers and fruit one needn't go to the botanical gardens. And the Rosenbaum children from the end of the block—always so primly dressed I used to think their housekeeper ironed their clothes right onto their bodies. Stay here—this sunny picture of the shiny round faces. No. Here's the cascade of names and faces—like a bolt of fabric tumbling off the tailor's workbench: Mama and Papa, Oma and Opa, Alfred's parents, his brother Hans, Grandma Meissen (she never knew I secretly called her that). A lucky lady. Who else got to die in their own bed? And only three weeks after her husband had passed in hospital; didn't even have to face life as a widow.

Lucky lady? How can you even think this way? Don't! But now the boy's face—can't shut it out. Bite your lip to stop it. Look at something else—the window, the sink, the grey, slimy water. Back to the plate—and now set it down.

The plate makes a clink as it touches the stone counter. Good, that flicks the switch off, the boy's face gone now. But right after that clink—another sound—a low rattle from the door.

Quick—the cutlery, rinse and just put it down. *Ach* . . . alright, line the pieces up symmetrically and dry your hands. Yes—on the apron is fine. Such a simple thing, and yet, a triumph. I'm alive, a mother, a wife, I have a home. So lucky . . . again with the lucky? Yes! Yes, indeed! Lucky. And happy? Almost, but for that tear that cannot be mended.

Now to the door. Squeeze past the three chairs. Look at them—tucked in tightly, straight backs kissing the edges of the table. The air is so fresh today, and the trees hug the slopes of Mount Carmel in a more vivid green. The light rain overnight must have washed the dust off the leaves.

She presses her ear to the door and listens. Is someone breathing rapidly on the other side? You are imagining things. You do that, you know, imagine things. So, open the door already, you'll see there's nothing there and get back to the chores. But you never know. Could it be . . . ?

She turns the flimsy lock and presses down on the door handle. It wobbles before the latch catches and releases. She opens the door and gasps. Her hand flies up to grab the doorpost but her knees buckle. The yelp of a wounded animal leaps from her throat. She collapses in the doorway.

Part I: October 1940

Chapter 1

Gertie awoke in the dark. In the faint light of the lone weak bulb at the far end, the slender phosphorescent hands of her watch showed 4:20. A long wait until dawn. When her eyes adjusted, she made out the outlines of mounds everywhere—people sleeping two and three to a bunk. She could *certainly* smell them. Taking only small sips of air did nothing to hold back the stench. People sweated so much in the hot, dank space, the fetid odor permeated every thimbleful of air.

How long had they already been on the *Atlantic*? Ten, twelve days? Remember the first days on board? You thought you'd never adjust. First the heat, blasting into the hold under the deck as if there were no walls separating it from the furnaces. Then the dense burnt-coal air; how could anyone breathe? By now she actually longed for that sickly-sweet smell; it was more agreeable than this reek of humans.

Can you blame them? Bathing in seawater only once a week, the salty brine did little to clean you and less to diminish the odor of bodies soiled by diarrhea and vomit. It left your skin with a lacey crust of salt. Don't, she ordered herself, folding her fingers into fists to stifle the urge to scratch. Think about those who couldn't resist: their skin flared red and bled. Infections were rampant and medications scarce; the most effective ones, Gentian Violet and Sulfa, critically low. She'd kept close watch over her Emil and cut his fingernails nearly to the quick, so he wouldn't break his velvety skin when he scratched. But can you make a four-year old remember not to scratch? Better not to bathe him at all, she had decided.

Gertie lifted her head to look at the lump that was Emil and Alfred, nestled into one another a handbreadth away. She was lucky, in her unluckiness—she was so big, she had a bunk all to herself. Though the bunk was less than two feet wide, she had learned how to accommodate her belly by lying on her side with her legs arrow-straight. Alfred and Emil shared their bed with their two suitcases and rucksacks. Alfred contorted his tall frame in the shape of a half-opened folding chair. He was pencil-thin, so there was enough room for Emil to squeeze himself into the triangle Alfred made with his bent knees. He's kind of a giraffe, Alfred is, Gertie chuckled, and Emil—a bear cub. And me, a hippo, my huge belly nearly scraping the floor. Quite the menagerie.

Gertie's eyes trace Alfred's rectangular face. So gaunt! She shakes her head. His dark hair is thinning on top. Already? He's not even thirty-two. The worrying or the physical exertion? She rests her eyes longingly on the small cleft in his chin. It's just a lentil-size indentation, but it makes a perfect nest for her pinky. She liked to rest it there after they made love. And his unusually long earlobes: strange, even ugly to most people, certainly to women. Did women look at him that way? Even here on the boat—when he was up on the deck, and she trapped down here?

Whatever those earlobes were to other women, she loved them. She used to kiss each one and talk to it on nights they were amorous. A stirring in her pelvis seemed to come from hundreds of miles across the sea. She sighed. Will that ever come back? She closed her eyes to savor the sensation, but it left her and now all she felt was pressure in her bladder. Ach, she is going to have to go to the bathroom; not yet, but soon. At least at this hour there was no line.

Even without a line, going to the toilet was an ordeal. She was so heavy in her pregnancy that her belly swayed with its own rhythm. Standing and walking, she had to cradle her belly in her hands to keep it moving with the rest of her body.

"I look ridiculous," she'd complained to Bronia early in the journey. "Look at me! A bulging-bellied chimp with long arms hanging to the floor."

"Oh, Gertie, what do you care? It's too dark and crowded down here for anyone to notice you anyway."

"On that point, you are right. And there are other advantages; no one sees my matted hair, either." Gertie touched her hair, so thick with sea salt it stood on her head like a haphazard pile of twigs. When she closed her eyes, she could still see the soft swells of her blond mane; how it had made three graceful waves from the part at the top of her head to just above her shoulders.

"*Ach*," Gertie said, "what I would give for a hot shower, shampoo, and a clean towel."

"Would you settle for a mirror?" Bronia asked and fumbled among her things.

"A mirror?" Gertie touched her fingertips to her cheeks. "How long since you've seen rouge?" she whispered to them. "And you two, lipstick?" she ran her finger along her thin, elegantly etched lips.

"And to think, Bronia, how much time I spent every morning back home, fixing myself up."

"I'll bet . . ."

"Well, I had a reputation to maintain! And now look at me."

"I'm looking. I don't see . . ."

"You don't? Skin chafed by sea salt, lips cracked and peeling, eyebrows grown wild. It's a patch of weeds up there!"

"You are still beautiful, Gertie."

"*Danke*. You're lying, but you're a good friend."

Gertie glanced at her watch: 4:28. In the soothing silence around her all she heard were occasional snores and the faint lapping of the waves against the side of the boat. Of course, there was also the constant rumble of the turbines, but she had learned to tune that out. Try to hold it a bit longer, so Alfred can sleep a little more.

She closed her eyes, hoping to doze, but instead her mind took itself to the steps ahead of her. Three times a day she had to get herself up to the deck to the so-called toilets. At least there was one benefit to the water and food rationing, she told herself. She remembered the last month of pregnancy with Emil only vaguely, too far away in so many ways from her present reality, but she was sure the bathroom trips were much more frequent.

She had come to loathe the *Toilettereise*—the voyage to the toilet. First, she'd try to make herself a little more presentable, smoothing her hair with dampened palms or hiding it with a scarf, then pulling on her oversized blouse to cover her belly. It was as if she were inside a moving tent. Lucky that Mama had insisted on the blouse. Once dressed, she snaked her way between people and luggage, careful not to step on a hand or foot. Every horizontal surface was occupied, from the upper deck to the lower hold, their "cave." And the stairs were getting harder and harder. She had to rest every other rung. If no one was watching, she went up by hauling her behind up from step to step. It was actually faster, and she felt safer staying low to the ground.

Once she got up on deck people let her go to the front of the line, and she thanked them warmly. The toilets, a long plank with holes cantilevered over the edge of the boat, had sheets of rough fabric marking individual stalls, providing minimal privacy.

Just thinking about the revolting stench of toilets made the urge subside. Who knew your body would do that of its own accord? She lifted her belly to relieve the pressure on her bladder. No hope of sleep now, though. Worries chased one another as marbles roll down a narrow chute. Food and water severely rationed, medical supplies dwindling, typhus and dysentery rampant. Thank God they got typhus vaccinations back in Vienna, despite the unpleasant side effects. But dysentery you couldn't inoculate against. She could catch it from anyone—Alfred, Emil, her friends. How much longer before they get there? What if it's more than a week? Or two? An icy chill shot through her despite the heat.

Chapter 2

She had hoped when they first boarded the *Atlantic* that the baby would wait until they made land. "God forbid, Alfred, I should give birth here," she'd said the moment they settled down on their bunks. But as the promised week-long sail went past two weeks, it seemed more and more likely the baby would come at sea. Thank God, there were five doctors among the refugees on the boat. She had seen the "Mother and Baby Clinic" set up in the small cabin on the deck. Everyone called it *The Panama Room.* Alfred said it was because a Panamanian flag was painted on its flat roof—their rather pathetic attempt to hide their identity. They flew the Panama flag as well, hoping to appease both the Germans and British with their supposed neutrality. She chuckled every time she said it— *The Panama Room!* It sounded like an exotic dance lounge or a gentlemen's club.

Enough! She told herself. Tomorrow you'll try to organize the basic necessities: food, water, medical supplies, and a few things to swaddle and dress the newborn. She'd brought no baby clothes, never imagining she'd still be on the ship for the birth. So many delays . . . Their journey unrolled in her mind like a spool of silk ribbon.

They left Vienna in late May only to learn in Bratislava, the gathering point for the journey, that they would be detained there until "all the permits are in place."

"Welcome to the *Patronka*," the Czech Jews had called out when the Viennese Jews arrived. The Czechs had already been there since January, when the Danube froze over. They no longer noticed the acrid smell of old gunpowder, which still made her shudder with nausea.

"An old munitions factory, Alfred," she remembered saying, "it's no place for a pregnant woman!"

"We'll only be here for a few days, Gertie. You'll feel better on the open water of the river."

Two months later they finally boarded the *Schönbrunn*, an "old glory" Danube paddlewheel. The passengers cheered as if they were only a few hours away from their final destination. Not that it was going to be a pleasure ride. There were so many of them crammed onto the boat they would have to stand most of the time.

"This is the *Schönbrunn*?" Alfred called out. "*Sic transit gloria mundi!*" he shook his head theatrically as they stepped onto the deck. Emil was asleep on his right shoulder, exhausted by both the waiting and the excitement.

"*Ja*, certainly not what it was in its heyday," Gertie sighed. "Not to mention that we have to sail under a Nazi flag."

"Yes," Alfred snorted, "the God-dammed swastika—"

"Alfred!" Gertie grabbed his arm, her face blanched with fear.

"It's all right, Gertie. At least we can say what we want now."

"I guess so," she let her breath out slowly. "But the boy . . . "

"Still sleeping," Alfred assured her.

They shuffled forward, carried by the river of people deeper into the boat. Gertie scanned the cabin as they entered. You could barely see the walls for the people jammed inside it. She looked up at the ceiling: the ornately carved wood was chipped, the painted moldings peeling, the chandeliers all replaced by bare bulbs on twisted wires.

"No glory left, indeed," Gertie said, her voice dark with foreboding.

They'd found a corner where Alfred stacked their two suitcases on top of each other. Gertie lowered herself down slowly, careful not to crush the luggage and Alfred carefully transferred Emil into her arms, hoping not to wake him.

"And to think, Alfred, how we used to stand on the dock back home and eye the passengers embarking onto the *Schönbrunn* with such envy."

"Sure, only the *crème de la crème* could afford a journey on the *Schönbrunn*. As a matter of fact, my parents did go on it soon after it was launched. To celebrate their wedding anniversary; their 10th, I think. Just before the war."

"Just before the war?"

"The other war, Gertie."

"Well, that was different."

Emil squirmed and sat up in Gertie's lap and his eyes grew bigger as he looked around.

"Why are there so many people, Mama?"

"That's what they call 'standing room only,'" Gertie said, more to Alfred than to Emil, then thought the better of it and said in a cheerier tone, "we are lucky, Emilein. At least we can sit down. Papa fixed it for us."

"Thank you, Papa!"

Alfred smiled and tousled Emil's hair, but Gertie could see he was still back in the "Olden Days."

"The famously palatial *Schönbrunn* turned into a huge tin of sardines at the hand of the damned Nazis," Alfred said, loud enough for everyone around him to hear. "It smells that way, too. A can of sardines left open too long."

"It does smell. *Pfui!*" Emil tried to join their conversation.

"Not much *Schön* left in this *Schönschiff*..." Alfred shook his head.

"Not much. But the Schönbrunn Palace hasn't fared any better. They turned half of it into military barracks."

"Much of Vienna is like that."

"Ja . . . it seems so far away now."

The trip down the Danube should have taken six days, but it stretched to almost a month. At every border crossing and every river port they had to appease and bribe the local officials to gain permission for passage. They passed Czechoslovakia, Hungary (at least Budapest was a beautiful sight), Yugoslavia, and finally a long stretch along the Romanian—Bulgarian border.

Don't think about it! Gertie warned herself. But it was too late. The image was etched on the inside of her eyelids. She had been standing at the edge of the *Schönbrunn's* deck with Emil by her side, holding more and more tightly onto the banister and his hand. They stared at a dilapidated boat with the strange name *Pentcho*, right in the middle of the Danube, listing to the left. They got close enough to call out to the big crowd on its deck.

A jumble of voices until a young, muscular man yelled: "Quiet, everyone! Let one person speak from each boat." A tall man with a wild beard stepped forward on the *Pentcho*. They had been stranded for weeks. The engine broke down and neither the Romanians nor the Bulgarians would let them dock at their shore. They were "enemy aliens" with no permits to stop in either country. By now they had run out of food and water, not to mention medical supplies. People on board had started dying.

Everyone started throwing things to the stranded boat; half-loaves of bread, sardine tins, water canteens. Gertie wanted to spirit Emil away from the scene, but it was too late.

"Why are people throwing things at them, Mama?"

"They want to give them some good things to eat," she said biting her lip to hold in her rage. "They are Jews, like us. Their boat is making a stop and . . . " Her voice trailed off. *Get him away!* she ordered herself. "Speaking of good things to eat," she forced out a cheerful voice, "I have some . . . candy for you!"

"Candy?"

"Yes, I saved two pieces. Let's go inside and get them."

"Look, Emil!" She said inside the cabin, "we have the whole place to ourselves! We can stretch out and lie down on the bunks. How nice is that?"

"Nice. I'm tired of sleeping sitting on Papa's lap. It's so crowded in here, Mama!"

"It is. Emilein. But not right now!" She lay down and pulled Emil over to snuggle next to her.

"It's going to be crowded for a few more nights, *Liebling*, so let's enjoy this now." Emil curved himself around her belly.

"Your belly is getting huge, Mama. Soon there won't be any room for me."

"Don't worry, Emilein, soon we'll get to Palestina and the baby will be born and we'll have big beds and our own house and plenty of room . . . " She stopped herself from getting carried away.

"That will be good, Mama. But now it's candy and story time," Emil said and laid his head on her chest. She handed him two small toffees.

"One after the other, alright? And suck them slowly to make them last longer."

"I know, Mama." He popped one into his mouth and cupped the other in his fist, clutching it to his heart.

Gertie began a new adventure story, this one about a pioneer settlement in Palestine. Emil was mesmerized and seemed to forget about the scene outside. As she had hoped, with the comfort of lying horizontally with legs fully stretched out, he soon fell fast asleep.

A loud bang startled her and she realized she had dozed off too. She grabbed hold of Emil.

"What's that, Mama?" he cried out.

Another two loud pops followed.

Emil buried his head in her chest.

She didn't know. They sounded like rifle shots but she wasn't going to say that to Emil.

"Oh, Emilku, don't worry. Sometimes when they rev up the engine it makes a loud bang like that. It probably means we'll be moving fast soon. But for now, put your head down and sleep a little more, while we can still stretch out." Emil scooted back down from Gertie's embrace. She stroked his hair and, in a minute, he was asleep again.

"Thank God he's asleep," Alfred said as he entered the cabin.

"Yes, he needed a good sleep."

"No, more than that—" he sat down on Gertie's bunk, visibly shaking. He gripped his fingers in such tight fists she could see the whites of his knucklebones.

"Up above . . . ""

"Yes," Gertie interrupted him, "what were those bangs?"

"Gunshots."

"Gunshots?"

"Yes. Several people from the *Pentcho* jumped into the water to swim ashore; some to the Romanian side, others to Bulgaria. All of them . . . "

He shook his head.

"All of them what, Alfred?"

"Shot by guards standing on the shore."

He covered his face with his hands as his body trembled. Gertie said nothing. She gently laid her open palm on his back.

CHAPTER 3

When they finally disembarked from the *Schönbrunn* in Tulcea, Romania, they saw hundreds of people lined up on the dock, amid a clutter of luggage.

"Look at all the people, Mama! Are they coming onto our boat now?"

"Maybe, Emil," Gertie said then turned to Alfred: "Are these Germans going back up the Danube?"

"Must be. Eichmann's devilish plan is working," Alfred said *sotto voce*, cocking his head towards Emil.

"They don't look that different from us, Alfred."

"Mama, there are boys like me," Emil tugged on her sleeve, "can we play together?"

"No Emil, they're leaving soon."

"Not fair," he whined.

"Not much different, with their suitcases and little children in their arms," Gertie continued her conversation with Alfred. "But they must be happier about their journey."

"Some are, but, as a matter of fact, many are being repatriated against their will."

"I'm sorry, Alfred, but I cannot feel sorry for them."

"Who does?"

"Look, there," Gertie pointed, "a pregnant woman. About as far along as me."

"Yes, Gertie, but *they* are going home!"

"So are we, Alfred!"

"After a fashion . . . after a fashion . . . " Alfred muttered.

How the wait in Tulcea dragged on! Day after day, promise after promise—camped in rough-hewn wooden warehouses, former granaries, with wheat kernels still stuck between the boards. "The ships are coming any minute now," the organizers reassured them. Meanwhile, the Romanian guards did everything they could to keep them docile. Those who had a little money to spare or a bottle of liquor got extra food and a few Romanian cigarettes, which they broke into four pieces and shared with their friends. The brand was . . . yes, "National." Everything had patriotic names. How she hated it. Non-smokers themselves, Gertie and Alfred traded their meager possessions for food. The memory of the dry salami made her tongue cleave to the roof of her mouth; an unpleasant sensation, yet a sweet memory. Would be nice, right now . . . Hungarian salami on the *Atlantic* . . . she laughed at herself, but her stomach was already growling. "Shush, you," she patted it.

She looked at her watch again: twenty-three minutes had passed. "Five more and then we go," she whispered, "patience."

Her mind back in Tulcea: how long had they been stuck —really imprisoned—there? Eight, nine days? Longer? But finally, the ships did arrive at the port, three of them.

"These they call ships?" Gertie had muttered when they'd lined up on the dock, ordered at dawn to get ready to board. "They look like patched-together floating crates!"

"Shush . . . " Alfred nodded towards Emil.

"You see the ships, my boy?" he said, mustering as much as cheer as he could.

"Yes, Papa. I see three."

"One of these ships will be ours."

"The only ship-like thing about these is their names," Gertie said, her voice low but harsh. *Milos, Pacific* and *Atlantic*.

"Are these sea-worthy, Alfred? How will these wrecks hold all of us?"

"Shh... don't frighten him."

Alfred hoisted the rucksack on his back, then Emil on his hip. He picked up one of their suitcases.

"You take the other one, Gertie. Let's go."

The long line of passengers stood in stunned silence. They shuffled forward a step or two at a time. Gertie dragged the suitcase along the rough pavement. Finally, they climbed aboard the gangplank and entered the *Atlantic*.

"As a matter of fact," Alfred picked up where he'd left off, trying to sound confident, "the man from the Jewish Agency was very proud of these boats."

"He was?"

"They bought them for a song. Fixed them up in two weeks."

"Fixed them up? Ours looks more like they barely kept it from sinking."

Alfred shrugged. Emil's head was now lolling on his shoulder. Gertie wondered if somehow Emil knew he must shield himself from the situation. No, she corrected herself: *You! You must shield him.*

They filed onto the deck. "But really, Alfred, isn't it much too small? We are more than 1,600, no?"

"We'll have to manage."

"Yes, we will," Gertie said between clenched teeth. "Does it have family cabins?" she asked, determined not to complain anymore.

"Cabins? I doubt that. The man said it was a cargo boat."

Gertie pressed her lips together. What was the point of her protests? Europe was locking its jaws around them. They were lucky to escape.

Hanging onto Alfred's arm, Gertie followed as he navigated the steps leading down to a barn-like hold. Row after row of narrow rough-hewn wood bunks lined each side, most already occupied. They moved through the aisle towards an area lit by three bare bulbs.

"Don't touch the wires!" a woman shouted at them from her bunk. "You'll get a bad shock."

"Thank you," Gertie said.

"My name is Bronia," the woman introduced herself.

"From Vienna? Am I right?" Gertie said.

"Indeed."

"We are, too. Gertie, Alfred, and our boy, Emil."

"Just past my bed there are two open bunks," Bronia said with the welcoming gesture of a stylish hostess. "Looks like you'll need one for yourself and one for your husband and son."

That was just two weeks ago, Gertie marveled now.

They had sailed side by side with the *Milos* and *Pacific* across the Black Sea and into the Dardanelles.

"The Three Musketeers," Alfred announced.

"Indeed," Gertie said, "but let's hope there are no sword fights ahead of us."

But once the boats passed into the Sea of Marmara, they lost sight of each other.

"*Arrivederci*," Alfred said, "we'll see you all in Haifa."

Chapter 4

Now she couldn't hold it any longer. She woke Alfred and they set out. Since no one else was awake, she hauled herself up the stairs on her bottom.

"Not bad, hah?" Gertie said at the top.

"Amazing how fast you do it this way."

"Ja. Not elegant, but very efficient."

Up on the silent deck Gertie breathed in the fresh air. Delicious. Despite everything, there were moments of bliss out in the open air. They passed someone sitting up wrapped in a blanket, then skirted around a young couple deep in hushed lovemaking. They pretended not to notice. Alfred pushed Gertie from behind as she climbed up to the toilet stall. She sank into the relief of letting go. The waning, still nearly full moon, lit their way back.

Near the stern, they heard voices, then silence, then a splash.

"*Yitgadal veyitkadash shmeh rabbah.*"

"What is it, Alfred?"

"*Kaddish.*"

"Someone died?" she whispered. "Did you know?"

"Yes."

"You didn't tell me!"

"It's like that almost every day, Gertlein. Typhus, dysentery..."

"You didn't tell me."

"I didn't want to upset you. You have enough to worry about."

"And they always do this at night?"

"Not usually. For most of them we have a proper ceremony with *Kaddish* and a eulogy before they are pushed overboard. Maybe this person had no one."

Back at her bunk, Gertie was so exhausted she fell asleep right away. When she opened her eyes, Emil and Alfred were already dressed and heading up to the deck. Only Bronia stayed back "to keep you company." But Gertie knew it was also to keep an eye on her. Everyone was nervous about the baby coming.

"Don't worry for a minute," Bronia said after Gertie listed all the things she would need if she gave birth on the ship. "I will ask the other mothers for a few things. There are several babies who must have outgrown their newborn outfits by now. I'll go on a hunting expedition."

"*Danke,*" Gertie smiled, "and some cotton towels or sheets—to make diapers."

"*Natürlich!* I know that, Gertie, even if I don't have a baby myself. My friend, Elsa, you've met her . . . "

"Of course, you two are inseparable."

"Well, she's investigated the diaper question already. The mothers tear tattered clothing people give them into strips and boil them with Lysol. Then they hang them on a clothesline up on the deck."

"Oh, yes, I've seen them flapping in the wind up there. That's at least one thing this blazing Mediterranean sun is good for. Bleaches better than any chemical."

"Elsa is a treasure," Gertie said. What a comical sight it had been the first time she saw them arm in arm. Elsa was as tall as Gertie, but much thinner. Her willowy frame was crowned by sleek black hair, that stood at attention by each cheek. Her mouth seemed set in permanent disapproval, perfectly fitting her role as the purveyor of gossip; putting the haughty in their place, tzek-tzeking at the dandies. Every inch of Elsa's height went into Bronia's width, every sharp angle into roundedness, all topped by curly brown hair. A beauty spot right above the left corner of Bronia's lip made it seem as if she was always smiling.

"Time for breakfast," Bronia said, looking at her watch.

"Go ahead. Try to find Alfred in line and remind him to bring me my rations."

"Or course. And if he is too busy, I'll bring it myself. But don't get your hopes up about either the size or the taste."

"I haven't for a while," Gertie said and went back to sleep.

Alfred's footsteps hammering on the steps woke her. He had Emil with him and her breakfast. She took the food and asked him to inquire at the Panama Room about food and supplies. "I'll keep an eye on Emil. He'll stay with me and rest."

"I don't need to rest!" Emil protested, "I want to be on deck with Papa."

"I'm sure, *Liebling*," Gertie tousled his curls, "but let's practice your numbers now. When we get to Palestina you'll go to kindergarten, and what if the children there already know how to count to a hundred?"

"I do too!"

"So, show me," Gertie said and made room for Emil on her bunk. She felt a tinge of guilt for using the practice as an excuse to savor the last few days, maybe only hours, with him as her only child. You're allowed, she told herself.

"I'll go up, then," Alfred said and took the steps two at a time. Gertie wrapped her arm around Emil and pulled him closer. After he recited his numbers, she began to tell him a story. Soon Emil fell asleep.

―――

Alfred returned with a forced smile.

"Well?" she whispered so as not to wake Emil, "do they have anything there?"

"As a matter of fact, they've stocked a small cache of food." He counted off on his fingers: "Eight tins of sardines. Three jars of jam—the ersatz kind."

"No matter."

"Six packages of dry biscuits, probably moldy by now."

"We can scrape off the mold. And?" She looked at him expectantly.

"Where was I?" Alfred put up his fourth finger: "powdered milk—they said enough for ten days, but I don't know if I believe them. They saw I was worried."

"Ja, I imagine so," Gertie sighed. Then she brightened up. "I also managed to save some food from our rations. And one water canteen. For the critical moment."

"How?" Alfred's raised his eyebrows.

"My friends. Mostly Bronia and Elsa, but others too. They've been bringing me little portions of their daily rations. Whatever can be dried, I save. The rest I eat and a few bites I give to Emil. He's hungry all the time now. You too, Alfred, I know."

Alfred took her hands. He leaned down and kissed each finger, then laid his palm on her stomach. "Huge, isn't it?"

"I'm better nourished than anyone else on board," Gertie said. "But you . . . " she shook her head, "you're getting so thin."

"A little bit. But I'm only eating for myself. And I don't need to keep my strength the way you do."

She worried about him, about the hard physical work: carrying huge pots of soup for dinner, stacking heavy sacks, coiling cables, heaving garbage overboard. He certainly wasn't used to this. His clothes hung on his frame like the scarecrows she had loved spotting in the fields on her family's trips to the countryside. She winced at the twine he cinched tighter and tighter to hold up his pants. But, she admitted to herself, she did like the new ropes of muscle in his arms.

In the afternoon Elsa and Bronia came back with two small packages. They laid the items out on Gertie's bunk.

"Hardly anyone has anything to spare," Bronia said, "but they were still generous. Look at this one," she picked up a light blue bonnet and twirled it around her finger. It's so small! Gertie thought, barely big enough to fit over a man's fist.

"Would you look at it?" Bronia exclaimed. She pointed to the tiny embroidery stitches around the rim, green arrow-shaped leaves and yellow daisies, each with a bright red center made with a tight knot.

"A grandmother's handiwork," Gertie said with a smile, but then her face darkened. "Ach . . . a world without grandmas."

"And these," Elsa said counting out ten cloth diapers, three baby outfits, and two receiving blankets, "enough for three days."

"And these soft rags for your bleeding," Bronia showed Gertie a small bundle.

"After three days we'd better get to land or we'll have to start laundering," Elsa concluded.

"I'll wash if we have to," Bronia said, "but I vote for getting there."

"Don't we all," Gertie said and began stacking everything into a neat pile.

CHAPTER 5

"Alfred, Alfred! Wake up. *Bitte.*"
"*Was ist?*"
"Wake up, Liebling. I need you."
"What's wrong?"
"Nothing. I mean . . . I have to throw up. The baby —it's pressing my stomach so much now."
"Coming!" Alfred sat up and swung his legs over Emil so as not to wake him. Gertie waited as he pulled on his sweater. He helped her to her feet and they maneuvered to the stairs.
"The usual method?"
"My method," Gertie sat down and one by one, hoisted her bottom up the stairs.
On deck they navigated slowly between sleeping passengers and their possessions.
"What's that noise?" Alfred said and looked over his shoulder.
"Don't bother with that now, Alfred. I really need to get to the railing!"
"Yes, Liebling. Hold my hand."
"What a relief," Gertie announced after her meager dinner went overboard.
But now she heard it too.
"What is it, Alfred? Can you tell?"

"Shush! It's coming from the other side of the boat."

"Yes, heavy scratching sounds."

"But now, that's something else, Gertie, like something fell into the water."

"Not another dead person, I hope."

"I don't think so, didn't hear of any deaths today."

Another plop.

"Stay here!" Alfred commanded. "I'll go see what it is."

"No, Alfred. I'm coming, too. I'm not that slow."

"Alright, but quiet! Be careful—who knows what it is?"

They circled to the front of the boat, tiptoeing as if they were thieves. Louder now, they could hear muffled voices. "What in the world is going on?" Gertie whispered. Reaching the other side of the boat, they saw a large sack fly overboard, landing in the water with a big plop. Then several smaller ones, plip, plip, plip.

Alfred held Gertie back with his hand, then inched along the railing. Gertie waited, counting her breaths. He returned, panting. "*Schrecklich!* It's dreadful! The sailors are throwing the coal overboard! Some in sacks, some with shovels."

"What on earth for?"

"God knows, Gertie. I must wake people —the Leadership. You go back to where we passed someone who was awake. Tell him to find the right people on deck. Then we'll meet right back here. I'll come back as soon as I can." Alfred raced off. Gertie gripped the railing and advanced towards the man they had seen sitting up. She heard Alfred's shouts ricocheting back from the steps to the lower deck, then other voices, shouting orders. Mayhem down below, she thought, and for once I am not stuck there.

Two much louder plops came from the stern of the boat. Leaning over the railing Gertie spotted two lifeboats in the water crowded with sailors rowing as fast as they could. What on earth? Where and why are they going?

Alfred returned, gasping for air. "The Greek sailors... they threw the coal overboard."

"And escaped!" Gertie pointed to the lifeboats.

"Yes, most of them did. But we captured the captain and locked him in his berth."

"Why? Why did they do this?" Gertie demanded.

"People are saying they got a message by Morse Code that Italy just declared war on Greece."

"What's that got to do with us?"

"The sailors panicked. They don't want to be caught up in the war. Maybe they were afraid they would be charged with transporting illegal passengers."

Gertie shook her head. "I can't say I'm surprised. All of them looked to me like nothing more than small-time criminals."

"That I have to agree with, but..."

"But what?"

"It's not irrational. There must be Italian warships not far from here at war with their country. But why throw the coal overboard?" Alfred was shouting now. "I fail to see how that helps them! What is the logic in that?"

"Alfred, they are criminals, not philosophers, their glorious Plato and Aristotle notwithstanding."

"Still, it makes no sense. That is not rational."

Gertie sighed.

Alfred took her arm. "Let's go down. Then I'll find out what's going to happen."

Gertie shot one last glance at the sea. The lifeboats were slipping away. They looked no bigger than toys now, and the sailors' silhouettes were outlined by the first light of dawn.

Back at her bunk Gertie found Emil in Bronia's arms. She gasped. He must have woken up from the shouting and been terrified. *Thank God for Bronia!*

"Mama, here you are finally!" Emil rushed into her arms. "Bronia said you would come right back, but you didn't! "

"I'm sorry, Emilein. I had to go to the . . . hmmm, the ladies room. But I'm back now."

"I didn't cry, Mama," he said, but his lower lip was trembling.

"I'm proud of you. Bronia, you are a Godsend!"

"Merely in the right place at the right time."

"Always in the right place, Bronia. *Natürlich*, as you would say," Gertie flashed her a thankful smile.

"Mama, why is everyone shouting?"

What should she say? How could she make the situation seem safe?

"The sailors decided to go home now," she said, raising one eyebrow towards Bronia, "because . . . we are close to their country, Greece. So now the boat is all ours."

"Hooray!" Emil spread his arms out. "The boat is ours!"

Gertie winked at Bronia, turned up her palms and shrugged.

"Maybe later you can go to the captain's helm," Bronia jumped in.

"What's captinelm?"

"Captain's - helm," Bronia spaced out the two words, "it's where the captain of the ship has a big wheel, like in a car, but bigger. With this wheel he steers the boat, going this way or that," she illustrated, her hands grabbing a phantom wheel.

"Can I touch the big wheel?" Emil beamed.

"Maybe. But not right now."

Bronia bent down to Emil's eye level. "For now, let's make a boat from paper." She scooped him up from Gertie's lap and took him to her bunk.

"I know how to do it!" Emil called out.

Gertie shot Bronia a smile of thanks. She settled herself on her bunk, exhausted by both the physical effort and her despair. Soon Alfred came running down the stairs. She'd never seen him like this. His grey eyes were narrow and fierce; his mouth a mere pencil line.

She inclined her head towards Emil and Bronia to caution him. He nodded and began speaking in his schoolboy English.

"It is now only very small mountain of coal. What exactly stands next to the furnace. Not more." Under his rage she sensed a panic he was struggling to hide.

"What we are to do now?" she asked, using English as well.

"There is no choosing. We must to sail the boat by our own selfs."

CHAPTER 6

In the Haifa harbor that morning the waves shimmered in the light of the rising sun, just a handbreadth above the hazy outline of the distant Galilee hills. Moussa slowly rowed his boat towards the dock, savoring the sound of the oars plopping into the water in an otherwise silent world. Thank Allah for the lucky morning! Less than an hour on the sea and his five buckets were filled to the brim with fish. "Come to me my friends," he had called out as the boat bobbed up and down. This habit of talking to the fish . . . embarrassing, but so what? No one heard him out at sea. Especially not today, with no other fishermen in sight.

He sidled up to the dock and jumped out, wrapping the rough rope around the weathered wooden post. He made a double knot, pulling the rope so tight it flayed a bit of skin off the palm of his hand, but he was used to that. With the seawater bathing his hands as he handled the fish, it would heal quickly, to be forgotten by tomorrow. He pulled the buckets out of the boat, and straightened his back. The edge of a dark brown robe scraping the pavement beside him caught his eye. Aha, one of the men from the Monastery. More luck. They're good customers, buying at least four or five good-sized fish.

He looked up at the man; he'd seen him before. He didn't know his name but remembered his gentle voice, his thick curls and the brave silky-fine hair sprouting on his chin, desperate to become a beard. Unconsciously, Moussa touched his own dark curly hair, cropped shorter but, otherwise, not much different. But his beard, should he let it grow, would be dense and full. The thought pumped him up a tad, making up for the awkwardness of standing face to face with the very tall monk. Next to him, Moussa appeared like a teenage boy just at the start of his growth spurt, despite his thirty-two years.

"*Marhabah*, my friend," Moussa greeted the man cheerily, "you are the one from the monastery who speaks Arabic, right?"

"Yes, I'm Lucas. I speak —so-so."

"Yes, Lucas. I am Moussa."

"Yes, I remember. But I don't know about 'Speak Arabic.' I'm learning."

"No, you're speaking! You speak well."

"*Shukran*," Lucas said and couldn't help the pride in his voice, "it's my job at the monastery."

"Your job?"

"You could say so. I'm good with languages, so the Abbot wants me to learn Arabic, to help our monastery with Arab merchants, visitors."

"I see —that's a good job. You are lucky. And today you are lucky, too, I have a lot of fish and you're the first customer."

"I am first?"

"Yes, first. Look out at the water; do you see any fisherman? No. They're all still out at sea."

The monk shaded his eyes and scanned the harbor.

"You're right. But what are the boats over there?" he pointed at two cargo ships, anchored about a hundred yards from the dock. He read their names out loud: "*Milos, Pacific.*"

"Those boats?" Moussa pointed, too.

"Yes, those boats. They look very crowded with things —I can't make out what they are."

"No," Moussa shook his head, "not things, people."

"People? You mean, the boats are so crowded with people?"

"Yes, many, many people, all crammed in."

"But these boats - they don't look like - how do you say *passanger* . . . people. What kind of people?"

"*Yahoud*. Hundreds, maybe a thousand. They came two days ago. Yesterday I got a job from an English policeman to take boxes and boxes to the boats. Food, medicine. I had to go three times."

"Now I understand," Lucas nodded, "that's how you know they are Jews? You spoke to them?"

"Not a word. The policeman said to me 'Keep your mouth shut.' He paid a good sum, so I kept my mouth shut." Moussa shrugged. "But I kept my eyes open. I saw what there was to see. I know they were *Yahoud*. So many. They looked terrible: no food, no water, clothes dirty."

Lucas remained silent, lost in thought, his eyes still on the boats. Moussa held up the biggest bucket, crammed full with fish snapping their tails.

"You want to buy fish now?"

"Yes, yes . . . but the Jews, what you think? From where did they come? Why are they there on the boats and not at the dock?"

"Escaping from the war, I think. They looked very bad. And the smell . . . " Moussa pressed his nostrils between finger and thumb, "it smelled like many are sick."

"Aha, you mean they are mmm . . . what's the Arabic word? *Réfugiés* —from Europe?"

"Yes - how you say: ref- u-gi?"

"Ré-fu-giés," Lucas repeated. "But why they still on the boats? Those boats don't look so safe."

"Why? That's not for me to ask," Moussa shrugged, but then added, "but I hear my friends talking."

"What they say?"

"Everyone knows the English won't let any more Jews come here, to *Falestin*."

"I see. They don't have papers to come here."

"I don't know think so. Anyway, we don't want more *Yahoud* here. There's no room for them."

"Well," Lucas began but thought the better of it. He'd have to tell Father Pierre about this. A humanitarian crisis. Perhaps the Abbot could intervene for mercy.

Lucas turned to the bucket of fish. "I'll take the biggest five fish you have."

Excellent sale! Moussa congratulated himself and lifted the fish out one by one, placing them on the white towel in Lucas' basket. Lucas folded the edges of the towel over the fish, tucking them in as if for a sweet night's sleep. He pulled out a fistful of coins from his pouch and opened his palm, letting Moussa pick out the needed payment. He'd bought from Moussa several times before and counted on him to be fair.

The fish seemed to jump out of Moussa's buckets into other customers' hands and soon Moussa sold out. He headed home, resolved to at least recite a prayer of thanks in addition to the regular *salat* ritual. It was a short walk through the busy main street to the quiet alley to his small house, a slipshod job, built onto the side of a larger one owned by uncle Abu Zbeid. His uncle had been the first one in the family to leave the village for the city. When, after the third miscarriage, Moussa and Youssra moved to Haifa to escape the scrutiny of everyone in the village, Abu Zbeid took them under his wings.

As a small boy Moussa had been a little afraid of him. His belly protruded too far. His thick moustache, which he twirled endlessly, looked so pointy at the edges, Moussa was afraid it would poke him. And the bushy eyebrows, threatening to meet in the middle of the bridge of his nose any minute, seemed to warn Moussa to stay away.

"Uncle, you should weed around those eyebrows a little," Moussa said when he was about ten. Abu Zbeid pinched his cheek. "You and your weeding!" Moussa was already famous in the family for his love of weeding. As young as five, his father already crowed about how good the boy was out in the field. "This little squirt can already tell the weeds from the plants. He'll outpace anyone on a row of wheat or watermelon."

Moussa actually missed those weeds. In Haifa, after several months of fishing he caught himself talking to the fish just as he had to the weeds he pulled out, apologizing for taking them out of their homes where they were so cozy. It was Abu Zbeid who had taught him to fish and bought him his small boat. It had been a very big outlay, way beyond Moussa's means. "*Inshallah*, if God wills it," Abu Zbeid had said, "you'll pay me back before my son needs to buy his own boat." Moussa was proud that he did, making one payment already in his first year as a fisherman. He paid back a fifth of the loan just before the start of Ramadan each year. He'd made the final payment that summer.

Chapter 7

Arriving at home, Moussa was still rolling the thoughts about his uncle's generosity in his mind, the way his own father rolled his amber prayer beads along his palm with his thumb. On the wall across from the door hung a mirror in a wooden frame with mother-of-pearl inlay, an extravagant gift from Abu Zbeid when they came to Haifa. "This is what makes a home," he had said when he presented it with great flair. Moussa felt embarrassed for the frayed prayer rug— the only other object hanging on the wall - and for the rest of their furnishings. The mirror made them look so drab and worn. Only Youssra's embroidery had brought a bit of color and the grace into their home.

But Youssra's creations resided with them only a day or two before she handed the finished work over to the woman who'd commissioned it. Moussa could see how each time Youssra endured a moment of grief separating from her handiwork. Once he even caught her crying. "The embroideries . . . " she confessed, "so hard to part from them. They are like my children . . . " She left the sentence hanging in mid-air. Moussa flinched and sucked his lips in. The tips of his moustache pricked the raw cracks in his lower lip. Those words had stung. He glanced at Youssra, shoulders crowded into her chest, head bent down. Yes, those words had shot an arrow of pain through her, too. In silence, they waited for the barbed knot in the air between them to dissipate.

Youssra broke the tense silence: "Some tea, Moussa?" He nodded, pushing the stinger deep into the corner where it always resided. It mostly rose up when he was alone on his boat or walking in the neighborhood with Youssra. They both knew full well that everyone here pitied them, just as it had been in the village. They hated the looks of sympathy. Youssra always said that behind them was gloating, especially by men Moussa's age. Many already had four or five children. He denied it every time, but he felt it too. Worse, he thought he could sense the neighbors' suspicions that their childlessness was punishment for some hidden transgression.

Sometimes, in his heart of hearts, Moussa wondered too. But what could possibly justify such punishment? He had always been careful to wrong no one and never deviated from the Quran's teachings. Youssra was the same. Back in their village, if you made one step off the righteous path, it was bound to come out. Everyone knew everyone else's business. Here in town, there was less scrutiny, but this community had its gossips too, and more than one self-appointed sin-sniffer.

Could Allah punish him for his thoughts, not actual deeds? The only ones he was ashamed of had come after the miscarriages. Or punish Youssra? But for what? When had she ever done anything that might offend Allah, or any person for that matter? Could it be that she was just too small? Her waist was not much thicker than what he could encircle in his hand, her chest easily mistaken for flat under the dresses with embroidered fronts. Were it not for her thick braid, she'd look more like a teenage boy than a fertile woman. But he knew of plenty of young women as diminutive as Youssra who were mothers, both back in the village and in town. Could Allah have been displeased with Youssra's bitter grief after each miscarriage, and the way she then drew herself inward? Often Moussa felt as if a cold wind blew from her body to his. Her lips pursed, she rocked back and forth, shaking her head, "*Kullu min Allah* —everything is from God."

He knew this seeming acceptance was just to cover over her

grief; he could tell from her detachment when she cooked and her defeated, hunched back when she embroidered.

He saw her pain, but did she see his? Understood how humiliated he felt in front of his friends and neighbors? In truth, he'd had momentary thoughts about a way out, taking another wife. He even had —hoping Youssra didn't notice —glanced at her younger sister and nieces.

But what if he did take a second wife and she lost the babies, too? After all, there had been several miscarriages in his family, not Youssra's. His mother had lost a baby girl before he was born and two between him and his sister Maryam. Two more after that, until she died from complications of the last birth. He was thirteen at the time. More than his own grief, he remembered his father clenching his fists and mumbling angrily. He was a boy, so no one explained the intricacies of pregnancy and birth, but the feeling of danger freezing his gut stayed with him.

"The curse," as he came to think of it, seemed to continue down the family line when Maryam miscarried twins, then a boy. Finally, she held onto one pregnancy in the hospital in Nazareth. She only has one child. Thank Allah —for the grandparents' sake—a boy.

Could it be something he carried in his blood? Somehow the male seed in his family fought with woman's seed? That even though in daily life both he and his father were blessed with peaceful homes, their seed couldn't adhere to the woman's? They could till the soil in their fields, but not their wives, as the Quran commanded? Maybe they failed the Quran's instruction for men to rule over their women. Did he and his father acquiesce too readily to their wives' wishes?

"*Salam habibiti*," Moussa greeted Youssra, who was hunched over her sewing.

"So early, *habibi?*"

"Very lucky day today, excellent catch!" Moussa grinned and

smoothed down his moustache in satisfaction. He showed Youssra the leather pouch bulging with coins.

"I had a good catch today, too," she said, lifting her embroidery to show him, a tiny dress. *Who has enough money to order an embroidered dress for a newborn?* Moussa wondered. *It'll only be good for two months, maybe less.* He swallowed his words; however he might ask the question would hurt Youssra.

"This one looks like you'll get very well paid for!" He came up with the right thing to say.

"Yes, indeed - a very rich lady. Ghazal, the wife of Abbas."

"Abbas the textile merchant? Your name is getting out, going higher and higher in society."

"It's good for business," Youssra forced herself to say, but then had to add, "but it's only money."

Moussa would have no idea what price she paid for this commission. The door hadn't banged shut behind Ghazal when Youssra's tears poured out. "Envy is your biggest enemy," her mother's words reverberated in her head, as they had so many times before. She was no more than eight when her mother had first said that to her, in the soft voice she reserved for important lessons. Youssra shook her head.

"What?" Moussa said, a layer of worry she rarely heard under his words.

"Nothing, nothing."

"I know, Youssra, some people have all the luck in the world. They seem to grab it from the rest of us."

Youssra put the fabric on her lap, smoothing it out. She pulled her basket of threads closer in to search for yellow and green.

Moussa emptied his pouch on the plain copper plate set atop a tripod, which served as their table. The coins clinked and sang as they hit the metal.

"*Alhamdulillah!*" Youssra exclaimed. She put aside her sewing and methodically picked out the half dozen largest coins.

"Put those away in our savings."

"Good idea."

Moussa opened his palm and Youssra dropped the coins in one by one. In the corner of the room, he crouched and extricated a small leather pouch from under a loose tile.

Chapter 8

At the bus stop, Lucas watched the morning fog recede from Haifa Bay, as if someone were rolling up the long sleeves of a flannel shirt. The bus arrived and Lucas entered, the basket wedged against his body leading the way. He took the only bench left open with two spots, and set the basket at his side. The bus drove down the main street and soon turned and began to climb up the slope of the Carmel.

Two stops later a young woman in a pencil-thin burgundy skirt got on. A little boy climbing up behind her called out, "Faster, *imma*! Go faster!"

"I'm trying," she said and, now on the top step, extended a hand to help him scramble up. She paid the driver and then looked around, surveying the crowded bus, with passengers already standing in the aisle. Lucas slid towards the window, placing the basket on his knees. The woman smiled and sat next to him, lifting the boy into her lap. She thanked him in Hebrew-accented English. Lucas bowed his head and smiled at the boy. That's safe, he assured himself, just keep your gaze away from her. Don't look at her pretty face, or that flattering skirt. He squirmed, suddenly remembering how he'd blush back home, when Thérèse from the next farm over greeted him at Sunday services. How tongue-tied he'd get . . . and how he'd stare at her two braids bobbing up and down as she threw herself into singing the hymns. "Lead us not into temptation" he silently chanted the *Pater Noster*.

The boy noticed Lucas smiling at him and puffed out his chest. "Look at the boat!" he said in Hebrew, pointing to the embroidered boat on the bib of his overalls. Lucas bent towards the boy to look. The boat was quite marvelous. Shiny-white long stiches outlined its side, circular ones marked black portholes, and three trim grey chimneys rose in the middle, each with three tiny puffs of smoke, no bigger than the head of a pin.

"*Mlechet machshevet*," Lucas used his well-practiced biblical Hebrew for beautifully-wrought work.

"What did he say?" the boy asked.

"That it's beautiful!" the mother answered, then turned to Lucas. "His grandmother made it for him. He is so proud of it. He got it a week ago and he has refused to wear any other clothes."

"Little boys, they love the boats," Lucas surprised himself by his ease talking to her. Then came the warning to himself: don't indulge yourself talking to her, using the boy as an excuse.

"Yes, they do," she smiled.

"But even more they love the trains."

"Yes!" she agreed and gave Lucas a quizzical look that he knew meant, "How would you know?"

"I had one when I am small boy, like he is," Lucas explained in halting English, forgiving himself the small lie, eliding the coveting with the having. She smiled and kissed the top of the boy's head. Lucas let his eyes rest for a moment on the boy. That was safe —as long as he kept his thoughts away from how attractive his mother was.

The boy made the motions of a boat rocking on waves with his chubby hands. Something that had been tied in knot after knot and crammed into a narrow crevice inside Lucas loosened. He knew; it was what he had glimpsed in his own father in precious moments with his children. He took a gulp of air, as if to swallow the wave of longing back down. "You would make a wonderful father," his mother's words rose up of their accord. "Please, don't," he begged the feelings. He wished he could cross himself to ward them off, but that would be taken the wrong way here, on this bus, next to this woman. He closed his eyes and visualized the gesture: forehead, heart, left shoulder, right.

It didn't work, so he admonished himself: "He had no son. You won't need one either. You have Him. But!" his gut wrenched. In desperation, he slipped his hand under the towel, sliding it between the fish. The slimy cold scales made him shudder in disgust. That worked.

And now, the bus was approaching his stop.

"Pardon," he said to the woman, "my stop soon." She stood up with her boy and let his pass into the aisle.

"Good day," she said and smiled at Lucas and the boy waved goodbye. Lucas smiled and waved back, then navigated towards the door.

Off the bus, he hoisted the basket higher up and wedged it against his hip. From here, it was a short hike on a paved path to the monastery. The basket was heavy enough to make him feel pleased with "his catch," not so heavy as to be a burden. He marched up the hill, letting the cool morning air dry his perspiration.

He entered the kitchen and Brother Matthieu turned from his steaming pots, calling out: "Ecce homo, *qui tollit piscatum mundi.*" It was his standard greeting, substituting *piscatum*—fish, for *peccata*—sins. It had taken a while before Lucas discovered the nooks and crannies in the monastery —the kitchen, woodshop, shoemaker's —where the monks let themselves have a good laugh. It was always the older, veteran monks who allowed themselves the levity, sure to first glance around to make sure Father Pierre was out of earshot.

Lucas slid the heavy basket onto the knife-scarred butcher block and raised the edges of the towel. Brother Matthieu bent over the glistening fish and took two sniffs. "Very fresh," he exclaimed and smiled at Lucas, "and nice size!" He pulled the fish out of the basket and lined them up on the chopping block.

"Like soldiers at roll call," Lucas said.

"Or monks at choir," Matthieu responded and they shared a chuckle.

"Off to that very choir now —that's my lot," Lucas announced and hurried out of the kitchen. He crossed the central courtyard, now warming in the sun, and ducked into the dark chapel, deeply inhaling the incense-infused air.

After lunch, Lucas had asked Father Pierre for an audience. The Abbot invited him to come to the library during the afternoon meditation. Now, pushing open the library's heavy carved-wood door, Lucas took a moment to let his eyes adjust to the dimly-lit room. Father Pierre was at his desk, leaning over a large open book.

"Yes, my son."

The Abbot kept his finger on the page to save his place. Lucas described the two boats he had seen at the port and what Moussa had said about the refugees crowded on board. Father Pierre kept nodding, but the corners of his eyes narrowed, lending him a skeptical look. "You must do something, Father," Lucas' voice quivered, "it's horrible."

The Abbot remained silent. Finally, he tucked a bookmark into the crevice between the open pages and spoke: "We are between Scylla and Charybdis, here ... in our Holy Land."

"Pardon?"

"Oh, you country boys; I always forget you learned nothing of the classics before entering the monastery," Father Pierre sighed.

"My apologies," Lucas bowed.

"It's as it says in the Prophet Amos, about the Day of the Lord. This you should know:

"As when a man runs away from a lion

And is attacked by a bear;
And he leans his hand on the wall
And is bitten by a serpent."

"I understand," Lucas bowed.

"Both sides—the Arabs and the Jews—are suspicious of us. In fact, many of them probably hate us. Tilt towards Ishmael more than towards Isaac, or the other way around, and we invite attacks; and perhaps not just verbal ones."

"But . . . "

"Listen," Father Pierre cut Lucas off, "on top of that," he pointed his long bony finger up, "we must 'Render unto Caesar' as our Lord has wisely taught us. We cannot go against the policies of the British authorities."

"Of-f-f c-c-course. But the suffering?"

"Indeed, the suffering," Father Pierre muttered. "We will mention them in prayers for the next two weeks—until All Saints Day."

"Prayers . . . ?" Lucas mumbled.

Father Pierre turned his piercing gaze towards him. "And I'll see about an act of charity, perhaps some supplies for the boats—blankets, medicine, and free copies of the Psalms."

Chapter 9

Alfred woke Gertie from an unsettled sleep. He sat on the edge of her bunk and took her hand.

"Emil went with Bronia for what Bronia calls the 'Boat Patrol.' She says it makes him feel important."

"Thank God for Bronia," Gertie said.

"So, we have a moment to speak freely, Gertie." She sat up. This was going to be a grim conversation.

Alfred told her that with no coal and no crew, everyone had been at a loss about what to do, until two men, one from Prague and the other from Danzig, had stepped forward.

"They don't really know anything about piloting a boat, but they are engineers."

"So are you, Liebling."

"Yes, Gertlein, but they are much more experienced."

She raised an eyebrow.

"As a matter of fact, the Danzig man worked on several projects in the Danzig port."

"So at least he has been next to some boats . . . "

"Gertie!"

"Sorry," she apologized. The situation was certainly not Alfred's fault. "At least we have a plan," she tried to sound reassured.

"Ja. We have a plan," Alfred said as he laced and unlaced his fingers.

"How much longer, do you think, Alfred, until we get there?"

"No one knows that. The truth is, no one has any idea where we are." Alfred spoke as if his throat were filled with pebbles. "We do have the captain," he tried to sound more upbeat. "He should know, but they found him in his cabin dead drunk."

"Maybe once he sobers up?"

"We hope so. At least now we know it's not enough to lock him in; you have to lock the liquor out."

Gertie forced a smile at Alfred before he headed up the stairs, and she went back to sleep.

She awoke and looked at her watch. God! Three hours had passed!

Her eyes darted from side to side. There's Emil, curled up into a ball on the bunk, his nose wedged against his stuffed donkey. *Everything's fine*, she told herself, but then realized the women in the neighboring bunks were talking very loudly, too agitated to keep their voices down.

"What is it? What's going on?" Gertie asked.

"The last of the coal has been used up," Bronia said.

"The last of the coal . . . " Gertie repeated. Slowly the words sank in.

"So now what, Bronia?"

"The engineers and the Leadership decided we would feed the furnaces with wood."

"The Leadership? What's that?"

"Sorry, I forget that you are stuck down here and don't really know what's going on upstairs. It's eight men, six from the Czech Youth Movement and one each from Vienna and Danzig, plus the two engineers. They have taken command of the boat."

"After the sailors absconded?"

"Well, before that, really," Bronia reclaimed her place. "Before this, they organized the lines for the toilets and the distribution of food and water. Also, cleanups, but those failed. It's so crowded there's no room to move people out of the way in order to clean."

"But Bronia, what wood? From where?"

"They are going to dismantle the deck and the cabins. And all the furniture."

Just then, four men with small axes came down the stairs and started hacking the bunks to pieces. Others broke the planks in half over their knees. A couple of the men had wrapped their hands with rags. Bronia rummaged through her rucksack and handed them an old kerchief and two socks with torn heels. A young, tan-faced man who seemed to oversee the work came over to Gertie.

"We'll leave your bunk for you. At least for now."

"Danke, that's very considerate."

All afternoon Gertie's ears reverberated with the cracking of wood. She had sent Bronia and Elsa up with Emil to look around after his nap. "They are cutting deck boards, breaking down bunks, pulling off wood paneling and throwing tables and chairs into the furnace," Alfred reported when he brought her the rations. "Even a piano was fed to the fire." They needed fuel, not music. The boat was eating itself.

Toward evening the boat quieted down. Alfred came down. "Don't worry, Emil is still with Bronia. The engineers worry about how much wood we have. They decided to run the furnaces only half the day. The rest of the time the boat will float."

"Float?"

"On momentum. Hopefully eastward, in the right direction."

"God help us," Gertie said under her breath.

"Ja, if only we believed in him," Alfred answered. "The religious people from Danzig are holding a special prayer service."

"Are you going?"

"No, of course not. Siegfried and I are trying to work out the direction of the prevailing winds."

If anyone could calm Alfred, Gertie knew it was Siegfried, his close friend from engineering school. They seemed so much alike in both personality and appearance that people sometimes confused them one for the other. Same body frame, slight stoop, wire-rimmed glasses always sliding forward on a beak of a nose. But Siegfried had neatly parted sleek hair and a thin well-groomed moustache. Alfred was always disheveled, his hair mussed and glasses smudged with fingerprints.

Chapter 10

The next morning Gertie watched as two young men in sweaty undershirts chopped the stairs to the deck in half. She was going to be a prisoner now. It would be too dangerous for her to try to climb the half-stairs. Alfred brought her a small enamel basin. "Whenever possible," he put his hand on her shoulder, "use this. Wait until there's no one around . . . if you can. I'll hang a sheet across the bunk." He cleared his throat. She could see the blush on his cheeks. He pushed the basin halfway under the bunk with his foot.

"Danke," she patted his hand.

"And try to keep Emil with you down here. It's too dangerous upstairs: broken boards, sawed-off banisters, holes in the floor."

"Of course," Gertie said, thinking that having Emil with her would protect her more than him from the grinding boredom and gnawing anxiety.

She and Bronia passed several hours with Emil, telling stories and playing games. But he was wound up like a toy train engine waiting to be released. When Alfred came to check on her later in the day, she told him to take Emil along.

"He is going stir-crazy down here."

"I can see that. And you, too, I'm sure."

"Find something safe for him to do on the deck. Some way he can feel he's helping."

"You're right," Alfred said. "Come Emil, come with Papa now."

"Keep a really, really close eye on him! Don't let go of his hand!" She had to say it, though she knew full well she could trust Alfred to keep him safe.

"I will, Gertie. Nothing will happen to him. He is perfectly safe with me!"

She nodded and pursed her lips.

Gertie turned her face away to hide her tears. She pulled her hands into taut fists at her chest.

Alfred touched her shoulder, then took Emil's hand and together they hurried up the half-steps.

Gertie tried to make herself stop worrying. She knew that everyone on board loved playing with Emil and looked out for him. He cheered them up with his innocence, always asking, "Can you see land? Are we near Palatschinka yet?"

Before, in Vienna, Emil had misunderstood when they talked about "Palestina" and started calling it "Palatschinka." Gertie and Alfred let him imagine he was going to the land of his favorite food. Oh, did he love palatschinkas! Her mother spoiled him with a stack of the pancakes made fresh every Sunday, rolled tight with different fruit fillings.

"See, Gertlein? See how he eats?" Mama would say. "You were never a good eater. Now I get my reward."

Gertie and Alfred had hoped that Emil's fantasy of 'The Land of Palatschinkas' would ease the departure from home and the harsh conditions on the journey. Once they got there, who knew what it would be like? Certainly not easy; surely nothing like Vienna, even if she could find the ingredients to make him palatschinkas.

On the boat, too, people humored Emil and asked what it would be like in Palatschinka. With a look of expertise on his beaming face he would explain: "You eat palatschinkas every day. For breakfast, lunch and dinner. And they have donkeys there!" He would pull out the donkey they had bought at *Kober*, his favorite toy store in Vienna.

"Like my donkey? His name is '*Esel mein Gesell*,' because he's my best friend, even though he is a donkey."

Emil would squeeze the donkey to his chest and sink his nose into the soft velvet and then come to Gertie for one of her "Esel Went to Palestine" stories. Caressing the spots on the donkey where the originally thick, lustrous velvet had been she'd whisper to herself: "Ach, if only half my stories come true." Would it be safe in Palestine? Had they merely exchanged one dangerous world for another?

CHAPTER 11

Gertie was startled awake. The baby! This is not just kicking. She opened her eyes and saw Alfred perched on the edge of her bunk.

"The baby will be coming very soon, Alfred. I can tell."

"It will come when it comes," Alfred put his hand on her belly. He looked around at the ripped-up bunks and shrugged. "We are as ready as can be."

Alfred promised to check on her frequently. He woke Emil and they went back up the half-stairs to the deck. Soon Elsa and Bronia came clomping down the half-steps.

Elsa plunked herself down next to Bronia and launched right in: "Wait till you hear this! Do you know Artur Kolenov?"

"The older guy from Vienna who always wears shorts," Bronia explained. "Tries to pass as half his age. You've seen him. His bunk is at the very end."

"I know who you mean," Gertie cheered up, "the one with the ugly knees."

"Well, yes, that's mostly what you would see at your eye level," Bronia chuckled.

"That's him," Elsa said. "And everyone's noticed his ugly knees, Bronia, not just Gertie. But he compensates for them with his perfectly combed pompadour."

"He carries a comb in his shirt pocket, day and night," Bronia exclaimed.

"So, who is he with?" Gertie pressed.

"Zdenka!"

"Our Zdenka from Vienna?"

"No, not her. The Zdenka from Prague."

"Natürlich," Bronia smirked, "you think ours would even look in his direction?"

"I don't believe it!" Gertie exclaimed, "that Prague one is half his age and twice his height!"

"All the better," Elsa said, "probably from up there she doesn't see his knees."

Gertie laughed so hard her belly shook as though it were a huge mound of pudding. But soon the heaves of laughter turned into wrenching anxiety. She turned to face the wall and nurse her worries alone. Bronia and Elsa whispered to each other and went upstairs.

"We'll be back soon," Bronia called out from the top half-step, "get some sleep."

Chapter 12

Gertie tried to stretch out her legs and release the spasms and cramps. She remembered these from her pregnancy with Emil, but then they had woken her up from sleep in her soft bed under a fluffy down blanket. That bed . . . as soft as a cloud. "Ach . . . " she moaned, but then she made herself face the inevitable: she was going to give birth on this haplessly drifting boat. They would never make land before the baby came.

She was lucky it was not her first birth. How could you stand this if it were your first time? And how lucky that Emil was such a little *mensch*, so outgoing and mature for his age. When they'd named him after the character in Erich Kastner's book *Emil and the Detectives*, they'd hoped he'd live up to the name. And so far, he had. He was clever and courageous, taking all their troubles as a great adventure. He almost never complained.

He was just a year old on their last trip down the Danube, in July of '37. Before everything. They'd stood at the side of the boat, Emil in her arms, and watched the turbulent plume of water trailing behind them. The river and its green banks were as beautiful as ever, but the darkness lurked. Like all their friends in Vienna, they were already anxious as they whispered among themselves about what Hitler might do next.

"Mark my words," Alfred said as he leaned over the railing, "it won't be long before he comes here. Every tyrant wants a victory parade in his home town."

"This is *not* his home town!" Gertie spat the words.

"To him it is. He became a man here."

"A man?" Gertie snorted, "more like a monster."

By the next summer, after the *Anschluss*, Jews were no longer permitted to take such trips. The Anschluss... the word ricocheted inside her head. Vienna, March 13, 1938. They had bitten their nails and trembled, along with all of the city's Jews, while it seemed their Christian neighbors averted their eyes. Alfred wanted to go out to the street to find a public phone to call their parents, but Gertie stopped him: "It's much too dangerous."

She allowed Alfred to go early the next morning. "Stay in back alleys, away from the main streets."

"Yes," he said and buried his wallet deep inside his jacket. "I'll go check on my parents first. Then I'll go to your parents. It's the most direct route."

"Yes, of course, and your parents are older. They'll be more terrified."

Alfred clasped her hand in thanks. He put on his wool coat and gave her a forced smile as he opened the door.

"Be careful!" they said in unison.

She could not fathom how she'd manage to pass the hours until Alfred returned. Carve the worries out of your mind, like you are slicing them off with a scalpel. She kept busy with Emil, letting his giggles fill her ears, as best she could. She made him tiny sandwiches with decorations from cheese, radishes and parsley: funny faces and little flowers. Then she settled him down to sleep.

I should have gone, she said to herself the instant Emil fell asleep. With my hair and my cheekbones and my nose, I could pass. And it would probably be safer for a woman; they wouldn't attack a woman. Accost and insult, maybe, but not assault. But maybe they would? Ach, the old rules were useless. And Alfred would never have agreed.

"Thank God you're here!" Gertie ran to Alfred when he finally returned. She wrapped her arms around him and squeezed hard. His body was rigid and his eyes were wide with a wild look. He opened his mouth but no words came out.

"What, Alfred?" she grabbed his sleeve. "My parents? Yours?"

"Both . . . all right. Very frightened, but safe."

"*Gott sei dank*!" Gertie called out as tears filled her eyes. She slumped, as if the air which held her body aloft had been let out.

"B-b-b-b . . . but, on the way back . . . " Alfred tossed his head sideways as if to shake something off.

"What happened?"

"In the street . . . " he began but his voice broke. She waited.

"With toothbrushes . . . "

"Toothbrushes? What are you talking about, Alfred?"

"They are making people scrub the pavement with toothbrushes."

"What? What people?"

"Jews. Anyone they catch," Alfred said. "Businessmen in their suits, professors, doctors, rabbis, too. I saw Professor Hirsch from the architecture faculty."

"*Gott im Himmel*," Gertie's hand flew up to her mouth.

"And then . . . Sieg . . . "

"Sieg?"

Alfred bit his upper lip, trying to hold himself together.

"Sieg? They made them do the *Sieg Heil*?" Gertie tried to help him say it.

"No. Not that. Siegfried."

"Your Siegfried? Oh, no!"

"At the far end of the line. On his knees. He didn't have his glasses."

"But he can't see a step ahead of him without his glasses!"

"Then I saw them, Gertie. On the cobblestones. Shattered. I stepped towards him and called out his name, but someone yanked me back and slapped his big hand across my mouth."

"Who?"

"I don't know him. A big, muscular man. He yelled at me: 'Don't! You can't help him. You're only putting one more of us in danger!'"

"He was right."

"I know. But I should have helped Sieg . . . "

"You couldn't. Now sit down," she said and guided him to a chair. She brought him a glass of water. He sipped slowly, closing his eyes.

"But why, Alfred?" Gertie said after a long silence.

"They made them scrub off slogans for the Plebiscite."

"Chancellor Schuschnigg's? The vote for a free Austria?"

"Yes, if that's what 'Free and German; Independent and United' means. But regardless, that world is gone now, Gertie. Gone. Maybe forever."

She said nothing, just tried to align her breathing with Alfred's to help him calm down.

"Thank God you got away," Gertie finally said. She cupped his trembling hands in hers and rested them on her chest.

The memory made her shudder. Up to that moment, Alfred's fortitude and trust in rationality had kept her steady. The atmosphere in Vienna was already tense when Emil was born in 1936. They sensed the trepidation behind people's polite smiles and handshakes when they brought him home. "Things will get better," they kept saying to each other. How could they have been so blind to what was coming?

But we've escaped! Think about the future, she instructed herself. Soon—so soon—the baby would come. Then they'd arrive in Palestine. Then . . . Everything will work out just fine, she told herself. She had never liked the phrase 'count your blessings.' Such a cliché. But this time she did just that: Alfred, Emil, the baby about to be born, the hope of a new life. Really, she was lucky. Lucky compared to almost everyone else: her mother and father, her grandparents, Alfred's parents, the rest of their family, their friends. How were they all surviving, trapped by war in their beloved, terror-struck Vienna?

"You won't believe this!" Bronia shouted to Gertie from the top of the steps.

"What?" Gertie sat up.

"Fried fish for dinner!"

"Fish? From where?"

"From here!" Bronia said triumphantly.

"Here?" Gertie couldn't follow, but her mouth was already watering.

"Well, Gertie, we are, after all, at sea, where fish live."

"Very funny. But how?"

"So, this afternoon, suddenly a swarm; or do you say a flock if they are flying? Anyway, these flying fish passed right over the boat. A lot of them landed on the deck. The Danzig people said it was a miracle. They brought out the Torah scroll."

"A miracle," Gertie blurted out. "Did any loaves of bread multiply?"

"Gertie, you don't have to be so sarcastic all the time!"

"Sorry," Gertie's face reddened. "I'm terrible that way. Ask Alfred."

"Here you go," Bronia handed her a plate and patted her arm.

"Danke," Gertie said, as she took the first bite.

CHAPTER 13

At the same twilight hour, Lucas sat staring at the verse in Chapter 9. He had begun reading it during individual meditation. When they were free to choose their own passages to study, he tended to favor his namesake. Reading the words of Luke made him feel a hint of a familial embrace, coupled with a lesson in humility: how high he had to aspire to follow in the apostle's footsteps.

He had read rather mechanically until this point. But now he was stuck. Something in the story of the multiplying loaves and the fish to feed the multitude of five thousand was troubling him. He closed his eyes and tried to let thoughts flow freely, waiting for the one that hit the nail on the head to come of its own accord.

It arrived with a thud: miracles. Or rather, the lack of miracles. The bitter disappointment. When he had departed Pamiers for Stella Maris, the grief of leaving his family was almost assuaged by his excited expectation that in the Holy Land he will behold real miracles. He was sure those still happened when his own feet traversed the paths that the Lord had walked. But five years later, much wiser at twenty, he knew his wide-eyed search for miracles when he first arrived was childish naiveté.

He returned to the verse to contemplate the allegorical meaning of the miracle, but all that came to him were the meals Brother Matthieu made with the fish he'd brought from the port. Matthieu didn't feed five thousand, but he did perform his own small miracle of the fish, making delicious meals that lasted for three days. The memory of Matthieu's fish soup catapulted Lucas back to his mother's kitchen and to his family seated around the heavy oak dining table. His parents' silent chewing and his siblings' antics. He missed his little brother Philippe the most. He touched the soft center of his open palm to his lips: how perfectly it had fit over Philippe's small shoulder! How often had he cupped the little bony mound, drawing Philipp close to his chest, to comfort him when he cried or hug him when they laughed together?

Philippe hung by Lucas' side, as though he were his little puppy. They shared bites of his mother's tastiest dishes and made-up games. Philippe's favorites were "sack of flour" rides on Lucas's back, and pillow fights.

"You are such a good big brother, Lucas," his mother would marvel. "Your older brothers certainly didn't treat you like this!"

She almost always added, "You would make a wonderful father," but once Lucas joined the monastery, she forced her lips shut.

Chapter 14

Earlier that same morning, Moussa had walked home with fish he had caught that morning glistening in his basket. Half-way down the alley leading to his house he stopped at a narrow door, its green paint peeling and scratched to the bare wood at the bottom. He glanced left and right to make sure no one was in the alleyway, then knocked twice, halted briefly and knocked twice again.

"Who is there?" a woman's voice called from behind the door.

"It's me, Moussa. I have some fish for you."

"*Alhamdulillah*," the woman opened the door. A baby was perched on her hip and a young boy appeared in the gap and pushed the door open wider. He was holding the hand of a toddler. Moussa lifted two fish from his basket.

"Go get a pot, Mahmoud."

The boy turned around and dragged his little brother behind him.

"How are you getting by, Amala?" Moussa asked in a hushed voice, careful to make sure no one heard him. He couldn't help a pang in his heart every time he said her name. It seemed like a cruel joke that she should be named for hope. Everyone now referred to her not by her name, Amala, but as "the *armala*," the widow.

"I don't know how," she sighed. "Right after Abu Mahmoud was killed in the bombing everyone brought food, clothes for the children, even some money. People said he was a martyr, a hero of the nation. *Eh*... he was just in the wrong place. That's a fisherman's luck—at the port to catch fish, instead he catches a bomb."

Moussa was shocked by the barrage pouring out of Amala's mouth. He'd never exchanged so many words with her, or with any other woman, except Youssra. All the more so now, during her *Iddah*, her confinement after her husband died. One was not supposed to converse with a widow.

But every word was like a hammer blow. It could have been him that day at the port in late July. He remembered he'd gone to sleep the night before with a crushing headache and runny nose. "What terrible luck," he had said to Youssra, "who gets a cold in the middle of summer?" In the morning his body felt as if he'd been lying under a pile of rocks all night. He stayed in bed and Youssra plied him with glass after glass of mint tea. He fell in and out of fitful sleep, then was nearly thrown out of bed by a thunderous explosion. In minutes the room had filled with the noxious smell of burning fuel.

"The whole port is a black cloud," Youssra yelled from the window.

"Another bombing. The Italians or maybe Hitler?"

"A plague on both of them," Youssra hissed.

Moussa felt queasy as the memories flooded him, but Amala didn't notice. "After Ramadan," she continued "everyone started a new season. No place left in their hearts for me and my three boys. If not for your fish every few days, we would have to beg. A woman with three boys and no husband! My oldest, Mahmoud, not even five. I can't send him out to the street!"

"Three boys under five," Moussa shook his head. *How can one person be so lucky and so unlucky at the same time?*

"I am sorry," Amala said softly. "I didn't mean to... I know how you pray for a child. And Youssra."

Moussa lowered his eyes and clenched his teeth. "A long time," he said, "ten years." An uncomfortable silence hung between them.

"Your Youssra," Amala finally said, "I know how she suffers. But she is an angel. The only one who helps me with the children. When you are out fishing, she comes here to help. Before Abu Mahmoud was killed and I could go out, I would come to her - to your house. She would take care of the boys while I went to buy food, or wash laundry. A few times she even said to me, 'Just go home and sit quietly for an hour. That's what you need the most.'"

"She is very kind. I know that," Moussa said.

"More than kind. And how she manages with the children even though she has none of her own! She has a magic touch," Amala gushed, but quickly stopped herself.

"These two fish are very nice, Moussa, I can stretch them to three days."

"Then I'll bring more," Moussa said. He turned to go but Amala whispered: "Moussa, I have been thinking." He turned around to face her again. There was a strange glint in her eye that made him uneasy.

"What?"

"If there is something I am good at, it's producing sons. You can see that."

Moussa nodded.

"But Youssra," she began, but halted. Moussa nodded again. There was no need for words.

"Well, in two weeks my Iddah ends. I can remarry. We could try—"

"Try?" Moussa felt his mind trying to catch up with Amala's.

"Yes, so we are sure. Before you decide."

"Sure?"

"That I'm pregnant. Before you take me."

"Take you?"

"As a second wife. Moussa, don't you understand what I am saying?"

"I, I understand. But you are moving so fast. You have a whole plan worked out?"

"I am desperate. And I have plenty of time to think."

"I understand. But how would you know? Doesn't it take a few months?"

"I always know right away. I mean—I did with the three until now."

"How?"

"How to say it?" Amala hesitated, "my . . . ahm - when we were girls we called them pomegranates - you know what I mean." She shot a glance at her bosom. "They begin to talk to me."

Moussa blushed. What could he say to this? Certainly, this was not an appropriate conversation for a man and a woman. He couldn't even imagine having it with Youssra. But deep inside he felt a tight knot loosen.

"Think about it, please, Moussa. It's what the Prophet did for the widows of his followers."

Moussa could not find the right words for an answer.

"You have some time to think about it, but not a lot. I can't go on like this for much longer."

Moussa nodded and turned to leave.

"Thank you for the fish, Moussa," she called after him.

Walking the short distance home, Moussa's feet rose in slow motion while his mind raced. "It's what the Prophet did for the widows of his followers," he repeated over and over. But how could he ever do that to Youssra? *Think!* he ordered himself, *think it through.* But his mind was a drunken see-saw of "yes" and "no." He'd better wait for the turmoil to pass, at least until tomorrow, pass the time with Youssra, Amala sealed deep inside him. He told himself he must ignore the invisible thread, thin as the strands of a spider's web, now stretching between his heart and Amala's.

He trudged home. Something inside him opened and closed; contracted and expanded in synch with his footsteps.

CHAPTER 15

Strong contractions woke Gertie before dawn. She looked at her watch: 5:10. She brought it to her cheek. Her parents had spent weeks searching for the perfect wristwatch as a wedding gift. She traced the delicate *Jugendstil* design of palm fronds around the oval face with her finger. She had worn it at her wedding and had not taken it off since then. Eight years ago; a life begun with Alfred in a world that was now gone. He had just graduated near the top of his class as an engineer. Sure to land a good job. They'd found a nice apartment in the Döbling neighborhood, north of the center of town.

Another contraction, and then a lull when she let her mind return to Vienna. How thrilled she'd been that they would be near the Vienna Woods. She always imagined being a mother and walking in the woods with her children, looking for mushrooms or wild blueberries. She would carry a large wicker basket and the children would each have a little one, woven from fresh strips of birch bark...

The next contraction yanked her back. She took a sip of water from the canteen that was stowed against the wall at the corner of the bunk. Another contraction. They were coming every ten minutes now, gradually getting more intense.

"Fifteen more minutes," she whispered to herself, "just a little more sleep for Alfred." He was so exhausted. At night he fell on the rough sack mattress so heavily and so fast, it seemed he was already asleep before he laid his head down.

In the quiet valleys between contractions, she returned to the late spring days before their departure from Vienna, the repeated discussions: was it wise for her, four months pregnant, to undergo the dangerous journey? And with no papers to enter Palestine legally? How could they risk going? But how could they gamble on staying?

Contrary to the way things usually went, it was her mother who was decisive and pushed for it. "Go," she'd said, "the second half of your pregnancy went easily last time. You'll get there in four or five weeks and you are due in November, plenty of time to find a good doctor. There are German and Austrian-trained doctors there." They knew of several who had gone, like their pediatrician, Herr Doktor Friedrich Klein. He'd left Vienna in August of '38, right after the decree prohibiting Jewish doctors from practicing medicine.

"Of course," Gertie said, "we took Emil to him for the first two years. We were sorry to lose him. He had a great way with small children."

"He did. And now we know how wise he was, too," her mother said. "The doctors who stayed here barely make it by treating Jews in secret. Look at Alfred's father."

"I know . . . though he does still see some of his old Christian patients. They bring him to their houses late at night through the back door."

"Really? That's so dangerous!"

"Yes, for both sides. But he's one of the best in Vienna."

Gertie's father asked her again about what precisely the emissary from Palestine said about the arrangements.

"The Jewish organizations working behind the scenes have boats already chartered for a trip from the Black Sea to Palestine," Gertie quoted word-for-word. "We just need to get there—to the Romanian coast of the Black Sea—and board the boats."

"But how is this possible? How can you leave here? How will you sail down the Danube?" her father shook his head as he pressed her.

It had been kept rather vague, she admitted. But from bits and pieces of information passed secretly from one person to the next, she and Alfred had worked it out. The Jewish organizations had made a deal with Adolf Eichmann, the mastermind behind the forced emigration of Jews.

"A deal with Eichmann?" her father looked nauseated.

"I know. Horrid! But it's to save Jews. The Nazis are repatriating Germans from all over - the Balkans and Czechoslovakia—and transporting them by river boats to Germany."

"Yes, I know about that; *'Heim ins Reich* - Home to the Reich' they call it."

"So, the . . . " Gertie continued, sour saliva flooding her mouth, "the boats have to sail back down the Danube for the next load of passengers. The deal is: Jewish refugees are allowed on those down-river trips."

"But why?" her father seemed unable—or unwilling—to grasp it.

"Well, first of all, the Jewish organizations are financing the whole operation and then some. Also, it fits into Eichmann's plan to get Jews to leave Europe voluntarily."

Her father looked as though he were going to vomit. "*Schwein, Schwein*," he muttered.

Gertie took his hand and plaited her fingers through his. "I know, Papa. It's horrible. But it's a way out." Her father looked up at her and she saw the question in his eyes.

"I'm so sorry, Papa. They only want young people. Those who can go and be *chalutzim*, you know, pioneers, to build the land of Palestine." Her father squeezed her hand and grimaced. "And with your heart, Papa, it's not possible."

"I understand," he untangled his fingers and caressed her hand. "And Oma and Opa. We can't leave them here."

"The trip will be hard, I'm sure, but not too long. 'Three or four weeks,' they said," she tried to break the ring of fear that held them tightly together. "And the Jewish community in Palestine," she quoted the Zionist Movement representative, "is working every minute to see to it that we manage to get into Palestine."

She saw her father's face as if he were right in front of her. He'd made one more plea for them to wait. "We have submitted applications for visas to America, Argentina, and Uruguay. Something will come through and we could stay together. I've even heard that the Chinese Consul is giving out visas."

"Yes, we heard too. Ho Feng, or maybe Ho Sheng. But to Shanghai? Is that realistic?"

"Shanghai, yes. Of course, it's far . . . " Papa's words trailed off without the definitive tones Gertie was accustomed to. But she and Alfred had already decided they must go.

Chapter 16

It was the very first incident in the street that she always remembered when she thought of their decision to leave Vienna, although much greater horrors followed. Maybe because she came to see that it was the very beginning of the end. She and Alfred were walking arm in arm along the Ringstrasse, huddling into each other against the cold. It was January 18, 1938. She remembered everything: the date, the sharp wind, the excitement lightening her steps.

Alfred was talking about the play they were going to see. She recalled how, the moment before the incident, she was getting impatient with his pedantic recitation of its historical background. *Nothing unusual there.*

A young man, sharply dressed in a cadet's uniform, passed them on the right.

"*Judeschwein,*" he yelled and spat in Alfred's face. "Get your filthy hands off our women!"

Gertie felt Alfred yank his arm away, ready to strike the man. She pulled it back to her side. "Don't, Alfred! You'll get us in trouble." Before Alfred had a chance to say a word, the man was gone.

"I would have . . . " Alfred seethed.

"I know. But what for?" she asked, knowing perfectly well it would have been to uphold his honor, and hers.

"It's my fault, Alfred," she tried to soften the blow, as Alfred unfolded his white handkerchief and wiped his face.

"Your fault?"

"My hair—how blond it is. And my features, too. I could pass for Aryan."

"You could," Alfred said bitterly, "maybe one day that will come in handy. Certainly, more easily than for me. My nose betrays me."

"That nose was the first thing that attracted me to you, Liebling," Gertie tried to lift his dark mood. "And that high forehead," she added. "Mama always said a high forehead was a sign of intelligence."

Alfred regained his bearing, exclaiming, "We are not going to let them interfere with our plans. We are going to the theater!" He threaded his arm through hers and began marching forward.

She didn't tell her parents about it. Why upset them? Later it seemed so trivial in comparison with what they endured. A few months after the *Anschluss* the legal profession was closed to Jews in the Reich and her father sold his law practice to Herr Von Richter, a very junior Christian partner whom he had taken on as a favor to his uncle, a distinguished client. Von Richter had a better family pedigree than test results, and they both knew it. He was thankful and loyal, though, even as anti-Semitic slurs became commonplace. He gave her father the most difficult cases "just for a quick glance," and paid him for his work, a pittance compared to his normal fees, but still something. Gertie's father's name, elegantly lettered on the glass front door, was scraped off and replaced by Von Richter's. He had to go in and out of the office through the service door in the back.

And then Kristallnacht . . . it broke her father. Despite Von Richter's name on the glass doors, they were smashed. True, almost all of Vienna's synagogues were shattered and burnt that night, but for her father it was this door that was his entry to the most sacred of places. Only jagged slivers were left of the grand Scales of Justice that had been etched onto the glass by one of Vienna's finest glass artists, with the beautiful lettering of "*Iustitia quasi torrens fortis*"—"Justice as a mighty river." In Latin, of course, rather than the original Biblical

Hebrew, which her father could not read. As a little girl she would press her finger into the grooves in the glass and trace the outline of the scales. The glass was so cold in winter that once her fingertip stuck to it. When she'd pulled it away it felt as though it had been burnt.

Gertie had never seen her father the way he was when he returned home that night. His eyes bulged and his upper lip was bloody because he had bitten it so hard. He held his head in his hands saying, over and over: "It's not possible; not possible to believe this." She led him to the armchair and had to lower him down into it. She brought him a glass of water, but he waved it away.

When her mother entered the apartment, he began to shake.

"The doors of his office," Gertie stepped in to save her father from saying the words, "smashed." Her mother sat next to him, her hand on his arm, without saying a word.

Gertie checked: seventeen minutes had passed. As painful as the memories were, they made the time go by. "A few more moments of sleep for Alfred," she told herself. Back she went: to the sight of one Jewish business after another ransacked and looted; the eyewitnesses who said the police and firemen stood by as synagogues burned, only moving to stop the fires when they threatened to jump to the houses nearby. And the rumors about hundreds of people arrested and shipped off somewhere, no one knew where.

Later they would piece together a list of friends, colleagues and clients who had been sent to Dachau and Buchenwald. Thousands of them. A few people they knew returned in the following two weeks and left Vienna again within twenty-four hours. They'd promised to depart immediately, taking only what they could fit in one suitcase. They left behind apartments, furniture, shops, pets and, in the most heartbreaking stories, aging grandparents and ailing parents.

Saying goodbye to Alfred's parents was excruciating. She'd accompanied Alfred but tried to melt into the corner of the living room. Alfred's father, a reticent man by nature, just shook his head. Alfred's mother seemed dumbstruck. All she could do was stand close to Alfred and stroke the sleeve of his jacket.

"I . . . we . . . we can't, I mean we won't come to the station to say goodbye," Herr Schiff stammered.

"Of course not," Alfred came to his rescue. "As a matter of fact, the organizers told us to instruct our families to stay home. To say our farewells at home. It's too dangerous for so many people, I mean Jews, to congregate at the train station. It would draw attention to our departure. We don't want that."

"Definitely not," Alfred's parents said in unison.

They hugged each other. Alfred's father repeated: "So sorry I can't go with you to the train." Alfred put a hand on his shoulder; the first time Gertie had ever seen that. Then Alfred turned to his younger brother, Hans: "Find a way out," he said to him and slipped a tightly folded roll of bills into his hand.

Chapter 17

A much stronger contraction rolled through Gertie's body, scattering her memories. Not much longer before the contractions overtake everything, she knew. At that very moment Alfred stretched his legs in his sleep and a sigh slipped out between his partially open lips. She thought he might be dreaming now and hoped it was of good things: the baby in her arms and Emil perched on his shoulders as they walk hand in hand on the streets of Haifa...

"It's coming, Liebling," she woke Alfred, "our little boat-baby is coming."

He sat up immediately and grabbed her hands. Emil remained in a deep sleep, wound up like a salt pretzel. Alfred began to breathe with her, exaggerating his inhalations and exhalations to help her slow hers down.

"We must get to the Panama Room right now," Alfred said.

"Yes, but go find someone. To help get me up the stairs. And wake Bronia up, for Emil."

"Of course."

Alfred stuffed his legs into his pants and pulled on his sweater, not bothering with a shirt. He leaned over and touched Bronia on the shoulder.

"Bronia, wake up. The baby is coming. You have to stay with Emil."

Bronia raised her head and stared at him for a second, as if she were still dreaming.

"The baby is coming!"

"*Ja, ja,*" Bronia grunted, "go!"

Alfred already raced up the half-stairs.

"I'm coming, Gertie. Don't worry. I'll lie next to Emil until he wakes up. You go!"

"As soon as Alfred brings someone to help me up the stairs."

"Of course," Bronia settled herself next to Emil.

Gertie counted her breaths awaiting Alfred's return, glancing at her watch every few seconds.

"So where is he?" Bronia asked. "Why did he run upstairs? There are plenty of people here."

"Alfred must be sure the person is reliable. 'Reliable and responsible,' it's a religion with him."

"With all of us, Gertie."

"*Ja* . . . I'm sure he's looking for Siegfried, they've been friends since engineering school. But really, anyone would do, even one of the Danzig people."

"Though it's harder to communicate with them, Gertie. Their Yiddish is very different from our German."

"Yes, but how hard is 'push' and 'up'?"

Gertie let out a big breath of relief when she heard Alfred holler: "Someone wake up the doctors! Someone come help me!" A minute later the half-steps rattled loudly as Alfred came running down with a man Gertie did not know.

"*Shulem,*" the man said. "I'm Yakob Hertz." He extended his hand to shake hers. She gave him a smile and waved off the formality. She was pleased to see he looked very strong, with a thick chest and muscular arms. He could handle the half-pushing, half-pulling needed to get her upstairs.

"So, we go now!" Alfred said.

Yakob pulled his fisherman's cap down tightly, keeping the

sideways slant the young men favored. They each grabbed Gertie under an arm and lifted her to her feet. It brought on a contraction so powerful she doubled over and shrieked. Alfred murmured reassurances. She let them more or less drag her to the bottom of the stairs, where they stopped to plan their ascent. The stairs were barely wide enough for one person.

"You go up first, Yakob. Climb backwards so Gertie can hold onto your hands."

"Good idea," Yakob maneuvered himself into position.

"Pull her up very slowly. I'll push from behind."

Alfred wedged himself against Gertie from below. "Elegant it is not," he said to her.

"Don't worry. I haven't been elegant in a long time," she answered. "Ach," she groaned with another contraction.

Each step had to be conquered by itself, with a pause for Gertie to catch her breath. Three times she had to stop for a contraction. *Just let me get to the deck before the water breaks,* she begged her body.

Chapter 18

On the deck Doctor Samuelsohn was already waiting for her. Gertie glanced at his long, fine-boned fingers, wrapped tightly around the handle of his dark brown medical bag. *Thank God he's here, an obstetrician.* He was from Prague but spoke flawless German; they would be able to talk through the labor. He took Gertie's arm, nodding to Alfred to keep holding onto her, and they stepped towards the Panama Room.

"Walking is the perfect thing," Samuelsohn said, "to help the birth process move along. The longer we can stay out of that tiny cabin, the better."

Gertie waddled, more than walked, back and forth by the Panama Room. A nurse arrived. "We disinfected the room last night," she assured them, "every wall and corner swabbed with Lysol. It's as clean as a proper hospital room."

The smell of Lysol seemed lovely to Gertie; she breathed in deeply. One more circle in front of the Panama Room and a gush of liquid ran down her leg. "*Sehr gut,*" Dr. Samuelsohn said, "now we can go in." He guided Gertie through the low door and signaled Alfred to stay outside.

"No, I must come in!"

"We'll be like sardines in there!" the doctor said, "Back home I would never allow it. Not in Prague and not, if I may say so, in your

Vienna. But here..." He motioned to Alfred to enter. "Cover yourself with the disinfected sheets. Head to toe."

"Of course."

"I am Klara," the nurse introduced herself, "German-trained, from Danzig." Gertie stared at her in amazement: she had brought her nurse's uniform and had kept it spotless and starched. She took Gertie behind a narrow curtain and helped her strip off her clothes, then draped her with a sheet. The doctor pulled a neatly folded gown out of his medical bag.

"*Alles ist bereit?*" he asked.

The nurse straightened her back, as if to salute: "Yes, doctor. Everything is ready."

"Good. You and the husband can help her get on the bed," he said, pulling on a pair of surgical gloves.

Just then Doctor Gruenbaum squeezed into the crowded room. Gertie and Alfred knew him by reputation from Vienna. He was a specialist in internal medicine, not an obstetrician, but their shared hometown made her feel more secure with him present. His milky-white palms and seemingly manicured nails comforted her too. How had he kept them in such pristine condition?

She held Alfred's hand, tightening her grip with each contraction. How ironic that had she been giving birth back home, Alfred would never have been allowed in the delivery room. Having him by her side was an unexpected boon. With every contraction she felt him get closer, trying to siphon off some of the convulsions from her body into his, to ease her pain. He counted the seconds out loud for her. She forced her mouth into a smile to show him it was helpful.

Suddenly, pressure exploded within her.

"*Schnell, schnell!*" the nurse called out, "it's coming very fast!"

Gertie lifted her head to catch the expression on Doctor Samuelsohn's face. He stood between her legs in a boxer's crouch, ready to catch the baby or pull it out.

"Push now! Go ahead!" he said.

She needed no encouragement. It was as if a train were ramming its way through her. She barely caught her breath between the pushes, closing her eyes tightly with each one to fully focus on the effort. A flash of searing pain, and she heard: "The head is here!"

"Just a few more pushes," the nurse said, pressing lightly on Gertie's abdomen.

"Push, Liebling. One more time," Alfred tightened his grip.

Somehow, she summoned another push and felt the baby's limbs slithering out of the birth canal. Alfred gave a shout when the doctor pulled the baby out fully and immediately, she heard the baby's first cry. She let her body slump back onto the bed. Done!

"A boy," the doctor announced, as he tied and snipped the umbilical cord. "And everything looks fine. *Mazel tov!*"

"*Sehr gut,*" she smiled at Alfred.

"Sehr gut," he repeated. "Our beautiful baby!" He wiped the beads of sweat from her forehead and dabbed the corners of his tear-filled eyes.

Gertie watched the nurse swaddle the baby and immediately reached out to take him into her arms. The nurse placed the baby on Gertie's chest and patted her hand. "We'll finish cleaning you up. You and your husband can turn your attention to your baby now."

"Danke," Gertie and Alfred said together.

"Dr. Gruenbaum will check the baby soon," the nurse continued.

Gertie turned her head towards Dr. Gruenbaum with a questioning glance.

"I did two rotations in pediatrics before choosing internal medicine."

"Sehr gut," Gertie said and cradled the baby in her arms while Alfred held her in his. This is how it's meant to be, she smiled to herself: a nest within a nest; that's a family.

A few moments passed, with Gertie luxuriating in their embrace. Dr. Gruenbaum came to her side and held his hands out. She passed the baby over, astounded at how hard it was to part with him, even for a few minutes. Away from her body, the baby suddenly seemed like not much more than a bundle of swaddling.

"Go, Alfred," Gertie said, "go out to the deck to announce the news. And bring Emil."

"Right away!" Alfred headed to the door.

"Wait!" Gertie called out. "What date is it? What's his birthday?"

Alfred took a folded paper out of his pocket; his hand-made calendar. "November sixth."

"November sixth," she repeated.

Out on the deck there was a small crowd waiting.

"Alfred, my friend! A papa again!" Siegfried slapped Alfred on the back. He held aloft a small bottle.

"What's that?"

"Well, as you would say, Alfred, 'As a matter of fact' it is a bottle of schnapps!"

"You're kidding! How did you get it?"

"From home," Siegfried said. "I kept it all this time; the last remnant of luxury from our old life."

"You've had it since Vienna?"

"Amazing, ha? And this is the moment to open it. No one will chastise my hoarding it till now."

"Le-Chayim! Le-Chayim!" the deck erupted in cheers.

Alfred opened the door of the Panama Room a crack and blew Gertie a kiss from the doorway. "I am no longer sterile," he said.

"That's all right," the nurse said. "We're done. Just wear this," she handed him a facemask and gloves.

"Everyone is ecstatic, Gertie. And Siegfried, he pulled out a bottle of schnapps! Who'd have believed it, here on the boat?"

Gertie got a whiff of the alcohol on Alfred's breath, seeping through the gauze of the mask. "Aha! And you've had some!"

"Dr. Gruenbaum is checking the baby," she said, pointing to the far side of the room.

"Thank you, Herr Doktor," Alfred half bowed.

"Alles ist gut," Dr. Gruenbaum flashed them a smile so broad there seemed almost nothing else left of his face.

"Now," he continued as he re-swaddled the baby, "of course we will postpone the circumcision until you're in Palestine, even if it's more than eight days."

"Of course," they both said.

"Actually, Alfred, that would be better for Emil's sake, too."

"You're right, Gertie."

Back in Vienna they'd decided not to circumcise Emil after he was born, even though the grandparents on both sides frowned on it. They thought—and their parents agreed—it was wise. Life was getting more dangerous for Jews in Vienna. Emil might be seen by other small boys in a public bathroom or at the nursery school where they'd already signed him up. Better put it off until the threatening clouds cleared.

Before finalizing their decision, they'd consulted with Doctor Klein, who agreed that there was no medical harm in doing it later, under local anesthesia.

"You'll have to explain it to him so it won't be frightening. Wait until he can understand a logical explanation."

"Maybe I will tell him that now he gets to look like Papa?" Alfred ventured.

"I don't know what Herr Doktor Freud would say about that exactly," Dr. Klein said, "with his Oedipus Complex and so on. You'll consult with a pediatrician there, perhaps someone trained in psychoanalysis."

In Palestine they'd find a psychoanalyst? Maybe. From what they'd heard, the German Jews brought their whole culture there, from Rosenthal porcelain to Bauhaus buildings and punctuality. Why not Freud, too?

CHAPTER 19

"All yours now!" Dr. Gruenbaum handed the baby to Alfred, who'd draped a clean sheet over his chest. Alfred embraced the baby tightly and kissed his head through the surgical mask. He passed him into Gertie's arms, which were already outstretched. She put him on the breast and he began to suck. She closed her eyes and gave herself over to joy.

"Are you ready, Emil?" Bronia was asking right outside the door.

"Yes! I am really, really, really ready."

"Let me just make these wild curls a little more presentable."

"Mama always says that, too. But it never works."

"I can see that. Can I at least fix the buttons on your shirt?"

"No!"

"So be it," Bronia said, "now knock on the door."

It was more of a bang than a knock.

The nurse opened the door and Emil rushed to Gertie's side. He looked at the swaddled baby.

"He doesn't have any nicer clothes?"

Gertie and Alfred couldn't help bursting into laughter. Emil looked crestfallen.

"You are so sweet to worry about his clothes," Gertie soothed him.

"The baby will get new clothes in Palestine," Alfred added.

"You'll help me pick out baby clothes," Gertie promised, "and some new outfits for you, too. You're so tall now—everything's too small on you."

"A new sailor suit! Can I have a new sailor suit with gold buttons? And the baby too?"

"Sure," Gertie smiled and pulled him into an embrace.

Emil put his head down on her belly. He looked at her with alarm. "Mama, where's your tummy?"

"Remember the baby was in my tummy and sometimes you could feel his foot kicking in there? Well, now he's out so, no more big belly."

"Does he look like you, Emil?"

"Not at all!" Emil seemed insulted. "His hair is all black and swirly and his face is so red and crinkly. And he is so, so tiny."

"He is, but he will grow up quickly. And when he does, his hair might look more like yours—brown and curly. It can change, you know."

"It can change? Will mine change?"

"No, just the baby's. And the color of his eyes can change too, because..." But she made herself stop the child development lesson.

"What's his name?"

"Benyamin."

She exchanged glances with Alfred. It was the first time she'd said the name out loud. They'd thought to call the baby *Yisrael*, but despite eschewing all superstitions, they were afraid to tempt fate. They had not arrived yet, after all. Better a more cautious name, but a Hebrew one, to buoy their hopes. They picked Benyamin with some help from Ernst, whose Hebrew was better. He'd suggested it: a playful name, since *"Ben Yam"* could mean "child of the sea." They immediately liked it, as it was also a living reminder of Alfred's grandfather, Benyamin Moses, buried in the dark, cold soil of Europe.

Bronia poked her head in: "Everyone wants to see the baby. 'Such a miracle,' they are saying, 'joy in the midst of our despair.'"

Gruenbaum frowned, but then relented, on condition that they keep the baby at least five meters away from the crowd.

"Yes," Alfred said, "just a quick peek from far away."

He took the baby and wrapped him in another layer of swaddling. "Go with Papa," Gertie told Emil, "So you can show off your baby brother."

They went out on the deck, the nurse several paces ahead, ordering everyone to step back. Cheers rang up from all sides: "Welcome to the world, baby! Soon you will be in *Eretz Yisrael*!" Then: "Photographer, photographer!"

Soon a tall, lanky man, about Alfred's age, showed up with a small camera.

"Korngold," he introduced himself with a small bow and positioned himself in front of Alfred.

"Here we go, hold the baby facing towards me."

"Perfect!" Korngold said and the shutter clicked.

"Maybe, just one more? With his older brother?" Alfred pleaded.

"Of course! We must have a photo of the big brother!"

He motioned for Alfred to kneel down with the baby in his arms next to Emil, their heads almost touching. Emil puffed out his chest. A wide grin splashed across his face, like a small slice of watermelon.

"Smile!" the photographer said and pressed the button.

"Well done, young man," he said, "you look like you'll be a very good big brother. And very handsome, too," he said, more to Alfred than to Emil.

Alfred thanked him profusely. "How lucky for us that you have a camera!" he added.

"Wouldn't go anywhere without it," Korngold patted the small box, "and rest assured, I will develop this as soon as I can. Once we're on land."

"Danke! But . . . how will I find you?"

"Shouldn't be too hard," Korngold said after a moment of thought. "How many photography studios could there be in the

Jewish neighborhood in Haifa? That's where I plan to settle. There are a lot of German-speakers there."

"Yes, I know. As a matter of fact, we plan to settle there, too. They say it's beautiful."

"So, once you get situated, ask around for the best photographers in Haifa. You'll find me at one of those studios," he said, as if it were a simple matter of two plus two.

"Good plan. Very much appreciated." Alfred rounded his arms protectively around the baby and headed back to Gertie, Emil trailing after him. "You can stay outside and play. Bronia will watch over you."

She had already arrived at their side.

"Thank you, again, Bronia. Can you keep him entertained a bit longer?"

"Enough with the thank you's, Alfred."

"That . . . "

Bronia cut him off. "Emil and I have many things to do and talk about. Right, Emil?"

"Many!" Emil said and grabbed Bronia's hand.

Alfred ducked into the Panama Room. He was barely past the threshold when Gertie put her hands out for the baby.

"Everyone loves him, Gertie! They said he is our good luck charm for reaching Palestine soon."

"Let it be so."

"And guess what! We even have a photograph of him."

"How?"

"Herr Korngold. He took his picture. And one with Emil. We'll get them in Haifa. We worked out the details."

"That's great," Gertie gave a half smile, "but let's just get to Haifa first. And safely."

"Of course, Liebling."

―――――――

Soon the cheers and loud talk on the deck subsided. Alfred went out to gather information. Gertie dozed off with the baby on her chest. When she opened her eyes, Alfred was by her side, his face dark. He took her hand.

"I talked to Siegfried. The last bits of wood were thrown into the furnace this morning. There's nothing left to burn."

"Nothing?"

"Nothing. We're at the mercy of the Mediterranean. Who knows if the currents push eastward? Is it reasonable to hope that we will simply wash up on the shores of Palestine?"

"No one knows?" Gertie sighed. "What about all the engineers on board? And all the important *Herren Doktoren Professoren*?"

"Gertlein . . . there's no point getting angry, or sarcastic."

"Sorry. I'm just tired."

They sat in silence. Gertie watched Alfred drift away from her and the baby, hunkered down into his own thoughts. It was as if Alfred were transparent; she could see how he rode the large waves of fear and small troughs of hope, with no anchor. She at least had the baby keeping her moored in a placid bay created by his immediate needs.

Chapter 20

Gertie passed the next two days in the daze of the birth and caring for the newborn. She gladly left the Panama Room, knowing it was needed for many people struggling for their lives. How lucky that her bunk had escaped the hatchets. She kept the baby shielded between her body and the wall. Emil came in and out, checking on her, touching the swirl of black hair on Benyamin's head, calling him "my little *Schwarzkopf*."

Late in the day Alfred handed her an army-style flask. "Gertlein, there's no more water and no more food on the boat. Our friends gave me this canteen. This is the last of the water. Try to stretch it as long as possible." She hugged the canteen to her chest, unable to hold back her tears.

"Please thank everyone for their kindness," she whispered. She turned towards the wall and scooped the baby as close into her body as she could. Eventually, she fell into heavy sleep and Alfred, knowing Emil was in Bronia's trusted hands, allowed himself to doze off too.

"There's hope!" Elsa's shouts woke Gertie up. Running down the steps. Elsa called out: "A speck. Black . . . on the horizon. Just spotted!"

"What speck?" Alfred asked as they both startled awake.

"Maybe a boat coming towards us. Maybe . . . help is on the way!" Elsa yelled and turned to run back up.

"Let it be true," Gertie whispered into the baby's conch-like ear. "Go up, Alfred. Then come tell me what . . . "

"Immediately," Alfred got up and took the steps two at a time.

"And find Emil," she called after him.

On the deck Alfred found Emil playing by the large pile of coiled ropes. His favorite spot: the ropes made a fortress, a palace, or a cave. Bronia was seated nearby.

"Come, Emil. Let's look for the boat together."

"The boat is here, Papa. We don't need to look for it."

"No. Not this boat. Someone saw another one—maybe. On the sea. Far Away."

"Another boat! Hooray!"

Alfred hoisted Emil up on his shoulders and snaked through the crowd. He grabbed the railing with one hand and held Emil's legs to his chest with the other, and glued his eyes to the horizon. Was there really a tiny black dot out there? He let go of the railing and took off his glasses, polished the lenses against this shirt. He put them back on and craned his neck forward. Yes, there was something out there!

"See it, Emil?" Alfred set him down by his side.

"No, I don't see nothing!"

"You will soon. It's coming closer, but slowly."

"Where is it?" Emil whined.

"Let's close our eyes and count to sixty twice. That's two minutes. Then, when we open our eyes, you'll see it."

"One, two, three…" Emil began. He chanted the numbers as if they were an incantation.

"Sixty. Open your eyes! There, Emil—see it now?"

Emil put his hands across his eyebrows as he saw the adults do.

"No," he said, dejected.

Alfred knelt down and stretched his arm along the side of Emil's head and pointed. "Follow my arm with your eyes and keep going, all the way to the edge. Where the water ends in a line. Do you see that? That's called the horizon."

"I see the ho-ri-zon," Emil repeated Alfred's enunciation, then yelled, "Papa, I see it! But it's not a boat, just a black dot."

"Yes, because it's so far away. But it's coming towards us. Soon you'll see that it's a boat. Or a ship, which is bigger than a boat. Let's do it again—close our eyes and count."

When they opened their eyes this time the dot had taken shape. Darts of late afternoon sunlight bounced off its side. Alfred hoisted Emil up again.

"Yes! It's a ship," Emil called out. Everyone around them cheered.

"I saw it!" Emil shouted, "I saw it first of all of you!"

Now Alfred could make out the bow and stern and a mast with a flag, not yet identifiable.

"Which flag is it? What country?" people asked each other.

Alfred took Emil down and worked their way towards where he'd spotted Fritz, famous for his sharp eyes. Fritz bent down to Emil's eye level: "So, did you see the ship, *mein Kleiner*?"

"Yes, Uncle Fritz. I saw it first of everybody!"

"A big ship, right, Fritz?" Alfred said.

"Definitely."

"And the flag? Do you see red on it?"

"I think . . . I see some red."

"What other colors? If red and blue that's good. Red and yellow, or green—that would be a disaster for us."

"Of course," Fritz agreed.

"Why?" Emil tugged on Alfred's sleeve, "why don't you like yellow and green? I like them!"

"I'll explain later, Emil. Be patient," Alfred cupped Emil's shoulder.

"Do you see blue now, Fritz?"

"Not yet. Blue doesn't stand out against the water."

"Look again!" Alfred insisted.

"Just wait, Alfred. What did you say? Be patient?"

"Very funny, Fritz. But, yes, wait. Keep an eye on Emil for a minute. I have to go tell Gertie."

"Sure," Fritz said, pulling Emil to his side.

"Gertie, a ship!" Alfred shouted running down the steps, "heading towards us!"

"What kind of ship?"

"We can't tell. Can't see the colors of the flag yet. I'm running back up."

"Go! But where's Emil?" her voice rose.

"Fritz has him. Don't worry!"

On the deck people huddled together, whispering, as Alfred threaded his way back.

"Papa, the ship is getting bigger. I'm being very patient-ly, like Uncle Fritz said."

"Let's count to a hundred," Alfred said, thinking it would ease the wait.

"We already counted, Papa. I don't want to count for the ship anymore. It should just hurry up already."

"Yes, it should hurry up already."

"Blue and red!" people began to shout.

"The British flag!"

"Gott Sei Dank!"

"Baruch Ha-Shem."

"The Union Jack," people cheered. Someone even belted out the first notes of *God Save the King*.

Alfred pulled his handkerchief out and swung it wildly above his head. It was no longer the gleaming bleached silk it had been in Vienna, but still serviceable as white. Now all the passengers were yelling and waving. Someone signaled S.O.S. with a large towel. Others held up empty water jugs to communicate their situation: no water, no food. Two women hoisted up a line with baby clothes.

The ship came near enough now that people could see the uniformed sailors rushing back and forth on deck.

"They see us!"

"Someone is signaling in Morse code!"

"Quiet!" someone called out, as if you needed silence to decipher the message flashed by the ships' floodlight.

Four men started writing down the code. The deck fell silent. Lips tightened; foreheads furrowed. The older men began praying. But within seconds the jaws of all four men dropped simultaneously. Alfred's face turned ice cold. He clasped Emil's shoulders to keep his balance. One of the men read the message out loud:

"His Majesty's Royal Navy regrets. This ship en route to battle. So sorry. Cannot help you."

"What?" Alfred shrieked and his knees buckled. Fritz grabbed him. People gasped, then shouted and punched the air with angry fists. Others knelt down on the deck, held each other and sobbed.

"This boat will be our grave, Fritz," Alfred said.

"And you just had the baby . . . "

The crowd froze in place. In silence, each person turned to his own heart, despair spreading like spilled ink.

Alfred dragged himself across the deck pulling Emil along, back to Gertie. She saw his face and immediately knew. Alfred sat by her and cupped the baby's delicate skull. He slipped one curl between his fingers.

"Mama, the ship went away," Emil whimpered.

Gertie glanced at Alfred. Neither one of them dared utter a word about the scenarios playing in their heads.

"It must have been in a hurry to get somewhere," she hugged Emil. "Maybe another one will come and visit us soon."

Thankfully, Emil soon began his usual chatter, about the ship's flag and the sailors running on the deck. He asked again where they were hurrying to, why they wouldn't stop to say hello. She pulled reassuring words out of her mouth as if they were a thick rope—one knot after the other. Alfred hugged the baby to his chest and rocked him. Gertie saw the wet corners of his eyes and averted her gaze. As night came, people filed in and, without a word, lay down, each hoping for the solace of sleep.

The next two days most people stayed huddled on the floor in the hold. Despair kept them silent and frequent naps, aided by the weakness of hunger, helped pass the time. Gertie felt so far from them, all consumed by shielding Benyamin from their breaths and sneaking Emil bites of her dwindling stash of food.

Chapter 21

At dawn people sleeping on the deck thought they were dreaming, until someone finally shouted: "Land! Land!" In minutes everyone was up on the deck, gazing in disbelief at a mountain-ringed shoreline ahead. They hugged their neighbors and wet each other's faces with tears.

"Go tell Mama! Quick!"

Emil maneuvered through the forest of legs and started yelling from the top of the half-stairs:

"Mama, Mama! Get up and come to the deck! It's a land!"

"Land?" she called back. She gathered herself up and swaddled the baby to her bosom.

"Hurry, Mama," Emil urged, now at her side.

"I'm coming! But Emilik, go slowly." Eyeing the half steps, she decided the only safe way up was on her bottom. She hefted herself up, one step at a time.

The passengers crammed the front of the boat.

"Do you know where Papa is?"

"Yes, I can find him!" Emil took her hand and led the way.

They wended their way through the crowd, as Gertie tucked the baby's face into her chest. Her ears buzzed with overheard speculations.

"It looks like the mountains of the Galilee."

"But it could just as well be the shores of North Africa."

"Really? What country?"

"Libya, Tunisia, maybe even Morocco."

"God forbid!"

"No telling how far we've drifted off our course towards Palestine. No one knew which way we should sail."

"Not once those Greek sailors abandoned us."

"Scoundrels."

Gertie passed a group of men making even darker predictions, certain the mountain range looked like southern Italy or Sicily. "We're drifting right into the enemy's hands."

"The Italians will have no pity for us."

"Would they send us back . . . ?"

"God forbid!"

"Don't listen to them!" Gertie admonished herself. She tightened her hold on the baby and followed Emil.

"Finally," she tried to catch her breath when they reached Alfred. "What do you think?"

Alfred just grimaced and pulled all three of them into an embrace. Gertie rested her head on Alfred's shoulder. They waited in silence.

"Look," a man next to them yelled and pointed to a motorboat heading their way from the harbor in the distance. He pulled out a pair of small ivory-inlaid binoculars.

"What was he thinking when he packed those?" Alfred blistered, "that he would be going to the opera in Palestine?"

"But thank God for them now!" Gertie hushed him.

Every head turned to the man with the binoculars. "Union Jack!" he announced.

"British! British!" shouts of joy erupted. Someone yelled "Rule Britannia!" *That's ridiculous,* Gertie thought. And yet, at this moment, yes, the English were their saviors.

"Gott sei Dank," Gertie let out a long-held breath, "we're at the mercy of the British, not the Germans or Italians."

"Let's hope they're more helpful than that warship," Alfred said.

As the motorboat got closer, the noisy chatter on the deck turned into tense silence. Suddenly Gertie realized her ears had been swathed in constant noise for weeks—the incessant talking and yelling, the rumble of furnaces. Now she heard only the gentle slapping of waves against the *Atlantic* and the purring of the approaching motorboat. Who'd imagine that the racket of a motor could be so lovely? Even the smell of the diesel fuel wafting over them seemed sweet.

The motorboat circled the *Atlantic*. Two naval officers stood at its helm, shading their eyes with their hands. Their uniforms shone so white in the glaring sun that Gertie had to squint. Each had at least a half dozen medals pinned to his chest.

"They are surveying the sorry state of our beloved *Atlantic*," Alfred said.

"Well, let them see just how miserable it is," Gertie answered. "Maybe they'll take pity on us."

The captain revved the engine, turned the boat around and headed right back to the harbor. The deck burst into a roar. Gertie and Alfred leaned their heads together to hear each other above the cacophony. "What now, Alfred? Is this a good sign or a bad sign?" Alfred shrugged: "Nothing to do but wait and find out."

They settled down on the deck in a small circle with Siegfried, Fritz and Ernst. Soon Bronia and Elsa joined them. "We're waiting for the boat to come back," Gertie told Emil with forced confidence.

Alfred cleared his throat: "It could have been worse, no?"

It seemed as if an hour had passed, but Alfred had his pocket watch out: it had only been twenty-three minutes when they spotted a much larger boat heading their way, low to the water with no cabins.

"A tugboat!" someone called out.

"Mama, Papa," Emil jumped to his feet, "can I go see it? I love tugboats!"

"Take him, Alfred, it's a good idea. I'll wait here."

Emil's excitement spread to the people nearby who got up and followed to line up at the railing. Eventually even Gertie got up and joined them. She stood away from the knot of people and held the baby facing forward as if he, too, wanted to see the tugboat.

Nearing the *Atlantic,* the tugboat blew out a big puff of smoke, accompanied by a sharp toot. "Hooray, Tugboat! You came to us!" Emil clapped and called out. Everyone around him laughed, the grooves of tension in their faces momentarily relaxed. The tugboat nearly bumped the *Atlantic's* side and a crewman threw a thick coiled rope onto its deck. Two young men on the *Atlantic* grabbed the rope and wound it around the metal bollard.

The tugboat's engine roared and belched out another puff of smoke. Gertie almost lost her balance as the *Atlantic* jolted and lurched forward. Bronia jumped to her side and wrapped her arms around her, enveloping the baby. With another jerk, the *Atlantic* regained its balance and smoothed its course. They were gliding forward with speed now. "Well," Alfred exclaimed, "this is certainly a different feeling than the floating of the past week."

"Papa, are we in Palatschinka now?"

"Almost, Emilik." Alfred said, overly cheery. "We are almost there!"

Inside the harbor Alfred pointed to the large block letters on a warehouse. "Can you read that, Emil?"

"Ja!" Emil said proudly: "L- I- M-A- S- S- O- L. What is it, Papa?"

"Limassol, the biggest port in Cyprus."

"What's Sei-Proos?"

"It's a big island not far from Palestine. Maybe we'll stop here to get food and water."

"And a bath?" Emil pleaded.

Gertie's mouth fell open. Emil asking to bathe! He must be terribly uncomfortable with the sea salt coating his skin. She promised him a bath in their new home, in Palestine. And a swim in the sea.

"Maybe a swimming pool is better, Mama?"

"Yes," Alfred chimed in, "we will find you a swimming pool."

"Remember how well he swam in *HaKo'ach* sports club pool," Alfred turned to Gertie.

"Sure, I remember, the only place in Vienna where Jews could swim by then. But he did swim well, like a little frog."

Chapter 22

The tugboat towed the *Atlantic* to the far edge of the harbor, where they were ordered to anchor.

"Look at this big, busy port," Alfred said to Emil, "fishermen, cargo ships, the British Navy—those are all painted grey. Can you count how many of each kind?"

"It's too many, Papa!"

"Try, I'll help you remember the numbers."

Satisfied now that Emil would be occupied for a good while—and seeing Gertie's nod of approval—Alfred turned towards Fritz and they began speaking in low voices.

Gertie couldn't make out their words, but she knew they were speculating about best- and worst-case scenarios. She closed her eyes and touched her cheek to the baby's face, savoring the moment: Emil counting ships, the baby in her arms, the fresh breeze cooling the harbor . . . it was almost serene.

But soon Emil began to wilt, spent from the excitement. She handed the baby to Alfred and told Emil: "Put your head in my lap and rest a little. You'll need your strength for later." Uncharacteristically, he didn't protest and snuggled into her. He was asleep in minutes.

They waited. After an hour three small boats approached. Alfred and Fritz stood up. "Three boats, each with about a dozen men," Fritz reported, "some soldiers, some sailors. I'd guess they'll come aboard to check our papers."

"Perhaps they'll first bring us some food and water," Gertie said, hopeful.

"That would be befitting of His Majesty's famed generosity," Alfred said, only half sarcastically.

The soldiers extended narrow metal ladders to make a gangway from their boats to the deck of the *Atlantic*. Six British officers came aboard. Instinctively most of the passengers stood at attention, as if they were soldiers at roll call.

"All the mothers with babies and young children, go to the front," one of the Leadership members called out. "And the sick and elderly too. Let them see how bad things are."

"Let them know," someone added, "that you, and all of us, haven't had food in days."

Gertie stayed put as she was already near the front of the deck. *They'll see me*, she thought and watched the British officers walk the length of the deck. People moved aside to make a path. The officers looked around, whispering to each other. They returned to the head of the gangway and signaled to the sailors on their boats, who immediately threw more ropes onto the deck. The officers tied them to the railing and the sailors, along with some porters, started hauling crates and large barrels up to the *Atlantic*'s deck.

"Food! Thank God!" a cheer went up once the crates were opened.

"And look, Gertie," Alfred pointed to the farthest boat, "four huge bundles of blankets and three crates of medicine. See the red crosses on the sides?"

As the crates were stacked and opened, Gertie saw faces smooth out, shoulders release, even smiles. Ordered to line up, each family received a loaf of bread, a canteen of water and three pomegranates. No one paid attention to the two British officers lugging a desk up to the front of the Panama Room, then arranging papers and card boxes in neat piles.

Alfred Gertie and Emil got to their feet. Once in front of the soldier doling out the rations, Alfred pulled his shirt out to make a little hammock for the food. They sat down in a corner and laid out the food. Emil opened his mouth as wide as he could and bit into the fist-size bread chunk Alfred had handed him. Emil ate with his eyes closed, concentrating every muscle on chewing and swallowing. Alfred gave Gertie a piece and her mouth flooded with saliva. She could feel the texture of the doughy bread before it had even touched her lips. She took a bite and closed her eyes too. What pleasure! She passed around the canteen. Each one of them gulped down the water, only now realizing how thirsty they'd been.

They barely restrained their urge to wolf down the whole loaf of bread. Alfred put aside half of it. Once the sharp edge of hunger and thirst was dulled, they turned their attention to the shiny red pomegranates. They'd never seen or eaten these before, but they knew about them—one of the biblical fruits of the Land of Israel.

"Remember, Gertie, at the Zionist Movement meetings in Vienna how the *Shlichim* from Palestine always raved about 'The fruits of Eretz Yisrael?' As a matter of fact, they had a list in alphabetical order: dates, figs, grapes, olives, pomegranates."

"Of course," Gertie laughed, imitating the self-important pronouncement: "The biblical fruits of the Land of Israel. The sweetest in the world!"

"Well, then let's try them!" Alfred picked up a pomegranate with a theatrical flourish.

Gertie cradled hers in her palm for a few moments, turning it this way and that. She touched the smooth skin to her cheek. A fresh piece of fruit! Heaven! She bit into it. Her jaw dropped with the shocking acerbic taste that set her teeth on edge. She looked at Alfred and Emil who had each taken the same hopeful bite that very moment. Their faces told her how hers looked.

They all spit out the piece of fruit. Emil looked not just disgusted by the caustic taste, but actually insulted by it; as if all his parents' promises about the land they were going to were shattered by this bitter bite.

"It's the worst thing I ever ate, Mama!"

"I agree. It's horrid. Maybe these are not ripe?"

"I never want this thing again!" Emil shouted.

"I understand, but once we get to Palestine, you'll have a Jaffa orange. Those are really sweet—the best in the world. I know—I ate one in Vienna."

As if he felt Emil's insult, the baby started whimpering. "Why are you crying?" Gertie shushed him. "You didn't have to eat this ghastly fruit."

"He is lucky!" Emil said heatedly.

Gertie patted Emil's shoulder, and settled herself against Alfred's bent knees, the baby at her breast. She waited the few seconds it usually took for the sensation of warm amber oozing through her body with the letdown of her milk. She felt as if the water she'd just had rushed into her breasts filling them up, her skin tingling with milk.

Fritz came over and saw their discarded pomegranates.

"Don't tell me you bit right into them!"

"As a matter of fact, . . . " Alfred started but stopped himself.

"You have to open them. You eat only what's inside!" Fritz exclaimed and showed them how to crack open the pomegranate and pull out the shiny red seeds one by one.

Now a British officer pulled out a megaphone and called for an ad hoc committee to present itself at the desk. Four men stepped forward without hesitation.

"Who are those men, Alfred? Do you know them?"

"They are from the Leadership."

"Maybe they should put a woman on the committee. She might be able to get more out of those stiff-upper-lipped British officers. Look at their faces, Alfred, they show less emotion than Big Ben."

CHAPTER 23

The sun was midway in the sky when the members of the ad hoc committee called everyone to attention. A young man from the Prague group, dark hair slicked down to the side, climbed on a wooden crate and spoke. The British Commanding Officer had informed them that everyone on the boat must be registered at the desk by the Panama Room. They must line up in an orderly row, families with young children first, then the elderly, then the rest of them. "Please cooperate with these instructions as best you can."

Immediately people started scrambling to their feet and heading towards the desk.

"One more thing," he called out. "Please quiet down and listen. The Commander also presented us with a bill for the crates of food and water, the medicine and blankets. Plus, a charge for the tugboat service."

People were dumbstruck. They shook their heads, as if to throw off the unbelievable words. Then a beehive of conversation started buzzing.

"We were stunned too," the man yelled over the swirling voices.

"Hush! Let him talk!" Fritz called out.

"We . . . we looked the Commander in the eye, and said in our best English, and I quote: 'But, sir, surely you can see that we have no money. We are refugees. We have nothing.'"

"Nothing, indeed!" people shouted.

"The officer listened, but he was unmoved. He told us to do our best."

"What would that be?" a woman asked bitterly.

"He said and I'm quoting him so you all understand fully: 'Given the situation, the British Crown would be accommodating and will accept valuables—wedding rings and other jewelry and personal items of value—in lieu of cash.'"

People shouted in dismay but soon grew quiet and each turned to their family and their belongings. Gertie caressed her wedding ring with her fingertip. She cast furtive glances at other people's hands, as they rotated their rings very slowly, as if their fingers would not release them. But she knew the rings should come off easily—they had all lost a lot of weight on the journey.

"The wedding rings or my watch?" she asked Alfred.

"The rings. We can get new ones in Palestine. They are plain gold bands. Your watch is irreplaceable."

"From my parents..." her eyes misted. Quickly she unfastened the watch and slipped it into her brassiere, hoping no one saw her.

"And I'll keep my gold fountain pen," Alfred whispered. "My father gave it to me when I graduated engineering school. I remember what he said, every word: 'May you sign many blueprints with it.' You know that until that moment, he had made his disapproval of my career choice eminently clear."

"I know. You were supposed to be a doctor and follow in his footsteps."

"Yes..." Alfred choked on his words, so Gertie supplied them, "but you couldn't stand the sight of blood."

"What's everybody doing, Mama?" Emil asked.

"Well, you... see..." She stumbled trying to figure out how to soften the blow and preserve his innocence. "You see, Emilik, everybody wants to thank the British for the food and the water and for helping us get to Palestine, so we're giving them some presents."

"Me, too!" Emil exclaimed.

Before she could say a word, he was running downstairs. Moments later he was back with his sailor cap in hand. He began to pull the now dulled gold-plated button off the front. It had an anchor embossed on it, matching the smaller ones on the buttons of his sailor suit shirt.

"Yes? No?" Alfred whispered in Gertie's ear. "What's more important? His beloved suit or his pride in participating with the grownups?"

"Let him make his own sacrifice, Alfred. The lesson will last longer than the suit."

Bronia, standing next to Gertie was clutching her *Magen David* necklace. With a sigh, she unfastened the hook and let the necklace slide into her open palm. She held it up towards Elsa and Gertie.

"Beautiful," Elsa said.

"Yes, it's stunning," Gertie agreed. "Try to imprint the shape in your mind. You'll find a jeweler to make an exact copy once we are settled."

"I'll try . . . " Bronia said, "and you, Elsa?"

Elsa opened her rucksack and pulled out a large silver stopwatch. "This fellow saw me break my 100-meter record at the gymnasium. Oh, I was fast in those days!"

"You were famous," Bronia said.

"But I guess it's time for us to say goodbye."

Their fellow passengers were already lined up at the desk. Women gave necklaces or earrings; men a gold fountain pen, wedding ring or pocket-watch. Some produced a small stash of English pounds they'd saved for their first weeks in Palestine. But Gertie also saw some hands slip quickly to push gold coins deeper into the seams of jackets as they put down copper ones or take off a cheap wrist watch while hiding a valuable bracelet. The pile on the table grew higher and higher. Finally, the officer shoveled everything into a large leather case and indicated it would do. The registration process would now begin.

Thanks to Benyamin, they were near the head of the line. A young lieutenant rolled the edges of his mustache between his fingers as the first passengers stepped up to the desk. The officers interviewed each person.

"This will take a while," Gertie said.

"The procedure is a good sign. The British are very competent in such matters," Alfred said. He proceeded to recite their present advantages, holding a finger up for each: they're no longer adrift at sea; they have food and water, also medicine and blankets. Their situation is being resolved. Gertie suppressed a sigh. He could be so pedantic . . . but now was not the time for her annoyance.

"Mama, I'm hot," Emil whined.

"It's not like home, Emil," Alfred explained. "This is the Mediterranean. It can get hot even in winter."

"Can I take off my shirt, Papa?"

"It's fine, Alfred," Gertie said. "Let him. He can put it back on just before we reach the desk."

Emil pulled his shirt over his head, not bothering with the buttons.

"Look at you!" Gertie marveled, "you're so tanned!"

"It's been hot up on the deck. I let him, sometimes . . . " Alfred said apologetically.

"I see. What else have I missed being down below?"

"All the men have been taking their shirts off while working on deck. Some even took their pants off and . . . worked in their underwear."

"And I missed that!" Gertie exaggerated her reaction. "He's so dark, Alfred! *Halb asiatische.*"

"So, he'll blend in with the Asiatic boys in Palestine. It'll make it easier for him to make friends."

"That's the least of our worries."

"Next!" the officer called.

Emil took two steps forward and saluted.

"A real salute!" the officer congratulated him.

"I practiced with Uncle Fritz," Emil beamed.

Gertie was close enough to the officers to see the embroidered name on the left pocket, McCormick, as well as the fuzz on his cheeks: *seems he hasn't started shaving yet.* She noted the other fellow, his pearly nails when he picked up his pen. She glanced at hers, cracked and caked with grime.

They laid their passports on the desk. Gertie apologized that they had no papers for the baby. McCormick looked shocked to hear he had just been born.

"Here?" he asked incredulously, "in these conditions? Has he been seen by a doctor?"

Fully aware that despite the limitations of her schoolgirl English, she was speaking with an air of superiority, Gertie informed him that, in fact, there were several first-rate European trained doctors and nurses among the refugees. The baby had been examined and pronounced in excellent health.

"Jolly good, then," McCormick said, oblivious to her condescending tone. He wrote down Benyamin's details: name, date of birth, parents' names. For "Place of Birth" he hesitated a moment, and then put down: "Mediterranean, territorial waters, status unknown. Nationality: To be determined."

The registration done, Gertie suddenly felt completely drained.

"I must sit down, Alfred, and eat something."

"Of course," Alfred took her elbow in his hand. "All of us," he said and guided them to the far corner of the deck where they sat on a large wooden crate. He pulled out the remains of the bread, wrapped in a rag, out of his rucksack and the third-full canteen. Emil immediately bit into his piece, but Gertie hesitated: "Is it safe to finish all we have?"

"Yes. No doubt the British will bring more food. Fritz saw a large box loaded up yesterday with sardine tins, probably for today."

"That would be heaven. As long as they don't bring more pomegranates."

The edge of her hunger dulled, Gertie put the baby on the breast and let the flow of milk restore her spirits. She looked at the sea, scanning the horizon. The white caps rolling by seemed to indicate the eastward direction of the waves.

"So how far is it from here to Palestine, Alfred?"

"Cyprus to Haifa . . . I'm not sure. Perhaps three hundred kilometers? I'll ask Fritz, he'll know more precisely."

"If so, how long of a sail?"

"If the British tugboats pull us and we depart early tomorrow, we'll sail overnight and be there the next morning."

Alfred pulled out the folded hand-made calendar he always had tucked in his pocket. "So that would make it . . . November 24."

"So, we're almost there," Gertie sighed with relief.

"Almost there."

Chapter 24

Lucas reached the end of the path in the olive grove surrounding Stella Maris. He sat down on a large rock, his body heavy from the afternoon's labors. The heated rock, warmed by the sunny day, soothed his sore muscles. What a treat to bask in the sun so late in the year —November 23rd—a mere week before the beginning of Advent! Enjoy this precious gift of the Holy Land, Lucas told himself, back home it's already frigid.

The olive trees always took Lucas back to the orchards spreading south of his village home. The silvery hue of the leaves had seemed brighter back home; a different variety or the glossy patina of childhood memories? His mood darkened. The sweet memories of tending his father's olives inevitably led to the bitter one of walking away from all of it.

He winced and raised his eyes towards the open sea, looking west towards home. But it made him sad, so he turned back towards the harbor. The sun's rays bounced off the waves, creating a mosaic of glittering golden swatches. A large ship towered over the other vessels at the port, its gleaming white deck high above the water. How did an elegant cruise ship make it through the Mediterranean in wartime? he wondered. Perhaps a British ruse, a battleship disguised as a passenger boat?

He followed the triple row of portholes, like beads on a long pearl necklace. Above them rose three thick smokestacks, symmetrically spaced along the length of the deck. "The Father, the Son and the Holy Ghost," Lucas chuckled, but immediately chastised himself for his irreverence.

How much more modest the single smokestack of the cargo boat he'd come here on... Five years had gone by, but he recalled every step he took from the dock in Marseille onto the deck, jam-packed with crates and barrels, and down to the cramped cabin shared with five other travelers, squeezed onto narrow metal bunks. It was the cheapest passage - all the Church could afford - as a passenger on a cargo ship.

But arriving at Haifa - how glorious! First the stunning view of the sandy coast and Carmel crest, then the curve around its tip and the glide into the quiet of the Haifa harbor, safely tucked into the eastern side of the mountain. He remembered disembarking and wondering: would he look ridiculous kissing the ground? His knees already on the pavement, he felt a hand on his shoulder and a voice said, "No, no, my son!" He looked up - a monk from the monastery - he could tell immediately from his thick brown robe and sockless feet in simple sandals.

"Here all you'd be kissing is the cement dock. Wait until we get to the monastery. There you can touch the real soil of the Holy Land."

Lucas rose. He towered over the middle-aged monk. He startled; the monk looked so much like his own father! Same squat, stocky guild, sunburnt lined face and thinning, grey hair.

"Brother Lucien," the monk stuck his hand out. "You must be Lucas."

"Indeed," Lucas said and bowed and shook the outstretched hand. It, too, was like his father's: a calloused, chafed palm and stiff, knobby fingers.

"I am the monastery's carpenter. That's why my hand's so rough. But my heart is not, and it rejoices in welcoming you. I came to bring you to Stella Maris, along with some lumber. I hope you don't mind," he pointed towards a donkey cart standing nearby.

Lucas bowed and hoisted his leather satchel on his shoulder.

Now he stretched out on the warm rock and closed his eyes, remembering the first time he saw the olive groves circling the monastery. How magical they had been that day, like a crown on a king's head. Now, they were just tomorrow's toil. What a long road he'd traversed, from home to this place, the journey - both physical and spiritual—begun the morning he left his family for the Carmelite monastery in Pamiers. He was only ten.

His father had taken him, in the wooden cart he used to carry vegetables to market. Papa's face had been stony. When they arrived at the city gate, he had said he could not take Lucas all the way to the monastery; too much congestion in the town's streets.

"You can walk the last part."

"Yes, Papa. I should walk the last part. I am a *pèlerin*, following my religious call."

At the entrance to the Pamiers monastery, Lucas looked up at the tympanum over the door, an elaborate carving of Judgment Day. No wonder people trembled in church. He certainly did . . . perhaps more than most villagers. He knew only two other boys who'd been called to the Church. The rest of them mostly fidgeted in their seats during prayers, impatient to get outside and play. He had eagerly swallowed the miracle stories of pilgrims who stopped in the village, a few days before they would reach Lourdes.

From an early age Lucas could stare for hours at the deep reds and blues of the church's stained-glass windows. He loved the smell of the candles and the scented cloud rising from the incense burner. He envied altar boys who walked between the pews swinging the intricately carved bronze censers. And the priest . . . his face always so peaceful and beautifully round. He looked so holy! And he clearly had enough to eat.

After five years at the Pamiers Monastery, visiting his parents only for Christmas and Easter, he was chosen from among all the novice boys to go to the Holy Land. His parents were elated ... and heartbroken. Such an honor! But would they ever see him again? The Holy Land was in their prayers, not in their geography. The Abbot assured them that after Lucas took his final vows the Order would arrange a visit home - around the time Lucas turned twenty.

Lucas saw his father put his hand on his mother's back to steady her. "I assure you," the Abbot said, "He will come back to you. For a visit, that is. He has given his life to the Church. You understand that, yes? You should be very proud of him." He flashed them a broad smile. It fluttered against their leaden, silent faces.

Tearfully, they let him go, thanking the Abbot for choosing him. It was a great privilege. Everyone in the village would look up to them. *And there would be one less mouth to feed,* Lucas knew his father was telling himself *and maybe a gift from the Abbot once or twice a year.* But the war broke out. His visit home was now two years overdue and no end in sight. He pined for his family every day, especially little Philippe and the "sack of flour" piggyback rides he gave him. Lucas' belly seized up in knots which, he knew, would still be there tomorrow.

Chapter 26

By late afternoon all the refugees had been registered. A damp chill rose from the water. Gertie and Alfred returned to the hold and tried to occupy Emil with word games and stories. Fritz came down to say that a shipment of bread and sardine tins had arrived, along with huge vats of tea.

"Tea time!" Alfred announced. "You can count on the British to serve you tea, even at sea. Even if they intend to throw you overboard tomorrow."

"Indeed," Gertie said, "still, their tea has milk and sugar in it, a great treat in our circumstances."

The deck was swarming with people. Alfred brought their rations and two canteens with tea back to Gertie's bunk. Emil began falling asleep as he chewed his bread. He put his head in Gertie's lap and soon he was asleep. Gertie nursed Benyamin and tucked him in the corner of the bunk.

Alfred wanted to recount all the possible scenarios for tomorrow, but Gertie cut him off: "What's the point of all these speculations? Let's focus on what we can do now: get some sleep."

"Where's my bread?" Emil asked the instant he woke up the next morning.

"Here," Gertie unwrapped the bread and handed it to him. He finished it in no time. "Is there more?"

"Papa is already in line for breakfast. Let's join him."

They went up the stairs, Emil first, then Gertie clutching the baby to her chest. She felt so light! What a pleasure to climb up without the belly!

After breakfast was served, the Commanding Officer announced that the *Atlantic* would be towed to Haifa. "There you will be informed of the next steps," he said, giving no hint of what those might be.

"Tomorrow —or the day after—we'll be in Palestine," Alfred hugged Gertie and Emil.

"We are so lucky!" Gertie leaned into Alfred and shut her eyelids tight to hold in her tears. She rolled her shoulders, as if a mountain of worries had just slid off her back. Her body felt soft and warm in a way it had not in months; not since she'd left home.

A tugboat twice the size of the one that had towed them into the harbor approached the *Atlantic* and its crew hooked the two boats together with heavy chains. A loud "Toot" sounded, and off they went. Suddenly time woke from its slumber and started flying. Gertie marveled at how quickly they set off and how smoothly the *Atlantic* rode the waves. She sat with Alfred on the deck all morning, cradling Benyamin and passing the time in conversation with friends and games with Emil.

"You should go down, Gertie, get as much rest as you can. We have a lot ahead of us. You've barely recovered from the birth." Alfred said it so tenderly she teared up. "I can keep the baby with me," Alfred added, "when he gets hungry, I'll bring him to you."

"Danke. And don't forget to keep an eye on Emil."

She spent the remainder of the day in sleep punctuated by vivid dreams and barely wakeful nursing. Mostly the dreams took her back home, to favorite childhood spots: the Vienna woods, the zoo, the Danube. Once she startled awake. She'd heard her father call her name with great urgency. He was choking. She'd tried to answer him but had forgotten her German. All she could say was "Ahh, Ahh."

Once, when Alfred brought the baby down to nurse, she asked about changing him.

"Bronia helped me," Alfred said sheepishly, "you know I'm not very good at it."

"Natürlich," Gertie smiled and sank back into sleep.

Was she really this tired? She asked herself towards evening, or was it that she could finally sleep, lulled not by the rocking of the boat but by a sense of security she had all but forgotten was possible.

Alfred and Emil lingered on the deck until the setting sun made the waves glisten and it turned cold. "Tomorrow, Emil. Tomorrow we will be in Palestina," Alfred hugged Emil. "We'll see the sunset from our own homeland."

"And eat our first Palatchinka!"

Chapter 27

Loud yelling from the deck jolted Gertie and Alfred awake early the next morning. They picked up the baby and Emil, still half asleep, and climbed up to the deck. The glow of the sun about to rise crowned the mountain ridge with a golden light.

People made room for Gertie, calling out: "Let the baby go to the front! Let him see it!" Alfred held onto Emil and, with Gertie in front, they maneuvered to the edge. She grabbed the railing, more to reassure herself that this was real, tangible, than to steady her stance. She glanced sideways; a row of knuckles lined the highest bar, chapped and cracked, wrinkled and smooth, sun-burnt and pale white.

"The Carmel Mountains! Alfred exclaimed, and added under his breath "Not quite as high as I imagined."

"Haifa?" Gertie asked

"Yes, we're here! Can you believe it, Gertlein? We are in Palestine!"

Emil swiveled his head side to side, scanning the mosaic of heads; hair bushy, thinning or bald, heads bare, kerchiefed, or covered with a yarmulke.

"Papa, what are they singing?"

"*Ha-Tikvah*."

"What's *Hatikah*?"

"*Ha-Tik-vah*. Our Jewish national anthem."

"What's anthem?"

"The song of all the Jews in the world."

"I think I heard it before."

"Could be, Emil. We sang it in Vienna sometimes."

Emil put his hand behind his ear, the way he'd seen grown-ups do.

"Papa, what is '*nefeshy-hudi*'?"

"*Ne-fesh Ye-hu-di*," Alfred enunciated. "It means a Jewish heart. *Yehudi* is *Jude*.

"*Jude?*"

"Yes. We say *Jude*. *Yehudi* is in Hebrew."

"*Ye-hu-di, Yehudi*," Emil repeated loudly.

"Why is everyone crying, Papa?"

"Because they are happy," Gertie said, seeing Alfred too choked up to speak, "so happy that we are finally here, in Palestine, in *Eretz Yisrael*."

"Why are they crying if they are happy? And you, too, Mama?"

"Grown-ups cry sometimes when they're happy."

"Why?"

"That's a really good question, Emilein. I don't think anyone knows."

Gertie lay her cheek on the baby's crown of black hair and let her tears wet his head. Alfred lifted Emil onto his shoulders, so he could ride above the sea of weeping.

As the singing subsided, everyone cheered and clapped, shook hands, and patted each other's back. Soon the tugboat turned in a northeastern direction and pulled them around the point of Mount Carmel. Now they could see the buildings in Haifa, then the warehouses at the port.

The tugboat swung to the far-right corner of the harbor and positioned them about fifty yards from the dock.

"Papa! I see my land. My *Palatschinka* is here!"

"Yes, Emil. We are home."

"Look, Papa, look how fast it is!" Emil yelled excitedly. A small British skiff was heading their way.

"Ja," Gertie called out too, "look at it - what speed!"

Within minutes the skiff reached the *Atlantic*. Two sailors in crisp white uniforms hooked a ladder onto the *Atlantic's* railing and a dozen British officers climbed on board. They surveyed the scene, their faces revealing their horror at what they saw. Their noses twitched from the putrid smells. The tallest one ordered silence and called out in a booming voice:

"Sit down, right where you are. Wait quietly and we will provide food and water. Then remain seated until further instructions."

Everyone sat down, leaving a narrow path from the aft to the stern. The officers walked around the *Atlantic* pointing at the skeletons of torn up wooden structures. One was jotting things down in a notebook while the others took positions at even intervals overseeing the seated crowd.

"What do you think will happen, Alfred?" Gertie's voice quivered.

"Not much to worry about now. We are here in Haifa; so close we can see people walking right there on the dock. Soon we'll be there too."

Emil tugged on Alfred's sleeve, "Look at that boat, Papa," he pointed to a large ship anchored nearby, "It's huge!" Alfred followed Emil's finger. "Yes, it really is big. As a matter of fact, that's a ship. Ours is a boat; that is a ship."

"Can we go on it, Papa?" Emil eyes opened wide.

"No, Emil. We want to get to the land, not go on another ship."

"It sure is big, isn't it?" Alfred turned to Gertie. "Looks like it was a luxury cruiser. See all those portholes? Three levels! And I see people on board. Look," Alfred pointed, "on the right side of the deck, near the third smokestack."

"Yes, I see. I wonder who they are."

She scanned the length of the three huge black and grey

smokestacks against the gleaming white cabins and bright blue sky. Each one had a narrow white stripe painted two thirds of the way up. Like wedding bands, she thought, touching her finger, to swivel the ring that was no longer there.

"Yes, a cruise ship. I wonder where it's been? Across the Atlantic, perhaps? The real Atlantic, I mean, not our floating wreck." She pointed to the side of the ship where its name was emblazoned on the white background. "*Patria*," she read aloud.

"Can you believe that, Alfred? *Patria!* A novelist couldn't have made up a more apt name for our situation."

The *Atlantic* bobbed in the placid waters of Haifa's harbor all day. Everyone savored the fresh bread and water and awaited instructions. The early dinner was a feast—biscuits, two hard-boiled eggs and two boiled potatoes per person, and, of course, tea. In the quiet that ensued as everyone hunkered over their food, a new British officer climbed aboard with a bullhorn: "Attention, please!"

Everyone hushed and quickly swallowed their last bites.

"Organize yourselves in groups of twenty-five. Each group will board a dinghy for transfer to the *Patria,* the large ship over there. Tonight, we will begin with members of your leadership and some of the younger people, so they can prepare for the rest of you to board tomorrow. At 7:00 AM you will line up in this order: families with small children, then the elderly, then the rest of you. The sick will be loaded last accompanied by your doctors and nurses, supervised by our medical staff."

"These British certainly know how to organize things," Gertie muttered.

The officer continued: "Once you arrive on the deck of the *Patria* you will remain standing with your group in rows of four. Small children and the elderly may sit down in their row. Others will remain standing. Further procedures will take place there."

"But they already registered us!" Alfred said, "why transfer us to this *Patria* to register us again?"

"Maybe they want to quarantine us there for a day or two, so doctors can separate out those with communicable diseases." Gertie offered.

"That's possible. That's logical. There are definitely a lot of very sick people here."

"How lucky that we are all healthy," Gertie said.

They trudged down to the hold. "For the last time!" Gertie said with a deep sigh as she sat down on her bunk.

Chapter 28

That same evening, Moussa and his father walked from the fields home for dinner, their shoes caked with mud. They reviewed the last few days' accomplishments: harvested the last of the olives, pruned the fruit trees and dug in fertilizer around each one, and weeded every row of new seedlings.

"Nobody weeds like you, Moussa," Bassem said with unusual warmth in his voice.

"Thank you, Baba. I still love it."

"Maybe you'll come back one day. Your half-brothers - all they want is the city. 'Nazareth,' they keep saying, 'that's where you can make it.' Who knows how they'll end up?"

"What do you mean?"

"I don't know what kind of trouble they get into. And marrying and giving me grandsons is the last thing on their mind."

"They are young, Baba."

Bassem shrugged. "Only you," he said emphatically, "can I count on. I need just one; one grandson. Then I can go in peace."

"We keep trying. But each time it . . . "

"I know. The curse . . . "

Moussa winced. They had never spoken of it. He was floored that his father called it by the same name.

"Maybe, you and Youssra should go to a doctor."

"A doctor? In Nazareth?"

"Not in Nazareth."

"Where . . . ?"

"In Haifa," Bassem said in a low voice, "maybe a Jewish doctor."

"What are you saying?" Moussa couldn't believe his ears.

"I hear they have the best ones. Just now coming from Europe. Trained in the best places there - Germany, France. Coming here to escape the war."

"That's true, Baba. I hear people talking about it: doctors, engineers, rich businessmen."

"That's what I hear, too. Maybe you've even seen them in the port. People say they're still coming, even though the English say they don't let them."

"I did! Just last week. Two boats, full of them. But I tell you, when I saw them, they didn't look like doctors or business men. They looked . . . wretched."

"That's refugees, my son; you can't tell the doctor from the beggar."

Moussa nodded.

"But think about it, please," Bassem pressed, "I have some money put aside for it."

Chapter 29

They lined up on the *Atlantic* deck well before 7:00 am, under the watchful eye of a British officer, rhythmically bouncing his baton into his cupped palm. A Leadership member walked along the row demarcating groups of twenty-five. Alfred and Gertie were in the second group.

When their turn came, Gertie handed the baby to Alfred and accepted a British sailor's arm for support. She swung into the dinghy, balancing herself in a wide stance. Alfred handed her the baby, then picked Emil up and passed him over to the sailor, who smiled and whooshed Emil through the air in a grand sweep.

"I'm flying!" Emil called in mid-air.

The sailor plopped him down in the dinghy at Gertie's side. Alfred passed over their luggage, and jumped in, disregarding the sailor's offered hand.

More families with children and several young men crammed into the boat. The sailor at the helm revved up the engine and they crossed the short distance to the side of the *Patria* in no time. They had to climb a long narrow metal ladder to get onto the *Patria*'s deck.

"Take the baby, Alfred and I'll watch over Emil," Gertie said.

Alfred clasped the baby tightly in his right arm and used his left to hoist himself up the rungs. Gertie put Emil in front of her, counting on her body to catch him, should he falter. Two men followed behind with their luggage.

As they stepped onto the *Patria's* deck, they saw that it was already crowded.

"Gertie, these people set out with us from Romania!"

"Yes. From Tulcea, of course!"

"They were on the *Milos* and the *Pacific*, remember? You thought their boats looked so much better than ours."

"And I was right. You can see they arrived well ahead of us."

"When did you get here?" Alfred asked a man standing near the railing.

"We got here on the *Milos* three weeks ago. The *Pacific* got here two days before us. The boats are there," he pointed to the far end of the harbor.

Alfred turned back to Gertie and pointed towards the two boats, "They do look better preserved than our *Atlantic*."

"Our *Atlantic* . . ." Gertie flicked her hand across her face, "I hope I never say *that* again."

Gertie and Alfred surveyed those around them more closely, seeking familiar faces. German, Czech and Yiddish mingled in their ears. Several passengers greeted them with recognition. They moved towards a small group of German speakers and tried to join the conversation. The new arrivals were pelting the veteran passengers with questions:

"Have you already registered with the British authorities?"

"How long do you think we'll wait on the ship before we go on land?"

A long-faced man with a stubbly beard spoke up, slowly and clearly, to make sure they comprehended the news. They weren't going to be allowed to get off the *Patria* and enter Palestine. They were *all* being deported to a place called Mauritius.

There was an uproar. Some protested the injustice, but most simply asked: "What is Mauritius?"

Alfred stepped forward saying that he, and other stamp

aficionados, knew this tropical island in the Indian Ocean because of the rare *Mauritius Two Pence Blue*. "Only five hundred *Two Pence Blue* stamps were printed, along with the *One Pence Red*, on September 21, 1847." *Even in these circumstances,* Gertie marveled, *his command of obscure facts doesn't falter.* And his audience seemed to welcome being lulled into the peaceful few moments of trivia.

"The two-pence stamps became so rare because nearly all were immediately used on invitations to the British Governor's annual ball. After the envelopes were opened the stamps landed in people's rubbish bins."

"And now," a woman called out, "it's our turn—into the rubbish bin!"

"Well . . . " Alfred stopped short. Gertie saw in his eyes that the absurdity of lecturing about philatelic history suddenly numbed him. The *Atlantic* passengers looked back at the veterans, hoping they would laugh off the information, but they remained silent and averted their eyes. Shouting erupted:

"This is not possible!"

"I can't believe it."

"It's too cruel to be true!"

"Surely the Jewish community in Palestine—the whole world—won't stand for this."

The veteran passengers just shook their heads, stony-faced, then followed orders to move to the back of deck to make room for the newcomers, who continued to pour onto the *Patria's* deck.

Alfred and Gertie joined the registration line. It moved swiftly. Soon they stood at the desk, facing two British officers.

"Madam, please put the baby down in the cabin on the right."

"What?" Gertie frowned.

"There, on the right. We've got a special cabin with bassinets for the infants."

So, I am "Madam" now. Of course, everyone knows the English are polite. Whatever happens, they are not Nazis. They're gentlemen. Everything will be all right. Just follow their orders.

She entered the cabin, trying to breathe out the twisted knots in her belly. The row of bassinets was under the watchful eye of a prim English nurse.

"All right, Madam. He is perfectly safe here. I shall supervise until your papers are processed."

"Thank you," Gertie nodded and kissed Benyamin on the top of his head. "*Kleiner Schwarzkopf,* I'll be back soon," she cooed, and settled him in the bassinette.

"It should not be long, so he probably won't wake up hungry before you're back," the nurse said. "If he does, I have my tricks, a good number up my sleeve. Been taking care of little ones going on thirty years now."

Chapter 30

The deck was even more crowded now, the lines much longer. Gertie glanced at the *Atlantic*, envious of their friends awaiting their turn, still blissfully ignorant of their fate. She joined Alfred at the front of the line.

"Where's Emil?"

"There," Alfred pointed to the right, "already feeling at home climbing the ropes."

"Those will keep him busy for a while."

"He sure loves those ropes . . . and the baby—sleeping?"

"Sleeping peacefully. The nurse seems very competent."

"We are almost done."

Gertie opened her mouth to answer but a deafening clap snatched the sound out of her mouth. A jolt threw her off her feet and slammed her on the deck, flat on her belly.

"*Gott im Himmel!*" she screamed. A rolling barrel walloped her head. She blacked out.

She came to, head throbbing. Her ears rang.

"*Hilfe! Hilfe*! Help me!" she heard a shrieking, then realized it was her own voice.

Emil! Alfred! She lifted her head to look but all she saw was a jumble of flailing bodies and tumbling cargo.

"Hilfe!" she screamed again but was drowned out by the others yelling for help.

Another monstrous roar and Gertie slid to the edge of the deck, crashing into wooden crates, barrels and coils of rope. Oh, God! Gertie gasped, the ship's keeling over! She wrapped her arms around a long beam and held tight. She raised her head and screamed: "Alfred! Get Emil!" She let go of the beam and crawled towards the nursery cabin: "Benyamin! Get Benyamin!" she panted with each breath.

"Help! Help! I have babies here!" Gertie heard the English nurse holler.

She inched forward on hands and knees. *Grab this! Push there!* she ordered herself, as if she had split into two people, a commander-in-chief and a dutiful soldier. She lurched for a thick rope attached to the mast and seized it with both hands. It flayed the skin of her palms. She managed to wrap an arm around the mast. The boat shuddered again. Another blast. The mast cracked in half. The broken shaft swept Gertie with it as it catapulted over the ship's railing. Flung into the air, she opened her mouth to scream but, at that instant, she was plunged into the sea. Salt water rushed into her mouth, drowning her voice.

She sank deep into the water and instinctively shut her eyes tight. The eerily calm commander-in-chief voice ordered: *Hold your breath! Don't open your mouth; don't swallow any water.* The broken mast she was still holding onto popped her back up. *Hold on, no matter what! Hold on!* A wave crested over her head. The sea salt scalded her eyes and singed her nostrils.

I can't see, I'm blind! She panicked, but then the commander's voice returned: *You must try. Blink your eyes open and shut; clear the salt.* In a moment she managed to make out the small shapes of people around her and the larger ones of crates, burlap bundles, barrels and wood planks. Heavy sinking items created vortexes all around her. *Hold on tight!* she ordered herself *Don't let go!*

"Gertie!" a scream penetrated her waterlogged ears.

That shout, it's near! Find it! She propped herself up against the mast and sought the voice.

"Gertie!"

There he was! Alfred! Gott sei dank! Only five yards away, flapping his arms to propel himself towards her. Thank God he's such a good swimmer. *Just keep your head above the water. He will get you! Don't swallow water!*

Alfred took two long strokes and grabbed hold of her and the mast. He took three deep breaths. "Now!" he yelled and thrust his hands under her armpits, pulling her up onto his chest. He pushed off the mast and started swimming backwards in an upside-down breaststroke, dragging Gertie towards the dock. She heard him gasping for air right by her ear and felt his muscles straining to keep her afloat.

"Emil! The baby!" she screamed.

The water around them was choppy with people shouting for help, and those trying to rescue them. Alfred kept looking back to avoid colliding with pieces of cargo that had tumbled off the ship's deck. He tightened his grip on Gertie. "Raise your head up!" he yelled right into her ear, "I'll get us there. Keep kicking."

A stranger pulled them up onto the dock. They collapsed on the hard stone.

"Emil! The baby!" Gertie shrieked, seawater spurting out of her mouth and nose. "My babies!" Gertie wailed.

She buried her face in Alfred's chest.

"What happened?" the stranger asked in Yiddish.

"We got thrown . . . off the deck," Alfred answered in German, panting, "he was near us . . . he must have been thrown off too."

"Who? Who are you talking about?"

"Emil, our boy! He weighs so little, I'm sure he got thrown far off the deck."

"He . . . was . . . right next to us. And the baby . . . in the cabin," Gertie added but began to swoon. Alfred held onto her.

"In the water," Alfred continued, as if snapping together pieces of a puzzle, "Emil's a natural swimmer. He would dog paddle. Somehow, he would swim. I know he would."

"Let's hope so," the man mumbled. "I must go . . . help others."

Gertie clutched her face in her hands. She tried to say something, but only ragged sobs came out.

"Gertie, Gertie! Someone will spot him and bring him to the shore. And Benya-" Alfred choked up. "You stay here, Gertie, I'll look for him, them!"

"Me, too!" Gertie tried to stand up.

"No, Gertie! I'll search. You must wait for me here, right on this spot."

"Right here? But . . . "

"Exactly! You must stay here. We must be logical. You watch the water and the people they're pulling out and I'll search everywhere. Maybe you will see him . . . them first. And there's the First Aid station," Alfred pointed to the right, "so this is *the spot* to be."

Gertie glanced over and saw nurses and medics amidst a jumble of stretchers, army blankets and bandages. Alfred was right. How, even in this catastrophe, does he manage to hang on to logic?

"You're right, Alfred."

"I'll find him!" he thundered and spun around to go.

"The baby!" Gertie called out after him, "the baby, too!" Her hands flew up to her chest, as if to grab her heart and hold it in its place.

She crawled a few feet away from the dock's edge and sank into herself. Her body seemed splintered into disconnected parts. Her eyes darted to the ship and the swirling water around it. Her hands flailed as if to grasp Emil and Benyamin out of thin air. The rest of her body was a granite boulder.

She looked around the dock in a frenzy, left to right, then across the water, which was filled with heads and thrashing arms. She couldn't piece them together into people. She couldn't comprehend the mayhem around her. British sailors were jumping into the water from their boats, others from the dock. Fishermen were launching their small vessels into the water. Ordinary people, some carrying shopping baskets, others leather briefcases, dropped their belongings and dove into the choppy water. Those on the dock—*who probably can't swim*—pulled people up from the water and wrapped their arms across their abdomens to help them bend over and vomit the sea water.

Calls for medics swirled around her. A young man approached her and offered a water flask. She sipped once, then shook her head. She could not take another drop. "My baby! A tiny newborn," she cried out to the man and to people passing by, "please look for him! And my boy, Emil, four years old."

Her voice barely carried past her own ears in the cacophony. British officers called out orders, vainly trying to establish order. A bullhorn barked at people to sit down, to stop screaming, stop running. Except for Gertie, everyone kept rushing every which way, yelling for help, calling out names. Parents called for children, husbands for wives and young ones for their parents.

Gertie wept and rocked back and forth, staring at the water and scanning the dock. She searched every face of those hauled out of the water, desperate to spot someone she knew, anyone who'd stood on the deck next to them, who might have seen Emil. She forced her lips shut to stop the shrieks that kept leaping out of her throat. Just keep looking! Anyone carrying a child? A baby? Where's that English nurse?

Chapter 31

Gertie gaped in disbelief at the *Patria* as it shuddered and listed further over. It was on its side now, half-submerged. Strange ... it looked so stable at this angle, as if this were its natural position. She squinted; yes ... there were still many people on the deck. Emil could be there —hanging onto something for dear life. *Please, please* ... perhaps he'd managed to hold onto the ropes where he'd been playing ... "

She called a British soldier passing by her and demanded in her halting English: "Why you not going to ship, save people still on the boat? My boy, my baby ... is there!"

"Too dangerous, now, Ma'am. The ship could sink suddenly and create a huge whirlpool that would suck our boats down."

"But, mister," she pleaded, "what happened?"

"Seems like an explosion."

"But ... " she couldn't find the words.

"We'll continue the rescue operation as soon as the Commanding Officer decides it's safe. There are clearly survivors still on the ship."

Now the Palestine Police and Royal Navy officers took charge more forcefully, pulling their billy clubs out of their holsters. Bullhorns blared, ordering everyone to line up and show their identification papers. But people kept on running and calling out names, looking at every face they passed. The most desperate ones were those, like Alfred, who were searching for their children.

Alfred returned and collapsed at Gertie's side. She knew. They stared at each other: how could it be? Both children drowned?

"Nein!" Gertie cried out and fell into Alfred's arms.

They sat in silence; eyes glued to the *Patria*. The sun had risen in the sky and dried their clothes, which were now hardened with crusts of salt. The bullhorns continued their exhortations.

"We must line up," Alfred stood up.

"No!" Gertie didn't move.

"Gertie, we must. Look," he pointed to a company of British soldiers marching towards them, rifles at the ready. He pulled her to her feet, wrapped his arm around her waist and dragged her forward.

"You must help me, Gertie, I can't carry you. Just come to the line. We'll register and I'll go looking again." He pointed to a row with passengers from the *Atlantic*. "Let's join them. They know us; maybe someone saw something."

Gertie didn't resist but didn't help either. She stared blankly at the faces, as if they were strangers, even those she knew well from their long journey. She heard several women suck in their breath and stifle a cry when they saw her empty arms.

An officer ordered them to stand in a double row and began counting them one by one.

"You are Group D2. Remember your individual number!"

The loudspeaker crackled: "Attention, please! Two small girls and one baby have been found. They are at Command Headquarters by the southern gate."

"A baby! A baby! Alfred!" Gertie shrieked. They moved as if a great wind had scooped them up. She'd never run so fast. They had to dodge shipwreck survivors everywhere. People jumped aside as Gertie cried out, "Our baby!" and Alfred, "Make way! Let us through!"

They arrived breathless. An officer had the baby in his arms, wrapped in an army blanket, only his button nose and feathery eyebrows peeped out of the cocoon. His eyes were shut against the bright sun. A corporal, flanking the sergeant's left, put his hand out to stop them three feet away.

"Sergeant MacMillan," Alfred addressed the officer by the name on his badge, "it is our baby!" Before anyone could say a word, another woman arrived. She was panting too hard to speak. Her husband followed and steadied her with hands at her back. Gertie stepped in front of them. "This baby, it is mine! He is born just two weeks ago."

"No!" the other woman cried, "I have one, too —just born."

MacMillan blanched and pulled back, tightening his grip on the baby.

"I'm not here to be a modern-day Solomon," he grumbled to the corporal by his side. "Every bloody single day in this God forsaken place," he added, "I wish we were back home."

"You're not the only one, Sir."

MacMillan took a deep breath and narrowed his eyes, looking from one mother to the other, and back.

"Do you have any m-m-marks . . . by which y-y-you can identify th-th-the baby?" "Damn that stutter," MacMillan silently cursed and hardened his jaw.

"Black hair," both women said in unison.

Gertie froze.

"W-W-What else?"

Silence first. Then Gertie said: "Uncircumcised."

"Mine too!"

MacMillan frowned. He stared at them, his thoughts gathering on his forehead. "But you . . . are b-b-both Jews, no?'

"Yes, but on the boat," Alfred took a small step forward, "no proper conditions."

"This b-b-baby was born on the b-boat?"

"On that boat," Alfred pointed to the *Atlantic*.

MacMillan looked shocked.

"An-n-nything else?"

Gertie closed her eyes and retraced kissing every part of the baby's body in the days after he was born. His chubby arms and thighs, his round, fatty knees and elbows, his sweet-smelling chest, his milky palms, and the velvety soles of his feet.

"He has a beauty spot, almost black, behind his left knee," Gertie said. The other mother remained silent, sucking in her lips. Her husband's fingers dug into her shoulders, knuckles standing out like small pebbles.

As if opening the most precious gift, MacMillan pulled at the end of the blanket tucked in around the baby's side. He glanced at the mothers to make sure they had summoned the strength for the moment that was coming. He unwrapped the swaddling, still damp with seawater. A pungent, clammy smell rose up. The corporal shut his nostrils with his finger and thumb, but Gertie inhaled. "Yes, it's him!" she called out. But then she wondered silently: could she really identify that odor as Benyamin's?

MacMillan nestled the baby in the crook of his arm as he unfolded his left leg. Gertie threw her face in, while Alfred held onto her. She gulped some air, then held her breath.

"Yes!" she screamed. "There!" she pointed to a black spot, no bigger than a small lentil. She held out her hands, tears streaming down her face. Alfred steadied her, and himself, holding onto her shoulders. "Ben . . . ya-min," his voice cracked, "our Benyamin."

MacMillan rewrapped the blanket loosely and put the baby in Gertie's arms. The other mother turned without a word, her empty hands drooping like lifeless limbs. Her husband embraced her and pulled her away. Gertie re-swaddled Benyamin and pressed him to her chest. Alfred wrapped his right arm around her back and his left around the bottom of the blanket, where the baby's feet were cocooned. They walked together crying and laughing, kissing the baby on every inch of exposed skin.

"Gott sei Dank! *Ein kleines schwarzes Pünktchen*; a little black dot!" Gertie wept.

"Kleiner Schwarzkopf, kleines schwarzes Pünktchen..." Alfred's voice cracked.

They found a wooden crate to sit on and tried to catch their breath. Gertie slowly softened her grasp on the baby.

"Emil, Alfred!" the beast of fear roared again.

"I'll go look some more."

"Yes, go!"

"I'll keep coming back. Don't move, Gertlein."

Gertie barely nodded; her head was suddenly too heavy to move. She laid her cheek on the baby's head for a moment, then settled him on the breast.

Chapter 32

Alfred scoured the docks in a methodical progression from the edge of the water to the big warehouses. He saw many children without parents. Some were standing rooted in place and crying, others were held by strangers. Teenagers wandered the length of the docks alone, calling out for Mama and Papa. Names pounded his ears: "Erich, Elena, Yosele, Franticzek, Miriam, Yakov, Zdenka." He winced at the familiar ones. "Emil!" he added his voice, shouting "E-meeel!"

He bent down to look at the face of each child he passed. No. Not him. A head of brown curls made his heart jump. He overtook the boy in three giraffe-like steps but no. After traversing the dock twice, he went back to the Command Headquarters to see if they had posted a list of lost children. He didn't see MacMillan, so he asked another sergeant.

"Working on it, sir," Sgt. Biddle said, "we post an updated list on the hour."

"So exactly next hour? *Punkt?*" Alfred instinctively reached his hand into the inner pocket of his jacket. Miraculously, his pocket watch was there. He pulled it out. It read 9:17; the moment he'd plunged into the sea.

"Working as fast as we can, sir. And you, in fact, are getting in the way," the sergeant added as he flicked a speck of dust off his left shoulder, right under the insignia on his epaulet.

"So sorry, sir. I come back in one hour."

"Some preliminary lists are already posted on the side of the building," Sgt. Biddle suddenly softened. "We've got a kind of 'Lost and Found Center' there."

"Thank you! I look now."

"Mind you, I expect it should take until the afternoon to have a complete list of survivors, let alone the missing."

Rounding the corner, Alfred had to lean against the building, unable to stop the violent trembling of his knees. Five pages of lined paper were tacked to the sidewall. He leaned in. Each page had two columns, side by side. "Survived" on the left, "Missing" on the right. They looked no different than a student's list of vocabulary words. He scanned the names, moving his finger across each row. Once, then again: Name, Age, Sex, Eye Color, Hair Color, Other Identifying Markings.

A four-year-old boy with brown eyes and brown hair was not listed. Alfred picked up the pencil dangling from a shoelace next to the list. His hand shook as he shaped each letter.

Alfred returned to the list hourly. Each time Gertie collapsed into herself when she saw him walking back, stooped like an old man over a cane, shaking his head. At mid-afternoon he sat with her for a while, just looking at her and Benyamin. She was staring, hypnotized, as the hull of the *Patria* kept dipping lower into the sea. Once in a while, the ship groaned, as if it were an old lady with rheumatism. By now most of it was submerged. The three smokestacks protruded from the water at a diagonal, the narrow white bands still visible. The grey tops blended into the clouds on the horizon.

Gertie kept her gaze on the part of the deck still above water. No matter how hard she looked and squinted, she couldn't tell if there were still people there. She followed every fishing skiff and British Navy patrol boat that returned to the dock from the carcass of the ship. At first, they had brought back passengers, some plucked from the ship's deck, others from the water. She could tell from the way some bodies dangled when transferred to shore, that not everyone was alive. As the afternoon wore on, more and more boats returned empty.

Alfred put his hand on her knee. She did not respond. Suddenly her gut convulsed. "Look there, Alfred," she pointed at the *Patria*. "Do you see something?"

"Where?"

"There, on the far right of the deck! Is that a child?"

"Gertlein . . . I cannot see anything. It's too far."

"Look harder!"

"I am. I'm sure if there were a child there, they would have brought him in by now."

Gertie bit her lower lip and said nothing. The salty taste still in her mouth mingled with blood. Alfred went to look at the list and scour the docks again.

When he returned Gertie was sitting in the same position, staring at the ship. She nursed the baby, but it felt as if her breasts were an artificial attachment, pumping milk out on their own. She did not answer when Alfred called her name. He sat down and caressed the baby's head. Finally, Gertie looked at him and told him she'd seen two men trying to jump into the water to swim back to the *Patria* to rescue their wives. They had to be restrained. Two soldiers hoisted each man by the armpits and force-walked them towards the warehouses. People looked away as the men shouted. Another man begged an Arab fisherman to take him back, but he refused. The people brought ashore collapsed on the dock calling out a name, or two, or three.

Chapter 33

In late afternoon British soldiers corralled everyone into new groups of forty, this time with military gruffness. No one, except Alfred, remembered the name of their earlier group. "So much for D2," he snarled. A row of soldiers, hands on the barrels of their rifles, stood behind the officer with the megaphone, who announced:

"You will now be taken to temporary safety in a British army facility. Board the buses in an orderly fashion, women and families with children first. Once the buses are filled, proceed to the army lorries on the left. Now!"

"No, Alfred," Gertie's voice rattled with a suppressed sob. "We can't leave yet. We have to keep looking for Emil. He must be here somewhere!"

"Gertlein," Alfred held her, "we have no choice. You see those soldiers? Their rifles? The bayonets at the ends?"

Gertie shook her head so vigorously her hair, matted with dried salt, slapped her cheeks and forehead. "No, please, no . . ."

"And" Alfred tightened his hold around her and the baby, "we are more likely to find Emil once we get there, to that 'British Army Facility.'"

"No."

"Gertie, listen. There are thousands of people here. It's total chaos. We'll never find him here. At the place where they're taking us, we'll sort things out. I'll speak with the officers right away when we get there."

Gertie shook her head but allowed Alfred to drag her up and forward. They were practically carried by the swarm of people moving towards the vehicles. Several buses at the front were already full, the drivers shooing people away and trying to close the doors. At the first bus they could board Alfred pushed Gertie from behind as she climbed the stairs. She held the baby in one arm, propelling herself up by gripping the door handle with the other.

Her body felt leaden. She needed a strap to lift each knee and drag up her foot at each step. It was not her weight, but a mighty force yanking her back to the dock, to the sinking ship, to keep looking, to keep calling "E- meel!"

Chapter 34

Gertie shuffled down the bus aisle, mechanically taking a package of dry biscuits a British soldier handed each passenger. They were already half crumbled in their cellophane wrapper. No matter, she could not imagine eating them anyway. *You must, though, for the baby; to keep the milk supply.* She dropped onto the first open seat and slid over to the window. Alfred plunked down next to her with a thud. He grasped the edge of the seat in front of him so tightly the skin on his bony fingers stretched to near translucence. "*Und, so*," he said under his breath, "forward, to God knows where."

Gertie settled the baby in her bosom and rested her cheek against the cool glass of the window. Through half-closed eyes she scanned the embarking passengers. *The dregs of humanity*, she couldn't help thinking as several elderly people doddered down the narrow aisle. Four young men followed, their faces contorted by the contradiction of rage and resignation. A tall woman came next, nearly carrying another woman about her age, whose pregnant belly seemed to barely hang on to her emaciated frame. "Hold on to hope," the tall woman exhorted. "What hope?" the pregnant one yelled, "with no husband? And my sister lost, too! I have nothing."

Gertie shuddered and clenched her teeth to stifle a scream. Alfred pressed his hand on her thigh. "Gertlein," he whispered, "don't listen to anyone else. It's not good for you. Try to eat the biscuit, for the baby's sake." She fumbled with the crinkly cellophane, then made a small tear with her teeth. The package split open, right where it was stamped with a silver imprint of the British Crown. The crown was cut in half. "So sorry, your Majesty," she said, shaking her head, "but thank you for these."

She pulled out a pinch of crumbs, but her hand seemed frozen in place until she marshaled the commander-in-chief's voice: *Open your mouth. Put the biscuit in. Chew. Swallow.* The hard pieces tasted vaguely of mildew, but she kept chewing. The sugar pumped a burst of energy into her body. She remembered feeding this kind of cracker to Emil when he started teething. Stop! she ordered herself. Stop the memories or you'll rip yourself in half . . .

Alfred handed Gertie his package of biscuits. "Tea-time! Biscuits and jam coming up, and a nice cup-o-tea, dearie," he announced in an exaggerated British accent. Gertie pushed the package back.

"Again, with your silly jokes, Alfred. Nothing is funny! Nothing!" She stopped herself, mortified that she was yelling.

"Forgive me, Gertie," he blurted out, chastened, "I don't know what to say. I don't know what to do." His voice cracked. He clasped and unclasped his hands.

"I know," she touched his arm and managed a forgiving nod.

Alfred moved a little closer to her, pressing against her. She forced herself to allow the warmth from his body to penetrate her skin and gave a nod to show him she appreciated it. He placed the package in her lap, then tucked his hands between his thighs, squeezing hard.

Gertie softened towards him. With her free hand she gently pulled out his right palm from the crevice he had made. She threaded her fingers through his. He glanced at her sideways, then brought their entwined hands to his lips and kissed the spot on her finger where her wedding band had been, a thin line of un-tanned skin.

Gertie made herself eat every bit of broken biscuit in her package and put Alfred's in her pocket. She draped the baby on her shoulder. He didn't wake. She was thankful that he'd slept and slept—nearly the whole time since they'd reclaimed him. "Lucky little baby," she whispered in his tiny conch of an ear, "you don't understand." She rested her cheek on his head for a fleeting moment of gratitude.

Chapter 35

But the moment passed in an instant. Panic leapt at her like a wild beast. She gasped for air. Screams for Emil exploded in her head. *Quiet,* she admonished them, *quiet down. It's no use.* She flattened her forehead against the windowpane, pressing hard until it hurt. She wanted to bang her head on the glass: *Emil, Emil, Emil,* with each slam.

"I can't take it . . . " She whispered to herself and shook her head. Her eyelids dropped down like a roll top desk whose hinges had suddenly broken. She dozed off, then startled awake in disbelief that she'd fallen asleep with the raging storm in her head.

The bus driver closed the door. Gertie looked back as they drove out of the port onto a busy street. Alfred got up and walked down the aisle, row by row. Gertie watched him holding onto the edges of the seats, swaying with the bumpy ride and questioning every single passenger. She couldn't hear him, but she knew what he was saying. "Four years old, round face, brown eyes, brown curls. Tall for his age, a smile showing gaps between his lower teeth and," and, as he'd promised her he'd remember to say, "a round beauty mark on his left ear lobe." People shook their heads, lowering their eyes.

Alfred returned and crumpled into the seat. "No one has seen Emil." He told Gertie what she already knew. A couple seated in the last row couldn't find their ten-year-old daughter, either. He touched the man's arm and whispered: "I understand."

The bus drove down the main road flanking the port. Gertie craned her head to hold the sinking *Patria* in view as long as she could. Finally, it slipped away. *What had actually happened? An explosion? An attack? An accident?* She wanted to ask Alfred but was afraid of the flood of sobs that would rush out if she opened her mouth.

Alfred looked out the front window. He scanned the shabby houses they passed in town. From the position of the sun, he surmised they were heading north along Haifa's main street, cluttered with shops and eclectic-style buildings on their left, and the bay on their right. The sun's late afternoon rays glowed on the hills in the distance. Someone called out: "The hills there—"

"That must be the Galilee."

"Look! Palm trees!"

"Like we heard about from the youth movement Shlichim."

"Like the pictures we saw!"

Soon the bus began to arc left and head west. They now faced the sun, steadily sliding towards the horizon. Gertie kept scanning the street, as if somehow Emil would pop up behind a house, around a corner. *You're losing your mind,* Gertie told herself when she realized she was even looking at the branches of trees they passed. She made herself close her eyes and remove one dart of torture.

Most of passengers on the bus quickly fell asleep, their heads lolling back and forth or bouncing as the bus turned and jerked. Alfred forced his eyes open and stared intently at the road, as if it were vital for him to know their route, as if he had to know how to come back. *If only he had breadcrumbs . . .*

Suddenly Alfred saw blue ahead. "Look," he touched Gertie on the shoulder.

She opened her eyes halfway. "What?"

"The open sea. Who can believe we came from there just yesterday? Who could've guessed what was coming?"

"*Katastrophe. Grosse Katastrophe.* That's what was coming."

Soon they were driving south on a narrower, rough road hugging the coast. The sun was about to plunge into the sea. Gertie watched the pink light of dusk spread across the horizon, decorated by scattered clouds turning crimson at the edges. Furious, she whispered, "How dare you be beautiful?"

Chapter 36

The same setting sun nearly blinded Moussa and Youssra as they trudged along the road home. The day-long journey from their Galilee village was nearly over.

"Look how beautiful!" Moussa pointed at the western sky, the horizon aglow in orange and maroon-edged clouds.

"Yes, beautiful!" Youssra agreed, a little surprised that Moussa noticed.

"A sky of gold; clouds of rubies," Moussa said in a soft tone, almost reverent.

Youssra raised her eyebrows. She'd never heard him talk that way.

"Allah is the greatest painter," Moussa continued, as if in a trance.

"Moussa, what happened to you? You sound like a poet!"

Moussa smiled at her proudly. Yes, let her see I'm more than just a fisherman. Sure, I can't read, but I have heard enough poetry. I have an ear for it. I've composed some; they're memorized. Should I tell her?

"It is beautiful," Youssra said. But then, speaking softly - not to splash too much cold water on him - added, "but soon it'll be totally dark and we have a ways to go."

"You are right. An hour to walk all the way. But maybe we can catch a ride on another cart."

"That would be nice," Youssra said, suddenly feeling the full weight of the burlap sack balanced on her head.

They had left the village at dawn after five arduous days helping their families with the labors of the turning of the seasons.

"How was the olive harvest in your family's orchard?" Moussa started a new conversation, burying the poems that were already on his tongue.

"Beautiful olives, so plump and shiny-black, the oil will run out of them by itself."

"Ours, too."

"But," Youssra added, "fewer this year."

"Same in our *basatin*. Olive orchards go like this - a see-saw. One year a big harvest, the next small."

He pulled on the straps holding the jug of olive oil slung over his shoulder, to hoist it higher up. His mind took him back to his father's fields, to how he loved the little clods of damp soil crawling up between his toes as he walked the freshly turned furrows. He feathered out his nostrils to remember the smell of the moist earth, inhaling tiny particles of dirt which sank to the bottom of his lungs, just above his belly. That was where he always felt their absence when the first rain washed Haifa's dusty streets. Though he'd grown used to the sea, the briny tang of seawater could never make him feel at home the way wet earth did.

They snaked their way along the gravel road, exhaustion settling deep in their muscles and bones. Getting back from the village to Haifa took all day; part on foot, part in a donkey-cart. The sacks full of dried chickpeas and carobs, and the jug of new olive oil got heavier as the day wore on.

"It was a good visit," Moussa said after a while.

"My family too, and I helped my mother finish embroidering two dresses for my little sister's dowry."

"The last one to be married off! That's good news for your parents."

"My mother is already talking about the next grandson."

"That's all she talks about," Moussa said. "Must be hard on you."

"Yes, but my sisters are very kind. They always thank me so sweetly for helping with their children."

"Of course, you're so good with little ones."

An awkward silence hung between them, like a beaded curtain—not a complete partition, but a veil, separating them.

"Amala," Moussa tried to part the curtain, "she told me too. How you help her with her boys. Especially now."

"She told you?" Youssra tried to hide her alarm. "I am sorry, I didn't ask your permission to go there. But she is desperate."

"Of course - it's a *farḍ*. Why would I oppose you fulfilling a good deed? Of course, you can go."

Youssra stepped more lightly, relieved that Moussa now knew and approved. But her cheer quickly vanished before a more familiar, painful feeling—envy. But how can you envy a widow raising three boys under five? she berated herself. Three boys, that's how, she answered. And me —three miscarriages. They all rushed in, a grim parade. The time the midwife held the "thing" - couldn't call it a baby - in her cupped palm; the time it was so small the midwife didn't bother finding it in the gush of blood; the time they didn't bother calling the midwife anymore. And after that, the times she didn't even tell Moussa about the bleeding in the middle of the night.

Immediately, she heard her mother's voice: "Envy is your biggest enemy." How did she always know? How did she see it even though Youssra hid her private thoughts and even some of her actions? Could her mother see the sharp arrows Youssra felt darting out of her pupils? Was it in her pursed lips—as if she'd just drunk a cup of vinegar?

Youssra sighed. The very first sting of envy was still so vivid: her older sister's first pair of shoes. Rasheeda had been so thrilled she'd worn them to bed. When *Yumma* discovered it in the morning she forbade it, instructing Rasheeda to line them up at the edge of her mattress. The next night Youssra kept herself awake and, the house silent, sneaked over and put the shoes on. She wore the shoes to bed too, telling herself it was only for a few minutes; she'll get up soon and put them back where they belonged. But somehow it was suddenly morning, Rasheeda wailing: "A thief, Yumma! A thief came at night and took my shoes!"

Their mother stepped in from the kitchen, her hands white with flour. "There's no thief, Rasheeda. You forgot to put them where I told you. Now go wash your face and I'll find them for you." The moment Rasheeda left the room Yumma sat next to Youssra and lifted the bottom of her blanket. Youssra turned crimson and buried her face in her hands. Yumma unbuckled the shoes and shoved them part way under the low shelf in the corner. She pointed to the shoes when Rasheeda returned: "There they are. And that's a better place to stow them than the end of the mattress, so keep them there."

Rasheeda looked puzzled but quickly got busy putting the shoes on and buffing the buckles with her sleeve. All day long Youssra avoided her mother despite wishing she could fall into her embrace and thank her. At bedtime Yumma leaned close to Youssra's ear and whispered those words about envy. Youssra let her tears flow. Her mother dabbed them and whispered: "Now you know."

She did know, yet she couldn't banish envy. It kept coming: when her brother Assif, two years her junior, started school, when her mother embroidered a dress for Rasheeda's twelfth birthday, and when, soon thereafter, boys started following Rasheeda along the village paths.

"Your turn will come too," Yumma told Youssra each time, but she couldn't wait, couldn't smile and nod, as was expected. Envy kept clawing at her heart, climbing up her windpipe and searing her throat till she could hardly breathe. The torture of shame, still there, every day. Worst were her hands which balled into fists whenever she walked past a pregnant woman. Thank Allah, she always managed to tuck them into her sleeve or clasp them behind her back, but in her mind, she pounded them into every protruding belly.

Youssra's hands clamped into tight fists now. She willed them to open; willed herself to pity Amala. Now, logic returned: "Wait a minute," she turned to Moussa, "Amala told you? You talked to her?"

Moussa cleared his throat with a triplet of small coughs. "I . . . I go to her, maybe once a week, to bring her fish. When I have extra. Since Ramadan ended people aren't bringing her much anymore."

"I didn't know you . . . "

"I'm careful. I look up and down the alley to make sure no one sees me at her door."

"You didn't tell me," Youssra said, unable to hide the hint of accusation in her voice.

"The highest level of charity is the one that is concealed. That's according to the Prophet."

"May he be blessed. It's good, Moussa. She must be so grateful. Such a fate. So lucky to have those boys, and yet so unlucky to have them."

"Yes, three boys, just like that: one, two, three; and now no father."

"At least she's lucky not to be carrying his fourth," Youssra said.

"You know it?"

"Yes, definitely."

"How can you be sure, Youssra? It's not so long since . . . "

"She told me. She knew already in the summer, right after the explosion. She always knew right away when she got pregnant before, with each of the three boys."

Moussa was not sure what to say; he'd never had such an explicit conversation about these matters with Youssra. He looked away and busied his hands adjusting the straps on his shoulders. In a flash one thought clicked into another, as though the teeth of a flywheel locked into place. There was a way he could get Youssra to propose exactly what Amala had. If he just proceeded wisely, laid the ideas out as one would place down stepping-stones. At first the slabs seem set at random spots, you step here and there, then suddenly you realize they make a path.

"How she'll manage with the three boys . . . " Moussa said, acutely aware of feeling both cunning and guilty.

"She'll have to pray for someone to marry her. As soon as her *'Iddah* is over."

"You think anyone will, Youssra?"

"With her talent for producing boys—someone will take her."

"Someone will."

"Yes, as an act of kindness. Like the Prophet did for his wives," Youssra agreed.

"Inshalllah," Moussa said and admonished himself not to utter one more word. He had laid down the first stone in the path.

Chapter 37

Up on the Carmel at that moment, the sky seemed on fire. Lucas had just come out of the chapel after Vespers, the Madonna's grace stretched like a protective membrane over his agitated mind. He wrapped himself tightly in his thick wool habit to fend off the fingers of frigid air climbing up from the sea. He circled the paved courtyard with his head bowed down, then raised his eyes and looked to the west. The dazzling sunsets here tore him up inside. On the one hand, the glory of the Lord's handiwork was right in front of him. How lucky he was to behold it in the Holy Land itself! But the very same grandeur made him so homesick, so lonesome for the softer hues of the sun descending over the hills that ringed his village. Today he felt more bereft than usual because the beauty of nature clashed so harshly with the doings of man.

In the morning they had heard a thunderous roar from the lower city, but it was not until afternoon that information reached the monastery. A ship in the harbor was either bombed from the air, torpedoed by a submarine, or exploded through other means. It sank with many people on board. The monks had discussed the news all afternoon, as Father Pierre turned a blind eye to the violation of their code of parsimonious conversation.

Brother Lucien thought an aerial bombing seemed most plausible —there had been many. But no one remembered hearing or seeing airplanes. Others argued for a torpedo: that would square with the lack of any visible attacker. There had been two other such incidents since summer; Italian or German U-boats reaching Palestine's coast.

"Maybe a shelling from across the port?" Donatien suggested, "or an explosion on the ship itself —accident or sabotage?"

The ship, they had learned from radio transmissions and Arab peddlers at the monastery gate, was full of Jewish refugees. Rescue operations had gone on all day but many were feared drowned. Were these the same refugees he had seen at the port a few days before, marooned on the two dilapidated boats? The ones he had beseeched Father Pierre to help? Had the Abbot done anything for them? Would he regret now that all he'd offered was some blankets, medicine, and Psalters?

But it was not his place to question, let alone criticize, Father Pierre. "Humility," Lucas had instructed himself and bowed his head. It was his seemingly eternal struggle; he needed solitude to muster it. Instead of returning to the chapel, he had gone out of the gate and headed to his favorite rock, to sit and look out west, over the expanse of the Mediterranean.

As the glow of the sunset began to subside the waves in the sea looked almost black. The headlights of occasional cars and trucks illuminated the narrow dark road hugging the coastline. Such disparate lives, Lucas thought to himself, up here and down there, on the road. And yet each one of us heading towards our own destiny. For a moment he let himself imagine that he could see past the horizon, all the way to his village and his family's home. And, his eyes closed, he saw his mother, bent over in her grief for him, her long-gone boy.

Chapter 38

After a long rough ride, as the sea popped in and out of view between the windswept hillocks in the darkening dusk, the bus turned right onto an even narrower road. Alfred tapped Gertie's shoulder. "We're here, wherever this 'here' is." She looked out the window. They were driving down a road lit by the last glow of the setting sun and weak floodlights on poles interspersed between tall palms. Despite herself, Gertie had to admit the trees were charming. The slim trunks rose up over two stories high from the salt-crusted sand. Their pompon-like green tops swayed in the wind.

The baby opened his eyes and seemed to look out of the window with purpose. She kissed his nose. "I'll knit you a wool hat with a pompom, Benyaminku." She clenched her teeth to stop the next thought: Emil had one.

They stopped at an iron gate flanked by a two-meter-high stone wall crowned with serpentine barbed wire. At the gate stood two soldiers. A tall officer, with "Palestine Police" embossed on his cap, poked his head through the driver's window and announced that they'd arrived at the British detention camp of Atlit. Then he lifted the heavy latch and swung the gate open. The bus rolled forward, gravel crunching loudly under its wheels. They passed a row of squat cabins on each side of the road with dark wood walls and mustard-yellow shutters, and stopped in a large square yard. Bright spotlights washed out the rose hues of dusk. The driver opened the door and a British officer climbed aboard, black billy club in his right hand. He slapped the club into his left palm as he spoke:

"Everyone will disembark in an orderly fashion, starting with the front seats. Outside you will line up to register; women on the right, men on the left. You will be given dinner and assigned to your barracks. No exceptions, no questions, no special requests. Proceed now. In silence!"

The passengers peeled off their seats one by one. No one said a word. Gertie handed the baby to Alfred and shuffled down the aisle. At the top of the stairs, she stood as if she had forgotten how one goes about descending. She held her breath and got herself down, stepping gingerly onto the ground. She winced at the grating sound of the gravel crushed under her feet. Alfred followed, nestling Benyamin against his chest. As soon as he was off the bus, Gertie reached out to take the baby back. She needed him against her bosom. Alfred wrapped his arm around her and cupped his open palm over the baby's head. He dragged Gertie forward and positioned her in the women's line, then stepped sideways into the men's queue.

Over the buzz of hushed conversations, he said to Gertie, "Tonight we'll ask everybody in our own barrack, and tomorrow everyone else."

Gertie nodded, too spent to form actual words.

"And I'll speak with the British policemen as soon as possible."

The refugees proceeded, single file, to the registration desks. From there they walked over to a long, narrow table where they were handed a mess kit with army rations: two cubes of minced canned meat, four dry biscuits, one packet labeled "meat broth," and two sugar cubes. They were marched towards the barracks, men on the left, women on the right. Gertie knew she had the baby to hold on to all night; she couldn't fathom how Alfred would get through the dark hours. He looked so bereft as he shuffled into the men's camp.

Gertie's group was led to the third barrack in the women's camp.

Out of the corner of her eye she registered the length of the row: at least ten barracks, maybe twelve. Inside the barrack were twenty army cots, ten to a side with a narrow aisle down the middle.

"You'll have to share cots," The British officer at the door informed them. The cots were jammed so close together you had to walk sideways between them to get through. Gertie found one towards the back, where women from a different group were already fumbling with blankets, trying to settle down.

"You, with the baby," said a skinny woman sitting on a cot, "we'll let you have this one all to yourself." She moved over to the next cot, where a heavy-set woman already sat and snapped, "Some people have all the luck."

Gertie nearly screamed, but she forced her mouth to stay shut. She sat on the brown blanket with PP embossed in a circle in the center and "Palestine Police" embroidered in shiny khaki thread in the corner. The blanket was rough and itchy, but she was too tired to care. She set the mess kit aside for later and laid Benyamin down in the middle of the cot. She picked up the thin towel from where a pillow should be and tore at the side with her teeth until she'd made a small rip. Grabbing the edges, she pulled hard and tore the towel in half. "Sorry," she apologized to her neighbors for the shrill ripping sound.

She rose and dipped the half towel in the barrel of water she'd noticed at the end of the barrack. She gently unwrapped the army blanket that had been Benyamin's swaddling since he was found. The baby whimpered as she cleaned his red, chafed bottom with the wet cloth and tried not to breathe in the sour smell. She swaddled him in the remaining half of the towel and wrapped up the soiled blanket and wet strip as tightly as she could, to trap the odor inside. She'd figure out how to wash them tomorrow.

A high-pitched tearing sound snatched Gertie's gaze away from the baby to her neighbors. Without a word, the woman at her right tore off a third of her towel and handed it to Gertie. The one on her left did the same. So did three women in the cots across the aisle. Gertie's eyes welled up. "There I go," she told herself. As far back as she could remember, what made her cry—in books or the cinema—was not tragedy and misery, but human kindness.

"*Danke*," she said, letting her tears flow, "you are so kind."

"You'll need it more than I will," her neighbor said. "What? You think we'll get a real bath here? Who needs a full-size towel?"

"Thank you. What is your name?"

"Miriam. But my friends call me Mimi. You can, too."

"Where from?"

"Prague. I came with a youth movement group."

"Ah, yes, the Praguers. We had some on the *Atlantic*." Gertie tried to muster a smile.

"I was on the *Milos*."

"But we're all in the same boat now, aren't we," Gertie said.

"In a way," Miriam agreed, "now it's those who lost a family member versus the lucky ones."

"You?" Gertie raised her eyebrows.

"One of the lucky ones. Most of us younger people are, since we came alone."

"Lucky . . . " Gertie groaned.

"But friends . . . " Miriam stopped herself and shook her head.

Gertie swallowed hard and looked into Miriam's eyes, which she saw were caressing Benyamin, now sleeping again in Gertie's arms. So young, Gertie thought to herself, what could she know about luck?

Mimi met Gertie's gaze. "How lucky *you* are—to have your baby."

"Nein..." Gertie shook her head and pressed back her tears. "Yes, but no. I have a boy, too. Four years old. We couldn't find him," she whispered.

"Forgive me! I only knew what I saw."

"Of course."

"On th-the d-d-docks," Miriam stammered, "I saw women who lost their babies. But I didn't know about your boy."

Gertie could say nothing more. She sank her face into the baby's swaddling, letting it swallow her tears.

Miriam got us and came to sit next to Gertie. "Tomorrow you'll look for him in the camp. I can help you. I can ask people. I heard there are some orphans."

"Orphans! Where?" Gertie cried out.

"In the last barrack, at the end of our row."

"I'm going!" Gertie swooped up the baby quickly and jumped to her feet.

"No," Miriam pulled her back down. "We can't now. We're not allowed out of our barracks. Didn't you see the armed guards at the door?"

Gertie let Miriam seat her down on the cot. "*Ja, ja*. I understand," she forced the words out between her tight lips, "later."

Gertie lay down on the cot and curled her body around Benyamin. She pulled the itchy blanket over her head, burrowing under it. She clutched him to her chest and he rooted for the breast. She helped him latch on. With the letdown of the milk, she let her tears flow. They soaked the rough sheet.

Chapter 39

With the first light of dawn Gertie bolted upright. She bundled Benyamin in every bit of cloth she had and tied him in a sling against her chest. Outside the white-washed stones marking the edges of the path showed her the way. The camp was silent. Sporadically spaced single bulbs on lampposts shone weakly. She hurried, walking faster than she had since their march down Vienna's streets to the Danube.

Reaching the last barrack, she was thrilled to see no one stationed at the door. She slipped inside. The bare bulb's wan light was enough for her to see that the barrack had the same ineffectual kerosene stove in the middle as in hers, giving off more noxious odor than heat. She tiptoed past the cots, checking each sleeping face. The children slept two or three to a cot, the smallest nestled in young women's arms.

Gertie focused on those Emil's size. Each face captured her eyes like a magnet. She halted her breath with each quick gaze, but then let go—*not him*. She bent down to look at the children held in the women's embraces. The faces were poorly lit, but she was sure she would identify Emil in total darkness if he were there.

Two small boys, pressed against each other on the farthest cot made Gertie's heart leap. She leaned over them and craned her neck.

"What is this? Who are you?" the young woman in the next cot sat up and demanded. Gertie startled; she hadn't realized anyone was awake. She tried to speak but only a stifled cry came out. She forced out an answer: "My boy . . . he's four. We haven't seen him since the explosion." She trembled so hard she was afraid Benyamin would slip out of her arms. She tightened her embrace, commanding every muscle she had to hold herself together. "I came to see. Perhaps he was here . . . but, no."

The young woman looked at Benyamin, his face peeking from the sling. "I am so sorry," she said softly, "but at least you have the baby."

"Ach . . . what 'at least'?"

Too many people had already said that to her. Each time it was like a kick in the gut.

"Forgive me. I'm . . . just so sorry," the woman's voice quavered. She got up and put her arm on Gertie's shoulder, supporting her as she shuffled out of the barrack.

Outside the fresh sea breeze stroked Gertie's skin with cool fingers. But inside her body live coals burned. She returned to her barrack and crumpled onto her cot. Her mess kit was there with last nights' dinner and an additional boiled-grey potato, a piece of herring, and a small sticky square of something she did not recognize. She settled the baby under the blanket and thanked her neighbor.

"Eat," she said, "It's not good, but it's good for you."

Gertie made herself smile and put the mess kit in her lap.

"What's your name?"

"Lilka."

"Danke, Lilka."

She stared at the food, unable to move. Then told herself, you must eat, in her mother's voice; for the baby, for Alfred, for E . . .

"Chew, chew, and . . . swallow," she chanted to herself silently. Everything tasted the same. She left the strange square thing for the end. When she picked it up gingerly between forefinger and thumb, it was a little slimy. She put it in her mouth and started chewing. She was nauseated by the overpowering sweetness and the way it made her palate and tongue feel desiccated and sticky.

"What is this?" she asked Lilka, forcing herself not to spit it out.

"They call it *halva*. It's an Arab sweet. Very nutritious, they said. It's cheap to make and never spoils."

"It never spoils because it's rotten to begin with."

Miriam entered the barrack and rushed to Gertie's cot. Gertie saw the question on her face and just shook her head. "I'm so sorry," Miriam whispered and retreated. Gertie picked up the baby and hugged him to her body, rocking back and forth with a singsong "Ben-ya-min, Ben-ya-min."

She felt the soothing warmth of the baby seeping into her breast, but her insides twisted and wound themselves like tightly coiled ropes. She was divided in two: a top half nursing Benyamin and a bottom half screaming for Emil. It was as if she were still pumping blood into the umbilical cord that had tied her to him. She sensed the cord the way one feels a phantom limb. She sank into nursing and watched the room. Some of the women were swapping clothes, others tried to disentangle and smooth down their hair with their fingers. No one had a comb, a brush or an extra blouse. Everything had been lost on the *Patria*.

Gertie burrowed into the bed, but Lilka called her: "No Gertie, you must get ready to go out."

"Go out? Where?"

"They're letting us see the men. An hour by the fence when we can talk to each other. You must find your husband. Maybe he's heard something . . ."

She bundled Benyamin up and walked out with the rest of the women. She walked along the fence, scanning the men's faces. She narrowed her eyes, as if that way she could avoid absorbing the pain in all of them.

It didn't take long to find Alfred. *Thank goodness he's so tall—easy to spot in a crowd.*

"Alfred," Gertie called out. He waved his hands above his head. She pushed her way to a spot at the fence across from him. She decided to spare him the orphans' barrack.

"Did you find out anything?"

"I tried to get permission to go back to Haifa to search. But the British won't let anyone leave the camp."

"Never?"

"Who knows? Not now, anyway. They gave me papers to fill out. A detailed description of Emil."

"That's something."

"The officer said that the papers are filed with both the British Police and the Jewish authorities in Haifa and, then he added: 'We will do whatever is within our power, under very difficult circumstances, which, of course, Sir, you must appreciate.'"

Gertie rolled her eyes.

"Don't make it harder, Gertie. I'll keep trying."

They stood silently for a moment.

"How are the conditions there in the men's barracks?"

"Conditions?" Alfred shrugged. "That's what they are—conditions. Certainly, no comforts. But it's not Dachau."

"Ours are tolerable," Gertie said. "We even have a kerosene stove, not that it does much good."

Alfred dug into his pocket and pulled out a thin, sausage-shaped parcel wrapped in paper. "Here, Gertie," he slowly passed the package between the fence wires. "A little extra food for you I saved from the rations. Sugar cubes and bits of biscuits"

"But Alfred . . . "

"You need it! The British claim the rations meet the daily caloric requirement. Maybe, but not for a nursing mother."

Gertie took the package, partially unwrapped it and fished out two sugar cubes. "At least take one back, Alfred," she pleaded and passed it back through the same gap.

"Danke," Alfred said and popped it into his mouth.

"It's too cold to be standing still," Gertie said, pressing Benyamin deeper into her chest and wrapping both arms around him.

"Yes, strange how the cold here is nothing compared to back home, but it really penetrates into your bones."

"Home..." Gertie sighed, "at home we had wool coats and hats, fur-lined gloves."

"Let's not dwell on that."

They paced in tandem along the fence. Alfred stopped near the captain overseeing their section. "Let me try again. To make a special appeal," he said to Gertie. He stepped up to the officer, halting his right hand midway, on its way to a military salute.

"Please Mr. Officer," Alfred began. His Gymnasium English made Gertie choke up; it made him seem like a little boy.

"You must have to understand. We have a boy. A small—kleiner, yes?"

"What?" the officer barely looked at Alfred.

"Our—boy—of—four—years," Alfred enunciated every word. "He is lost yesterday in explosion of *Patria* ship. You must give help to us to find him. I must to the docks to go, to find my boy."

"What? What docks?"

"At Haifa Port."

"Sorry, Sir. There's no such option," the officer clicked his heels and turned to leave.

"But you must!' Alfred cried out. "You must to help!"

"Ach, Alfred. It's enough," Gertie put her hand up. "Come, this is no use."

Alfred interlaced his fingers so tightly that they whitened as the blood stopped pulsing through them.

"Let's continue," Gertie spoke slowly, as if to a child, "I'll look on my side. You look on yours."

Alfred just stared ahead.

"Some of the women have small children with them," Gertie added. "Maybe someone... is taking care of him until we find him."

"Maybe," Alfred managed a whisper.

She saw in his eyes how he wished he could find solace in her words.

Gertie maneuvered the baby's arm through the square gaps in the barbed wire fence, pushing it towards Alfred. Alfred cupped his hands over the baby's tiny fist and kissed his soft skin. He extended his fingers through the next hole to touch Gertie's hand. He looked away, trying to hide his tears.

"Alfred, Liebling, just keep asking everyone. And fill out the papers carefully. Remember to mention the beauty spot by his left ear and the scar on his right knee."

"I know, Gertie."

"*Meine Liebe*," she whispered to him.

A sharp whistle sounded and the bullhorn announced that "visiting hour" at the fence was over. They turned and headed towards their barracks. Gertie asked one woman after another: "Have you seen my boy? Emil. Four years old. Brown curly hair. Small gaps between his bottom teeth. A beauty spot... " Each woman lowered her eyes and shook her head. A few touched Gertie's arm. Others hugged themselves. None could bear to utter the word "no."

Gertie's voice got weaker and her steps heavier. Gradually the extraneous words peeled off, like the thin skin of an onion before you cut into its bitter flesh. She whispered in a raspy voice: "*Mein Kind, vier Jahre alt*. Four years old..."

Chapter 40

Alfred waited for her at the fence the next morning. At first, they just shook their heads at each other. She lifted Benyamin towards the fence, but Alfred turned his face away, pressing his lips together, she knew —to hold back tears. She settled the baby back into the sling.

"I inquired again with the British officer in charge of my section last night," Alfred finally spoke. "This one, on the late shift, was nice, went out of his way . . . "

"A British officer nice to us?"

"He was, Gertie. He wrote down Emil's name and age and my description and said he would check both the full roster of survivors and . . . "

"What do you mean 'the full roster'?"

"Those here and those in Haifa hospitals. You know that there are many injured people in hospitals, Ja?"

She frowned, "But of course! How hadn't I thought of that until now?"

"And also . . . " Alfred said grimly, "the full list of bodies recovered from the water."

"Bodies . . . "

"But most of the drowned are still trapped inside the ship under water."

Gertie covered her eyes.

"He told me he has a boy at home."

"Who?"

"The British officer. Two years old. In Glasgow. Born after he shipped here. He hasn't seen him yet."

"So, he can understand?" Gertie's eyes filled.

"Yes. But... this morning he found me at the breakfast line and just shook his head and turned up his hands."

Gertie gripped a section of wire between two barbs and pressed her forehead against it.

"No touching the fence!" a British soldier immediately called out and raised his billy club. "Step back at once!"

"Schwein," Alfred hissed under his breath.

"Shush, Alfred, it won't help us."

In the afternoon a young woman from the orphans' barrack came in with a baby girl, about six months old, in her arms. "Do you recognize this baby?" she asked every woman she passed. No one did. She said she'd been to every barrack. No one knew who the baby's parents were. They'd probably drowned. Nobody knew their names, or the baby's.

CHAPTER 41

The next day the British announced that they could all go for one hour to an area of the camp where a double fence with a narrow strip of "no man's land" separated them from a section housing the refugees from the *Atlantic.*

"They're the lucky ones. They didn't make it onto the *Patria*," Alfred said when Gertie found him in the crowd.

"Yes, and we thought *we* were lucky to be at the head of the line."

"We thought a lot of things that were wrong," Alfred said with such violence in his voice that Gertie flinched.

"Still, let's be thankful for this time together, Alfred." She handed him the baby. He scooped Benyamin into his chest and held him as tightly as he could, short of making him cry.

Gertie marveled at how light she suddenly felt. No wonder. She'd been holding the baby for three days straight. A pang of pain for Emil hit her so hard she nearly doubled over. Alfred jumped to steady her. She did not have to tell him what had happened.

"Let's look for our friends," Gertie said. They found Fritz on their side of the fence and Alfred nearly collapsed into his arms. They called out to the other side; Gertie first for Bronia and Elsa, then Alfred for Siegfried and Ernst. Names mingled and clashed in the air, like paper airplanes sailing over the fence. People on the *Atlantic* side called out a name and from the *Patria* camp either someone answered, "Yes, I'm here," or there was silence. Someone would then say: "We haven't seen him," or, "We think she drowned."

Alfred and Gertie called out that they were there.

"Gott sei Dank!" Bronia shouted back. "And the children?"

In silence, Gertie lifted Benyamin up. Bronia nodded, brought her palms to her heart and lowered her eyes.

Finally, the calling died down. Gertie looked out to the white curls of the surf. Until this moment it hadn't occurred to her that they were by the sea, the same sea where Emil . . . She leaned on Alfred's arm.

Some *Patria* survivors yelled to the *Atlantic* passengers for any personal items they could spare, since they had lost everything in the explosion. "Wait," many *Atlantic* passengers called out and ran back to their barracks. They came back quickly and assorted items began flying over the fence: shirts and pants, underpants and bras, small towels, shoes and socks, combs and small pieces of soap.

"It's not raining cats and dogs," Alfred said wryly, "it's raining shirts and socks."

Gertie winced. *He has a talent for bad jokes, if one could call it a talent.*

"Ach, Alfred . . . just watch your head."

Another day passed, grey and cold. Then a spurt of rain washed the dusty camp, followed by a bright winter sun that warmed and almost cheered them, some of them, at least. In the evening the temperature dropped quickly as the day slid abruptly into night. Her Geography class at the Gymnasium came back to Gertie with a wallop. The teacher had droned on and on about how in regions near the Equator, nightfall was sudden, "As if someone had thrown a blanket over you."

Part of her longed for the slow, silken dusk of Europe, but another was thankful that night came so fast. Once it got dark, everyone raced through their dinner and then slid into their beds. Sleep temporarily erased the fears and frustration that inhabited daylight. Gertie would wake just barely a few times during the night to nurse, and once to change his soggy swaddling. But though her body was awake her mind stayed in the cocoon of sleep. Thankfully, her dreams took her back to her distant childhood, and didn't unlatch the iron box of her present nightmare.

Chapter 42

"It's December first today," Alfred said when he found Gertie across the fence.

"It is?" She was shocked.

"Yes, we've been here a week. Here's the calendar I started the day we got here." Alfred pulled it from his pocket, unfolding once, twice, and again.

"A week since..." Gertie shook her head and clutched Benyamin to her chest.

Alfred was numb too. Finally, she asked: "Have you heard any more about what might happen to us? The women in my barrack don't know anything."

"Only rumors. The men pass these tidbits from one to another, like precious stones. But they're useless. On the other hand, the news we get from the *ghaffirs* is reliable, I think."

"The *ghaffirs*? What's that?"

"Yes, Gertie, Jewish policemen that are part of the Palestine Police. They have strict orders not to fraternize with us refugees, but they find opportunities out of sight of their British commanders. They pass along whatever they can."

"So, what do they say?" Gertie asked skeptically, afraid to get their hopes up.

"They keep telling us that the Jewish community here is doing everything possible to help us. '*Kol ha-Yishuv itchem*—the whole country is with you.' They say that over and over."

"I've heard that, too. What's "Yishuv?"

"Their word for the Jewish community here. There's a kind of quasi-government as the leadership."

"Quasi . . . it's all 'as if', the so-called reliable information too," Gertie snarled.

"Well, there is something to it," Alfred said emphatically. "The ghaffirs reported that there were rallies and strikes in all the major towns in the country. The Yishuv leadership was meeting with the British authorities."

"What good will that do?" Gertie wondered out loud, her tone less harsh now.

"One ghaffir heard that all the way in America, Stephen S. Wise, the most important Jew in America, has met with Lord Lothian, or Lothiar . . . something like that—the British Ambassador to the United States. And there are efforts to appeal directly to Churchill."

Gertie rolled her eyes.

"You must keep your spirits up, Gertie," Alfred pleaded and placed his open palm against the wire fence. All she could do was nod.

Gertie did not believe the rumors that began to circulate that the *Patria* explosion had been the doing of the *Haganah*, a last-ditch effort to disable the boat so it could not sail. People reported hearing the ghaffirs explain that it had been the only avenue left to stop the British plan to deport them all. Negotiations in Palestine and London had failed. The British were determined to demonstrate that they would fully implement the White Paper's restrictions on Jewish immigration to Palestine.

Like most of the refugees, Gertie and Alfred had already heard of the Haganah in Europe. "The leading clandestine Jewish militia in

Palestine," the Shlichim had said proudly, "the moderate wing of the Jewish opposition to the British occupation."

Alfred said these were not just rumors: he had heard is all from Fritz, who "knew the right people to ask." A Haganah member disguised as a port worker had smuggled explosives onto the *Patria* two days before the morning they'd come on board.

"So, before we were to board?" Gertie asked.

"Yes, but . . . "

"But?"

"The man handed the leather bag—it looked like a lunch bag or tool satchel—to a refugee the Haganah had recruited and that night he snuck the bag into the engine room. But it failed to explode. The next day, a new detonator arrived on the ship the same way. The next morning the passengers were instructed to all go up to the deck to organize a ship-wide cleanup, to start right at 9 am."

"How great, just in time for us!" Gertie's bitter words cut the air like knives.

The explosion was only supposed to damage the turbines and disable the ship, Alfred explained with forced patience. With nearly 3,500 passengers on board, it would be declared a humanitarian emergency. The British would have to let all the refugees onto land, and then . . . things would work out somehow, perhaps a compromise with the British high Command or maybe, at worst, a breakout they'd organize from the detention camp. But instead, the bomb had ripped off a huge section of the hull and caused the boat to capsize.

"That was our explosion," Alfred's face contorted, "and why the ship keeled over and sank so fast."

"Impossible to believe," Gertie hissed.

"The operation succeeded, but the patient died," Alfred seethed. "This they call a plan?"

Alfred had asked the ghaffirs: "Was too much dynamite used? Or was the hull of the boat badly deteriorated? Did the British know that? If so, how had they imagined the *Patria* would make the long journey to the Indian Ocean?" No one knew and it seemed that no one was willing to question the Haganah's leadership. The colossal disaster had stunned the Yishuv into silence.

They had never before felt both gratitude and murderous rage towards the very same people, at the very same time. But soon, most of the refugees—now prisoners—stopped talking about it. Many hardly spoke at all. Gertie and Alfred as well. Once they'd asked every single person about Emil, they fell into day-long silences. Even during the daily "Visiting Hour" across the barbed wire fence, they said little. Gertie cocooned herself around the baby. As he drained the milk out of her breasts, she felt he was pumping a thin stream of life force back into her body. If not for him, she thought, she would have just laid her body down to die.

She tried to pass her strength to Alfred across the fence. She stood holding the baby towards him, holding his little hand in hers and waving it, cooing, "Say *Auf Wiedersehen*, Papa." Alfred tried to force a smile, but his face was shut. She watched him lift his hand to wave listlessly to the baby, as if his arm weighed a hundred pounds. She watched him drag his feet along the fence, as if they were shackled in chains.

"What's the commotion?" Gertie asked on the way back from breakfast the next day, Benyamin sleeping at her breast, tucked tightly in a sling. Everyone was rushing towards the camp fence. A cloud of dust rose from the direction of the gate.

"New people coming," a woman Gertie didn't know told her.

"New prisoners?" Gertie asked and shifted the baby to her shoulder.

"So it seems."

In a few minutes they saw them, a sparse line of men and women, some limping with canes, others on crutches or with arms in white-bandage slings. Gertie recognized some faces from the *Atlantic* and understood. These were the *Patria* survivors who had been in hospitals until now. *So few? There must have been more. So many died?*

As soon as they separated to enter the men's and women's camps, Gertie approached the first woman in line who was hobbling in slowly.

"From the *Patria*, yes?" Gertie asked, to be sure.

"Yes. I broke my leg and my arm. Was in the hospital until now."

"At least you are better now."

"My leg is, but what good is it? Stupid, stupid, me—and the rest of us here—we followed orders obediently."

"You mean . . ."

"Of course, the smart ones escaped from the hospital. On the last two days."

"Other women?"

"And men. Even children."

"Children!" Gertie yelped.

"Yes, they were in a different ward, but they disappeared too. The Haganah saw to it."

"There were children . . ." Gertie said, more to herself than to the woman.

"But not me, stupid dutiful me," the woman muttered bitterly.

But Gertie no longer heard her. She pressed Benyamin to her bosom and ran towards the fence. "Alfred, Alfred," she yelled at the top of her lungs when she spotted him, "there were children!"

Chapter 43

The loudspeakers summoned everyone at Atlit to the main courtyard. They were to stand at attention and await an important bulletin. Gertie rushed there and found Alfred. She handed him the baby, who squirmed and began to cry. Alfred shushed and bounced him. He settled down and Alfred kissed the top of his head, closing his eyes for a precious moment.

"What do you think it is, Alfred?" Gertie asked surveying the courtyard, looking for their friends. "And what date is it? How many days have we been here?"

"Does that matter?" Alfred shrugged, but he handed Benyamin back and pulled the calendar out of his pocket.

"It's December 5th, see?" he pointed to a small square he had already crossed out. "We've been here ten days."

"Unbelievable," Gertie held back tears.

Alfred rounded her shoulders with his left arm and encircled her and the baby with his right, holding them in an awkward embrace. She let herself sink into him. In a minute they'd have to stand apart as she approximated, as best she could, standing at attention with the baby in her arms. They had only touched each other, body to body, that one time by the fence across from the *Atlantic* passengers. That had been six or seven days earlier, but it seemed to Gertie as if weeks had passed.

Alfred kissed Gertie's hair and the cold tip of Benyamin's nose. They walked to the center of the courtyard and stood among their *Atlantic* friends. The British camp commander stepped up onto a platform. Everyone tensed up, at attention. The commander raised a bullhorn and read the formal announcement:

"The British Mandate in Palestine declares that His Majesty's Administration will not deport the survivors of the S/S *Patria*, pursuant to a special dispensation of mercy issued on the grounds of the horrors they suffered on board said ship. They will be allowed to remain in Palestine legally, per international custom for survivors of a shipwreck. But let it be noted that their number will be reckoned as part of the annual Jewish immigration quota."

Gertie clutched the baby and fell into Alfred's arms. She let herself sob.

"There is more information," Alfred hushed her, "you have to listen!"

The commander continued: "You will remain at Atlit for the period necessary to make arrangements with the local Jewish authorities to find housing and process your papers. Everyone must maintain order and cooperate with all instructions. There will now be one hour a day for family visits, to be held in this courtyard. Only married couples and families with children qualify."

A chaotic jumble of shouts and sobs filled the square.

"Quiet!" the commander shouted. Everyone hushed. "There's an addendum," he announced: "The other illegal immigrants—those who came on the *Atlantic* and had not yet boarded the *Patria*—will remain in custody. They will not be allowed to remain in Palestine. More information will be forthcoming."

The crowd parted as if an order had been given. All the *Patria* survivors moved towards the platform while the *Atlantic* passengers retreated to the back in utter silence. Alfred and Gertie stared as Bronia and Elsa, Ernst and Siegfried, and other acquaintances from the *Atlantic*, turned around and walked back to their camp. At a loss for words, Alfred marshaled his habitual humor: "Lucky for us we got blown up." Gertie winced.

Several nights later Gertie woke up, thinking the baby was crying. She pulled him to her breast, but found he was fast asleep. What was it that woke her? Yes, there was definitely someone crying somewhere, but not in the barrack. She tucked the blanket around Benyamin and got out of bed. She tiptoed to the door and opened it a crack. A whoosh of frigid air startled her and sharpened her senses. Yes, she could definitely hear women—not crying, screaming!—and men shouting; and a distant rumble of truck engines.

It was too dark to see anything, but she could tell the sounds were coming from the *Atlantic* camp. She went to Miriam's bed and shook her shoulder: "Wake up, Miriam! Something's going on." Miriam lifted her head and opened her eyes, squinting to make out Gertie's face.

"What's wrong? Is the baby sick?"

"Get up! Something's wrong—on the *Atlantic* side."

"The *Atlantic*? But we're on the Mediterranean here," she laid her head back down.

"Not the ocean, our boat. The people from the *Atlantic*."

Miriam rose now, pulling her blanket with her, a walking tent. She followed Gertie to the door and opened it wide. A blast of cold rushed in and Miriam pulled the blanket tighter across her chest. After a moment of tuning their ears to the sounds outside, they could distinguish between the women's high-pitched screams, men's wild shouts, and gruff voices, barking orders.

"The *Atlantics*! The deportation." Miriam cried out.

"That's what I thought," Gertie said. "What should we do?"

"What can we do?"

With a loud shout Gertie woke up all the women. She yelled over everyone's confused stares and questions, explaining what was going on. The din turned into stunned silence. Now Miriam stepped in: "We should all yell and scream as loud as we can. Maybe we can cause enough of a commotion that they'll have to come here and we can stop the deportation."

"Yes, yes!" some women called out and jumped up from their beds.

"You are dreaming," a woman near the door stood up, "the British soldiers on that side can't hear us from there. Not with this noise going on around them. The most we might accomplish is getting a beating from the soldiers guarding our barrack."

Everyone quieted down. They heard the rumble of trucks, the crackle of crushed gravel signaling one departure after another. Some women counted the trucks as they passed by; others covered their ears or burrowed under their blankets. Gertie returned to her cot and crumpled down. She slung her arm over her eyes. She was shivering. She was thankful the baby started to fuss and she could put him on the breast.

In the morning Gertie rushed to the fence to find Alfred. She couldn't wait until "Family Hour." She saw him approach in a slow shuffle and waved her hand in the air calling out: "Did you hear, Alfred? They took our *Atlantic* friends, all of them!" He came near her, but she couldn't stop yelling, "Before dawn. We heard the screams and the trucks rolling out!"

"The ghaffirs told us," Alfred said, "in detail." He recounted the description of how the *Atlantic* passengers attempted to resist by stripping naked. "All of them—men and women—lay naked on their beds. Can you imagine how they must have shivered there?" Alfred asked, shuddering. Gertie winced.

"They wouldn't move when the officers ordered them to get dressed and get on the trucks. They beat the men with billy clubs and rifle butts and up-ended their beds. Then they dragged them out of the barracks, two policemen to a man, and threw them into the trucks."

"I can't . . . " Gertie choked up.

"The ghaffir said that most of the men were bleeding and bruised. It was the same at the women's barracks."

"They beat the women, too?" Gertie gasped.

"It didn't get to that point."

"How do you mean?"

"The women were lying naked on their beds, like the men. But they knew from the shouts that the men had already been stuffed into the trucks. They had the trucks driving off. The British soldiers pulled the women off their beds one by one."

"Naked?"

"They threw blankets over them and yelled at them to cover up. Then they forced them onto the waiting trucks and off they went."

"We heard it, Alfred, the long row of trucks passing on the gravel."

"And the last truck," Alfred added, "the British filled with bundles of blankets. In every barrack they piled all the personal possessions in the middle of one blanket, tied it in a big knot and threw it onto the truck."

"Do we know for sure where they are taking them, Alfred?"

"They say to Mauritius. The same as we heard on the *Patria*."

"But how? There is no *Patria*."

"They have a new ship. The ghaffir said they brought another ocean liner. It will be a long trip. Three, maybe four weeks."

Gertie shook her head. She swayed side to side to calm the baby who had started fussing. Her eyes smarted.

"But once they get there, they'll be alright, no? Our friends . . . " she pleaded more than asked. "Maybe we'll even be able to write to them? Through the Red Cross?"

"Let's hope so," Alfred tried to muster a reassuring tone.

"Bronia, she'll manage," Gertie bit her lip, "she's tough. But Elsa—remember how she suffered from the heat on the boat? Those horrible sweat rashes all over her throat and armpits."

"Yes. I saw them."

"And in places you wouldn't have seen, Alfred. Places you men don't even have."

"That sounds very uncomfortable. But, as a matter of fact, we have our own men-only spots for sweat rashes."

"I can imagine," Gertie gave him a sympathetic look. "How will Elsa survive the tropical weather?"

Alfred shrugged. He pushed his hand through the fence to touch the baby's swaddled feet. Gertie grasped his hand and brought it to her lips.

"Thank God they got their typhus inoculations before they left Vienna," Gertie said with the small relief of something positive. "And they had some Quinine in case of malaria. Did Siegfried get the inoculation, too?"

"I'm not sure, we didn't discuss it. But probably so; you know what a careful planner he is."

"That's for sure."

"Not that it helped him much until now . . . "

Chapter 44

It got dark so early now that Gertie often found herself skipping dinner and going to sleep by 6 pm. But today was different. The British soldiers and administrative personnel were trying their best to create some Christmas cheer. They set up a Christmas tree of sorts—a spindly pine—and hung it with small lights and silver-paper stars. Gertie was surprised to find she felt sorry for them. Their homesickness hung on their faces like rubber masks. And it seeped into her.

"Remember," she said to Alfred at the fence, Benyamin wrapped in several layers to keep him warm, "how beautiful Christmas was in Vienna?"

"I remember, but I can't say I long for it. We were lucky to get out alive."

"Of course!" Gertie agreed, but then after a moment added, "but it's so harsh, so drab here, so . . . "

"Prisons usually are," Alfred sneered.

"So, there's no harm in remembering something beautiful. The snow, the decorations in the store windows, the Christmas trees . . . " Gertie became defensive.

"I suppose not," Alfred relented.

"How Emil loved the . . . " the words slipped out before Gertie could drop the shutter.

Alfred winced but softened when he saw the tears in her eyes. "He did love it all! Especially, I can admit now, the Christmas tree at your parents' house."

"We had such a big fight about it, remember?" Gertie dabbed the corners of her eyes.

"I do, Gertlein. How foolish it seems now. I'd have ten trees year-round if . . ."

"We mustn't lose hope, Alfred."

"We mustn't." Alfred nodded and turned to go back to his barrack.

Part II: 1941

Chapter 1

"Good riddance," Gertie hissed on a grey damp day in early February, as they exited Atlit's gate. They were thankful to be among the first people released from Atlit. Their turn came right after those whose relatives in Palestine could take them in. Two buses waited for them on the gravel road just past the gate. A rotund man with a shiny bald head welcomed them on behalf of the Jewish Agency in the high tones of a radio announcer: "*Bruchim Ha-Ba'im*! Welcome! You are finally really here in your homeland. We have two buses from Egged, our premier bus company, to take you to Haifa."

Everyone looked at the buses and tried to marry the man's obvious pride with the faded pale blue buses, sides marked by rusty gashes, dust-crusted streaks running down the windows. "Look at that bus," Alfred whispered to Gertie pointing towards the prominent forward-thrusting engine hood with horizontal grillwork in front, "it's got a Jewish nose!"

"Alfred," Gertie poked her elbow at his side, but chuckled together with the two men standing right next to the. Others around them were muttering too.

"Today you are free!" the man continued. "In Haifa you will be taken to your own apartments to start your life here. The sooner you settle into a normal routine the better for you and for all of us, who are trying to build up our country."

"Humph," Gertie said under her breath, "*They* are trying to build a country; we are just an unfortunate inconvenience."

"Oh, Gertie!" Alfred chided her, "can't you just be grateful for once? Don't you see how lucky we are?"

"Lucky?"

"Don't you see that, Gertie? So many people will be waiting in Atlit much longer. Not to mention our friends and everyone else in Mauritius. I bet they're not sitting on the beach there."

Gertie swallowed hard. He was right. Despite everything, she should be thankful.

"It's thanks to the baby," Alfred added, "we have priority."

Maybe . . . she hugged Benyamin more tightly into her chest, saying nothing. She was sure Alfred, too, wondered if it was actually because of Emil.

She scanned the group. Indeed, it included other couples who had lost children. To her left stood the Sterns; she had heard their story their first week in Atlit. She couldn't help recounting it, as if a film projector had been turned on and she couldn't find the "off" switch. The father and his son, Peter, four years old just like her Emil, were on the deck at the moment of the explosion. Mr. Stern had a passenger he knew hold on to Peter as he ran down the collapsed stairs to the cabin where his wife was trapped behind a crushed door. He managed to kick out half of the door, crawl into the cabin and drag his wife out from under the wrecked bunk beds that had buried her. They scrambled up the smashed stairs on their hands and knees, seawater already at their chests. When they got up to the deck both Peter and the man Mr. Stern had entrusted him to were gone. Two days after they arrived in Atlit, Peter's body was found in the shipwreck.

They boarded the bus and, once seated, Alfred asked to take the baby. He hugged Benyamin to his chest and brushed his cheek against the top of his head, whispering, "I have to make up for lost time, so much lost . . . time."

They drove along the road hugging the coastline. There are those sand dunes, Gertie thought, the palm trees, glimpses of blue, again … This time the trip seemed much shorter and soon they were at the outskirts of Haifa. They headed south on the busy main street flanking the port, navigated around donkey carts, small rickety trucks, porters loaded with bulging sacks, rushing pedestrians, and street vendors hawking tea or pastries. Alfred pointed out the larger Arab stone buildings with their arched windows and carved doorways, porches with ornate balustrades. "Classic Arab architecture," he said. Gertie didn't really listen but nodded all the same. She knew how much his little lectures helped him regain his equilibrium.

A line of refugees snaked from the bus to the desk where three women with lists of names assigned each family to an Agency official.

"*Guten Tag*, my name is Gershon," a lanky man with round glasses who, in another life, could have been Alfred's brother, introduced himself: "from the Jewish Agency. And Berlin before, where my name was Gerhard," he added to explain the flawless German. They shook hands and he showed them to his small truck.

"Your apartment is on the Carmel. The neighborhood is called *Hadar Elyon*. You'll feel at home there."

"*Ha-Dar El-Yon*," Alfred tried to pronounce it.

"You'll be with our kind of people. You can manage easily in German, until you learn Hebrew."

"Thank you," Alfred bowed slightly, "that will make it a little easier."

"You'll get information about where you can learn Hebrew," Gershon continued "and get help finding a job."

"A job, yes. That is most important!" Alfred said. "The sooner the better. Perhaps a job where I can get by in German. I am a certified engineer, you know."

"You'll give your information to the Jewish Agency representative who will come to visit you at your new home. He will also give you your starting allowance—not much but enough to get by for a few weeks if you are careful how you spend it. For now, my job is to get you from here to there and start you off with this modest sum." He pulled an envelope out of his tattered leather bag and handed it to Alfred, who slipped it into his pocket. They'll look at the amount later, Gertie knew, not polite to do it in front of their benefactor.

"As far as a job, I will tell them to send an employment consultant as soon as possible. But you understand, we have many people to deal with, many to find homes for, not to mention jobs."

"Of course."

"*Also, Nach vorne,*" Gershon opened the passenger side door. Gertie climbed in and stretched out her hands to take Benyamin. Alfred passed him and climbed in.

"*Kadimah!*" Gershon said turning the key, "a good word for you to learn. It means forward, something like 'Let's go.'"

"*Ka-dee-mah,*" both Alfred and Gertie repeated out loud.

CHAPTER 2

"It's a long way?" Alfred asked.
"There are shorter ways," Gershon answered, "but they are very steep and the streets are very narrow. Anyway, I am taking you by the scenic route—you'll see a bit of Haifa." They drove circling Mount Carmel and climbing up. Gertie watched the small Arab-style stone houses give way to modern buildings as they ascended. Here and there she spotted the influence of Bauhaus, symmetrical minimalist rectangles, rounded balconies, elegant square windows. So, they're not so behind the times here! Bauhaus is still considered avant-garde by many in Vienna. Maybe they would fit in more easily here than she'd thought.

As they climbed, Gershon pointed west to the open sea and then right ahead of them, to a massive two-story stone building with a row of evenly spaced rectangular windows and a large cupola with a cross rising above it. "Stella Maris," he announced, "a Carmelite monastery."

"A monastery here?" Alfred was surprised. "The Zionist Shlichim never mentioned that."

"Indeed, built centuries ago. There are others, too. See up there —the olive grove?" Gershon pointed just below the wall, "the monks work their groves and fields in their long brown habits, winter and summer, totally disregarding the local climate. It's a little touch of Europe right here in our Levant."

"A little touch of Europe . . . " Gertie muttered and shook her head.

"Europe is finished," Alfred declared.

"For us it is . . . " Gershon agreed.

Finally, after a slow drive on a busy main street in the area Gershon told them was called Hadar, they turned into a quiet lane. "Your street!" he announced in a booming voice. I would call this an alley more than a street, Gertie thought, but she was still thankful to have arrived. They stopped in front of a three-story building. Its drab cement walls were streaked at the corners by rainwater leaking from the gutters, but it had good-size windows and the entrance and stairs looked spacious and clean.

Gertie handed Alfred the baby and jumped out. She approached the stairs and inhaled. Yes, someone had already washed them that morning and used a healthy dose of Lysol. A good sign, she signaled to Alfred. He put Benyamin back in her arms and pulled their small bundle from the back of the truck—items they had received in Atlit from donations by the Association of Viennese Jews in Haifa.

They followed Gershon up the stairs to the second floor, down a dim corridor. Muted voices seeped out from under a few doors. "It's mid-day," Gershon said, "so it's nice and quiet. In the evening you'll have more noise, but you'll get used to it."

He pulled a ring out of his bag with over two dozen keys on it. He flipped through the keys from left to right, as though they were pages of a book.

"Aha, here you are, my friend. You can't hide from me! Number 203!" He removed the key from the ring and wiggled it into the keyhole.

"You need a special touch in getting this one in," he said to Alfred, "you'll see. You'll get the hang of it." He unlocked the door and pushed it open.

"Bruchim Ha-Ba'im: welcome to your new home!" Gershon called out and opened the door with the flourish of a luxury hotel's bellboy. The room was small but bright, light streaming in through a window on the back wall. It smelled of fresh whitewash. Truthfully, a rather acrid smell, Gertie thought to herself, but so welcome now.

Two narrow metal beds were pushed against opposing walls, no more than five steps between them, constituting "the middle of the room." *The beds can be pushed together,* Gertie noted. On the far side was a tiny kitchen alcove with a sink and a small stone counter. Abutting the counter was a tall, narrow cupboard and past it, to the right, two narrow doors with small opaque-glass windows. The room was saved from being dismal by the bright sun and fresh breeze streaming in through the window.

"There are a few provisions in the cupboard to make your first meals. Between that and the smell of frying onion and garlic which will be a constant here . . . you won't go hungry. Tomorrow you can go to the local *makolet*—that's the name of the neighborhood grocery—and buy what you like. Ask anyone on the street to point you in the right direction. And that, there," Gershon continued, leaving no opening for questions, "on the far side, is your toilet. The other door is your shower and sink. It's tight, but you can get a decent shower in there. No bathtubs here in Palestine. You knew that, right?"

"Yes, it's not a problem." Alfred said. "As a matter of fact, showers are more hygienic."

Gertie suppressed the sigh inside her. She loved long soaks in a tub. *How long had it been since her last? Almost a year. Ach . . .* she shook her head.

She sat down on the bed: as she'd expected, a thin mattress. She peeled off the bedspread: off-white sheets and two faded army blankets with frayed edges. At least no 'PP' on these. Between the beds, pushed under the window, was a wooden crate padded with another blanket.

"Not too bad as a makeshift crib," Gertie said to Alfred.

"And this will do fine as a table," Alfred pointed at another crate—this one turned upside down in the middle of the room. Two straight-backed chairs flanked it; on one of them was a small pile of towels and on the other a stack of clothes.

"These are donations gathered from the Jewish community of Haifa," Gershon explained.

"That's very kind," Gertie said.

She slid the cradle-crate towards the bed on the right and laid Benyamin down. He wiggled a bit but remained asleep.

"Perfect size for . . . " she gestured towards the space left between the crate and the other bed, then clamped her lips to hold back her tears.

"Ja," Alfred swallowed hard. He turned towards Gershon and asked, "What if we need another bed?"

"Another bed?"

"A small one, for a little boy."

"A little boy?"

"If we . . . " Alfred began but couldn't finish the sentence.

Gershon waited.

"We . . . will be . . . looking," Alfred pressed the words out one by one, "for our . . . "

"Our boy, Emil," Gertie finished the sentence for him.

"If and when . . . you'll tell our office and we'll find one," Gershon assured them, "at least a mattress."

Gertie and Alfred each nodded but couldn't speak.

"I'll go now," Gershon broke the awkward silence. "I'll give you our office address if you need any further help. In a day or two a woman will come from the Organization of Viennese Immigrants to help you with household things," he said to Gertie, "where to shop. How to find the things you need for the baby."

"That will be very helpful. When precisely?"

"We're not well enough organized to tell you that," Gershon apologized, "and no telephones, of course . . . but if you are not here, she will leave a note on the door and say exactly when she'll come the next time." He handed Alfred a folded piece of paper and shook his hand, then Gertie's.

"Thank you for everything," they called after him as he headed down the hallway.

Chapter 3

Gertie sat on the bed and started sorting the small pile of clothes. She was delighted by a woman's hat, made from deep brown felt with a little black and yellow feather tucked into its silk ribbon. The hint of luxury cheered her for a moment, reminding her of the days she was known as a *Modische Dame,* among her Vienna friends.

"This is ludicrous," Alfred said. "What's it good for? Are we going to the opera?"

"Alfred, why are you are always so . . . pragmatic?"

She twirled the hat around her index finger. "It was nice of someone to think that a woman would want something with a little dignity and style in her new life. Just like whoever set up the room for us tried to cheer it up with these flowers. I think they are wild roses." She touched her fingertip to the feathery petals, tracing the pink hued edges.

She stepped up to the open window, feeling the sun's rays on her skin. "It's so balmy, Alfred, in February . . . In Vienna, you have to wait until May for such sunshine. Come stand here, feel it."

Grudgingly, Alfred came to her side.

"Our view!" she drew her hand across the window, rather surprised by her own cheerful mood. She peered out, to see what view they actually had. Rays of sunshine reflected off the water in the harbor and blinded her momentarily, but then she gasped: "There it is!" She pointed to the hulk of the *Patria* lying sideways, three smokestacks jutting out at a diagonal, just above the water. Alfred looked and recoiled. He stepped back and sat down on the bed with a thud. The baby started wiggling and making tiny squawks. He'll wake up soon, Gertie thought, it will be a welcome distraction.

Alfred pulled the envelope out of his pocket, opened it and laid the bills on the crate-table: One Palestine Pound note and two 500 *mils* notes.

"How long will that carry us, Alfred?"

"I think for a couple of weeks."

"We'll manage, somehow. I had some gold coins sewn into the hem of my coat," Gertie said, "but so much for that."

"Ja, they're at the bottom of the harbor."

Gertie raised her hand to stop him from getting any closer to this dangerous terrain.

The baby started to cry, and Gertie picked him up. She touched her tightly sealed lips to his soft cheek. After a long nursing session, she bounced him on her shoulder, awaiting his sweet burp. She laid him down in the crate and cooed at him. His small fists flailed above his face, and he kicked his feet until the bits of woolen cloth wrapped around them for socks unraveled.

"Look at him, Alfred! He's pretty cozy in his little box. He likes his *kleine Krippe*—his little crib."

"So, it seems." Alfred barely looked at the baby.

"Alfred, at least we have a home now. Our own, here, in Palestine."

"A home . . . Ja."

"But we can't stay here now!" Alfred shot up. "We must go make inquiries and look for him!"

"Of course," Gertie sprung to her feet, too. She picked up a sweater from the pile on the chair and put it on. She eyed the lovely felt hat, and then shook her head and pulled out a man's sweater and wool scarf. "Take it, Alfred. It will get cold once the sun starts to set."

She bundled Benyamin in the woolen shawl, and they went out

to the street, not sure how to find people who could help them follow the thin thread of hope they still held onto. Perhaps Emil was found that day, rescued from the ship or the water by someone and brought ashore. With the trauma he suffered, the chaos on the dock and the jumble of English, Hebrew and Arabic thrown at him, maybe he could not say his name, or his parents' names. Perhaps he was taken to a hospital, and no one knew who he was, like that baby girl back in Atlit, then was scooped up in the escape from the hospital.

Or maybe the British only appeared to be well organized but, in fact, had no system for matching the names of survivors? They wouldn't have known what to do with him—a lost boy—but to turn him over to the Jewish authorities. And then what? Where would they have taken him? Could he be somewhere now where they did not know who he was and didn't know to look for them?

Outside, the stone and cement houses gave back the heat they had stored all day from the bright sun. The halo of warmth kept the chill of the late afternoon air at bay. Alfred tried to start a conversation with the man at a newspaper stand, thinking he was likely to be in the know. He didn't speak German and instructed them in English: "Go there," he pointed to the grocery store, "they are *Yekkes*—like you. They speak your language."

The grocer was attending to several customers in his cramped but meticulously organized shop. Gertie propped Benyamin on her shoulder and followed the grocer's every move as he hopped from section to section, up and down a step ladder, pulling items off the shelves to fill each customer's order. She made a mental note of the prices he quoted on basic items: 100 grams of a cheese that looked like the Emmental back home, a bottle of milk, fresh bread and yesterday's loaves, canned vegetables. Gertie squeezed Alfred's hand when the grocer bid *"Auf Wiedersehen,"* to the last woman leaving the store.

Alfred greeted the shopkeeper with, to Gertie's taste, exaggerated politeness. He explained their inquiry. The man's finely wrinkled face registered sympathy. He rested his hands on the apron covering a belly of substance that somehow made him look especially friendly. He had been in his shop on the day of the explosion, he said. "Everything flew off the shelves. Such a catastrophe. It took more than a week to piece together what had happened. We were all in shock. So many victims. It must have been a nightmare for you..."

They nodded silently and looked at him expectantly.

"I think, yes ... I do think I've heard there were orphans."

Gertie gasped. The baby let out a cry. She was squeezing him much too tightly. She loosened her grip and she leaned into Alfred.

"Go on," Alfred said.

"It seems logical," the grocer said, almost to himself. "But where are they—that, I don't know." He mulled it over for another minute, then promised he would do his best to find out. "I know people, people with connections, knowledgeable types. Come back tomorrow afternoon. I hope to have more information for you."

"Thank you!" Alfred and Gertie said in unison, clasped each other's hand and turned to leave.

"*Moment, Bitte!*" the grocer said. He handed Gertie the end of a cheese wheel and half a loaf of bread. "From yesterday, but still good." He looked at the shelf behind him and reached for a small package of Twinings tea. "Those British, they are making it hell for us here, but they do know how to make a cup of tea." Alfred dug his hand into his pocket for coins. The grocer waved him off.

"This is to welcome you; make you feel at home." He stepped around the counter and extended his hand to Alfred, and then to Gertie, "Grunewald," he said.

"Schiff, Alfred," "Gertie," they each said and shook his hand.

"Come back tomorrow afternoon," Grunewald called after them, "I open at four o'clock sharp."

Chapter 4

"Yes, I have the information!" Grunewald announced before they were fully through the door at precisely 16:00. "The children—the orphans—from the *Patria* are all in a boarding school further up on the Carmel in the new *Achuza* neighborhood."

"Achuza neighborhood," Alfred repeated, committing the name to memory.

"It's called '*Achuzat Yeladim*,' meaning '*Kinder Platz*'—something like that. It's a boarding school and orphanage combined," he plaited his fingers together to illustrate.

"How many *Patria* orphans are there?" Alfred asked.

Grunewald did not know.

"A few? Many?" Alfred pressed.

"I'm not sure."

"How do we get there?" Gertie jumped in.

"There are buses that go there twice a day, but they're not terribly reliable. The best way is to hire someone with his own donkey cart."

"A donkey with a cart?"

"Yes, here we have no horses and carriages like in our day in Vienna, Berlin. But it's still wheels. And they go, not in style, but..."

"So we go with a donkey," Gertie said, "it doesn't matter."

"Whatever they have here is fine," Alfred hastened to add.

"There are both Jews and Arabs who take passengers anywhere

in town. It would cost double with a Jewish driver, but then you can communicate with him. If you know some Hebrew, that is."

"Only Kadeemah, Bruchim Ha-Ba'im and Shalom," Alfred apologized.

"*Boker toff*," Gertie added.

"It should be *Boker Tov*," Grunwald emphasized the soft "v" sound, "but who can say that? Anyway, not much of a vocabulary. The Arab drivers will know those, too."

"But is it safe for us to go with an Arab?" Alfred and Gertie both asked in the same breath.

"Pretty much. Back three, four years ago, during the Arab Rebellion—then it was dangerous."

"Yes, we heard of troubles of some sort, back in Vienna," Alfred said, "but no real details."

"Ja, 36 to 39, that was terrible. More than one Jew was knifed on the streets of Haifa."

"And now?" Gertie asked anxiously.

"Now it's safer. The British crushed their revolt. Very brutal."

"We didn't know." Alfred said.

"Yes, killed two, maybe three thousand of them. But also gave them what they wanted—the White Paper."

"That, of course, we know about. That's why we had to come illegally."

"Of course, we know what you have been through," Grunewald said, "the whole country . . . "

"Was behind us," Alfred and Gertie parroted. Grunewald looked at them with a puzzled frown, but said nothing.

"So maybe we save our money?" Alfred looked at Gertie.

"As long as Herr Grunewald thinks the Arab drivers are not only not-dangerous, but also trustworthy."

"Oh, yes, no problem there," Grunewald reassured them. "They want their fare, just like anyone else. Make sure you pay at the end, not at the beginning."

"Of course," Alfred said. He was no fool, he wanted to say, but let it go.

"But go tomorrow. It's too late now. You don't want to get caught up there in the dark."

"I understand," Alfred said. "As a matter of fact, that is exactly our plan. Tomorrow morning, first thing."

The grocer walked them to the door and pointed down Herzl Street, in the direction they would go to find their ride.

———

Gertie slept poorly and heard Alfred toss and turn for much of the night. But they didn't speak. They got up early and Gertie settled Benyamin in a carrying sturdier sling she had made from a sheet. She draped his baby blanket and her shawl over him. "Take your sweater Alfred," she could not stop herself from saying. He slipped it on and wrapped a scarf around his neck.

"Look, Gertie," he showed her the piece of paper on which he had written out the words Achuzat Yeladim in Latin characters and, with only two mistakes, in his rudimentary Hebrew.

"Very smart to write it out, Alfred."

"Let's hope the Arab donkey driver knows how to read," she said under her breath.

They walked down Herzl Street and found a donkey driver napping on the seat of his cart. The driver's face was buried in a ragged *kaffiyeh*, which he had wrapped twice around his neck, and once over his head. The harness lay limp in his hand, which Gertie noted was rough with hardened blisters.

Alfred cleared his throat and called out in his Viennese accented Hebrew: "Bokr Toff!"

"Yes, Sir?" the donkey driver shook off his sleep.

"Achu-zat Ye-la-dim, Ja? Achu-zat Ye-la-dim. *Verstehen Sie?*"

"*Betakh!* Sure!" the man nodded vigorously.

"*Yallah!*" he gestured to the cart. Then, recalling the few words he'd mastered in German, added: "*Gehen, gehen, Bitte schön.*"

Alfred beamed. "He knows where it is, Gertie."

"I see that, Alfred. I, too, understand his German." She swallowed hard. *No time for Alfred's little insults —perhaps unintended? —and her veiled retaliations. Was he oblivious?* She wondered, as she often had before.

Alfred supported her as she climbed into the cart, her hand wrapped around the bundle that was Benyamin, then hopped up and squeezed next to her on the narrow bench.

"I am Ali," the donkey driver said and flashed them a polite smile.

"Alfred and Gertie," Alfred tipped the hat he wasn't wearing.

"And is baby?" Ali asked pointing to Gertie's bosom.

"Yes, baby," Alfred said, "very small one."

"I drive you very careful for baby," Ali said and turned forward.

"*Yallah!*" he yelled and slapped the donkey's side with a thin dry reed. The donkey proceeded with a clip-clop of its hooves on the paved main street, then less loudly on the gravel of narrower alleys. The road was rough, but the driver had a steady hand.

They climbed and climbed. In some places it was so steep Gertie had to brace herself against Alfred. The unfamiliar terrain made the ride seem very long. Gertie's eyes rested momentarily on every scene they passed, but she took nothing in.

They arrived at Achuzat Yeladim, the Children's Estate, their hands sore from clutching the side of the cart. Gertie climbed down, holding the baby tightly as Alfred steadied her. Alfred showed the Arab driver the coins in his hand. He gave him half of them and put the other half back in his pocket.

"I think this way he will understand we want him to stay here and wait for us."

"Hopefully, but try to explain it in simple words, as best you can."

Alfred spoke slowly: "You to sit here. We to go there, inside.

You to stay here. We to come back." He pointed from the driver to the cart, from himself to the gate, then curled his finger indicating their return back to the cart. Next, he pulled out his pocket watch and showed it to the driver. He traced a half-way arc on its face, demonstrating a half hour. "*Halbe Stunde*, only *Halbe Stunde.*" He could not call up the English.

"Half an hour," Gertie said.

"Yes," Alfred said, "half hour. Half hour we go back. Down to Hadar, *Herzl Strasse*. More money, *dinars*, for you."

"All we can do is hope he understands," he said and took Gertie's arm.

As they walked towards the gate, they both glanced back and saw that the driver had remained in place, leaning on his cart.

"Looks like he is waiting for us," Alfred said with a hint of triumph in his voice. "Once I showed him the time, he got it. It's lucky I still have that watch."

"I didn't know you had it!"

Alfred reminded her how he'd stuffed it deep into the inner pocket of his leather jacket just before they'd lined up in front of the British officials on the deck of the *Patria*. It was a snug-fitting, dark brown "bomber jacket," the kind they had called "*battledress*" back in Vienna.

"You may not remember Gertie, how you'd mocked me for dressing up for the procedure. You said, if I recall correctly: 'It's not the British Parliament or an audience with His Majesty. We can look as bedraggled as we have been throughout this whole journey.'"

She certainly remembered. Alfred had his standards and she had often bristled at how respectful he was of authority and formalities. Back on the *Patria* it had seemed mostly comical, maybe even pathetic. But she knew that it helped him feel like a man—dignified—if he could just look the part.

"And it works?"

"Indeed, thanks to the *battledress* you laughed at. It fit very tightly around my hips and I had the zipper pulled all the way up. The watch remained in my pocket when we were thrown off."

"That's amazing!"

"It stopped, of course, when we plunged into the water. Precisely at 9:17."

Gertie felt her pulse quicken. She made herself slow her breathing.

"9:17," she repeated.

"In Atlit," Alfred continued, oblivious to the tremor in Gertie's voice, "I found Motke Zilber. Did you know him?"

"Motke Zilber? Yes, maybe." Not really, but she was thankful Alfred was extricating her mind out of the dark hole.

"A jeweler from Vienna. He made a miniature screwdriver from a woman's hairpin and opened the back of the watch. 'Lucky for you,' he'd said, 'it's well made. After I clean and dry it, it should work fine.'"

"And it did?" Gertie was incredulous.

"As you can see," Alfred said triumphantly, "it does!"

She bit her lip to stop her thought from jumping to her lips: *the watch survived but our Emil is gone.*

CHAPTER 5

They entered through the simple iron gate, latched high up where only an adult could reach it. They crossed a small courtyard and found the office. The door was open; they stepped in. All Alfred could say to the secretary sitting erect at the small desk was: "Mein Kind... from *Patria*."

"I understand," she nodded. She got up from her chair, pushed it carefully back against her desk and told them to follow her. She glanced at the baby as she passed Gertie. Gertie stiffened, ready for "At least you have the baby." But it didn't come, and Gertie let her breath out slowly. They followed the secretary whose low heels clicked and reverberated in the empty corridor.

She led them to another office and knocked on the door. They heard a chair dragged across the floor and several heavy steps. The door opened a crack, and the secretary stuck her head in and whispered a few words. With a high-pitched squeal, the door swung open.

"The Director," she announced gesturing towards the short, balding man in the doorway. He was rather chubby and his smooth, fleshy cheeks gave him a child-like charm. His roundness made his presence comforting.

"Welcome, *kommen Sie herein*," he said, shaking Alfred's hand, then Gertie's. He let his open palm hover over the baby's head for an instant but didn't say anything.

"Gott sei Dank," Gertie said, "you speak German."

"Of course," the director said. "Bitte," he pointed towards two straight-backed chairs. They sat down while he settled into the armchair behind the desk. Gertie propped Benyamin up, noting the director's smile when he saw the small face peeking from the folds of cloth. She turned her head sideways and, shielding it, licked her ring finger and put it into Benyamin's mouth to sooth him. Alfred told their story in painstaking detail and Gertie described Emil from head to toe, his curly brown hair and big brown eyes. "People always remarked about his intelligent eyes," she said.

"A very bright boy. You could see it in his eyes," Alfred echoed her.

Gertie mentioned the beauty spot on Emil's left ear and his widely spaced lower teeth.

"He was wearing a sailor suit and a knitted woolen vest. He loved the suit's gold anchor buttons, but who knows if anything remained of it . . . " Gertie's voice trailed off.

The director listened; his head tilted to the left.

The right must be his good ear, Gertie thought.

"Indeed," he began in a measured tone, "there are some boys at the orphanage who are *Patria* survivors."

"Yesss?" All the air Alfred had held in his lungs came out in a whoosh.

"Yes. Some girls, too. Mostly they are older, but two of the boys we have more or less fit the description and the age."

Alfred and Gertie jumped up from their chairs. The director raised his hand.

"Please sit down. We'll go in fifteen minutes. The children will be having their mid-morning snack then. It is a good time to watch them without causing a commotion."

He apologized: he must think about the welfare of all the orphans. After all, they must understand that many of the children hoped their parents would come to reclaim them.

They sank into their chairs like deflating balloons.

"And this one?" the director asked, pointing at the baby.

"He was born on the boat, the *Atlantic*, just before we arrived here," Gertie said. "Somehow, he was saved from the *Patria*. We don't know how."

"Someone must have thrown him overboard," Alfred added. "He was found floating on a small mattress in the water."

"The British found him." Gertie said. "A miracle . . . "

"But not our Emil . . . " Alfred said in a raspy voice. He put his hand on Gertie's arm. She fought to hold back a gush of tears.

"But not our Emil," she repeated.

They waited in the director's office, Gertie rocking the baby nestled in her arms. She stared at the clock on the wall for a while, then circled the room with her eyes. It was furnished with the bare minimum; a desk, chairs, two bookcases and a tall filing cabinet. The desk was piled with carefully stacked folders. She saw neat block letters on the top of each one, but she could not make out the words. The names of the children? The bills?

She looked past the desk at the bookcases, heavy with thick volumes. There were many titles in German, on child psychology and pedagogy. She could make out a few of the names she would have expected: Sigmund Freud (for an instant Gertie was nineteen, so peeved at his "Penis Envy" she nearly threw the book at the wall, but then she was won back with his book about jokes,) Carl Jung, Rudolf Steiner. Near those, the titles *Kinder und Spiele*, and *Kinder und Trauma*, stood next to each other, as if "play" and "trauma" belonged together.

There were only two pictures on the wall. One was of Theodore Herzl; the famous one of him leaning over the hotel balcony in Basel, the very picture Gertie remembered rousing them with Zionist sentiment at their youth groups in Vienna. The other was of Janusz Korczak, surrounded by children from his famous orphanage in Warsaw. *What was happening to them in the midst of Europe's war?* Before she could stop it, her parents' faces flashed before her eyes.

She looked at the clock again. A minute and a half had passed. "Just count quietly and slowly," she told herself, "from one to sixty, thirteen times. Then the wait will be over." The baby stirred and let out a cry. Gertie nestled him on her arm and ran her forefinger from the middle of his forehead down the bridge of his nose, caressing the downy skin between his eyebrows. She'd often soothed Emil to sleep that way when he was a baby. Soon she felt Benyamin's weight sink into her arm; he was asleep. She touched Alfred's arm softly, trying to pass to him the strength she felt. She'd wait twenty-four hours in this office, watching this clock, if that was what it took.

The director remained quiet as well, lifting one piece of paper after the other from the stack on his desk delicately so they wouldn't rustle. Gertie was certain he had a lot to do that morning. She appreciated that he let them take precedence over everything else.

"You know," he began, but halted.

"Yes?" Gertie looked up at him and Alfred leaned forward.

"Um . . . I am not a religious man at all, never have been. But right now, I wish I could offer some sort of prayer for you."

"Thank you. Us also," Alfred said, "not religious. But yes . . . at this moment I do wish I could pray."

"Just last week," the director continued, "another pair, parents like you, came. They found their daughter. I haven't ever seen such joy in this humble office."

Alfred wrapped his arm around Gertie's back. She clung to the baby. "But," the director hastened to add, "none of the other orphans have been claimed."

They continued to wait in silence. The ticking of the clock filled the room.

Chapter 6

"It is time," the director finally said, with a mixture of relief and tension. The waiting was hard, but they all knew the next step would be much harder. He motioned for them to follow him through the narrow corridor to the other wing of the building. They walked along a whitewashed wall hung with children's paintings. Gertie couldn't bear to look at them; she fixed her gaze on the balding back of the director's head.

Now they could hear children's voices. Alfred's shoulders rose towards his ears. Gertie tried to regulate her breathing, matching it to her walk; three steps for in-breath, three for out. She heard Alfred inhaling and exhaling with his slow stride, counting his steps too.

They entered the dining hall through a side door. At first all she saw was a sea of heads, bobbing up and down and bouncing side to side. The children were fully engrossed in eating and conversation. Only the caretaker, a middle-aged woman with an ample bosom and shiny double chin, noticed them. That was exactly what the director had in mind, Gertie realized. She began to scan the children who were seated in groups according to age. She sensed Alfred's gaze, as if it were a spotlight beam, running alongside hers. They quickly found the four and five-year olds' tables. Their eyes vaulted from one face to the next. A glance was long enough to take in the details necessary to answer the question "Emil?"

There was one boy facing the other way and gesturing to his friend across the table who had the right curly brown hair. Gertie felt her heart jump into her throat. She touched Alfred's arm. "That one?" she motioned with her head. "Maybe . . . " he said in a hushed voice. She could feel Alfred's pulse race.

"We need to see his face," Alfred whispered to the director, pointing to the boy. The director nodded and quietly led them along the wall, across the room. They held their breath. Gertie shut her eyes as she took the last two steps. She caught herself mouthing a prayer. *So unlike her! She had never felt anything for any God, angels, or ritual. She was too modern for that; but this moment had a logic all its own.*

She opened her eyes and looked straight ahead. Her face blanched and she leaned into the wall, faint—as if a tap had been turned on and all her body's fluids gushed out. She looked at Alfred. He was bracing himself against the wall too, his eyes shut, his face empty. They took each other's hand and looked at the director. Alfred barely managed "No. Not our boy."

They walked back in silence, thankful that the baby's sudden fussing filled the void. Gertie propped him on her shoulder and rubbed his back. His cries turned into a soft whimper.

"Thank you . . . for your kindness and your time," Alfred squeezed the words out. "Danke," was all Gertie could muster.

The director accompanied them all the way to the gate.

"I am so very sorry," he said as he held Alfred's palm much longer than a handshake called for. "I don't know if this helps, but you are not the only ones. Thank God you have the baby." His voice sank. Gertie lowered her eyes. Alfred uttered a hollow "Yes . . . "

The director held the gate open for them. They stepped out and he lifted the latch into place, careful not to let it bang. Gertie willed herself to raise one foot at a time and propel herself forward, as if she were lifting a hundred pounds with each step; pulling a rubber boot out of knee-deep mud. Alfred took the baby as she climbed onto the donkey cart, not even registering surprise or relief that it was still there. He handed Benyamin back to her and at that moment she held him as if he were just a bundle of cloth. Her hands felt so weak she was afraid he would slip out of them.

"Hold him, Alfred," her voice was barely audible. He took Benyamin and put his hand on Gertie's shoulder, but she felt no warmth from it. She sat silent and ice-cold.

"Yallah? Gehen?" Ali asked.

"Yallah, gehen," Alfred parroted.

The driver pulled the harness and slapped it on the donkey's back. With a slow trot, the donkey headed down the hill. They sat through the bumpy ride without a word.

When they arrived back in town, Alfred pulled out all the coins remaining in his pocket. He dropped the whole pile into the driver's cupped hand, not bothering to count. The driver bowed and thanked him profusely: "Thank you, Mister, danke!" After a second, he added, "*merci, todah, shukran!*" and hung a sack of grain on the donkey's neck.

They started up the stairs. Each step pounded in Gertie's ears: "No Emil, No Emil, No Emil." Inside the apartment Gertie dropped down on the bed and took Benyamin back. He was now crying and rooting for the breast, his swaddling soaked through. His little fists were clenched tight, and he flailed furiously when she unwrapped him and changed his diaper. He was ravenous and Gertie was thankful he'd waited until now.

She sat nursing and weeping. Alfred poured a glass of lukewarm water from the thermos they had filled that morning. He handed her the glass. She tried to smile in appreciation, but her mouth refused. She sipped some water, then gulped it down, suddenly feeling parched. She left a third of the water for Alfred. "Here, you should drink too." He drained the glass and put it down on the windowsill.

Benyamin soon fell asleep. Gertie put him in the crate-crib and flopped down onto her bed. She covered her eyes with her forearm, the tears making two rivulets on the sides of her face.

"No, Gertie, don't cry now," Alfred pleaded. He never found a comfortable way to be with her when she cried. It was a sore point between them. His view was that you grit your teeth and lock in your tears. Not just Alfred; it was their whole European upbringing, a total worldview. She never saw her father cry, no more than his moist eyes on the day she left. But her mother was different. She did allow herself to cry and didn't hide it. "Just let the bucket empty out," she would say. "When you let your tears flow out, they are salty. If you hold them in, they turn bitter."

Gertie pulled her arm more tightly over her eyes. She couldn't stop. A loud sob escaped her taut lips.

"Ach . . . Alfred. If only you hadn't let him go to the ropes. If only you had held onto his . . . "

She stopped herself mid-sentence. The room was suddenly suffocating.

"Oh, God, Alfred," she called out and sat up. "I didn't mean it! I just can't . . . "

She glanced at him, but he had already turned away. All she saw were his hunched shoulders.

"I'm going for a walk," he hissed. He stepped out and slammed the door. Gertie collapsed back onto the bed, sobbing loudly now. She cried and cried. When her bucket emptied and her strength was sapped, she drifted off.

Alfred returned over an hour later. She looked at his face: its curves had turned into sharp angles.

"Alfred, I am so sorry," she started; her voice cracked. He raised his hand and pursed his lips.

"Don't. We shall never speak of this again." His voice was flinty and his jaw locked. She nodded. There was nothing more she could say. She instantly knew that Alfred would never again let those words touch his tongue. From now on, all she could do was lacerate herself with them.

Silently she rose and prepared a small meal. The words she'd spoken lay between them, an obsidian rock with razor sharp edges. It would always be there.

Two weeks later Alfred announced that he got a job at an architecture and engineering firm. Gertie did her best to congratulate him. If her enthusiasm did something to thaw the iceberg between them, it took a long time to melt. Perhaps it was simply the routine of going to work in the morning and coming home for dinner that helped. Even though Alfred had been hired at an entry-level position, well below his qualifications, there was something to talk about every evening. Something beside the continued fruitless search for Emil.

They had asked at every possible office and put notices in the *Palestine Post* and the Hebrew papers. Maybe, through some inexplicable twist, someone had seen Emil on the *Patria's* deck right after the explosion, or in the water. The dock had been filled with people—Jews, British soldiers and policemen, sailors from a warship docked nearby, and Arab fishermen—didn't one person see him?

But no one came forth. They only got condolences. The only ones that meant anything to Gertie were from *Patria* survivors, especially those who had also lost family. As more survivors gradually came out of the Atlit detention camp and settled in Palestine, Gertie and Alfred sought them out. But they came back from each meeting empty handed. When they had spoken to every single *Patria* passenger they could find, they stopped frequenting the cafes where *Patria* survivors met. They shut themselves out of the community the survivors clung to.

They carried on as if walking in a thick fog. Only the baby, with both his crying and his cooing, broke through the darkness. He was their lighthouse on a rocky coast.

Part III: November 25, 1940

"Just because it didn't happen, doesn't mean it isn't true."

Chapter 1

On the dock Emil wandered in a daze, his ears still ringing from the explosion. His clothes had dried, but they were stiffened by sea salt. The knitted vest was mostly shredded and his beloved sailor suit was ripped and only one gold-plated anchor button was still hanging by a fraying thread. He was cold and his skin chafed. He was getting weak and hoarse.

"Mama! Papa! Where are you?" he kept shouting. "Mamapapa! Mamapapa..." Soon his calls thinned and dwindled until he finally opened his mouth and there was no voice left. His legs hurt so much he could no longer walk. His knees wobbled when he stood still.

Find a place to sit.

Why are they rushing everywhere?

They look so scary. Like policemen and soldiers.

Papa always said don't talk to strangers and go far away if you see a policeman. Or a soldier.

They are yelling so loud, but I can't understand what they're saying.

Don't let the policemen see you! Emil could hear up his father's voice.

Hide from the policeman!

He covered his face with his hands so the policeman could not see him.

Hide where?
Like in playing Hide and Seek. Find the best place to hide.
Go look! Quick!

Toward the edge of the dock, he spotted a heap of wooden boxes of all sizes. Some were facing up towards the sky, others on their sides, like open faces looking at him.

There!

He threaded his way through the forest of people's legs.

They are stinky.
I am stinky too. From the sea.
Mama will make me take a bath. This time I even want to.
Mama! Where is she? And Papa!
I must find them. But I am too tired.
First, I must rest, and hide. My legs can't walk any more.
Sit down.
I want water, too.
And I'm so hungry.
Where is Mama? And Papa?
When will they find me already?

He found a large crate and squeezed into it.

It's my little house for now. Until the police and soldiers go away.

He settled himself inside and laid his head down on his palms, pressing them together to make a pillow.

I am here! he wanted to let Mama and Papa know, but when he tried to call to them no sound came out. *Mama,* he whimpered in his head, *I am so tired. So cold...*

He scrunched his knees into his tummy and hugged them to his chest. His eyelids felt as heavy as the wooden roll-down shutters they had back home. In a minute they were shut, and he was asleep in the crate, his body tightly folded —an origami boy.

He slept for hours, rounding himself into a smaller and smaller ball as the night grew frigid. He awoke in a black sea of confusion. His body ached everywhere. He rattled with cold, shivering. His tongue felt as though it were sandpaper.

So hungry! What would be good to eat right now? Maybe chocolate? No, hot chocolate! And Germknödel, the dumpling with a plum in the middle, the Sunday treat. How he loved those! Or a warm slice of Apfelstrudel... His mouth watered, which gave him a slight relief. But his stomach was twisted into a pretzel and it hurt. There was no way to find food now; it was black all around. He was scared of the dark, so he closed his eyes again, in order not to see it.

Chapter 2

He woke up with the light of dawn. He raised his arm; it hurt. A lot. He stretched his legs—they hurt too and knocked against the side of the crate. He looked at his legs and arms; they were covered with bruises.

What happened? Why was he inside this smelly box?
And then he remembered.
A huge boom!
So loud, his ears burst.
People screaming.
Sliding down—whoosh!
Ow! Something crashed into him.
Falling!
So fast . . . and then so slow.
Splat into the water. That hurt!
Cold. Stinging. Salty water in my eyes, in my mouth.
Did that happen?
When?

The vivid memory was vanishing, the way dreams did when he opened his eyes in the morning and tried to tell them to Mama.

Mama! Emil tried to scream but no sound came out. And Mama did not come. He closed his eyes and called for Papa in his head. No Papa came either. His teeth rattled. He pulled his knees into his chest again and wrapped his arms around them. He kept his eyes shut tight and wished as hard as he could for Mama and Papa, for a blanket, for a little water, for . . .

He counted to ten with his eyes closed; to give the wishes time to arrive, then opened them into narrow slits. Nothing. *What now? On the boat, when there was a commotion, Papa said, "If you ever got lost, you should just stay right where you are. Mama and Papa will always find you."*

So, I should just stay here. Right here on this spot.

They will find me.

Soon, please . . .

He put his head between his knees, pressing on his ears. In the silence he tried to remember how his parents' voices sounded when they called for him:

"*Emil, Emilik! Komme! Herkomme!*"

They are coming now, very soon, he assured himself.

He laid his cheek on his knee. His eyes drooped shut again.

"*Ich komme, Ich komme,*" he called back in his dream.

Chapter 3

Moussa was the first fisherman on the dock at dawn. A thick, steel wool grey cloud on the water linked the sea and sky into one. He could only see a few steps past his feet. He pulled his fraying jacket tightly around himself and wrapped his kaffiyeh twice around his neck. The dense fog penetrated the layers of clothing as if they were flimsy sheets of tissue paper. He hunched his shoulders to protect his neck from the fog's icy fingers and thrust his hands into his armpits to warm his fingers.

He squinted, trying to pick out his fishing boat among the hodgepodge of small vessels tied at the dock. All he could make out were vague outlines. The dock was utterly empty and silent, but for the delicate lapping of the wavelets against the sides of the boats. Nobody else is out yet? Sure, who'd want to be here this early on such a cold morning? He himself would rather not, half-frozen ... but he had missed five days of fishing visiting the family in the Galilee village and must make up for lost time.

"Just be extra careful out there," he said to himself, in a barely audible voice. It will be tricky to navigate into the open water in this cotton wool of fog; pray the sun burns it off quickly.

Moussa pulled his hands out of their armpit caves and rubbed the ache in the small of his back. From the penetrating cold or still from the walk and ride home yesterday? More likely the ride; the constant trundling of the cart on the stone-strewn path. And the long hours of trudging on foot. When you walked you wished you were riding, but in the donkey-cart you bounced so hard, you wished you were walking. All that day he'd pined for his small fishing boat and its smooth glide over the water.

Crouching by his boat now, he touched the worn wood at the top of each oar, where his palms had left a darkened, smooth band. Thanks to Youssra - she made him rub olive oil on his hands every morning. At first, he'd protested: "Youssra, I'm a man. I don't need to smooth my hands with oil!" But she was right, it protected his palms from getting chafed by the sea salt, saved him from the fate of fellow fishermen whose skin cracked until they bled. How did she know these things?

Funny, how much he'd missed his boat over those past five days, he thought as he stepped inside it. He unrolled the tight bundle of netting stowed in the bow. Before the milky light of dawn had turned into day, he was nearly ready. He just needed a bit of twine to repair a tear he'd found in the net. There was nobody out to ask if they could spare some, so he walked toward the far edge where people left broken things: boxes, pieces of wood, short sections of rope or fabric. He would tie together two or three small pieces to make the length he needed.

Moussa peered between the crates and poked his foot into piles of indefinable debris. There—that bundle of rags looks promising. He bent down and pulled on its frayed edge. A small arm! A foot! He dropped the rag and jumped back. Wait . . . really? He crouched down and looked more closely. Yes! A child's foot and forearm. He peeled the rag off. A sleeping boy, thumb nestled in his half-open mouth.

Moussa leaned in close to the boy's face and smelled the sweetness of his breath, faint but detectable despite the reeking torn clothes. He touched one of the boy's brown curls with the very tip of his finger. For so many years he had longed for that exact motion.

He couldn't help himself. He had to stroke, ever so lightly, those soft cheeks, the small fists, and the scabby knees.

The boy opened his eyes but shut them immediately. He fluttered his eyes twice more until he finally held them open. A flash of puzzlement, then fear. Moussa could tell. "Don't be afraid," he murmured, "*Kulchi Wakhah* —everything's alright." The boy stared back; his eyes quickly turned from curiosity to terror. A moment later they went blank. Moussa put his hand on the boy's shoulder and asked in a near whisper: "What's your name, *walad*? Where are you from, boy?"

The boy opened his mouth, but only hoarse guttural noises came out, then stifled cries. He jerked his fists and knees into his chest. Moussa recoiled—the boy's limbs were covered with purple bruises.

"What happened? Who hurt you?"

The boy said nothing and began to tremble. His eyes remained open unnaturally wide, pupils huge, but unfocused. Moussa asked the boy his name again; one more effort he already knew was futile.

Suddenly Moussa understood everything. The boy is mute. He's been beaten, probably repeatedly, and abandoned by his parents. He must still be terrified of their blows and hiding from them. So, any man would frighten him, especially if he happened to be about his father's age, which Moussa might well be. He'd heard of cases like this: crippled children, "idiots," deaf and mute, abused until their families would no longer keep them. Having such a child made you a pariah in your clan. Boys like this would be subjected to endless taunts and cruelty, their sisters couldn't find suitable husbands. Often these children died young, under unclear circumstances. Or they disappeared and no one ever mentioned them again.

He brought his face closer to the boy's and spoke slowly, exaggerating the movement of his mouth, in case the boy could read lips. "Don't worry, *walad*." For an instant he saw a glint of panic in the boy's eyes, but then it was as if they were switched off. Moussa caressed the bruised arms, which the boy still held stiffly against his chest. He told him he was safe, no one would hurt him anymore. But he saw that his words didn't sink in. He needed something more primal.

Food! Moussa pulled a pita from his small satchel and handed it to the boy. The boy smelled it and turned it this way and that, wrinkling his forehead. Moussa gestured for him to bite into it and took a piece of his second pita and put it in his mouth. "*Tayeb.* It's good," he said, and smiled broadly. The boy quickly stuffed half the pita into his mouth and chewed with his eyes closed. His face smoothed and his arms relaxed.

That's it —he must be really hungry! Moussa handed bite-size pita chunks to the boy, one after the other. He left only a handful of olives for himself. The boy ate as if his entire being were needed to accomplish the task. When he finished, his eyes rested on Moussa, scanning him from head to toe. He touched his own hair.

Like mine...
The man's hair - brown, curls.
His eyes. Look at his eyes. Also brown.
Maybe he is an uncle?
But I don't know him from before!
Still...
Maybe Papa sent him to find me?
But what is he saying? Why can't I understand anything?
Don't know.
Scary.
Be careful!
Be quiet.

Moussa tried to catch the boy's gaze when he thought he saw a glimmer of connection, or recognition. But then a flash of terror and the eyes turned vacant, the body rigid.

CHAPTER 4

Lucas headed to the port very early that same morning. It was his turn to buy fish for Stella Maris. He shivered in the bone-chilling, thick morning fog and clasped his cloak tightly at his chest. The vapor of his exhalations hung in front of him for an instant, then came to rest on his cheeks. But he considered himself lucky. Whoever's turn was on Sunday had to carry a much heavier load for that day's festive meal. Tuesday was an ordinary day with the customary sparse supper. In fact, he had been surprised when Brother Matthieu asked him to buy fish for the day. Tuesday, like every weekday, was usually vegetarian. But it being early winter, Brother Matthieu said he had no fresh vegetables and the Brothers were getting really tired of the summer produce he had canned.

"How about one of the geese?" Lucas offered.

"*Mon Dieu* —no! I must fatten them up for Christmas. Just a few fish would suffice, even small ones. I'll make a stew, a bouillabaisse of sort. More for flavor and variety than filling up on."

"Bouillabaisse?" Lucas raised his eyebrows.

"I know," Matthieu said with an exaggerated sigh, "without all the good stuff, *moules, langoustine, oursin* . . . " Matthieu smacked his lips as he reeled off the seafood favored in Marseilles.

"But," Lucas pressed, "it's not my turn. I just went last week."

"Exactly, that's why I called you. You got such beautiful fish last time, you must you have a knack for it. Or you know the best fishermen." Lucas didn't mind the compliment but reminded Matthieu "the port may be under curfew - with that ship exploding yesterday. Certainly, there would be strict police controls . . . "

"Maybe. But this early in the morning?" Brother Matthieu waved off the concern, his hand waving one of his big spoons. "Before dawn they won't be in place yet. I really need this fish."

"I understand," Lucas said, and his stomach growled, perhaps in agreement with the cook.

"You know how the Brothers get when they're hungry," Matthieu said and then added with a smile: "if you do get into the port and, indeed, there is a curfew, there won't be many people there. You'll get a great price."

"I'll do my best."

Arriving at the port before sunrise, Lucas was not surprised that he passed no one on the silent wharf. The dense fog made it hard to see much along the dock, let alone over the water. He passed one small fishing boat after another, all tied to weatherworn posts. He stepped with great caution —it would be easy, and disastrous, to slip into the frigid water.

Chapter 5

Moussa picked the boy up; he was much lighter than Moussa had expected from the length of his limbs. He must be very thin under those ragged clothes . . . Moussa thought, not surprising for a child abused and cast out. Moussa unwound the kaffiyeh from his neck and wrapped it around the trembling boy. He hugged him tightly into his chest to warm him with his own body heat.

He carried the boy to his boat. He would take him along for a short fishing trip; he must have some fish to sell this morning. He put his left foot into the boat and balanced, his right still on the dock. The boy exploded in terrified grunts and struggled against Moussa's embrace. Why? Somehow, Moussa surmised, in this child's pain-filled past a boat had been a menace. Had his father gone so far as to try to drown him?

Moussa jumped back and lowered the boy to the ground where he cowered, his arms pulled tightly into his chest. Moussa crouched down, tied the boat to the post, and reassured the boy: "Don't worry, no boat today. *Salaam aleikum*, boat." He hoisted the boy up on his hip, his arm rounding his knobby back. Moussa melted inside as the boy's weight sank into him and his head nestled on his shoulder. Just then, a man in a dark brown robe came calling out: "Fish? Anybody have fish?"

"Must be a monk from the Stella Maris," Moussa said to the boy, though he doubted he could hear, let alone understand.

"*Marhabah*, Moussa," the monk hailed. "I am Lucas. You remember me, yes?"

"Yes! You are the one from Stella Maris who can speak Arabic."

"Speak—a little, yes. Not so good."

"Good enough! You came early today."

"I hoped to be lucky —and here you are!"

"Sorry, my friend, but I have no fish now. I must take this boy home," Moussa tilted his head towards the child in his arms.

"Ah, your boy? You brought him with you in morning?"

"No, he is not my boy," Moussa raised his voice. "I have no boy. I found him."

"Ah, this boy, he run away from home?"

"Maybe . . . I found him just now, hiding there," Moussa pointed to the crates at the dock's edge. "Maybe he ran away. Or maybe his family . . . threw him out. They hit him really badly. Look at his arms, and his legs," he pointed to the bruises.

"Oh, that look very bad," Lucas shook his head. "You ask him where is his parents?"

"He doesn't talk," Moussa slid his finger across his lips.

"No?"

"Not one word. Maybe he's deaf, too." Moussa touched his open palm to his ear.

Lucas bent over, examining the purple bruises on the boy's arms and the angry red swatches on his legs.

"Who could hurt such a boy? Such a beautiful boy?"

Moussa shrugged and asked, "What do I do? Where can he go, this little boy?"

"Hmm . . . where he come from is the first question," Lucas said, frowning as he tried to sort it out in his head. "Maybe," the words came before the thought was fully formed, "he's from the ship that yesterday, how do you say it - *est explosé* - go boom."

"Explode? A ship exploded yesterday? What are you saying?"

"Yesterday morning, yes, a very big ship exploded right here in the port. Many people—*Yahoud*—were on the ship."

"Here?" Moussa asked in disbelief.

"Right there in the water," Lucas pointed to the harbor waves. "It's there, but the fog on the water is so thick now, we can't see it."

Moussa squinted and scanned the harbor but saw nothing. *Yahoud, what if the boy is . . .* Moussa shuddered. He tightened his embrace of the boy, as if to hold onto the sweetness that had already seeped deep inside him. The boy started squirming in the tight press and Moussa loosened his grip. The boy slid down and stood with wobbly knees, clutching his groin.

"Look," Lucas pointed, "he needs to go pee-pee."

Moussa looked this way and that, then picked the boy up and stood him at the edge of the dock.

"You go pee-pee to there," he pointed to the water. The boy looked at him with blank eyes.

"Alright. I'll help you." Moussa crouched and gently lowered the boy's pants, then pointed at the water again. A thin yellow stream arched into the sea.

Moussa rose and whispered to Lucas: "You see him? Down there?"

"I see," Lucas whispered back.

"So, my friend, he's not Yahoud."

"I see, so not that . . . "

"What do we do now?" Moussa pressed, "Where will he go?"

Lucas wrinkled his forehead, his mind racing for an answer.

"You take him home now. He must needs water, clothes, maybe doctor."

"Maybe . . . " Moussa echoed.

"Then you ask to all your neighbors, your fishermen friends: who is lost a boy. You find out."

"Find out . . . " Moussa repeated as the overwhelming feeling he must take care of the boy—or was it more —swelled in his chest.

CHAPTER 6

Heading home with the boy hoisted on his hip, Moussa noticed a row of British police jeeps and a company of soldiers standing in formation listening to orders at the gate to the dock. What now? Some kind of trouble? A curfew again? That would explain why he was the only fishermen around. The fog had been so thick when he arrived that he hadn't see the soldiers, but he noted plenty of them now. He had no desire to tangle with them. He sneaked out between the warehouses where he would not be seen.

Out of the port, he breathed and sigh of relief. He started talking to the boy again, telling him that he was taking him home and recounting the treats Youssra would have for him. It hardly mattered to Moussa anymore that the boy was probably deaf and mute, he was already thinking of him as his boy.

Just outside the harbor, a truck rumbled past them, and the boy turned to follow it. *Alhamdulillah!* Moussa mouthed the words of praise. Thank God he hears fine! Maybe he can speak too, but has lived in such fear that he dares not say a word? Which would mean that he hears me and understands but doesn't believe a word I'm saying. Why would he, with what he's been through?

"Moussa, my friend," he admonished himself inaudibly, "it will take time to gain his trust. Time and patience." He knew without a shred of doubt that he could be as patient as need be; as patient as dry, cracked soil waiting for the first rain. He had been waiting ... nearly ten years.

On the main street the eerie quiet of the dock gave way to a jumble of sounds and commotion: donkeys clomping on the pavement, drivers calling their animals and each other, motors revving up, trucks rolling down the street, and honking car horns. The muezzin summoned men to prayer, clashing with the vendors hawking fresh pita or steaming tea.

Moussa inhaled the pungent-sweet smell of pita and his tongue came alive in his mouth. His stomach reminded him all he'd had all morning was a few olives. "Soon, Youssra will have her pita baked by the time we get home," he told his grumbling belly. But then he passed a small bakery and had to stop to buy the boy a sweet. Why not start right away showing him he'll be well treated? Can't go wrong with baklava.

He bought a large piece and asked the shopkeeper to cut the baklava into four small ones and lay them out on wax paper. He picked up one between thumb and finger and swung it around as if it were a little bird, about to fly into the boy's mouth. He opened his own mouth to demonstrate. The boy opened his mouth and Moussa deposited the baklava on his tongue. As he began to chew, the boy's face opened, melding both pleasure and surprise.

Mmm ... That's good.
But so different.
Not like Oma's Apfelstrudel.
Oma? Where's Oma?
What happened?
And Mama! and Papa?
Where are they?
Papa said to wait. They will find me.
But when?
They didn't come ...
Maybe this uncle will bring me to them?

Please!

Moussa stared at the boy, alarmed by the look of terror on his face. Why would he seem scared of baklava? Had never tasted it? Could his family be that poor? Or maybe —yes, this is more likely— he'd asked for it and they beat him for asking.

"Eat, eat! It's good," Moussa said. "Everything is fine. Don't be afraid." He put his hand on the boy's quivering shoulder and placed another piece of baklava in his mouth. "All for you!" Moussa said in a cheerful voice, moving the remaining pieces in a big arc from the counter to the boy's mouth. The boy chewed and closed his eyes again. Moussa was relieved; whatever the boy was frightened of won't happen to him again. He's going to have a new life now. A grin spread across Moussa's face. He was smiling, he told himself in wonder, happy... How long since he'd felt this way?

Moussa decided to buy two more pieces of the honey-fragrant baklava. One for the boy and one for himself. Why not? Ramadan had been over for more than two months now, he hadn't tasted sweet pastry since then. He stood the boy down and popped a piece into his own mouth with his left hand and into the boy's with his right. *Like two birds, flying side by side to the nest, invisibly tied to each other.* He licked the drops of honey congealing on his fingers. *Yes, this was a good first step towards becoming a father. I, Moussa, a father. Finally ... finally I can look my own father in the eye.*

He picked the boy up, ready to head home. The boy was shivering. No wonder - his clothes were torn in so many places they provided no warmth. As he tucked the boy as far as he could inside his jacket, Moussa caught a glimpse of a gold-plated button hanging by a thread from the top of the boy's shirt. Strange button, he thought, maybe special to the boy? Maybe he would be sad to lose it? He pulled the button off and stuffed it into his pocket for safe keeping.

CHAPTER 7

Moussa turned the last corner on the path home. The boy had fallen asleep in his arms, head lolling on his shoulder. The aroma of fresh-baked pita hovered above the narrow alley and Moussa smiled, knowing it had already filled his house. His nostrils flared and saliva washed his tongue. He stopped at the small gate of his house. Under the doughy-sweet smell of the pita he detected the biting trail of smoldering embers from the *taboun*, the outdoor mud oven. His stomach urged him to go in right away, but his head cautioned to hold off for a moment: he needed to prepare his explanation for Youssra.

He conjured up her delicate frame and her almond-shaped eyes, the shiny whites like polished marble, accentuating the dark pupils. He thought of her long braid, her great pride. "This is my beauty," she would always say as she rubbed olive oil on her hands and then smoothed her hair out between her glossy palms. Moussa loved to watch her braid her hair —a rare treat —as he usually left before she turned to it in her morning routine. She talked to each strand of hair: "Now it's your turn. Be good. Go around your friends and don't bunch up." Often, she'd turn to him and joke, "I know it's for my hair you married me. What will happen when it turns grey?"

Think! And fast! Moussa instructed himself. No doubt Youssra will have compassion for the boy and be drawn to him. But will she accept him as the gift from Allah that he was? Will she let herself love him as her own despite the mystery of where he came from? Despite his handicap?

Moussa swung the gate open and walked in, taking a big gulp of air before stepping into the house.

"Thank Allah you are home! I was so worried!" Youssra called out.

"What's to worry about?"

"Didn't you hear?" Youssra began but then saw the boy in Moussa's arms and stopped. Her mouth hung open. "What's this? Who is he?"

Moussa shushed her. "Let me put him down first." He went to lay the boy on top of their rolled-up mattress, pushed into the corner.

"Wait," Youssra whispered. She went to the other side of the room where she kept her clothes in a large basket and pulled out her best scarf, made from the soft wool of the first year's shearing of her family's lambs. She draped it on top of the mattress and signaled Moussa to put the boy right on it. Moussa lowered him down slowly. The boy's arms and legs flailed as his body settled on the mattress, but he did not awake. Youssra's face contorted in pain as she noticed the bruises, while covering him with a blanket. She touched her fingertips to his salt-stiffened curls. She hummed a lullaby Moussa hadn't heard since his own boyhood.

Moussa settled himself on a low stool and motioned Youssra to sit by him. She seemed reluctant to leave the side of the sleeping boy. She stepped away with her eyes still on the boy and took the stool next to Moussa. He told her about the morning, step-by-step, drawing the story out until it reached what he thought was its inevitable conclusion.

But Youssra asked: "Shouldn't you go to the police?"

"The British Police?"

"Yes. See if they have a report of a missing child."

"I can't, Youssra."

"Why?"

"The British police. They have me on a list. It would be too dangerous."

"A list?"

"I didn't tell you," Moussa said with an apologetic shrug, "didn't want you to worry. They caught me fishing during curfew. Six months ago."

"You didn't tell me!"

"I could have gone to jail," Moussa added, "or, worse, lost the boat."

"Lost the boat?"

"Yes, Youssra, they're very strict. They confiscate your boat. But I was lucky. The officer was kind and let me go with a warning. But he wrote down my name."

"Your name . . . " Youssra mulled it over, "but there are many Moussas."

"I had to give my address too. I was so scared I didn't think to lie about it."

"That's bad, Moussa."

"I know. And today, this morning, there was a curfew too. I didn't know it when I got there but I saw the British policemen when I left the port."

"Yes, exactly! That's why I was so worried."

"What could I do?" Moussa turned up his open palms. "I snuck out. Thanks be to Allah, no one stopped me."

"Lucky!" Youssra let out her breath, "because it's a huge one, this curfew. Everyone is talking about it."

"Why? Another curfew —how is that big news?"

"This one is. That's what I was trying to tell you. Yesterday a ship exploded in the port."

"A ship exploded, yes . . . the Stella Maris monk said something about that, too. What was it?"

"It was yesterday, while we were on the way from the village. With *Yahoud* on it. Hundreds, maybe thousands! All the neighbors were talking about it, such a commotion."

"But that has nothing to do with us," he reassured Youssra.

"Nothing?" Youssra asked, a blade of fear slicing her voice, "what about the boy?"

"Nothing to do with it! He's definitely not from the *Yahoud*."

"You know it?" a glimmer of hope brightened Youssra's voice.

"I know it," Moussa said definitively. "We saw it," he pointed delicately to his crotch, "when he peed."

"You saw it —so, you are sure?"

"I'm sure. Probably he is from one of our families, lost or ran away." Moussa put his chapped palm on Youssra's hand.

"But even so," she answered, "his family . . . they might have gone to the police."

"If his family is looking for him, we will hear about. I don't need to go to the police."

"If you went . . . " Youssra halted.

"They would know I broke the curfew again."

"It's in Allah's hands, then," Youssra said, "*Kullu min Allah*."

Youssra got up and made mint tea. They sat watching the steaming glasses cool. Moussa sipped his tea slowly. When the glass was drained, he slid the small mound of sugar at the bottom into his mouth with his pinky.

"The boy is a gift from Allah, Youssra."

"Yes, a gift from Allah. But . . . "

"Of course! We will see if his family is looking for him. That's first. But if not . . . "

"If not?"

"If not then he belongs to Allah. The Merciful One brought him into my path. We will take care of him for His sake."

"He belongs to Allah . . . " Youssra repeated and squeezed Moussa's arm.

"That's what we'll call him: *Moulk-L'illah*," Moussa said. He followed Youssra's gaze. Her eyes traced the boy's face with such tenderness Moussa felt his own body softening.

"Moulk-L'illah," she let the syllables roll on her tongue. "Moulk-L'illah. It's beautiful."

"Yes."

"Moulleek," for short, Youssra added after a couple of repetitions.

"Moulleek?"

"Yes. Moulleek. And it starts like your name, Mou, Moussa. You are Abu-Moulleek now."

"I am Abu Moulleek . . . " Moussa's face filled with a broad grin, "and you—you are Umm-Moulleek."

Chapter 8

Youssra tiptoed to the sleeping boy. She touched her fingertips to his shoulder. Moussa saw how she strained to hold back the hug aching in her arms. The boy didn't move. His breath was slow and even. Moussa turned to the alcove kitchen and bit into the fresh pita, his empty stomach suddenly his master. He marveled at how he could be, at one and the same moment, both ravenously hungry and totally satiated.

Youssra joined him and filled a pita with hummus and chopped olives. "Here, Moussa, it will taste better with this." Moussa flashed her a thankful smile. "Some more tea, too, Moussa?" He thanked her and she turned on the antiquated Primus kerosene cooker. She put the kettle on and placed a pinch of tealeaves and two mint sprigs in a glass.

"What will people say, Moussa? How will we explain this?"

"What will people say?" Moussa repeated, measuring out each word as if it were medicine. "You know what people have said until now. Not to our face, of course. 'Something wrong with them. A punishment from Allah.' So now they'll say Allah finally smiled on us."

"They'll say that?"

"Look at me," Moussa leaned closer to her, "we will tell them this and no more: Moussa found an abandoned, beaten child. No one's claimed him. Allah sent him to us, and we will care for him."

"May the Merciful One be blessed," Youssra responded and bowed for a brief moment.

She poured the steaming water into the glasses. Once the tea had thawed him all the way to his toes, Moussa stood up.

"I didn't even launch the boat today, let alone catch any fish. But Ali has a moving job for me this afternoon. But before, a little more tea, please . . . " Moussa said sheepishly.

"Maybe you should forget about Ali's job," Youssra said after refilling Moussa's glass. "Stay home today, it's safer. The English may be looking for people."

"Looking for people?"

"That's what I heard. For anyone who knows anything."

"Ah, yes, looking for suspects. Who could have done this?"

"Who could have?"

Moussa put the glass down on the copper plate table and rubbed his hands together to warm them, his palms nettled by the rough skin.

"And the boy —how do you think he got there in the middle of this?" Youssra asked, a tremor in her voice.

"Only Allah knows. Maybe he was there from before and ran to hide when the explosion happened? Yes, I think so . . . " he added, "he smells like he was there a while, in that crate."

"That's for sure," Youssra took a demonstrative sniff. "Well, if he's lost, we'll hear soon enough. His family will get the word out."

"Yes, they would."

"So, we wait, Moussa?"

"We wait."

Chapter 9

The boy slept well past midday. When he awoke, he had that vacant stare again, wide-open eyes focused nowhere. Moussa spoke to him gently to reassure him. Youssra sang to him and brought him bites of pita drizzled with honey or stuffed with dates. He ate everything quickly, averting his gaze, and remained folded into himself.

Now Youssra wrapped her arm around his waist and pulled him up to stand. He did not resist, but he didn't step forward, either.

"You bring him outside, Moussa. He must have a bath."

"Good idea!" Moussa noted the boy's briny odor again. He crouched at his side and said: "Come, let's walk together." He tapped the boy's knee, but the boy did not move. Moussa wanted to urge him to do what he'd loved at that age: step onto the tops of his father's feet, letting his father "walk" him across the room in a giant's stride. At first, he would face towards his father, his face barely above *Baba's* knees. He'd cling to his father's legs as if they were stone pillars, afraid he would fly off otherwise. Later he was brave enough to face forward, his father holding him by the shoulders.

But it might frighten the boy, he thought, so he picked him up and carried him out. Youssra was waiting behind the house with a tin basin set next to the taboun which she'd raked to bring back live, red coals. She fed the fire till it cast a warm ring around the basin.

She thinks of everything, Moussa marveled and lowered the boy to the ground. "Here's your treasure, habibti."

The boy stood still and stiff as Youssra peeled off the reeking, torn clothes. Moussa offered to discard the ragged clothing, but Youssra said she would wash them and mend the tears; the boy might get comfort from having his old, familiar clothes. *She knows that, too,* Moussa marveled again.

When the boy stood in front of them totally naked, his hands pinned against his chest, Moussa quickly scanned his body.

"What a relief," he whispered to Youssra, "no additional bruises."

"And he isn't self-conscious about being nude," she said, "thanks be to Allah, he hasn't been touched in a bad way down there."

"Alhamdulillah, but better get him in the water before he freezes."

"Of course!" Youssra knelt by the boy.

"Ali is waiting for me," Moussa said.

"So, you are going?"

"I can't afford to let Ali down. He might not give me another chance."

"If you have to, then go," Youssra shrugged her shoulders. She didn't need him now, anyway. Bathing a child was women's work.

"Goodbye, Moulleek. *Baba* will be back later," Moussa said and left.

Youssra lifted the boy's feet for him and guided them into the warm water, one at a time, then sat him down. She took a peek. Yes, as Moussa had said, not circumcised. A puzzle . . . even if he's from a family of ours, from around here. They'll talk it over tonight.

The boy seemed to thaw in the warm water. His shoulders released and his face smoothed. He wiggled his toes and made small splashes with his hands. Youssra soaped him from back to front, rinsing every crevice of skin. She lathered his matted hair and cleaned his ears. When the water got cold, she lifted him out and dried him with her own towel, softer than Moussa's. They'll get him his own tomorrow. Maybe Moussa can find one with colored stripes; a boy should like that.

She dressed him in Moussa's shirt. It reached nearly to his toes, swallowing him in a comical king's robe. She cinched the shirt around his waist with a length of twine. She had an urge to make him a crown of leaves and flowers, but he might not understand and be frightened. "Soon," she whispered to him, "soon we'll play games together."

She took him back in and offered him more pita. He took a few bites but chewed very slowly. Soon his eyelids began to flutter. She laid him down and pulled the blanket up to his chin. In minutes he was asleep. She had a lot to do but couldn't tear herself away from his side. She brought her face close to his curls, now shiny and fragrant from the soap. Something yielded deep inside of her, an inner part that had been knotted and hard.

What all the herbalists' concoctions and healers' amulets and prayers had failed to achieve, this boy had done. Will it work on Moussa, too? On whatever the "curse" was that made his babies come unglued from her womb? It was him, his family's curse, she never had a doubt. Of course, she had never told him. He always hunched his shoulders and looked away when anyone mentioned a baby, even when she talked about her own sisters. That hurt; what else did she have to tell him about besides her family?

Maybe now she could stop sneaking drops of herbal brews into the soups she cooked for him? How many excuses had she invented to explain the odd flavors he detected? "The fish was ... eh ... smelly, so I had to put in anise; the vegetables were overripe, so I put in a lot of *za'atar*." What an inventive cook she had become. Which reminded her —time to start cooking for today.

After their simple dinner of *majadra* and leftover pita, the boy in a deep sleep, Youssra said: "I saw it when I gave him his bath, like you said. So, what do you think?"

"Well, it makes no sense that the boy is an infidel. What, a child of one of the English soldiers?"

"Yes, doesn't make sense, but did you try to speak to him in English, just to be sure?"

"I tried all kinds of words. He didn't understand."

"And he said nothing the whole time?"

"Nothing at all. Not any sound that could be a word in any language."

"It's strange."

"Yes, strange," Moussa agreed, "but maybe he is too frightened? You could see fear in his eyes. And those bruises."

"Terrible!" Youssra cried out. "We must be careful, very gentle with him. Maybe he'll start talking in a few days?"

"Maybe. But Youssra, you must realize . . . he could be mute."

"I do. Either way, I think he is from ours," Youssra said in a decisive voice Moussa rarely heard. "Maybe he was born sick, very small, maybe premature? The parents decided to postpone the circumcision."

"Possible. But he looks like he is four, maybe five. So wouldn't they've done it by now?" Moussa asked Youssra as much as himself.

"Maybe once they saw that he was . . . mute, they gave up on him. You saw all the bruises. They hit him —a lot."

"That's what I thought," Moussa said.

"So now we wait. Tomorrow we'll find out if a child is missing."

One more piece of the puzzle weighed on Moussa's mind. "His clothes, did you see? They're strange."

"Yes. Very old and torn. But at the beginning, they were nice clothes."

"City clothes, no?"

"Yes. Even you, Moussa, can see that?"

"Not as well as you."

"So, who would dress their boy like this, Youssra?"

"A rich family, here in the city. No one dresses this way in the village."

"Someone who likes the British, you think?"

"Maybe, at least likes their money . . . their nice things, good cloth, cigarettes."

"Or making money on them. Plenty of people in Haifa have done really well for themselves doing business with them," Moussa said in a tone Youssra could not decipher: was it disdain or envy?

Suddenly Moussa remembered the gold-plated button. He pulled it out of his pocket. "Look, Youssra, I forgot about this until now. This was on his shirt, falling off. I took it to show you. And to keep for him."

Youssra examined the button in Moussa's open palm.

"It's from what's called a 'sailor's suit.' Little boys —they love them. They make them even for babies."

"Babies?"

"Yes! The English brought them here; now everybody wants them. Even some of us, the rich families."

"So, you think he comes from a rich family?"

"Only Allah knows. Sometimes the rich mothers give their children's worn-out clothes to the women that clean their houses."

"Really?"

"Sure. One time Fatima brought me such a suit to mend. It was torn in several places. But I managed to fix it. It looked almost new."

"It had this kind of button?"

"Not at first. All the buttons were missing. But Fatima, she's clever. She found them in a shop near the house of her lady. Saved her money and bought three. I put them on every other buttonhole."

"You are so good with your sewing," Moussa said with genuine admiration.

"I learned well from my mother."

Youssra went to the shelf where she kept her sewing. She reached up to get it down but dropped her hands. "No, I am too tired today."

"No wonder, Youssra! What a day, ah?"

"What a day . . . Perhaps we should go to sleep ourselves"

"Yes. We have another big day tomorrow."

"Yes, Moussa. We must make inquiries to see if anyone is looking for him."

"You don't think we'll hear about it anyway, from neighbors, in the shops?"

"Maybe," Youssra said and unfolded the mattress and rolled out the blankets, "but we can't just wait. Maybe his mother is looking for him."

"But the bruises?" Moussa pressed.

"That could be the father. If he has mother, she would be looking for him."

"What do you mean 'if he has a mother' Youssra?"

"You haven't heard of such cases, Moussa? Where are you living? The mother dies, the father remarries and the new wife has her own son . . . it becomes terrible for the child. It's how it goes."

"You could be right. I didn't think of that."

"You wouldn't . . . " Youssra said but then saw Moussa wince.

"I didn't mean, Moussa . . . We'll see what Allah brings tomorrow."

Chapter 10

The next afternoon Moussa came home and laid a package wrapped in old newspapers in a large bowl next to Youssra's chopped onion greens and mint leaves.

"The boy?" he asked.

"Sleeping again. That was his day: ate and slept, ate and slept."

"That must be good for him."

"Yes. Good fishing today?" Youssra looked at the bundle in the bowl.

"Open it, you'll see."

She tore off the newspaper. "Chicken, Moussa? Have you banged your head on something? And six eggs?" she unwrapped a second smaller bundle. "And sugar!" she gasped opening the last packet - the smallest of the three. "We can't afford this!"

"I want you to cook the chicken with the eggs and sugar; like we do for a mother after she gives birth."

"But . . . " Youssra choked up.

"No 'but.'"

Youssra crossed her hands on her chest and let her tears flow. It felt both awkward and right. "If you'll take some bites, too," she finally said when she regained her composure.

"I will. And our boy."

"And our boy."

At dinner Youssra spoon-fed Moulleek small pieces of chicken. He chewed and swallowed but his gaze still wandered. He did seem hungry, so Youssra kept the train of mouthfuls going for a long time. In the end, he had eaten more than she had. Only a few bites remained for Moussa. Youssra wiped his mouth and Moussa carried him to the outhouse and raised the shirt he was wearing as a *jallabiya*. He peed as if in his sleep. Moussa brought him back in and laid him down on the mattress. Youssra sat by his side stroking his hand and singing lullabies. He fell asleep quickly.

They treated him the same way in the coming days, spoiling him with a treat every day, sweet or savory. Very slowly he began to loosen his limbs and move on his own, with purpose. But he still said nothing. He seemed to like the pita and the pastries, but barely touched the olives and hummus, or the *labane* and salted hard cheese.

Moussa bought a towel with indigo bands, a striped-blue shirt and matching navy knee-length pants. They had agreed to dress him like a city boy, not in the *kumbaz* of village boys. Youssra was thrilled, but the boy did not seem to react much to either the towel or the new clothes. Could he possibly be already used to such niceties? If so, why would a well-to-do family cast him out? Was there a graver problem than the muteness? These worries ate at them at first, but as the days passed his intelligence and sweet temperament became more evident and the anxiety lifted.

"Patience," Youssra said to Moussa again and again, "and trust in Allah. The Merciful One has brought the boy to us for a reason. He would not give us a gift —a blessing —that would turn into a curse."

"This may help, too," Moussa said and pulled a large blue glass bead on a braided leather string from his pocket.

"A *harazeh zarqa*?" Youssra asked, worried that the traditional amulet for a newborn baby might be going too far.

"It can't hurt, can it? Keep the *Jinn* away . . ."

She nodded yes, this time keeping her tears pooled under her eyelids.

She began knitting Moulleek a sweater from wool she'd brought from the village. It had not been dyed, so it would be a drab beige, but it would be soft as her kisses and as warm as her embrace. She showed him how to hold up his hands, straight up from his elbows, so she could loosen the skein of wool by wrapping it around them. Around and around, she went, praising him for his patience and steadiness with each circle. She thought she saw a smile raise the corners of his mouth for a fleeting moment.

Days, then weeks, passed and they heard of no one looking for a lost boy, even though they had asked their neighbors and Moussa lingered on the main street near store entrances and cafes listening for rumors. Nothing. One day Moussa overheard four young men at a tea shop, drinking and talking loudly. They were dressed in English style. Several cigarettes sat on the table between them.

"The ship was already anchored at the dock!" the tallest man, a thin moustache on his upper lip, as if to underline his beak of a nose, said with an air of authority.

"I know," a chubby man on right answered, "they say there were many Jews on board."

"Many! Dozens and dozens," the tall man flung his hands up, "I talked to fishermen who went in their boats to try to save them . . ."

"What are you talking about?" a skinny guy with a pockmarked face interrupted. "It was hundreds. Maybe a thousand." He picked up a cigarette from the table and flipped it between two fingers.

"Are you sure?" the fourth man, sporting a thick handlebar moustache and slicked-back black hair, asked in disbelief.

"Yes, I know it! And the British police took them to a prison camp, outside of Haifa somewhere. No one knows for sure who made the bomb go off," he said. "Word is the British blame the Jews —their underground army."

The chubby fellow, his hair sculpted with *Brilliantine* into a showy curl astride his forehead, jumped in bragging that it was the heroes of the Arab resistance —to show the Jews that the Arabs won't let more of them come into Palestine. "It's not enough that the British said so. We, the people of *Falestin* have to take matters into our own hands!"

"If only we were so well organized," the handlebar mustache fellow snickered, his fleshy lips turned down dismissively.

"Yes . . . " said the skinny pock-face, "since the end of the Revolt we can't find our hands and feet."

Moussa picked up his basket and walked away. Was this explosion in some way connected to the boy, after all? Had he run away in fear when he heard the explosion? Or, perhaps more likely, his father set him aside as he pushed his fishing boat into the water to help the drowning and . . . never came back; drowned too? But what, then, about the bruises? Can a father beat his own child black and blue but still rush to rescue strangers?

Chapter 11

At home he sat down to relish his lentil stew. Youssra was settling the boy down for a nap, singing him village lullabies. As soon as the boy drifted off to sleep Moussa spoke up: "I must go to the Qadi to ask for his opinion and instructions since we haven't heard of anyone looking for a boy."

"The Qadi, really? Isn't his nose buried in the Quran?"

"Youssra!" Moussa chided her for the disrespect then added, "he may read the holy books all day, but he has people out on the street. They make sure he knows what's going on."

"Alright then, Moussa, go to him. Maybe he can investigate this more. A child can't just go missing."

"Not if his family wants him . . . " Moussa said softly.

He washed his face and scrubbed his hands with Youssra's olive oil soap, hoping to get the fishy smell out. He put on a clean shirt and performed the *salat* ritual, adding a silent prayer, which he barely admitted to himself asked for the boy's family not to be found.

"Do you think I should bring the boy with me to the Qadi?" he asked Youssra as he prepared to leave. She mulled it over, a frown on her face.

"No. The boy would be too frightened. Tell the Qadi what he looks like. Don't forget to mention the bruises. And how scared he was, still is. If the Qadi needs to see him, ask him politely to come here."

"That's good, Youssra. That's what I'll do," he said and got up to leave. He stepped over to the mattress and lightly caressed the boy's curls, then left.

At the Qadi's home he had to wait a while, as two others were ahead of him. His stomach heaved but the heavy lentil stew stayed down. He rehearsed his questions but once inside the Qadi's *madafeh* they vanished. He told the simple tale of how he found the boy, his angry bruises, his fearful eyes. The Qadi had not heard of any missing boys. Moussa offered Youssra's theory of a dead mother, a father with a new wife and son, who wouldn't want to publicize the missing boy. The Qadi nodded skeptically but said he would have his "street ears" perked up for any information and consider all the recent marriages and births.

"I will call for you if I hear anything. And if not, you go on your way loving this boy as your own. He deserves that."

"Thank you," Moussa whispered and nodded.

"And you and Youssra do, too," the Qadi added as Moussa was already half-way out the door.

"So?" Youssra asked the moment Moussa opened the door.

"He doesn't know anything. Hasn't heard of any missing boys. But he'll check."

"He'll check? How?"

"He has his people on the street. And I told him your idea. He'll go through his list of recent marriages and baby boys. He'll tell me if he learns anything."

"And if not?"

"If not, he gave us his blessing."

"Thank you. Thanks be to Allah . . . " Youssra mouthed and let her tears wash her face.

Part IV: November 26, 1940

"Doubt gives birth to a thousand stories."

CHAPTER 1

But perhaps it was Lucas who said on that frigid morning: "What we do now? Where he will go?" He squatted down to look into the boy's eyes. They seemed dulled, as if staring at something that was not there. But Lucas felt an invisible thread pulling him into the velvet brown pupils. His hand extended of its own accord to engulf the child. He halted it in mid-air and it hung awkwardly between them. Lucas tucked his hand inside the rope that held his robe at the waist. *Slow down!* he admonished himself.

He asked the boy his name in several languages. First in his native French, then in his schoolboy English and finally in his biblical Hebrew. The boy seemed to listen but gave no response. Moussa said he had, of course, already tried Arabic, but got no answer either. All he could tell Lucas was that the boy seemed very hungry. He had given him all the pita he had. He showed Lucas his empty satchel. The boy was probably thirsty too, Moussa said, but he had no water with him. He brought his *jarra*, the ceramic water jug, with him only in summer.

Lucas scanned the boy's bruised body again. A tender quiver ran from his gut to his chest. Whose child is this? Where did he come from? Why was he beaten like that? What should he do? Lucas tilted his head towards heaven, waiting for answers. How he wished he could talk to someone right then. If only another Brother were here with him. He'd made his initial vows only a few weeks earlier. He was barely past a novice! How should he know what to do?

But . . . maybe this was no accident. Maybe this was his first true test as a man of God. How many times did Father Pierre admonish him along the journey as an acolyte: "You will be tested again and again. Sometimes you'll know it when it happens; other times you'll only understand you had been tested when we talk about it in your weekly lesson. Or in Confession."

Confession . . . Lucas winced. It had been the highlight of his week as a young boy in the Church. He remembered the glow he felt after confession: the sensation that his heart had turned pure white. Of course, it was red; he knew that. But he felt it as if it were as white as a gleaming christening gown. Confession lost its magic that night he overheard some older novices joking in hushed, yet coarse, voices about the little sins they made up for the Abbot: gluttony (sneaking second helpings), sloth (nodding off during silent meditation), stealing (a bit of sugar from the pantry), sexual temptation (thoughts about women); all to cover up their true transgressions with their own bodies and with each other.

He had felt his face turn crimson and thanked God for the darkness in the room. Fools! Did they think that because no candle burned in the room, God couldn't see them sneer? That just because they were whispering, He didn't hear their words?

Now he knew, as if a light had shone. Of course! God is not just watching him. God is calling him, loud and clear, to save this poor child. The lines of scriptures were already on his tongue:

For I was hungry and you gave me meat,
I was thirsty and you gave me drink,
I was a stranger and you invited me in,
I needed clothes and you clothed me,
I was sick and you looked after me.

This child is all of that. Even a stranger, yes, a stranger in his own family. How else could you fathom them casting him away?

"*Mon Dieu!*" Lucas said out loud. Right here, right now, was his chance to walk in God's path, as the Lord has said: "Let the little children come to me." His own moment of *Imitatio Dei*: he hadn't dared hope to get this gift so early in his religious journey.

Chapter 2

"I will take the boy," Lucas put his hand on the child's shoulder, "to the monastery."

"Ah, to Stella Maris; to the *frères*."

"Yes. We'll take good care of him. We have other boys already. People bring them to us, little ones, orphans; or sometimes we find lost ones on the streets, like him."

No need to explain to Moussa the ins and outs: that the Carmelite Order had changed its normal contemplative, hermetic life when the war broke out. "The hour demands more of us," Father Pierre had said, "someone in this bitterly torn country needs to step in and heal the ravages of the war. We will take care of orphans, at least until it ends." They had already taken in a dozen boys. If this boy were really mute, as the fisherman had reasoned, he would find the monastery a reassuring place. While their order was not as extreme as the Trappist monastery in Latrun on the road to Jerusalem, they did adhere to speaking as little as possible, morning and evening greetings and, after that, only words essential for the tasks of daily life.

"Good. You take him," Moussa said. "Maybe you can make him all better."

"Yes," Lucas said, "and you ask all people you know in your neighborhood: is a family looking for their boy. If you find parents, you will tell me next I come here for fish —in one or two weeks."

His lips formed the words "if you find the parents," but his heart already sealed itself against that possibility and the thought —maybe I won't come down here for a while—flashed in his mind for the briefest moment. He quickly pushed it into the strongbox where he kept illicit desires locked up. Lucas put his arm around the boy and then gestured towards his empty basket: "And fish? You have any fish? I need just a few today."

"No fish. I was with him the whole time. Now that you take him, I'll go to fishing." Moussa began to loosen the rope tethering his boat to the wooden post.

"But I must have fish," Lucas said. "What I do?"

"Look, there's my friend, Mahmoud," Moussa pointed toward another fisherman just bringing in his first haul.

"I see. I get Mahmoud today."

"Yes. I'll hold the boy for you." Moussa offered.

Lucas glanced at the boy, unsure for a moment, then walked over to Mahmoud's dinghy. He looked in. There was a large pail with a meager catch, but enough to fill his basket more than half-way. He didn't want to wait, neither for better fish nor for better prices. Not, he knew, for someone looking for a boy, either. The boy needed attention.

"Shukran," Lucas said as he paid the price Mahmoud named. He hooked the basket over his shoulder and took hold of the boy's hand. It trembled in his palm, as if it were an injured gosling.

He waved good-bye to Moussa, already pushing off from the dock, and took a step forward. But the boy stood still, frozen in place. "Yallah," Lucas said, "we go. *Allons-y*." The boy didn't move. Lucas bent down and picked him up, hoisting him on his hip. The boy's body was limp and lighter than Lucas had expected.

Heading towards the port gate, Lucas noticed only now that several Palestine Police Jeeps were stationed there, with a company of soldiers standing at attention. He walked past them hoping he would not have to explain the situation. They did not stop him. Was it his monk's robe or the small child he was carrying that made them leave him be? Either way, he thanked Saint Christopher, seeing the patron saint of travelers carrying the Christ child across the gushing river in his mind's eye.

On the main street, heading to the bus stop, Lucas gave himself permission to call a street vendor selling baklava. He did have a weak spot for the pastry, but he was thinking of the boy. He set the basket of fish on the pavement and the boy beside it. He bought three pieces and brought one up to the boy's lips.

"Humm," Lucas said and mimicked biting off a piece.

The boy opened his mouth and took a bite. He chewed mechanically, as if his mouth operated independently of the rest of him. Then another. By the third bite, he chewed eagerly. Lucas thought he'd even seen a hint of a smile. He called over an old man selling tea from a brass tray and copper thermos. He asked for extra sugar and, after paying, swirled the hot liquid in the glass to cool it down and melt the sugar. He lifted the glass to his lips and took a small sip. Almost cool enough. He blew on it some more, then raised it to the boy's mouth. The boy grabbed the glass and slurped down the warm tea. His eyes seemed to regain their spark. Now Lucas realized he himself was parched and hungry. He bought himself a glass of tea and bit into the *baklava*.

After the third piece of baklava and draining the glass of tea, the boy looked at Lucas for the first time. Nothing like sharing food and drink to make a bond between strangers, *to* get a child to like you, Lucas told himself. For a momentary flash, Lucas was back at home, sneaking little pieces of his pear tart to Philippe.

Now he picked up the basket of fish, then bent down to pick up the boy. But before he could hoist him up, the boy began to squirm, then grabbed himself in the crotch. "Aha!" Lucas exclaimed, "you need pee-pee. Of course." He put the basket down and squatted by the boy, gently pulling down his pants. "*Alors*, pee-pee!" The boy clearly understood him as he let out a yellowing stream, splashing the stones. Lucas couldn't help himself and took a peek. At the monastery they were so very guarded; he had last seen a boy's penis before he left the village, when he and his friends bathed naked in the river or held peeing-distance contests. Hmm, he thought, the boy isn't circumcised. Don't the Muslims do it in infancy? Maybe it's only the Jews? He'll have to investigate. Could the child be the son of a Christian Arab family?

The boy gave a small smile of relief when he was done. Lucas helped him pull his pants up and then hoisted him up to his hip, picked up the basket and headed to the bus stop. Before he fully caught his breath, the bus came. He placed the boy on the first step and gave him a small nudge to go up. The boy clambered up the stairs easily. He slid into the first open double seat and melted into the corner.

Lucas settled himself close to the boy and set the basket of fish beside him. The tangy smell of the warming fish tickled his nostrils. He ran his eyes from the boy to himself, to the basket of fish. In order of importance, but not in order of good fragrance —the boy smells as bad as the fish! Lucas chuckled to himself. He sniffed twice: sweat, urine, maybe even feces, and salt. How long had the boy been on the dock? Hours? Days? Had he wandered around? Gone into the water? Or perhaps he just hid among the crates Moussa had pointed to, surely, strewn with rotting seaweed and caked with salt.

How long since his family had cast him out? Lucas wondered. He watched the boy closely as the bus climbed up the hill, to see if he would react in any way to different neighborhoods and sights they passed. That could provide a clue to where he came from. But the boy was withdrawn, staring aimlessly. He showed no sign of recognizing anything. His head started bobbing up and down as he began to drift off. His eyes shut and his small hand slowly slipped out of Lucas' gentle grasp.

Now Lucas could observe the boy more closely. Thin, but physically well developed. Four or five years old? Something like that. His clothes were threadbare and torn in several places, but they had once been a well-made sailor suit. One small gold-plated button with an embossed anchor was still dangling on a flimsy thread near the collar. Over the shirt the boy had a knitted sleeveless sweater, its edges so frayed it would unravel with one touch. It looked handmade, by his grandmother, perhaps?

Someone had taken good care of this boy; bought him nice clothes, knitted him a sweater. So why beat him so brutally? Why abandon him? Lucas didn't realize he was shaking his head as he ran through these questions. An evil stepmother? A brutal father; a drunkard, maybe? A widowed mother remarried, her child not wanted? No, that's fairytales. But didn't some of the boys in his village back home tell such stories. May something is terribly wrong with him.

Lucas shrugged and let his body weight drop fully into the seat. He tried to slow down the thoughts spinning in his head. At his stop, Lucas hooked the basket on his shoulder, plucked the boy from the seat and settled him on his hip. The boy was still sleeping; his head dropped onto Lucas' shoulder. Lucas got off the bus and the driver revved up the engine and headed off, leaving behind a haze of gasoline fumes. As he started up the path the boy woke up and looked around for a moment, then laid his head back down. Lucas spoke to him and pointed towards the monastery's towering silhouette on the mountainside.

Climbing up, flanked by olive groves, Lucas was right back in his village in the south of France, carrying his little Philippe home. Look at me! At the other end of the world, carrying a boy the age Philippe was when I left home. The gush of longing for his brother and fierce determination to protect this child made Lucas almost lose his footing. He steadied his legs and hugged the boy more tightly to his side.

Chapter 3

"For Thy glory," Lucas mouthed as looked up at the monastery's imposing dome and called up to the statue of Mary that stood inside, in the small chapel he favored. A Madonna with Jesus as a small boy —three or four years-old —seated on her lap, facing the worshipper with a benevolent smile, one hand raised in benediction, the other open in a gesture of receiving. Over his years at Stella Maris Lucas had grown to love that Jesus in a more personal way than any other icons. Sure, he had been taught over and over that the ultimate spiritual moment was the Crucifixion. He knew he should feel most elevated, closest to glimpsing salvation, when he beheld the Christ on the Cross. But at this statue of Mary and her son, he had felt something else. A more embodied love - an amber liquid flowing throughout his whole body.

How he'd cherished that image; how his arms had ached to hold the child in a protective embrace. Gratitude and certainty rolled through him. It had not been only a test of his faith; the boy was a gift from God. *"Donum Dei,"* Father Pierre would say. *"Don de Dieu,"* Lucas said to himself in his native French. It's beautiful! Maybe, with Father Pierre's permission, he will name the boy Dondieu. "Dondieu," he whispered. It rolled off the tongue like pure water.

Nearly out of breath, Lucas pushed open the monastery's gate. Despite the early morning chill, his face was moist with sweat. His robe was damp at his hip, where the boy seemed welded on. His own sour sweat mixed with the far more rancid smells of the boy and the pungent fish. But he hardly minded. Deep inside, he felt a sweetness he had never known before.

He delivered the fish to the kitchen without exchanging a word with Brother Matthieu. Peeking into the basket, the cook gave Lucas an approving look. It turned into a puzzled frown when Matthieu noticed the boy. Lucas rushed out without giving him a chance to demand an explanation.

He headed to the library, to find Father Pierre. At its door, Lucas tried to steady his breath and rehearse his sparsely worded explanation. "Courage," Lucas admonished himself in a whisper and stepped in.

"Yes, my son?" Father Pierre lifted his eyes from the page after. Along silence. The boy raised his head from Lucas' shoulder. He moved his gaze slowly in a half circle, as if enchanted by the books and the stained-glass windows. No wonder, Lucas recalled the first time he had seen the luminous *vitrages* in the grand church in Pamiers: the magnificent rosettes facing each other in the transepts and the narrow lancet windows along the nave's sides. How tiny he had felt in their presence! He had opened not just his eyes, but his mouth, as if to swallow the shafts of color beaming down. Throughout his childhood, he would imagine God as bursts of brilliant reds and blues.

Lucas shrank back from Father Pierre's piercing stare and annoyed frown. Suddenly it changed, as Father Pierre noticed the boy. He looked surprised, Lucas thought, but then saw a fleeting smile. Did the Abbot see the boy's charm? In an instant, Father Pierre's expression changed again, now seeming pained. Was that a pang of something? Lucas wondered, a tiny flash of . . . regret? Maybe. So many of them at the monastery carried a buried sadness. Homesickness for sure, but at least for some Brothers, grief about renouncing having children of their own. He himself? Yes, he'd had more than one moment of longing for his own child, for a family. The others must, too. Some clearly poured their ache into their tender care for the orphans.

Father Pierre motioned Lucas to come closer and nodded, giving him permission to speak but, Lucas knew, not a word more than necessary. Lucas was brief: meeting Moussa, the boy's bruised limbs and silence, and that he was uncircumcised—perhaps a sign something already seemed wrong at birth. Then the boy's hunger and willingness to come with Lucas. The moment of revelation; the realization that he had been called to save...

"But perhaps that was... presumptuous?"

"You did the right thing, my son. With war all around us, God calls us to peace and compassion."

"In His name, for His glory," Lucas bowed his head, then quickly added "And I told the fisherman to ask in his neighborhood, see if anyone is looking for a missing boy. Of course, if his parents turn up..."

"Of course," Father Pierre nodded, but his eyes traveled far away.

"We will raise the boy," he continued, "as Proverbs tell us 'in the ways of pleasantness and the paths of peace.' With time and proper guidance, this boy will come to serve our Lord."

Lucas held his breath. That was more words the Abbot had addressed directly to him since his arrival at Stella Maris. He breathed out and his body softened. The weight of the boy in his arms seemed lighter. Was this what he had studied about and prayed for daily: grace?

Father Pierre bent towards the boy and addressed him in Arabic. The Abbot had mastered it through dealings with their neighbors, more fully than Lucas, certainly enough for everyday life. The boy's eyes followed Father Pierre's lips. Without a doubt, he could hear; but he did not respond. Father Pierre tried Hebrew, an odd mixture of Biblical phrases from his days in Seminary and simple ones he had learned from the Jews in town. Still no reply, just a blank stare on the boy's face.

But, Lucas noted, when he and Father Pierre switched from the Latin the monks generally used to their shared native French, the boy seemed more attentive. Was he perceptive enough to realize that they were talking about him? Children were like that. Lucas had noticed that with the boys in the monastery. They seemed to have extraordinary hearing—"elephant ears" the Brothers called it —when he monks talked about them.

With a final nod and a momentary smile at the boy, Father Pierre let Lucas know the audience was over. "Show him that this is his home now," he told Lucas.

"Yes, Father." He stopped at the door and turned back stammering, "One m-m-more thing, please."

Father Pierre just raised an eyebrow.

"I'd like to name him Dondieu. To commemorate the miracle."

"Dondieu, Gift of God," Father Pierre repeated slowly. "Yes, that's a good name."

"And also... could he sleep in my cell for the first few nights? I'll put a small pallet at the foot of my bed?"

Father Pierre knitted his eyebrows together and pursed his lips.

"It's likely," Lucas tried to buttress his case, "he's never slept in a bed alone. Regardless of where he came from, he's shared it with siblings."

He thought back to his own bed at home, crowded by three of them, jostling for a soft spot on the lumpy straw-filled mattress. Yes, blankets were hogged and stolen, elbows landed in faces and feet in shins, but it was so warm and comforting. His first nights in the monastery in Pamiers, he felt so alone, tucked in so tightly that once he splayed his feet left and right, he couldn't move them. And Father Damien, settling the boys to sleep in the dormitory with his thundering voice: "Lie still! Hands over the blanket, in prayer. No wiggling and no talking!"

The boys hated Damien's "sleeping monk" position. They joked about it in the daytime, calling it "*Mantis Orantes*—Praying Mantis."

They giggled as they chanted in mangled Latin: "*Mantis Orantes sine Peccatis.*" But late at night Lucas often heard the youngest boys crying softly and the older ones breathing heavily. It was not until after his twelfth birthday that he began to understand the pressing temptations of his own flesh and the meaning of "*sine peccatis* - without sin."

"It would help him feel at home here, adjust to his new life," Lucas said, shocked at the gush of words and trying to firm his voice to cover over the desperate imploring.

"No," Father Pierre said after a moment of reflection. "It will make it easier, yes, but it will not help him. It is only out of the heart of loneliness and despair that we find God." He quoted the Psalmist in his practiced, chiseled Latin:

De tribulatione invocati Dominum
Et exaudivit me in latitudine Dominus.

"You understand, my son? It is 'out of tribulations' that we call God, invoke His grace and find Him. In the Hebrew—yours is good enough to make it out, no?"

Lucas' mouth was dry and he felt a wobble behind his knees. He squeezed out the words: "Yes, Father, though it's harder than Latin."

"Indeed," Father Pierre nodded and seemed to soften; Lucas hoped he wasn't deluding himself.

The Abbot cleared his throat. "So, in the Hebrew is says '*min ha-meytzar*,' which our Saintly Jerome translates as 'from tribulations,' which it is, yes, but literally it means from a narrow place."

Lucas nodded and tightened his embrace of Dondieu.

"You see, my son, loneliness, fear, despair; they all press us into a narrow crevice. But when we pray from that narrow cleft, God hears us. And He answers '*Ba-Merchavyah*'. You know what it means, right?"

"In the great expanse. *Ba-Mer-chav-yah*," Lucas repeated like an obedient student.

"Good, my son. Your Hebrew really is impressive. And I understand your Arabic is good as well."

"Not bad, Father. The two languages help each other, like sisters."

"Sisters, indeed. If only their peoples could get along like sisters instead of tearing each other and our Holy Land to bits."

Lucas just nodded. Father Pierre returned to the biblical verse: "So, what is this expanse? The *'latitudine'* of King David? Not a physical expanse, but the openness of finding salvation in God."

Lucas lowered his head. His mind understood the lesson; his heart refused it.

"That is how this little boy will find Him too," Father Pierre concluded. "Our Lord will answer him, whether the boy knows how to pray properly or not. If he cries in his loneliness, that will be his prayer."

He waved his hand to let Lucas know it was time to go, but then added in a warmer tone: "And he will be with other boys who've lost their parents. They will understand and help him. Even without words."

Lucas bowed. The boy's body suddenly felt cold, almost inert against his side. He opened the door. Father Pierre called after him: "You can ask Brother Donatien to switch with him tonight and help Brother Michel put the boys to sleep. Brother Donatien will appreciate the night off and you can tuck the boy in."

It was better than nothing.

Chapter 4

The first order of business now was a proper meal for the boy. And for himself—he had no idea he was so hungry! He checked the sundial in the middle of the courtyard. Lucky, just about time for lunch. How could the morning have gone by so fast? He carried the boy into the Refectory and sat him down by his side on the hard bench. The room was warmed by the heat and luscious fragrance emanating from the kitchen. Did he already detect the bouillabaisse simmering? The boy leaned against him and circled the room with his eyes. He looked at his empty plate and then up at Lucas. "The food is coming. Very soon," Lucas said and put his hand on the boy's shoulder.

Lucas watched the faces of the Brothers as they filed in and took their assigned seats. Everyone was silent, as the Rules required, but Lucas felt he could hear the buzzing in their heads. There was no avoiding the inquisitive stares. The children ate in their own room, supervised by two monks, joining the adults only on Holy Days.

Father Pierre rose and spoke about the boy Brother Lucas had saved. "We are all blessed today to join in this sacred deed." The Brothers glanced at Lucas and the boy and put their palms together, bowing their heads in their direction. Lucas stood up: "His name will be Dondieu."

Steaming bowels began to flow out of the kitchen, the monks on duty setting them down on the tables. Lucas marveled: this might turn out to be the most important day of his life, his personal *'Ecce, Homo!'*—the day he heard God calling him. The monks chanted the Grace before meals. The quotidian phrase filled Lucas' heart in a way it never had before: "*Benedic, Domine, nos et haec tua dona . . .*" He heard every word as if for the first time. He wasn't asking God for His blessing; he was giving thanks for the miraculous gift he'd already received. He closed his eyes; his body felt as if it were floating.

When Lucas opened his eyes, he saw that someone had already filled his plate and the boy's. Lunch was simple, as usual; a soft patty of cooked barley with a dab of butter in a little crater in the middle, slices of roasted turnip and a glass of lukewarm tea clouded by a few drops of milk. Lucas watched the boy, who had already started eating: how well he handled the cutlery! He was using the spoon to eat the barley but the fork to pick up the vegetables. And he chews with his mouth closed. Where did he learn these table manners?

When the "Amen" concluded the Grace After Meals, Lucas stayed seated at the table with Dondieu. Everyone passed by them bowing towards Lucas and smiling at the boy. Face after face beamed at them, from the smooth ones with only the first heralds of a beard to the bushy chins of veteran monks, latticed by wrinkles. Everyone out, Lucas wiped the corners of the Dondieu's mouth with the edge of his wide sleeve and dabbed the film of milky tea on his upper lip.

Lucas rose and helped Dondieu down. From the kitchen door, Brother Matthieu signaled them to come in. Lucas felt the grip of the boy's small hand tighten. Did Brother Matthieu's scrawny frame, scraggly beard, and long bony fingers scare him? But when Brother Matthieu handed him a bowl with honey-drizzled wheat porridge, the boy smiled.

"What a treat, Matthieu!" They never had anything sweet, except on Holy Days. And sweetened with honey—heavenly! Dondieu seemed to think so too. He swallowed each bite with his eyes closed and licked each teaspoonful until the metal shone.

Next was hygiene - the boy needed a bath badly. Another challenge, as they normally bathed only once a week, on Fridays. They boiled big vats of water to have enough for everyone to take a lukewarm, hasty dip. Lucas turned to Brother Matthieu; he had already shown his kindness to the boy. He nodded and set about boiling a large kettle of water.

While the water heated, Lucas took Dondieu to the clothes storeroom, lined with shelves of outfits sorted by color and size. The youngest boys wore loose pants and a tunic that hung down to mid-calf, woolen for winter and cotton for summer. They were all a dull beige that tolerated stains more forgivingly than the monks' everyday brown robes and holiday whites. Lucas fumbled through several piles of clothes, eager to leave the chilly room, though the mingled smell of the olive-oil soap and borax was pleasant.

He held a tunic against the boy's frame, just as his mother had done when she lined up all of them at the beginning of each season to measure for lengths of shirts and pants. Mostly, Lucas had gotten what his older brother had just outgrown and handed his own outfit to his younger brother. So, it went down the line from Martin to Lucas, Lucas to André, André to Jacques, and Jacques to Philippe. Lucky Marie, the only girl among them, never had to wear hand-me-downs. But by the time she was nine, mother had already started her sewing her own clothes and helping with the boys'.

Every turn of the seasons his mother had something special for each child, newly sewn or knitted. His all-time favorite was a dark brown felt cap when he turned six. He loved feeling the felt between his fingers, turning the cap face up, its mouth open to catch his mother's love. At first, he wore it only to church. Mama beamed when she saw how proud he was. What she didn't know was that Lucas slept with the cap every night, carefully folded and stuffed inside his nightshirt, against his chest. Later, he wore it to school. Eventually, it was so stretched out he put it over a cap his mother had knitted three winters later. He still had a section of it with him, secreted under his pillow. Mama would be flabbergasted to learn that . . . but also charmed. He could see the smile that would light up her face.

Suddenly it dawned on him that the cap was the same deep brown as his monk's habit. He remembered the rush of feelings he could not name when, as a small boy, he saw the brown robes of the priests. Did that cap play some role in his attraction to the Church? Was he, more literally than he'd ever realized, a "man of the cloth?"

Lucas shook the memories away, noticing now that the tunic edges bunched on the floor. He held three more against the boy's frame until he found one the right length, then added matching pants. He pulled a double-strand rope from a thick coil and wrapped it twice around Dondieu's waist. The boy's eyes darted from the coiled rope to Lucas' face. He began to tremble. "Don't be afraid," Lucas said as he cut the rope to length. He bent down to the lowest shelf, pulling out sandals. He held them out to gauge the size, then crouched down and took out a smaller pair. He stuffed two coarse-wool socks into the sandals and put them on top of the pile. He folded the tunic over the sandals, making a neat package, and tied it with the rope. With the bundle tucked under his arm, Lucas picked the boy up and headed back to the kitchen.

Brother Matthieu had gone, leaving the kettle on the fire and a large enamel basin in the middle of the room. Next to it he'd left a folded towel, a washcloth, and a small bar of soap. Lucas traced the smooth rim of the basin with his finger, marred by one chipped spot. It was halfway full with lukewarm water. Who would have thought Lucas marveled, that a boy would draw out sweetness even in Brother Matthieu? Certainly not a sweetness anyone had ever seen before. Is it something special about this boy or something about us, Brothers?

A hiss and jet of vapor announced the boiling water. Lucas wrapped a thick rag around the handle and picked up the heavy kettle. He poured in half the kettle and dipped the base of his wrist in the water. Not quite. He poured in more and tested again. Nice! Considerably better than the barely lukewarm temperature the Brothers were used to. He took the boy by the hand and pointed to the basin, the bar of soap, the towel and the clean clothes. Lucas began to peel the boy's clothes off. He didn't resist.

His outfit was frayed and torn in several places. A rancid smell shot up as Lucas removed the pants and underwear. He pulled the little sailor-suit gold-plated button off the last thread still connecting it to the shirt and placed it in the middle of his palm. "I'll save this for you," he said, slowly closing his fingers over the button and patting the closed hand. He hoped it assured the boy he would keep it for him, not steal it. "Please, God, help him understand," Lucas prayed.

He gathered the clothes into a small pile, lifeless and smelly. He'll turn them into cleaning rags; they weren't worth more than that. Seeing Dondieu naked, Lucas shivered. Perhaps it was chillier in the room than he realized. He held the boy under his arms and lifted, then sat him in the water. Dondieu pulled his knees to his chest and trembled, but after a few moments in the warm bath her seemed to return him to himself. He stretched his legs out and made little waves with his hands. He fanned his feet back and forth and curled his toes. He giggled when a small fart bubbled up between his legs.

Lucas took a glance to verify what he had already seen. Indeed, uncircumcised. So, not Jewish. Most likely an Arab boy. Muslim or Christian? Do the Christian Arabs circumcise too? He thought so . . . but needed to check. Other possibilities? British—a child of a soldier or member of the civilian administration? German - from the German Colony near the port? But the boy certainly doesn't look like either group . . . That's just too far-fetched.

He picked up the soap and washcloth and started scrubbing the boy's back. When he moved to the bruised arms and legs, Lucas tried to touch them as lightly as he could. The boy seemed upset at the purple splotches. "I know. It hurts. Soon it will be better," Lucas said, then added, though he was pretty sure the boy did not understand, "No one will hurt you ever again! I won't let them."

Lucas handed Dondieu the lathered washcloth and pointed first at his own groin, then at the boy's. He understood and scrubbed himself between his legs, then made soap swirls around his belly. Lucas thought he saw a smile begin to form on the boy's lips and grinned back.

"Now your hair," Lucas rubbed his hand around his own head. The boy was very cooperative, shutting his eyes tightly when Lucas lathered him up. Evidently, he was used to being bathed and having his hair washed. Another puzzle... could it be that the boy's parents abused him but still took such good care of him? What changed everything so drastically that they would beat him and cast him out?

He rinsed the boy's hair several times, getting off every bubble of soap. Clean now, the hair was so fine and smooth it slipped between Lucas' fingers like a thick liquid. And such a rich brown —mahogany? That sounded good, though Lucas really had no idea what mahogany looked like. He lifted the boy out of the basin when the water cooled and wrapped him in the towel. He patted him dry, hugging him to his chest: to keep the boy warm or because of the feelings swirling up inside him?

He wondered if being uncircumcised would trouble Dondieu. Most of the other boys at the monastery had been circumcised before they came. But some of the youngest ones, he had heard from Brother Donatien who oversaw them, were not. Perhaps the fisherman was right —the parents delayed it because he was too small or frail? Or they saw from early on that something was wrong? Maybe this is it: they'd sought one cure after another for his muteness. When all failed, they turned to violence.

Lucas knelt to put socks on Dondieu's feet and buckle his sandals, wishing he could have socks too. The Holy Land is nowhere as cold as home, but it's too cold for bare feet in winter. But that's the Order's practice, no point in complaining about it or wishing for socks. Heading down the long corridor, Lucas tried to teach the boy his name. He pointed to himself and said "Lucas," then to the boy, saying "Dondieu." Back and forth, back and forth, until it seemed he'd understood.

Chapter 5

They entered the dormitory and found an unmade bed. Lucas sat Dondieu on the adjacent one and pushed down on the mattress to show him that it had some bounce. He went to the cupboard and pulled out sheets, a small pillow and two wool blankets. Meticulously, he laid out the bedding, tucked in the blankets and fluffed up the pillow at the head. He'd done this for himself every day since leaving home as a mechanical chore. Who knew it could feel so tender and sweet to do it for someone else?

As soon as Lucas was done the boy crawled into the bed. His head sank into the pillow, his ring of curls looking, for just a fleeting moment, like a halo. The boy scrunched himself into fetal position. He nestled his right thumb in his mouth and drew his left hand into a fist by his cheek. Lucas pulled the blankets up to Dondieu's chin and tucked them around him, making a tight cocoon. He leaned down to kiss the crown of Dondieu's head but stopped himself midway and straightened up —too soon. Instead, he began the *Pater Noster*. Before he reached "Thy will be done," the boy was asleep.

He did not want to leave Dondieu's side. He would practice his silent prayer and meditation right there. To augment his devotion, he kneeled alongside the bed on the hard floor, facing the half-moons of the boy's closed eyelids and timing his swaying to his soft exhalations. He recited prayers for a long time, then fell into silence.

Gratitude welled inside of him, a gentle tide slowly rising from the pit of his stomach into his heart.

His shins began to ache, and his toes were so cold they had stopped sending his brain any sensations. He wiggled them to get some blood circulating but felt nothing. He rose slowly and sat on the bed next to Dondieu's. His eyelids drooped. He drifted off, wandering among images of mothers holding children of different ages; swaddled at their bosoms, hoisted on their hips, seated in their laps.

A loud jumble of boys' voices startled Lucas awake. "*Silencio!*" commanded a deep voice. They hushed and scrambled each to his own bed for their afternoon rest. Some stayed on top of their blankets and held their hands in prayer at their chests, eyes counting the wooden beams of the high ceiling. Others burrowed inside their bedding and closed their eyes.

Dondieu awoke. He looked befuddled, then terrified. Lucas knelt at his bed and brought his face close to him.

"Don't be afraid. I am here. *Tu es en sécurité. Tute tranquillo.*"

If only he could say it in Arabic! What words did he know? He ran through his vocabulary: *Marhabah, Shukran, Salaam Aleikum. Maybe Salaam?* It means something like "peace." No! It also means "good bye." Dondieu would be frightened. He had enough words for buying fish, but not for soothing a frightened child. He'll have to learn them.

He took hold of Dondieu's hand and hummed, hoping he'd fall back asleep. But he didn't. Instead, he stared at Lucas, and next methodically scanned the room. Then Lucas' face, the room and back again.

"Good then, Dondieu. Looks like you slept enough for now." Lucas helped Dondieu extricate himself from under the blankets. "The boys have to take their afternoon rest now, but you already rested, so we can go look around." Without having fully thought it through, Lucas had decided to explain everything to Dondieu, whether he understood it or not.

Dondieu's face was shiny clean and plumped by sleep, but his eyes returned to the bewildered stare of the morning. Lucas put him up on his hip and walked through the hallway into the enclosed courtyard. It was pleasantly warm, heat rising from the stone pavement that had baked in the sun all day. In the middle was a small water fountain and sundial, surrounded by a rockery with the first narcissus flowers of the year already in bloom. Lucas squatted down and brought Dondieu close to the flowers so he could smell the sweet fragrance. The boy inhaled and sneezed, then wrinkled his nose. Lucas laughed and rose, transferring him to his other hip.

He headed to the main chapel, bowing to enter through the low door. Inside, it took a moment to adjust to the dim light. Lucas drew in the musty smell of extinguished candles and sweet, almost cloying, residue of incense. Halfway down the center aisle he stopped and raised Dondieu up, pointing to the crucifix above a table laden with six lit candles. The silver-plated loincloth of the crucified Jesus and full robes of Mary and the Magdalene flanking him, along with the massive silver candlesticks, reflected and refracted so much light, Lucas was momentarily blinded.

"*Deus*, Dondieu. Look - *Jesus Christus*," he pointed up. Dondieu raised his gaze and let out a piercing cry. He covered his eyes and buried his face in Lucas' shoulder, then grabbed the end of Lucas' sleeve and pulled it over his head.

What happened to the man?
There's blood . . .
On his hands. And his feet.
Is he dead?
He lifted the edge of Lucas' sleeve and peaked at the crucifix.
Yes. He looks dead.
But also, he looks . . . I have seen him before.
One time. In a very big house.
Beautiful colors in the windows.
And a funny smell. My nose itched.

Who is he?
"Jesus Christus," this one said.
"Their God," Mama said.
Then the baby cried. The baby?
Yes. Our neighbors'.
A new baby. She cried because they put her in the water.
Why did they put her in the water, Mama?
Mama!
Where is Mama?

Dondieu clutched at Lucas' chest. Tears streamed down his face. Lucas hugged him tightly and chastised himself. Much too soon! What was he thinking? The boy has probably never seen a crucifix. The wounds oozing blood, the thin ribs nearly poking out of the translucent skin—it must be terrifying for him!

"Shush, shush," Lucas said and hurried to the door. He had a lot to learn about how to take care of the boy, of any child, for that matter. He made himself a mental note, though: he's certainly not from the German Colony. Those people are very pious. And English? most likely not either, they'd go to church at least on Christmas and Easter.

He carried the boy in his embrace, heading outside. Then rounded the corner and entered the smaller chapel; no Crucifix there. With Dondieu still cowering in his arms, he knelt down in front of the Madonna with Jesus on her lap. He held Dondieu and whispered soothingly to him, whispered and waited. He didn't move an inch despite the cold floor biting into his knee. Finally, Dondieu lowered his hands and looked up.

"The Madonna," Lucas pointed towards the altar. "There — Mama. *Maria Sancta. Mater Christi.*" The boy's ragged breath slowed down. His body softened and Lucas loosened his hold on him, setting him to stand at his side. He could finally rise and sit on the bench, massaging his frozen knees. Suddenly the boy bolted forward and one, two, three, clambered up the altar steps all the way up to the statue. Lucas stared, stumped by what was happening in front of his eyes. He himself had not yet been permitted to go up those steps. That honor was reserved for Father Pierre's hand-picked monks who ascended to light the candles or to drape embroidered bags brought by pilgrims as offerings, onto the outstretched hands of Mary and Jesus.

Dondieu climbed up on his hands and knees and wedged himself into Mary's lap, across from the Boy Savior. Like a little monkey! Lucas marveled but, immediately gasped and called out: "God in Heaven! What do I do now?" Is the offense of the boy in Mary's lap greater than the commotion sure to arise if he pulled him off by force? And could he dare get close enough to the statue to remove the boy?

"Please, Lord, have mercy," he begged, "don't let anyone come into the chapel now. He's just a little child who doesn't know better."

Better to act quickly. The Holy Father will forgive this transgression, committed in order to prevent a greater disgrace. Lucas climbed the steps on his knees, head bowed in supplication. At the top he stopped and looked at the boy, who had stretched his arms across Mary's robed abdomen. His face glistened with tears. As gently as he could, Lucas peeled Dondieu's fingers, one by one, off the Madonna's light blue robe and placed the boy's hands around his own neck. He wedged his hand under Dondieu's bottom and lifted him up, embracing him and murmuring softly. The boy whimpered, looked one more time at the Madonna and then buried his face in the folds of Lucas' habit. On tiptoes, Lucas carried him out of the chapel.

He took Dondieu back to the dormitory and settled him under the blankets. The boy was not crying any longer, but his eyes had returned to their vacant stare. Lucas sat on the edge of the bed watching Dondieu drift off to sleep. He woke him in time for dinner and carried him to the Refectory.

Lucas tried to enjoy the bouillabaisse Brother Matthieu had clearly labored over all afternoon, but his mind raced far from his taste buds. What an enormous task he had taken on himself: to make the boy feel safe. Could he? He'll need help from above, the same benevolence Dondieu had sought in Mary's lap.

Meanwhile, Dondieu slurped his soup with relish. "Thank You for that," Lucas mouthed, and put his hand on the boy's shoulder. After evening prayers, they returned to the dormitory and waited for the other boys to arrive. Brother Michel and Brother Donatien, who enforced the silent bedtime preparation with rigor, shepherded them in. Brother Michel was very tall and had an imposing black beard, while Brother Donatien was shorter and softer, but had the booming voice. In combination, the boys seemed sufficiently afraid of them to lie obediently in their beds in total silence.

Lucas nodded and gestured towards the sleeping boy. He signaled Donatien to come over and offered to take the rest of his shift, supervising the boys until every last one of them was asleep. Brother Donatien was surprised but thankful to be off duty for the evening; he was out the door before Lucas needed to offer a reason.

Part V: April 1, 1941

Chapter 1

"Next week is Passover," Alfred said during dinner.

"Of course! You can't miss that here. Unlike back home..."

"And that is what's great about being here," Alfred said, a bit didactic for Gertie's taste.

"Ja, Ja..." she answered.

"My colleague at work invited us to their family's Seder," Alfred spoke more softly now.

"Ach," Gertie sighed, "that's nice but it would be so hard, with who knows how many children there. But it's very nice of him."

"Maybe we should go, Gertie."

"I couldn't bear..." Gertie swallowed hard, "to listen to some other four-year-old sing the *Ma Nishtanah*."

Alfred nodded but didn't say anything. He reached across the table for her hand. She let him lace his fingers through hers and kiss her knuckles.

"I know, Alfred, I know you're trying to help me to move forward, but..."

"I understand, it's only been four months."

"Four months!" Gertie called in alarm, "how is that possible?"

At Easter services in the big chapel, Dondieu stood in the boys' choir, his spot fixed by his height. It took a while before Lucas, and many other Brothers, realized that he was singing out loud. He had a beautiful voice!

"How can this be?" Lucas asked Father Pierre after the service concluded. "He cannot speak, but he can sing? And so well —both the melody and every word of the hymns?"

"An enigma . . . " Father Pierre said, clearly puzzled too. He would consult the Abbess at the Carmelite nunnery nearby. Sister Margareta had a deep knowledge of human nature and medicine.

A week later Father Pierre called Lucas to the library.

"Abbess Margareta had never seen such a case herself, but she's read about it."

"Read about it?"

"In medical books. She has a small but excellent library. She said there are documented cases of children who don't speak but are not actually mute. A child psychiatrist in Switzerland diagnosed it, not long ago. She showed me the article, in German, of course. He named it Selective Mutism."

"But why?"

"That is not clear. It's an unusual condition, she said."

"But what causes it, Father?"

"Some children become mute after a traumatic event, or grave illness; others, for no apparent reason. Sometimes they outgrow it, sometimes not."

"Can we cure it?"

"There's no treatment. Nothing she knew of."

"Should we," Lucas began but hesitated. It was not his place to suggest this.

"Should we what?"

"Consult a doctor? A German-trained one, m-m-maybe."

"There are good ones in town," Father Pierre agreed, "especially among the Jews coming in the last few years. Top universities. No question about that, but . . . " his voice trailed off. Lucas waited.

"Nevertheless," Father Pierre continued as if he'd come back from a long journey, "I have complete confidence in Sister Margareta. She's as knowledgeable as any of them. And why call attention to the situation? What would we say when the doctor asks for a history?"

"But when Brother Nicholas was so sick . . . " Lucas stopped himself. Better not seem so brazen.

"That was different," Father Pierre frowned, "it was his appendix; he needed a surgeon. I debated between the Italian Hospital —easier for me to communicate with them —and the other options: the new municipal hospital the British are so proud of or Rothschild Hospital. Hard choice."

Father Pierre leaned back in his chair and pressed his fingertips together, slowly swaying his head, as if he were weighing the options right then. Lucas marveled at how free the Abbot was in conversation, forgetting Lucas was just a junior monk. He must be lonely! Lucas was stunned to realize. Keep quiet, he instructed himself, let him talk.

"But in the end," Father Pierre leaned towards Lucas, "I decide to go with Rothschild. Better a private Jewish hospital than a government-run one. And for the reason you mentioned: the German-trained surgeons. They must be the best we have here."

"Brother Nicholas certainly got better fast!" Lucas finally dared speak up.

"He did. But surely our prayers helped too."

"Of course," Lucas bowed.

"Tender care, and patience is all Sister Margareta advised. And that, I trust, I can count on you to provide, my son."

"With perfect faith, Father."

CHAPTER 2

"Next week is Mawlid al-Nabi," Youssra reminded Moussa. "I think Moulleek is comfortable enough with us to bring him to meet our families."

"Might as well take the plunge and satisfy everyone's curiosity. Surely word has already traveled back home anyway."

"Everybody will be in a good mood for the Prophet's birthday," Youssra offered, "so they'll go easy on us."

She sewed Moulleek another outfit—this time a qumbaz, the short version of a jellabiya, which village boys wore, so he'd feel at home there. Her fingers ached to embroider it, but her head said no: boys didn't wear embroidered clothes. *Just a small bird? A boat?* She bargained with herself, *boys like boats. But no, she shouldn't: people will ask questions, the other boys would tease him.*

She gave him an extra-long bath, lathering every inch of skin with a new soap bar. She washed his hair, knowing full well it would get dusty on the long road home. Moussa, meanwhile, rehearsed the story in his mind, but the fear of his father's disapproval kept unraveling it, like a thread pulled out of the edge of fraying fabric.

They went to Moussa's parents' home first, as custom dictated. They stepped through the small iron gate into the yard, enclosed by a chest-high stone wall. The paving-stone path was flanked by patches of vegetables growing for the kitchen's daily needs: onion, garlic, dill, cabbage and radishes. Lined up like soldiers against the white-washed wall were potted mint and parsley, lush in their bright green leaves.

Moussa's nostrils filled with the pungent smell of each plant and his mouth flooded with saliva, awakening his longing for his mother's cooking. Youssra inhaled deeply. Moussa thought he heard a small sigh of yearning. He hoisted Moulleek up higher on his hip as Youssra's whispered in his ear: "Smell this, habibi. *This* is the village."

With each step down the path, Moussa felt the familiar tightening in his gut. He hunkered into his sweater, though it wasn't cold. In fact, the day was blessed by a caressing warm sun. Moussa silently counted the paving stones left between him and the door; twelve altogether, each chiseled by his father into a perfect hexagon. It was one of Moussa's earliest memories. How old was he then? Close to four? Too young to retain details, but the image was vivid: his father sitting on a low stool carefully striking each stone with a small hammer, one small chink after another.

"See," Bassem had said to Moussa proudly as he passed his white-dusted palm along the edges, smoothing the corners, "six sides, each exactly the same length as the others. Just like the Dome of the Rock." He met Moussa's puzzled look. "You don't know it yet —you are too little. I'll take you one day to Haram al-Sharif, in Al-Quds. Oh, it's beautiful —the tiles, more blue than the bluest of skies."

That moment of emotions, of wonder at beauty, never returned. It was replaced in one blow when Moussa's mother died by a stern silence and a rigid face. During the days of mourning Bassem never spoke and, right after the first three days receiving condolence visits, he went back to the fields. Their aunt brought food and showed Maryam how to make simple dishes and bake pita in the taboun. Moussa helped his sister build the fire and tend it. They managed to feed themselves and their father and helped each other bear his stony, mute presence. Moussa passed his fourteenth birthday during the forty days of mourning. No one mentioned it. At the time Moussa didn't think he cared.

On the forty-first day his father started building a second room onto their house. He wouldn't talk about it, just instructed Moussa how to mix the mortar and layer the stones, mostly by pointing wordlessly at what he needed. In the month it took to finish the room he gave no hint of its purpose. Moussa asked Maryam what she thought, but she was only ten and looked to him to figure it out.

"Maybe he is finally building the Madafeh that Yumma wanted so much?" Moussa said.

"Maybe. How many times did she say it was a proper guest room that made a man important in the village?"

"Every time someone visited, as I remember," Moussa answered.

"Yes, every time."

When the room was done Bassem hung up a prayer rug and a mirror in a wooden frame inlaid with mother of pearl. In the middle of the room, he placed a highly polished copper-top table and two tripod stools with embroidered cushions. He set a beautiful copper pitcher on the table. They'd never had any decorations on the walls before, nor such lovely furnishings. It was the beautifully framed mirror that made Moussa certain the room was in honor of his mother. She would have cherished it so.

Two weeks later he realized bitterly, how naïve he had been. His father brought home a new wife; Afeefa, a young bride just one year older than Moussa himself. It was extremely awkward. Was it because she could have been his sister? Or because his father did for her what he'd never done for Moussa's mother? The bitterness grew when his father told Moussa that he had set up the new room as a bedroom for himself and his new bride. "You and Maryam will stay in the old room," he said.

Moussa couldn't stop his upper lip from curling up in surprise, right where, for a while now, he'd been furtively stroking the light fuzz heralding a moustache. He dared not say a word. He thought his father winced—just a bit - as he went on: "You must understand; you're not a child anymore. She is a young woman. Very . . . what can I say? Lively."

Moussa, lowered his eyes.

"You know what I mean Moussa, yes?" his father added.

The question hung in the air, swinging between them like a pendulum. Finally, Moussa whispered "Yes, Baba," and turned to leave, hoping his father thought he'd accepted it.

"What?" Youssra gently elbowed Moussa's side, as he stopped halfway down the path.

"The usual," he muttered, mad at himself for succumbing to the old feelings.

"Just ignore it," Youssra whispered in his ear as his father opened the door. He must have spotted them through the narrow window on the left.

"Marhabah!" Bassem called out and flashed them a welcome smile. It was immediately replaced by a puzzled frown which added a new wrinkle to his furrowed brow. He searched Moussa's face for a clue.

"It's Moulleek. Call Afeefa. I'll tell both of you all about him."

"She is in the back, picking some herbs. I'll get her. Come in!"

Bassem walked out and rounded the corner while Moussa and Youssra went inside. They sat down on the rolled-up straw mats, covered with colorful rugs, Moulleek tightly wedged between the two of them.

My legs itch. What is it?

He touched the rug under him with his palm.

This rug. Very scratchy.

Like something else...

Old man. A little like this one. Itchy blanket on his knees.

And his moustache. Always scratched me on the cheek.

Why on the cheek?

He kissed me. He said: 'Mein Kleiner.'

Kleiner... he always called me Kleiner.

I know! Opa!

And there was Oma, too. She hugged and kissed too. But she wasn't itchy. She was so, so soft.

The house —not like this at all!

Maybe this one is for the Opa and Oma of now?

They said this morning: Abu and Yumma. They said, "very old, but very nice."

But why? Where are Opa and Oma?

And Mama and Papa!

No!

Moulleek began to shake. Youssra wrapped her arms around him and sang to him softly. "He must be frightened, Moussa. Please make them understand."

"I will . . . try," Moussa swallowed, trying to wet his tight, dry throat.

"Tomorrow, we'll repeat this at your parents. This should be good practice."

"At my parents it will be easier, Moussa; they already have five grandsons."

Moussa bit his lower lip. Was there a veiled barb there - suggesting the infertility was his family line's curse? No, it wasn't like her to needle him with that. But maybe, in her worry, she's not as careful as he knows she usually is, stepping on egg shells not to take any shots at his manhood?

"Just tell the story simply," Youssra squeezed his hand, seeing his hardened jaw.

CHAPTER 3

Moussa knitted his fingers together and twirled his thumbs around each other. He sat stiffly, trying to suppress the trembling inside him. When his stepmother came into the room carrying a tray of baklava, he loosened his fingers and his jaw. Afeefa took slow steps towards Moulleek, and murmured, as if it were their secret: "You like baklava, don't you?" Moulleek's face lit up. "*Tfadal!* Take one! And you can have another when you finish."

After encouraging Moulleek to take the biggest piece, Afeefa passed the tray to Moussa and Youssra, and finally to her husband. With the honey of the bakla*v*a in his mouth Moussa's tongue relaxed. He laid out the story of finding Moulleek piece by piece, as if he were setting up a game of backgammon. He assured them no one responded to their inquiries about a missing child; explained that Moulleek didn't speak but was very bright and happy. Bassem looked at the boy intently, then at Moussa's face, and finally at his own rough palms, which, with his fingers laced together, made a small nest.

Afeefa spoke up, filling the awkward silence: "He is a gift from Allah, as good as any son."

"I said the same, Afeefa, exactly the same words!" Youssra jumped in.

"She did," Moussa said, "the first words out of her mouth."

"That's his name," Youssra added, "Moulk-L'illah—Moulleek."

They all looked at Bassem. He held his gaze steady on the boy, but didn't say anything. Youssra could tell that Moussa was biting the inside of his cheeks. She knew he couldn't, so she spoke up: "So what do you say, Abu Moussa?" Bassem pressed his thumbs together, then rolled the right around the left, forwards and backwards. Just like Moussa, Youssra noted.

Bassem cleared his throat, "Yes, a gift from Allah, praise be to Him. And, one day, when your half-brothers Yassin and Ahmed finally marry, inshallah, they'll produce more grandsons. From our blood. You understand, Moussa, yes?"

"What about them getting married?" Moussa seized the opportunity to steer the conversation to a safer subject, "any prospective brides?"

Bassem and Afeefa both shrugged their shoulders and turned their palms up with an anemic "kullu min Allah."

"Every other young man in the village is already betrothed, if not married," Afeefa said.

"Even Yussuf?" Moussa asked; his childhood friend had a reputation as a ladies' man.

"Yes," Afeefa snorted, "even that rascal."

"But he's older than Yassin . . ." Moussa tried to counter Afeefa's bitterness. She shrugged.

"Well, what about the two of them?" Youssra came to Moussa's aid.

"So far," Bassem said, "all they want to talk about is Nazareth: the shops, the bustling streets, the opportunities if you open a small store."

"Better Yassin should have a store in Nazareth than where he was two years ago . . ." Afeefa said.

Moussa nodded. He certainly didn't want another bitter discussion of that. How his father had railed against it! Moussa had felt a little guilty, but had admit to himself that it was a bit of a relief from father berating him for leaving the village.

"Better leave it," Bassem said, then clamped his lips shut. But he couldn't help himself. "'Youth to the hills!' —that was a foolish thing. Yassin couldn't stop talking about *Al Tawra*, the Revolt. And what became of it? *Bukra fil mishmish* . . . " Bassem hissed.

"Yes, you are right, nothing much came of Sheikh Al Qassam, 'our great hero.'" Moussa agreed.

"We shouldn't have let him go," Bassem interrupted, "so many got killed and injured. Everyone remembers that Al Qassam died—a martyr, but what about the rest of them? No more than boys . . . "

"What could we do?" Afeefa raised her hands.

Youssra elbowed Moussa; he should drop the subject. But he had to say one more thing. "Still . . . you should be proud of him!" he said, rather more loudly than he'd intended.

"Proud . . . " Bassem sputtered.

Afeefa shook her head.

"Yes, I'm sure he was brave. Do you think he . . . you know?" Moussa asked.

"We don't know," Bassem said in a tone that Moussa knew meant he better not ask any more questions.

"You mean," Afeefa whispered, "with a gun?"

"Or . . . a knife."

"He hasn't said anything," Afeefa said, "but I see something in his eyes. A darkness that wasn't there before he went."

"No hint? No clue if it was British soldiers or Jews?" Moussa asked.

Both Afeefa and Bassem shrugged.

"Well," Moussa knitted his fingers together again, as he spoke, "he'd done his duty. You should be proud of him."

"And what about you, if you're such a hero?" Bassem asked, a sharp edge to his voice.

"Me?" Moussa coughed. "It's as we say: the fingers of your hand are not the same as mine. I can't do those things."

"Those things?" Bassem wouldn't leave it alone.

"You know—guns, knives, bombs . . . "

"Moussa, the little one!" Youssra shushed him. Moussa halted but Bassem was still staring at him. Moussa squirmed. He had to say something to defend his honor. "There are other ways to support the *Jihad*."

"Other ways?" Afeefa and Bassem both asked.

"Other ways. Things, you know —illegal things—things had to be brought in to supply the fighters. I have a boat . . . "

"Moussa!" Youssra called out; her hand flew to her mouth.

"I'm sorry, I shouldn't have said anything."

The room seemed to ice over. Moussa felt as though he were in a morgue.

"At least Yassin's back home safe," Youssra broke the silence.

"Alhamdulillah!" Afeefa answered and laid her hands on her heart.

"A store in Nazareth, *heh*? Both of them?" Moussa shepherded the conversation to safer shores.

"Yes," his father said, letting out a breath of relief. "That's how it is with the young men, now. Many in the village. They want to be fancy city-people; not have to work the soil with their hands."

"Someone—Jameel, do you remember him?" Afeefa jumped in, "he even wanted to open a store in the village."

"In the village?" Moussa said, incredulous.

"Yes. *Majnoun!* Everybody laughed at him," Bassem said. "So, he went to Nazareth, too, like your brothers."

"Flew there —couldn't stay a day longer," Afeefa said.

"Give them time, Umm Yassin," Youssra tried a conciliatory tone, "they'll understand once they have their own children."

"Inshallah," Bassem and Afeefa said in unison.

Chapter 4

"Now I better start on our dinner," Afeefa announced and rose up. "Yassin and Ahmed may have gone to Nazareth, but they still come home for my cooking. Fancy or not, no restaurant there is better."

"I'll help you," Youssra jumped up and pulled Moulleek along with her, following Afeefa through the bead curtain into the kitchen.

"Let's go look at the basatin," Moussa suggested, hoping that among the fruit trees the tension with his father would ease. He always felt closer to him in the orchard than in the house. Especially after Afeefa came. For so long after the wedding his father's eyes seemed trained only on Afeefa. When the two boys, Yassin and Ahmed, were born less than two years apart, Bassem's chest appeared to lift and widen. But then a miscarriage, and a second and a third. He caved in again; his face took on the appearance of rough tree bark. Only once did Bassem say anything to Moussa, when he'd come to help with the olive harvest. "The curse has returned," he hissed as they walked together, stooped with sacks full of ripe olives on their backs.

"At least you have two more sons," was all Moussa could think to say that day.

"The basatin; good idea, Moussa," Bassem opened the door, "we've had good rains so far this year. Everything is growing fast, the weeds, too. Maybe you'll want to get your hands dirty and pull some out. Nobody weeds like you used to..."

Moussa smiled and instinctively cracked the joints of each finger, an old habit. He did it before he started on a patch, his own peculiar way of readying —blessing, even? —the fingers to draw each weed out of its home in the earth.

As they walked out of the village, approaching the family plot, Bassem said softly: "I know you had to leave, Moussa. You had your reasons."

"Yes."

"You do love the land, though? The fields?"

"I do, Baba. You know that," Moussa said.

Bassem squatted down at the edge of the field. "You must take an oath for me, Moussa," he said while sliding the delicate spears of the new wheat between his thumb and finger.

"An oath?" Moussa lowered himself to his haunches beside his father. He couldn't help uprooting a few weeds at his feet as he waited for an explanation.

"An oath, yes," Bassem wrapped his calloused palms around Moussa's right hand. The hardened, rough skin somehow felt soft and soothing. Moussa raised their joined hands gingerly, still puzzled.

"When I'm gone," Bassem started, and his eyes misted over for a moment.

"Inshallah it will be many, many years from now," Moussa rushed to say.

"Inshallah," his father echoed. "You must come back to the village and farm our land. Your brothers might get the idea of selling it. Money is what they want."

"Money?"

"Yes. Our plot would fetch a good price, especially with the Jews buying whatever land they can get their hands on."

"Yes, I've heard about people selling," Moussa said. "Traitors," he added under his breath.

"Traitors? maybe. Greedy, that's for sure. And probably lazy. It's hard work, every day, every year. No vacation, like they have in the city."

"I have no vacation either," Moussa said, squirming because he sounded defensive.

"I know. But the land —that's the important thing. We must keep it in the family. It's not ours to sell. Only to hand to the next generation."

"Of course. An oath, yes," Moussa raised his hand higher with his father's fingers laced through his.

They stood up together. Bassem scanned his land all the way to the row of acacias that marked its border.

"And I will teach it to Moulleek, I promise you," Moussa said.

"Good. Teach him that. And how to weed. Even if he's not our blood. Working the land will . . . make him."

They walked from the wheat patch and on to the vegetable garden, then toward the olive grove and the orchard with lemons, pomegranates, and two figs, one producing green figs, the other purple. Moussa had loved those fig trees; so perfect for climbing. A grapevine trailed from a small arbor where he and his friends sometimes spent the night in summer. Past the vine were almonds and then apricots, Moussa's favorites. The fruit was so sweet, if you picked it fully ripe, the flesh was a thick honey. You could suck it in with one slurp.

They entered the orchard and, unconsciously, both bowed as if entering a mosque. Their feet were already bare—no need to take any shoes off. They each leaned in close to the fruit buds, turned a fragile branch this way and that.

"Very good, Baba, looks like it'll be a good crop this year."

"Inshallah, if the weather cooperates, yes." Bassem fluttered his fingertips along a few more buds and turned around, starting back towards the house.

"Dinner should be ready by now. Your stepmother doesn't like it when I'm late."

"'Doesn't like it' is a very nice way of saying it," Moussa said and they both laughed and hastened their steps.

"He does have exactly your curls and your eyes," Bassem said just before he stepped through the door.

Chapter 5

As the days warmed Moulleek spent more time outside. He made friends with the neighborhood boys his age, who seemed to accept his muteness easily. He joined their games with pebbles and sticks, hide and seek, and climbing the few trees in the neighborhood. Moussa and Youssra still worried and sent him out each morning repeating: "Don't let anyone hurt you. Come right back if they're mean to you." Youssra confessed to Moussa that she often stood in the backyard rehanging laundry she's already taken down, or stepped into the narrow lane carrying a basket, pretending she had some errand to run, just to keep an eye on him.

What they feared happened only once. He rushed through the door and tried to slither himself under the rolled-up mattress. Youssra hurried to his side but he covered his face with his hands and turned his back to her.

"What's the matter Moulleek? What happened?" she tried to hug him but he shook his head violently and curled around himself, trying to bury his head between his knees.

No, no!

Hide!

But it's Yumma. She won't hurt you.

But the boys will. That game they played: "Itbakh el Yahoud."

First just a regular chasing game. Then they started with those words.

Louder and louder.
"Yahoud, Yahoud!"
"Itbakh—kill"
Run away!
Yahoud is Yehudi.
Like when they were singing and crying . . . on the boat: Nefesh Yehudi.
Yehudi is Jude!
Ich bin Jude.
Who said?
He said.
Who —Baba?
No, not Baba. Papa.
Papa . . . Papa?
Not Baba. Much taller. All different.
Papa!
Where is he?

Moulleek was sobbing and grunting; his body convulsed. Youssra wrapped her arms around him and rocked him.

"Something bad happened?" she tried again. "The boys scared you? Mahmoud? Mustafa?"

He just heaved in sobs. She couldn't piece anything together. She let him cry until he was spent, the bawls turned to whimpers. She rocked him until he fell asleep.

It was late spring when Lucas realized that Dondieu had fully adjusted to monastery life and routines. Everyone agreed that he was quick-witted. Much of the time they nearly forgot he was mute. Often Lucas caught sight of a boy pouring his heart out to Dondieu, who would sit with him in total concentration, sometime holding hands. Clever little boys, Lucas thought to himself, they've found themselves their own confessor; probably much safer than a priest.

Lucas spent time with Dondieu whenever he could. So that the other boys did not envy his special affection, he devoted more time to playing and talking with them as well. In truth, he wasn't surprised how much pleasure it gave him. They reminded him of his younger siblings' antics, especially tricks for getting out of doing their chores. Instead of annoying him, they charmed him. They opened what he imagined as small drawers in his heart, drawers that had long been shut.

Part VI: June 10, 1941

CHAPTER 1

The sun's rays bouncing off the water of the Haifa port momentarily blinded Gertie when she looked out the window. She couldn't tell, even after adjusting to the glare, whether the three chimney tops of the *Patria* were still sticking out above the water. If they were, they were so small now you couldn't see them from this far. The sea was very calm today, its surface a glassy expanse. So quiet . . . you could say peaceful, she thought to herself. But she couldn't. She couldn't use those words.

Yet those were exactly the words Lucas said to himself as we walked along the dock, looking for fishermen who'd come in with a good catch late in the afternoon. The heat of the day was giving way to the gentle afternoon breeze coming off the harbor. Thank God for that; he hated sweating in his thick dark robe. They didn't think of the Holy Land's summer sun when they chose deep brown as the color of the Order's vestments.

He'd never been sent to buy fish this late in the day, but he had grown to like this errand, his turn coming up every few weeks. In truth, it was partly the opportunity to sneak a little piece of baklava on his way back to the bus. It was a struggle, though: half the time the monastic vows won, the other half, the sweetness. Today, he assured himself, he would definitely resist! There won't be time anyway. He needed to rush in order to get back to the monastery in time for Matthieu to cook the fish.

Father Pierre had summoned him right after lunch. "We just heard we have distinguished visitors, the Abbots of the Trappist Monastery in Latrun and the Pater Noster in Jerusalem. They will arrive in time for dinner."

"Such an important visit? Why?" Lucas blurted out before he had a chance to decide if it was proper for him to ask.

"For consultations," Father Pierre answered and, for reasons Lucas couldn't fathom, went on to elaborate: "Like ours, their Order is worried about the safety of the monks here in the Holy Land with the war going on. If the Germans conquer Palestine, who knows what will happen to them? Not to mention the hostilities between the Jews and the Arabs. Danger all around."

"It is d-dangerous, isn't it?"

"Indeed . . . A Trappist emissary from France is coming to evaluate the situation."

Lucas was quite sure it wasn't his place to ask, but still . . . "And you, Father, are you worried about our safety?"

Father Pierre frowned. Lucas understood he had gone too far. But then the Abbot put his hand on Lucas' shoulder and said: "No. I have no fear. We have good relations with everyone in Haifa and have our Lord to rely on for our protection."

Lucas bowed.

"So, I need you to go to the kitchen and get the cook's order for tonight's meal."

"Right away, Father."

He hurried to the kitchen. Brother Matthieu was cooking a hash from the lunch leftovers. A small pile of chopped vegetables near the pot promised a slight improvement in taste.

"The fish for the visitors. What shall I get?"

"You'll get there late in the day, Lucas, so you can't be picky. Try to find three at least this big," Matthieu spread his hands about a foot apart.

"Be sure to smell them. If they have been there since early morning, they'll already stink. You want fish caught later in the day."

Lucas picked up the wicker basket from the hook on the wall and Brother Matthieu handed him a pouch of coins and a neatly folded white towel.

"Wrap the fish in this to keep them cool."

"I'll do my best," Lucas said, already half-way out the door.

At the dock now, Lucas looked left and right, shielding his eyes from the blinding light reflecting off the water. The sun had already started its arc towards the west side of the Carmel, so he must hurry. Once it sank below the crest the harbor would quickly grow dark and cold in the mountain's shadow. He passed many boats tied to their wooden posts and empty. The port was much quieter than he was used to from his morning forays.

This may be harder than he'd thought. He scanned the water to see if any boats were coming into the port. There was one on the left and another one about forty meters behind it. They are rowing towards the dock at a leisurely pace. "Hurry up!" Lucas urged them.

A thunderous explosion knocked Lucas to the ground. The basket flew out of his hand and rolled on its side. It settled about twenty yards away, its mouth gaping open towards Lucas, who lay flat on the ground covering his ears. After a moment Lucas willed himself to lift his palms and listen. A plane engine roared above. *Aerial bombardment! There might be more. Take cover!*

Lucas darted his eyes from side to side, searching for a place to hide. To his right was the exposed dock. To his left, amid a jumble of empty wooden crates, he spotted a fishing boat set upside down. For repairs, he guessed, then berated himself for this wasted thought in an emergency. He ran towards it with his torso folded half-way down, scooping up the basket as he passed it.

He crouched and slid into the squat space under the boat.

"*Ay!*" a man shrieked. Lucas realized the squishy mass he had stepped on was this man's hand.

"*Pardon!*" Lucas called out, forgetting just then how to say it in Arabic. He scooted sideways, away from the man's hand but making sure he was fully under the boat. Before his eyes adjusted to the dim light another explosion rang in his ears. Then the roar of a plane overhead. The noxious smell of perspiration assaulted his nostrils. Fear, Lucas noted, and less than stellar personal hygiene.

Once his eyes adjusted, he could make out the face of the man whose hand he had nearly flattened. He motioned to Lucas to scoot further in: "Tfadal, please, sit here. It's a good hiding place."

"Shukran," Lucas' Arabic came back. He braced himself against the hull but recoiled from the slithering fish scales under his fingers. He flicked off the scales that had stuck to his hand. His touch had stirred up the stench of dead fish. He wrinkled his nose, as did the other man.

"Now we must listen if the aero plane comes back," the man said.

"Yes," Lucas agreed, and they both cocked their ears. The sound of the plane engine was growing faint.

Lucas stared at the man; he looked familiar. But more importantly, he was grimacing in pain and holding his right palm tightly over his left upper arm. "What happened?" Lucas asked. The man removed his hand: three deep gashes had torn the flesh and immediately began to ooze blood.

"I help you," Lucas said and pulled the towel out of his basket and tore at the edge with his teeth, ripping the towel into three makeshift bandages. He wrapped each one around the sliced flesh, making a tight knot at the end to staunch the bleeding.

"After, you go doctor. He do it better," Lucas admonished.

"Shukran," the man's facial muscles loosened, softening the taut mask of pain.

As the rush of adrenaline subsided, Lucas realized he did know him.

"You Moussa, right? I buy fish from you."

"Yes! You buy for the monastery, Stella Maris."

"Yes, I'm Lucas, Frère Lucas." He extended his right hand for an awkward shake.

They sat quietly, smiling at each other. Lucas strained to hear anything that would signal more danger.

"How are you, my friend? And your *frères* at Stella Maris?" Moussa picked up the conversation. "It's hard because of the war, eh?"

"Hard," Lucas agreed, "but we safe in the monastery. The frères, the boys. For you it's hard too, yes? Not very safe . . . "

"Everything all around is bad, and the port —it's not safe. But I am alright, and my family. I still go fishing, so we have enough to eat."

"Now quiet. We listen!" Lucas said and placed his index finger across his lips. Moussa raised his finger to his lips as well. In the silence, the stink of the dried fish skeletons reasserted itself. They both wrinkled their noses as they breathed in.

"For smell this is really bad, but for hiding, is good," Lucas said.

Moussa squeezed his nose between the finger and thumb of his uninjured hand. "Yes, not a very good smell. But . . . I think we better stay here little more time. Wait for quiet."

They cupped their ears with their hands at the same instant. Moussa chuckled, pointing from his ear to Lucas' and back. All they heard was the faint rumblings of a few trucks and an occasional car horn beeping.

"And the boy? How is the boy?"

"Good. A very good boy. A very clever boy."

"And he does everything?"

"Yes, he does everything, just right."

"And talking?"

"No talking."

"Not one word?"

"No."

"But he hears fine?"

"Yes. He hears everything and he understands very well. And he's always very nice. A very sweet boy."

They sat for a minute, each lost in his own thoughts.

"Is he ever sad?"

"Maybe . . . sometimes he sits quietly, by himself. But no crying."

"He looks like he is happy most of the time?"

"Yes. Happy. He smiles, he laughs."

"Good. That's very good."

They hushed again. After a while Moussa stuck out his head beyond the rim of the upside-down boat and looked around. "It looks quiet now. What do you think? The aero plane, is it gone?"

"Yes, I think so. I hope."

"What do you say?" Moussa asked, "Aero plane —of the Italians? Or Hitler?"

"Italian, I think," Lucas said, mostly to reassure himself.

With no sight or sound of a plane overhead, Lucas crawled out. Moussa came right after him.

"Now I must get fish and go back to monastery," Lucas announced.

"Nobody will sell fish now!" Moussa laughed. "But come to my boat. I have a few in my bucket —from before."

They straightened their backs and shook their legs, then headed towards Moussa's boat. The dock was empty. No one else had emerged from their hiding spots yet. They walked quickly, their ears cocked for any sound.

"Halt! Do not go near the boats!" an order rang out. "We are still considered under attack. Find shelter immediately!"

Lucas and Moussa looked at each other. Moussa shrugged: "Sorry my friend. No fish today. Better go home now to be safe."

"Yes, you're right. Fish is not as important as to be safe. You also go home."

Together they hurried away from the dock to the main street where, as they parted, they heard the "All Clear" siren sailing above the roofs of the city.

When Lucas arrived back at the monastery he entered the kitchen, ready to apologize for coming empty-handed, Matthieu rushed over to him and hugged him. *That's never happened before,* Lucas marveled.

"We were so worried about you!" Matthieu dropped his arm, feeling a bit awkward now. "We heard the bombing and saw smoke in the port area. We were so worried . . . "

"Yes, it was nearby," Lucas said. His voice quivered; it was only now that he realized how terrified he had been.

Matthieu never asked about the fish.

Chapter 2

Finally! Gertie exhaled as she heard the "All Clear" siren. "It's safe to come out," she said out loud to herself. She'd been huddled under the bed with Benyamin. The cold of the tile floor had seeped into her bones. Still, being cold on a June afternoon was not so bad; almost a treat. She had managed to keep Benyamin comfortably nestled in her arms, so much so that he had dozed off. After laying him down in his crib she rolled her shoulders and twisted her neck left and right. Thankfully, Benyamin continued to sleep. She needed to calm herself and snuff out the flashes of memories ricocheting in her head.

She tried lying down, but she was too agitated. She sat squeezing her head in her hands and digging her elbows hard into her thighs. The pain was comforting. And then not. She wrapped her arms around herself and swayed back and forth. "Emil . . . Emil . . ." she chanted in a rhythmic singsong. "Go ahead," she told the tears streaming down her face. She wiped them on her sleeve when they reached past her mouth. "Empty the bucket."

Alfred! She gasped and the sobs broke. He's at his office. It's far enough from the port . . . I think. I hope. Windows probably shattered. Hopefully he wasn't next to one. Please, let it be so.

She made herself take a few deep breaths. He'll come home as soon as he can. Surely, they will let the employees leave once the sirens stop. He'll be home soon. Better if she's done crying before he arrives.

Fear rushed in. She hurried to the window to look at the port. The smoke swirls were already high up in the sky. No huge fire, thank God! But who knows what damage? Were people killed or injured? When will all this end? She shook her head. And what is it like back home in Europe, where the real war is? Must be ten times, no, a hundred times worse. How dangerous is it in Vienna? When will they hear something from home?

Traffic started up on the street, then voices, loud conversations. But no screams, she noted, so everyone nearby must be fine. Now the waiting... until Alfred got home. He must be even more worried than her. And thinking of Emil, too, for sure. But... not one tear. How on earth does he do that? How does he bear it?

She looked at her watch. The hands seemed to crawl. Benyamin started crying; she welcomed the distraction. She warmed up a bottle and hugged him to her chest as he sucked. Minutes later the handle jiggled and the door opened.

"Gertie! Gertie! Are you here?"

"Yes, Alfred. I'm here. We're fine."

"Gott sei dank. I was so worried."

"No need to worry. We are far enough from the port. You? The office? All safe?"

Alfred wrapped his arms around Gertie and Benyamin. "Everyone and everything is fine. The windows rattled and books fell, but nothing serious."

"Thank God!"

"My inkwell toppled and spilled. Ruined the drawing I was working on. But that's hardly a tragedy."

"Hardly."

Alfred dropped down into a chair, as if he were a sack of potatoes. Gertie put Benyamin in his crib and handed him his favorite stuffed animal—a grey-felt donkey with a little bell around its neck. She brought Alfred a glass of water.

"I hid under the bed with Benyamin. Lay on top of him."

"I went under my desk. Kind of silly, but still."

"Did you . . . ?" Gertie stopped herself.

"Yes. I was back there in an instant."

"Me, too, Alfred."

"I had to recite the alphabet backwards to make the . . . the screams in my head stop."

"Did it work?"

"As a matter of fact, on the fourth time it started to."

Gertie took Alfred's hand and touched it to her lips. She wanted to say she was glad he could stop it, but she couldn't get the words out. Alfred couldn't speak either.

He rose and opened the door. "Rudi next door has a radio. I'll go see what they are reporting."

"Good idea, Liebling. But don't stay too long."

"I know.

Chapter 3

The moment Alfred left Gertie sank onto the bed with a thud. She closed her eyes, but images of the *Patria* flashed by. She forced her eyes open to stop them, got up and tucked in Benyamin's blanket, then stood at the window scanning the port. A cloud of smoke still hovered. The door opened.

"What did you find out?"

"An aerial bombardment. At least two planes were spotted."

"Do you know who, Alfred?"

"The Italians, it seems."

"Mussolini's brave *bambinos* . . . "

"Better than the Germans."

"And how!"

"Anyway, Gertie, there were 'All Clear' sirens at the port and in the lower city. As a matter of fact, we can go back to —"

"To what? What the British call 'business as usual?'"

"Do we have another choice?"

She shrugged.

"Another glass of water, Alfred?"

"That would be nice. I had no idea I was so thirsty."

"Sit and catch your breath. I'll get it."

Gertie came back from the kitchen with two glasses of water.

"Let the cloudiness settle first," she set the glasses down at the table. After a minute they each took a big gulp.

"Oh, Gertie, I forgot, in all this mayhem!"

"The bread? Don't worry . . . "

"No, not the bread. Big news!"

"News? Ach, news is generally bad," Gertie waved a tired hand.

"No! This is good!"

"Shush! Don't wake the baby. But tell me, good news these days would be something."

"I have very good prospects for a new job. Excellent prospects, as a matter of fact. A real job, as an engineer in a very significant building project."

"A real position as an engineer? Finally, Alfred!"

"A real position. And a very important project—a new central bus station."

"A bus station? That's a big project?" Gertie said skeptically.

"As a matter of fact, this one is very big. The lead architect is Werner Wittkower, one of the most important architects in Palestine. Not from here originally, of course."

"Of course."

Alfred marched right on: "He trained first in Berlin and then at Stuttgart University. He came here in the early 30's. Saw the writing on the wall. He was part of the Bauhaus—actually an off-shoot of it called Der Block."

"Alfred, never mind those details. What's this bus station?"

"A new, up-to-date station. Very big and modern; maximum efficiency. There are many engineering challenges. They started construction last year and now is the most complicated phase. They need more engineers and people familiar with European-scale train stations, which, I certainly am! Very ambitious. It's to be an architectural landmark."

Gertie's thoughts flew to the train station in Vienna, the *Südbahnhof* where they had boarded the train to go to the Danube riverboat dock south of the city center. The last memory of home.

"Better to have the passengers get on the boat out of sight of the city's inhabitants, so as not to attract too much attention," the organizers had instructed them, "and not one word to anyone except your immediate family!"

Gertie's breath froze in her windpipe. She felt faint. She leaned over and put her head between her knees.

"Gertie, what's wrong?"

"I'm alright. Just . . . remembering the train station. In Vienna. And how that reminds me of our parents, who couldn't come see us off. And now—what do you think is happening to them?"

"We can't know, can we?"

"Not really, but . . . " Gertie pressed her hands across her chest, as if to keep it from cracking open.

"So better not to think about it," Alfred said firmly.

"I try not to, Alfred. I try! Every morning when I wake up, I tell myself to lock those thoughts in a vault. Our parents . . . and Emil."

"Me, too."

Alfred came over to Gertie and put his hands on her shoulders. He handed her the water glass. She took a few sips.

"Go on, Alfred. You were saying?"

Alfred cleared his throat: "A very ambitious project. A thoroughly modern station and an architectural landmark."

"Yes, you said that already," Gertie tried to restrain her impatience. "But in this provincial town? How many buses do they imagine will ever come here? Even after the war?"

"That's the thing, Gertie. Not here. In Tel Aviv, the new city. All the architects and engineers think Tel Aviv is the most important town in this country. There are already dozens and dozens of Bauhaus buildings there. It's the city of the future."

"Tel Aviv? I heard it's built on sand dunes."

"Yes, some people up here on the Carmel look down their noses at it. But it's already the biggest town in the country. It's the only one that will be a real city—the center of new life. It could be . . . a new life for us."

She clamped her mouth shut and waited for her mind to catch up with her gut.

"Alfred, I can't."

"Don't say that so fast. Think about it. I'll go for a walk with the baby. Give you some time by yourself." Before she could stop him, he had the baby in his arms and was out the door.

She rose and walked over to the window. She looked out, finding the spot where she knew the hulk of the *Patria* lay underwater. She'd stared at that spot every morning, silently mouthing Emil's name. Had it become her daily prayer?

She turned away and ordered herself back to the chair. She sank into to it and let her arms dangle to the sides. She tried to imagine Tel Aviv. Had she seen any photographs? Read any descriptions? Nothing came to mind; only how far it would be from Emil.

Alfred opened the door and slunk back in. He handed her the baby and began warming a bottle in the kitchen.

"So?"

"Liebling, I know this is the opportunity you've been waiting for. I know the work they give you now is way below your skill level and your expectations, not to mention the salary. But . . . " she stopped.

"But?" Alfred knit his brow.

"I can't."

"You can't?"

"I can't leave here." She tipped her head towards the window. Alfred mumbled something and went to the window and looked out.

"I understand. But it's the best chance for us. For a new life."

"A new life?"

"Yes. I know it will be hard for you, Gertlein. But it would be better . . . not just for me and our finances. For you, precisely for you." He came over and put his hand on her shoulder. All she could do was press her lips and squeeze her eyes shut.

Chapter 4

A week passed between them with no more than "Good morning," "Good night," and "Dinner's ready." Gertie saw Alfred stiffen when she looked his way, but she couldn't bring herself to start a conversation.

"You can't punish me forever, Gertie," Alfred finally broke the spell at the end of another mute dinner.

"I am not punishing . . ."

"You are, Gertie! Even if you don't mean to. You haven't said more than ten words to me since that afternoon."

"I just can't."

"I know it's hard for you, but you can! You must think of me too. And of Benyamin. Let the past go. Try to consider a new start."

Gertie pressed her temples and said nothing. Finally, she laid her hand on Alfred's tightly knit fingers.

"You are right this time, Alfred. I know it."

Alfred laced his fingers through hers and waited for her to continue.

"How do we restart, though? I'm willing, but I don't know how."

"Maybe we begin by going back to where we last saw Emil, to say goodbye to him in our hearts, to close that open drawer."

"How?"

"We'll find Mr. Korngold. See if he has those photos he took on the *Atlantic*. One of them has Emil holding the baby."

"How do we know he's here? Don't you think he was deported with our friends? You didn't see him in Atlit, did you?"

"No, but . . . there were so many of us, it was such chaos."

"Chaos, for sure. But if he were with us, that camera and film would have been ruined in the water."

"Maybe, but some people managed to hang on to the deck until they got rescued. So, it's not impossible."

Gertie sucked in her cheeks and tried to push back the tears welling in the corners of her eyes.

"You do have a good head for all logical possibilities."

"Thanks," Alfred said hesitantly, not sure if it was a compliment or criticism.

"It's a good idea, Alfred," Gertie softened towards him. "You are absolutely right!"

"For once . . ."

"Don't."

"Agreed then, Gertie? Tomorrow afternoon I'll come home early from work."

"Agreed."

They set out after the heat of the day had given way to afternoon sea breezes. Gertie put the baby in the creaking buggy they'd bought second-hand and draped thin gauze over it, in case the mosquitos came out early. They walked down to Herzl Street looking for photographers' studios. They didn't find any on the first few blocks, so they entered a small bookshop that displayed some prints of holy sites in Palestine.

"Would you know about a photography shop near here?" Alfred asked the owner.

"Sure, there are several," the middle-aged balding man said, his accent immediately telling them he was "one of them."

"We're looking for a photographer named Korngold. Have you heard of him?"

"Korngold . . ." the shop owner mulled it over, "a German?"

"Viennese," they both answered. "He came here in the last few months," Alfred added.

"Aha, then probably at Leopold Studio. He's from Vienna, too. Just half a block down the street, on the opposite side."

They found Leopold's studio in minutes. Inside, before they had a chance to utter a greeting, Mr. Korngold called out: "The parents of the *Atlantic* baby! Wait . . . Alfred and Gizella? No, Gertie, right? My goodness, you found me!"

"Yes, we spoke to the book shop owner and he guessed you'd be here."

"Yes, I'm here. Oh, look at the *Kleines Kind!*" he stood on tiptoe and peered over the counter into the buggy. Gertie picked Benyamin up and showed him off.

"Ach, look at his smile," Korngold gushed. "I remember taking his picture the day he was born—like it was yesterday. And your boy?"

"Emil," Alfred said.

"Yes, Emil."

Their faces fell. Korngold looked down. The silence was suffocating.

"He was lost," Alfred finally said, "on the *Patria*. We never found him."

"I'm so sorry," Korngold pressed his hands to his chest, "I saw the explosion. I was still waiting on the *Atlantic* for my turn to be transferred."

"Then how did you manage to stay here and not get deported to Mauritius?" Alfred asked.

"On the dock I went looking for my friends who'd already boarded the *Patria*. Especially one—a girl. We had a little thing going on the *Atlantic*.

"Really? Who?" Gertie asked.

"Zdenka. The one from Vienna. Not the other one, from Prague. She had her guy; the one who was so much shorter than her, remember?"

"Of course! And I knew your Zdenka a little, also the other one and her beau, Artur. He was famous among the girls for his ugly knees."

"Really? Who sees knees?" Korngold marveled, "and who cares?"

"Women do."

"What do you know!" Korngold gave Alfred a knowing look and shrugged.

"And he insisted on wearing shorts all the time," Gertie added. "But that hardly matters now. They were from the young Czech group, so I expect they were deported to Mauritius. But did you find your Zdenka?"

"Yes. We were lucky."

Seeing Gertie recoil at the word "lucky," Alfred stepped in: "And then?"

"When the British loaded us onto the buses Zdenka and I decided to stay together, no matter what. When we got to Atlit, I went with her and the *Patria* people instead of the *Atlantics*. Only later did it become evident that I was smart . . . or, rather, a lucky fool."

"Indeed. But," Alfred furrowed his brow, "I didn't see you in the camp?"

"I hid. I couldn't face all of you, what you went through. And that you'd see me carry on with Zdenka . . . "

"You two carried on?"

"We were young and in love. I was ashamed, but still. What can I say? A fool in love and in luck."

"So, you got to stay in Palestine with us from the *Patria*," Alfred summed it up.

"Yes, with Zdenka. We claimed we were married. No one had papers to prove anything."

"But most of my friends—my closest friends—were all deported to Mauritius. Yours too, no?"

"Yes," Alfred said, "we have no idea what exactly happened to them; only from the newspapers, that they got there."

"I know much more!" Korngold exclaimed. "I have letters."

"Letters?" Gertie's hand flew to her mouth.

"Yes. They've sent letters to Haifa, to the *Organization of Patria Survivors*. I'm involved. We haven't seen you."

"We couldn't," Alfred said. "After we asked everyone about Emil ... we couldn't keep coming."

"I understand. But there may be some letters for you. No one knew how to find you," Korngold said apologetically.

"We had no idea!"

"I will look at the bundle of letters we've been keeping. If there are any for you, I'll bring them here."

"Thank you!" Gertie said, "look especially for letters from Bronia, Elsa, or Siegfried."

"I will. And I do have the photos from the boat. Not here, in my apartment. I will find yours and bring them too. Come back in two days."

Alfred thanked Herr Korngold more formally than Gertie thought fit the situation, but she shook his hand. "Danke. And say hello to Zdenka. Maybe we can all meet?"

"We're not together anymore."

"No?"

"No. It was the 'love affair on a boat' syndrome. That and the *Patria*—she was on it, I was not. Once we were here ... I don't know. We just went in different directions."

"I understand," Gertie said softly. "It's very hard to stay together after such a terrible ... " She took Alfred's arm and pushed the buggy, heading out.

"Letters, Alfred!" she exclaimed once on the street. "Can you believe it?"

"We don't know yet, Gertie. But let's hope so," Alfred said as he laid his hand over hers on the buggy's handlebar.

Chapter 5

"Yes!" Alfred called out before he'd fully opened the door: "Two letters! One from Siegfried and one from Bronia. And he found the negatives and will print the photos. We are to come back next week for those." Gertie set Benyamin in his crib, hoping the few toys in it would keep him occupied. Alfred laid the two letters on the table; he'd already opened Siegfried's letter, but not Bronia's.

"Are they alright?" she couldn't wait to find out.

"Basically. Safe. Not exactly well, but safe."

"Gott sei dank."

She sat down and opened Bronia's letter, readying herself for whatever news it bore. Five, she counted the onionskin airmail pages; covered to within a few millimeters of the edges in neat, miniature handwriting.

>Dear Gertie,
>
>Where to begin? First, let me explain: all our mail has to pass the British Censor. I tried to write in English, but I couldn't. Not yet. So, this letter may take three months to get to you. I am trying to learn English because once I can write in it, the letters will take less time (we're allowed to write in English, German or French). I've been reading "Murder on the Orient Express" (there are not many choices here) with a dictionary. I have read it three times already: hopefully by the fifth time I'll know every word.

I have so much to tell you about things here, but first I must ask about you. You and Alfred and Benyaminku . . . but most important—Emil? I pray that you found him! In fact, I catch myself praying to God for you even though I never believed in anything of that sort.

If not . . . I can't imagine how you bear it. Can you still hold on to some hope?

Bronia had left the bottom third of the page empty. Gertie put it face-down and dabbed her eyes, then moved on to the next page. Out of corner of her eye she saw Alfred playing quietly with Benyamin. She teared up again, now in gratitude to Alfred for allowing her to immerse herself in the letter.

I don't know how much to tell you about our voyage here. We sailed on the Johan De Witt, which the British Navy commandeered after the invasion of Holland and brought to replace the Patria. The crew treated us so nicely! They overfed us with butter and cheeses. But that seems like a century ago now. We arrived at Port Louis in Mauritius the day after Christmas, on the third night of Hanukkah. The first two days of Hanukkah, no one felt like celebrating. But as the sun set and the ship anchored in the harbor, we lit three candles. We sang the blessings (this ordeal is teaching me more than I ever knew about being Jewish . . .) and stood on board, enchanted. Around us it looked indescribably beautiful: the gently moving azure sea, the red, pink and violet aura of the sinking sun. Mountains, hills, rocky formations covered in the lushest green. The lights came on at shore and we saw cars and heard horns blowing, which told us that it's not a desert or a wasteland; it looked like a civilized paradise. Everything was so beautiful, almost surreal.

The next day we went ashore and boarded buses which brought us here. The road was lined with magnificently blooming trees, cacti, palms, sugarcane fields. We saw the native people, Chinese, Blacks, Indians, Creoles and <u>so many children</u>, jump and wave, yell and laugh, and throw flowers at the buses. They called out in a frenzy of welcoming, "Bienvenues Messieurs, Mesdames les réfugiés!" "Welcome the refugees!"

Then we arrived: a big stone building with a closed, massive iron gate in a high stone wall and new, unfinished looking corrugated tin huts—His Majesty's Prison. Each man was put into a tiny individual cell in the stone building and we, women, in the huts. It was pretty clear that the women's camp was built for us. We could choose with whom to live. I live in a hut that has two rooms with five beds in each room and an additional room with ten beds. Elsa is in a bed next to me, thank God. She sends her regards. She suffers terribly from the heat, but she is strong and there is plenty of material here for her "daily reports."

At first, I thought: I'll never get used to this! Flocks of horrid flies all the time; I never saw so many flies in my life! You cannot get rid of them. And the strange taste of the water and the food made me sick to my stomach. Outside it rains and rains. It's not even rain; it's torrents of water that suddenly start to spill down from the sky. And as suddenly as they start, they also stop, and, immediately, the sun shines, or rather the sun burns in the bright blue sky. And everything is vaporized into steam, and everything grows at a fantastic rate. Too much fertility, too much vitality, too many colors, too many varieties of plants. We, Europeans, greatly admire this, but we miss the tepid light rain, the subtle colors, the delicate stars of home.

The women's camp is managed by policewomen, some English ones (who came here from their service in Palestine), and some French ones, drafted in Mauritius. They are very nice. In fact, it is not clear to me exactly what their job in "policing" us is. The men have it harder, though each one has his own cell (big enough to lie down straight or sit crossway with your back against one wall and your feet touching the other).

Pretty quickly we started to make ourselves at home. The

British authorities repeat their slogan every day: "Keep the people occupied." We tried to somehow normalize things. The camp has a kitchen where they cook our meals. You can work there and, if you do, you eat there for free. The food was very meager at first, but now they distribute all kinds of "delicacies," such as a teaspoon of condensed milk per day, or Marmite, a kind of vegetarian spread (do you have it there, too?), horrid tasting but full of vitamins.

There are all kinds of initiatives. Someone has opened a coffee house! He has an oil burner, so he gets a pot and boils water, and people come to sit there and drink and talk. He puts something in the water to make it brown, but it's a well-kept secret whether it actually is either coffee or tea.

There's a canteen, a laundry, a carpentry shop and even a workshop manufacturing rag dolls. Those are so successful that there is even demand for them from outside the camp. A school has been established with the support of the British. Anyone who knows how to teach anything is a teacher.

And there is a hospital about a half hour's walk, intended only for us. Two doctors and nurses from Mauritius work there, plus the doctors and nurses from our group. I volunteered to work there as a nurse's aide. The shift lasts eight hours and we work non-stop, an exhausting job that does not allow me to think and care too much about anything else. Indeed, when I am working, I am so tired that I fall into bed and immediately fall asleep. This way I push aside my worries and I feel I contribute something valuable.

Sometimes we see a policeman accompanying two men in white coats carrying a stretcher; on it a body covered with a sheet. We know that there is a typhus epidemic. You cannot defend yourself from the lice and flies and mosquitoes. I feel confident because I received a vaccination back home (as did you, I think,) and I have some Quinine I brought from home, so I believe that no Anopheles mosquito would dare bite me. This "security" is my main defense.

So, Gertie, as you see —we live. Day by day. How long we will be here only God, or rather, His Majesty, knows. We know very little about what's going on at home and in Palestine. We get newspapers a month or two late. Big news we hear from the British policemen (they have radios). But to our real questions—what's happened to everyone; our families, our friends?—no one has any answers.

You can write to me here. It will take a long time to arrive and, as I said, it has to pass the British censor. So, if you can write in English that would be better. Tell me everything that will still be true two months after you write it.

Don't lose hope.

Your Bronia

Gertie folded the pages in half and rested her palms on them, as if to keep them quiet. Alfred sat by her and touched her hand.

"What does she say? Is she all right? And Elsa?"

"She tells so much and in such vivid details. I feel like I am there."

"What's it like, Gertie? Siegfried didn't say much about everyday life."

"Here, read it yourself. Nothing's there that's not for you, too."

Alfred fingered the fragile paper, admiring the handwriting: "Very good penmanship; makes it easy to read."

"So, something good came out of our Gymnasium education."

"Yes. Though it certainly didn't prepare us for much else . . . "

As Alfred read the letter, his face told Gertie where he was. A wry smile at *"Bienvenues les réfugiés,"* a grimace when he got to the typhus and the dead. When he finished, he folded the letter back and smoothed the crease line with his fingertip. "When she says, 'Don't lose hope,' it seems like she is talking more to herself than to you."

"I know what you mean. I'll write to her right away. It's been four months since she wrote this, plus the two months it will take for my letter to get to her."

"*A* long time to hold onto hope," Alfred said, "so it will be almost a year between when she saw us across that fence in Atlit and when she hears from you that we never found him."

"I envy her, Alfred. I know it's stupid, but to her . . . he's still with us."

"It may be stupid, but I understand."

"You do? Even though it is completely irrational?"

"I do, Gertie. I feel it too."

She cupped his hands in hers and they sat in silence until Benyamin began to cry.

Chapter 6

"So, you'll think about it?" Alfred said after supper a week later.

"About what?"

"Tel Aviv," Alfred said in a near whisper.

Gertie coughed but could not bring herself to say the words "Tel Aviv" out loud.

"Give me two days. Can you wait that long?"

"Better not to; I suspect there are other candidates. But I understand." Alfred got up from the table and carried the few dishes to the sink.

"Danke," she whispered.

Gertie spent much of the next day by the window, staring at the port. Each time she walked away she felt as if a piece of flesh had been flayed from her body. She rocked with Benyamin in her arms with her eyes closed, trying to imagine the white-washed new buildings of Tel Aviv. But the rounded Bauhaus balconies she knew were there became large open maws threatening to swallow her.

When Alfred came home from work, all she could do was shake her head. His shoulders slumped, reminding her of how he'd looked at the fence in Atlit. She lowered her eyes and pursed her lips.

"I'm so sorry," she finally said, "I can't leave here. Not yet. Something else will come up. I'm sure . . . another opportunity."

Alfred nodded and clenched his teeth. After a long silence

he said, "Let's hope so. Meanwhile, shall we go to Herr Korngold tomorrow to get the photos? He should have them printed by now."

"Not tomorrow. Not yet. Give me a bit more time to prepare myself," Gertie whispered, almost begging. Alfred just nodded again and went out for a walk.

The summer heat in July and August made Gertie irritable and the baby suffered from heat rashes. Alfred thought it was better not to bring up Tel Aviv where he'd heard it was hotter and muggier, or any other ideas for a move. Around Rosh Hashanah seemed like a good time to again raise the possibility of a new beginning. Gertie no longer categorically refused, but she gave him no encouragement. She agreed to discuss any "realistic new prospects," but nothing came up. Alfred gradually accepted that his slow rise in his firm might be the best he could hope for now, at least at this time of war, with everyone beset by anxiety about whether the seemingly invincible German army would soon invade Palestine.

Chapter 7

"You know what day it is today, Gertie," Alfred said at breakfast, as she leaned over Benyamin who was squirming.

"I know what day —it —is . . . today," Gertie said seeming to nearly choke on each word. "It's November 25, one year since." She turned her back to Alfred and rocked the crib. Alfred stared at his plate.

"I'm sorry," he finally broke the silence, "I just thought I should say . . . there will be a memorial at the dock this morning."

"I know. All the *Patria* people will be there."

"We should go too, Gertie."

"I can't, Alfred. Not yet. Next year . . . maybe. Next year I think I could."

"So, nothing?"

Gertie took a deep breath and stepped away from the crib, Benyamin now back asleep. She walked to the window, training her eyes, as usual, on the spot where for months she'd watched the *Patria's* three smokestacks inch closer and closer to the water, until they finally disappeared. She no longer remembered the very last moment she'd seen them, but she still knew the spot.

"Not nothing. You're right, Alfred. We need to go. We'll go . . . tomorrow, the day after the ceremony, us alone. I can do that."

"Us alone," Alfred echoed. It was one step forward.

Moussa headed towards the port that morning, happy to have Moulleek with him. It made the time go by faster and he felt more comfortable talking to the boy than to the fish, as he did when he was out alone. It had taken months and much patience to get Moulleek to enjoy going on the boat. Moussa still remembered how he had panicked that day he found him when they'd approached the boat. Hot summer days had helped. Moulleek first learned to enjoy sitting on the dock and dangling his feet in the cool lapping waves. Eventually he let Moussa take him into the boat and, step-by-step, accepted going out to sea. Now he loved sitting on the bench and dragging his hand through the water.

As they entered the dock Moussa saw a large crowd blocking the way to his boat. They were standing close to each other, all facing the sea. At the front a man standing on wooden box said: "*November, der fünfundzwanzigste.*" "November" Moussa understood: the English name of the month. He edged closer to crowd, holding Moulleek's hand tightly, telling him: "Don't worry, they won't notice us." They stood listening. Moussa caught a word here and there. The one they kept repeating was "Patria," which he didn't understand.

Just then the man at the front put the megaphone down and the whole crowd started singing, a slow, melancholy song Moussa had heard once or twice. Some kind of special song of the *Yahoud*. He bent down to explain it to Moulleek and saw the boy was trembling. He hadn't dressed him warmly enough . . . Youssra was right. He picked Moulleek up and pressed him to his chest to warm him up.

The singing ended and the crowd began to disperse. "Just a few minutes," Moussa whispered in Moulleek's ear, "and we'll get to the boat. I have an extra sweater there." Moussa took a few steps back from the path people took to go out. Some were talking to each other in hushed voices, others walked in silence. No one paid any attention to him and Moulleek. But just as the last of group filed past, a tall man with a camera hanging from his neck halted in front of Moussa. Moussa shrunk back.

"Sorry," the man said, "but the boy, your son? He's so . . . so beautiful."

"Yes, my boy," Moussa answered, "very sweet boy he is."

"Yes, very special. The eyes, the curls," the man said, more to himself than to Moussa. Then he turned to the woman next to him. "Zdenka, look at this boy! Doesn't he look just like that boy on the *Atlantic,* of that Viennese family that had a baby on board?"

The woman peered into Moulleek's face. He shuddered and buried his face in Moussa's shoulder.

"I sorry," Moussa said, "he very, how you say . . . scared with people."

"We are sorry," the man said "it was not proper."

"Korngold," he added and stuck out his hand to shake Moussa's, indicating there were no hard feelings. Moussa shook the offered hand; what else could he do?

"What was that boy's name? Do you remember, Zdenka?" Korngold asked as they walked away.

"Emil. And the baby was Benyamin."

"Ja, of course, Emil. I took his picture holding the baby on the deck. Baby Benyamin and Big Brother Emil. I'm still waiting to give it to the parents."

"The parents?"

"Yes, they found me at the photo shop last summer."

"And they didn't come today?" Zdenka raised an eye brow.

"I'm not surprised. Must be too hard for them. They never found Emil."

CHAPTER 8

Lucas got the idea of celebrating Dondieu's birthday on the day he'd found and saved him. Most of the boys at the monastery didn't know their own birthdays, so they held a group celebration right after the New Year. But Lucas yearned for something special, just for Dondieu. He'd make it a private thing between the two of them, of course, so the other boys wouldn't be envious. And he needn't worry about Dondieu boasting about it; he still did not talk. It seemed now like he might never speak.

Two days after the monks celebrated the Carmelite All Saints Day in mid-November, Lucas came into the kitchen. "So, Brother Matthieu, are you planning a special treat this year with the first harvested oranges?"

"Yes, I always do something special. I'm still pondering what to make this year."

"Last year's marmalade was wonderful!" Lucas gushed —a little more than he had intended to. "I can still taste it if I close my eyes."

"Yes, that was a good one. But it takes a lot of sugar. This year my supply is lower."

"I see," Lucas nodded, "so maybe a dish with oranges more of a garnish than the main ingredient?"

"Exactly! Ever thought about taking up cooking?" Matthieu made as if to poke Lucas in the rib with his wooden spoon.

"Not a bad idea . . . It would be a nice change of routine from praying and studying."

At dinner Brother Matthieu signaled to Lucas to come into the kitchen. Lucas ducked in: "So, do you have a plan?"

"I have a great idea! Maybe talking with you influenced my thinking towards a French dish: crêpe Suzette."

"Crêpe Suzette! Oh, my, you're going to make me miss my mother terribly. Hers were divine."

"I'll use cooked oranges instead of honey," Matthieu said, more to himself than to Lucas, "and I have enough butter despite the shortage. You can get by with a small amount. And then a slice of fresh orange on top. Did your mother use anything besides honey and butter on her crêpes?"

"Sometimes a garnish of fruit—poached plums or pear. We didn't have oranges. But she did always tell us that it was supposed to be an orange."

"Yes, that's the traditional garnish. A drizzle of Grand Marnier too," the cook smacked his lips.

"Of course. Oh, you are making my mouth water! But Grand Marnier?"

Matthieu whispered in Lucas' ear: "I have my own home-made orange liqueur that I cook here, so I'll use a bit of that."

"I can't wait. When?"

"Friday."

"I'll definitely come help you. In the afternoon?"

"Yes."

"Friday afternoon," Lucas smacked his lips and left the kitchen.

"I have a special surprise for you, but don't tell anyone else,"

Lucas whispered to Dondieu the next morning right after prayers. Dondieu looked at him with a frown.

"Sorry, what am I saying?" Lucas grimaced, then told Dondieu there was going to be a very special treat on Friday that the cook was making especially for him, to celebrate his birthday. "But the other boys don't know it's especially for you. We don't want them to get jealous. So, it's our secret." Dondieu smiled and gave Lucas a hug, then ran off to join the rest of the boys in morning chores.

At dinner on Friday, Brother Matthieu stood up, his face glowing, announcing there was a special treat to celebrate the beginning of the orange harvest. A cheer went up:

"Can he outdo himself from last year? That marmalade was amazing!"

"And the compote two years ago?"

"And the fresh orange slices sprinkled with sugar and cinnamon the year before? That was my favorite."

"Yes, that was delicious. But a bit too simple for Brother Matthieu's culinary ambitions, don't you think?"

"You're right. So, I'll bet it's something fancier this year. Did you see the smile on his face?"

"Very promising!"

Brother Matthieu called for volunteers to help serve. With a small army of helpers, the platters started pouring out of the kitchen.

"Crêpe Suzette!" Matthieu declared with great flourish. "A glorious French dish. *Bon Appetite!*"

The monks controlled themselves with great effort, politely serving each other. But the boys needed several loud reminders from Brother Michel to slow down, keep quiet and serve each child in turn. Lucas watched Dondieu look at the crêpe on his plate first, then take a deep inhalation of the tangy-sweet orange and melted butter. He chewed his first bite with his eyes closed.

Mmmmm, so good.

Special for my birthday!
So good!
I know this dish . . . I had it for special times before.
But different.
It looked different. Rolled up, not folded like this.
And the taste?
Sweet like this, but not with oranges.
With something else.
Red.
Red and sweet. Strawberries. Other berries too —from the forest.
Not crepe suzze.
What?
Pa . . . La . . .
Palatchinka!
Oma made it for me. In the little house. In summer.
Oma. And Opa.
Where did they go?
No. We went.
"Say goodbye to Oma and Opa," Mama said.
Mama was sad. Oma and Opa too.
Mama? Where did Mama go?
Don't ask about Mama.
Eat.
Eat the palatchinka.
No Mama. Only palatchinka.

Dondieu hunched his shoulders and shut his eyes even tighter. Finally, he opened them and looked at his plate. Someone had cut the crepe into bite-size pieces. He lowered his head down and shoveled the pieces into his mouth, barely chewing before he swallowed.

Lucas looked over the heads of the other boys hoping to catch Dondieu's eye. He only saw Dondieu's curls hovering above his plate. He must really like it! What a great idea that was! He took a bite from his own plate—delicious! This first bite is for you, Mama. Not as good as yours, of course; no crêpe will ever be. He went down the list, each bite dedicated to another family member. Philippe's was the last bite. Lucas savored it and smiled, seeing Philippe's stuffed cheeks in front of him. Who says you can't be in two places at the same time?

Chapter 9

Two days after they'd gone to the Haifa port, Gertie told Alfred she was taking Benyamin for his one-year photos. "I know I'm three weeks late. I couldn't do it until after we went down there . . . for Emil."

"Of course," Alfred said, "you needed to close that book first . . . "

"What 'Close that book!'" Gertie flew at him, "never!"

"Gertlein, I didn't mean it that way," Alfred pleaded.

She was shaking as she looked away. She made herself turn towards him, "I know, Alfred. I am still so . . . "

"I understand," he said and stood up to hold her. She let him.

"Can you at least ask Korngold for the photos from the *Atlantic*?"

"Yes, Alfred. Do you think he still has them? It's been so long since we went there."

"I'm sure he does. He's like us—what do they call us here?—Yekkes. Everything in proper order. Always."

She bundled Benyamin in a sweater and a wool shawl and set out. It wasn't actually as cold outside as it'd been the week before. The sun warmed her back as she pushed the buggy up the street. She tried to push away the cloud that had burst between her and Alfred by making herself go through the motions of window-shopping. The new winter coats were in; she let herself covet the more stylish ones.

She entered Korngold's studio and was pleased to see there was no line.

"Frau Schiff!" Korngold called out as if he'd been waiting for her for days, "such a pleasure to see you!"

"Mine, as well, Herr Korngold," she said and pulled Benyamin out of the buggy. "The Kleiner is here for his one-year picture. A little late, but he's still just one year old."

"I can't believe it's over a year since I took his picture on the *Atlantic*," Korngold said as Gertie got Benyamin situated for the camera. All she could do was nod.

"I understand, Frau Schiff . . . I was just thinking about your Emil too."

"The anniversary?" Gertie asked.

"Yes and . . . " he stopped and steered himself another way. "I didn't see you and Alfred there."

"We couldn't. It was too hard. We went the next day."

"I understand," Korngold said softly, "and I see . . . that's why you never came back for the pictures from the *Atlantic* that I printed for you."

"Yes, too hard," Gertie nodded, shutting her eyes to stop the ears from spilling over.

Korngold seemed to disappear, sinking into his own thoughts for a moment. Then shook his head and said to himself: "No, I must tell her."

"Tell me what, Herr Korngold?"

"That day, the 25th, when you didn't come . . . "

"Yes?"

"There was a man there, an Arab—a fisherman I assume—with a boy. That boy, he looked so much like Emil. The same eyes, the brown curls."

"Like Emil?"

"Yes, I told Zdenka. She was walking with me after the ceremony. I was so startled that I stared at the boy and scared him."

"That's bizarre," Gertie said, but then waved her hand. "What of it, though? How does it help us? Even if he has a doppelganger."

"Sorry, Frau Schiff. You're right. It doesn't help one iota. I'm sorry . . ."

Korngold ducked under the camera's dark cloth and Gertie propped Benyamin up, hoping he would smile without her prompting him.

When she returned home, she realized she'd been so upset by Korngold's reporting about the Emil look-alike she had forgotten to ask about the photos from the *Atlantic*. You didn't forget, she chastised herself, you suppressed it. Who were you punishing? She had no answer, but she knew she'd have to tell Alfred in such a way that he wouldn't volunteer to collect the photos himself. She knew now that it was still too soon.

CHAPTER 10

At Stella Maris Lucas had taken part in preparing to celebrate Christmas with more enthusiasm than ever before. In previous years everything had reminded him of how much he missed his family: the decorations, the hymns, the candles. Even the cold winds, although nothing like the winter gales whooshing down from the slopes of the Pyrenees, made him homesick. This year was so different! He thanked God every day: everyone had accepted Dondieu so quickly and he, in turn, had already adjusted to life in the monastery. He, too, seemed excited by the holiday preparations. He helped hang cypress bows and laughed with the other boys when the pungent branches made him erupt into a long series of sneezes. His eyes twinkled as he looked at the candles placed in every window and at the base of the altar. He beamed as he joined the boys in rehearsing an abbreviated Passion Play; his role —a smiling cherub, no words needed.

The chapel was filled with cypress branches and everyone seemed to breathe more deeply than usual, letting the pungent, fresh scent of their sap cleanse their lungs. Bunches of pink wild crocus added color, their nearly translucent petals like tiny lit candles against the dark green boughs. Lucas remembered them popping up in the hilly apple orchards around his village. How heart-broken he had been when as boy —five? six? -—he picked a handful for his mother but they wilted within an hour. His mother had wiped his tears and told him they were the kind of flower that couldn't leave its home: "They only last inside in their bulbs." That's how they hung them in the chapel now, nestled on damp moss inside small wicker baskets, the roots at the bottom of each bulb still clinging to a bit of soil. They carried the rose hues of Gaudete Sunday until Christmas Eve.

At Midnight Mass, Lucas stole glimpses of Dondieu whenever he could avert his gaze from the altar without being noticed. Dondieu stood with the boys, joy on his face. Did he really understand the miracle of the birth of the Savior? Did he remember the day Lucas found him and saved him? Did he comprehend his own miraculous rebirth?

As the year came to a close, many Brothers commented to Lucas that, despite being mute and at first seeming not to comprehend what was said, Dondieu had learned the rules very quickly and knew what was expected of him. Even Father Pierre glanced with a smile in the boy's direction at the conclusion of Vespers. Dondieu kept his head bent during the service and, at times, seemed transported. Unlike the other young boys, he never fidgeted during prayers.

He was becoming a bit of a pet of the older boys. Maybe they were intrigued by his sudden appearance? Or by his silence? They, after all, had to struggle mightily to keep their voices hushed and their words to a minimum. Lucas smiled when he overheard some boys joke: "Not talking is easy for him!" They called him *"Puer Purus - Pure Boy,"* saying he was years ahead of them in his monastic discipline. Something about Dondieu made them say it lovingly, without malice or envy. They let him enter their games and listen to their conversations. He clearly wanted to be near the other boys, engaged in his own silent way.

CHAPTER 11

As the months went by, Moussa and Youssra heard no word of a missing boy and Moulleek seemed to adjust. The child he had once been slowly returned to the small body that had seemed hollow at first. "Moulleek" became an ordinary word in their daily conversations, though they each still stopped once or twice a day to marvel and thank Allah. Youssra rolled the name on her tongue with such tenderness it made Moussa's chest ache. Maybe he was even a little jealous, he had to admit to himself.

Youssra started singing again. First low-voiced lullabies at Moulleek's bedtime, then old village melodies while she kneaded the dough and pounded the chickpeas. Moulleek remained mute, but his eyes followed everything with growing interest, his body regained its verve, and his curls bounced with excitement. He even took to the hummus and olives.

Moussa and Youssra could see that he was really bright. He learned their daily routines quickly. In the rainy days of the winter, he was eager to help Youssra in preparing meals, sweeping the floor and washing dishes and clothes. On sunny afternoons he went into the stone-bordered yard behind the house and helped Moussa spread out the nets to dry and repair. His delicate fingers were a huge help for Moussa in tying small knots.

They watched Moulleek grow less fearful, though he continued to cower in terror at loud noises. They were careful: never raised their voices, avoided banging a copper pot or dropping a bucket on the floor. They never hit him, though they had certainly each received their share of swats and slaps growing up. Youssra dictated how to treat Moulleek with tenderness and a set routine. If he knew what to expect, he managed very well despite his handicap. Day by day he became more of a regular boy.

It was only in the middle of the night that Moulleek occasionally seemed to struggle with a terrifying monster. He thrashed around in his sleep and sometimes cried out. Unintelligible words. Once they thought they deciphered something; he seemed to cry out "Hilfe!"

"Why the grass for weaving baskets?" Youssra asked.

"Indeed . . . why hilfe?"

"Maybe his father used thick strands of it to beat him?" Youssra offered.

"Maybe. That's a possibility; I think you are right, Youssra."

"How awful!"

Youssra thought it was best not to weave fantasies about the abuse Moulleek had suffered, but they did speak about how they could undo its damage. Moussa kneeled down and brought his face close to Moulleek's when he spoke to him, talking in his softest voice. He kept a hand on Moulleek's shoulder whenever they ventured outside their house and courtyard. He loved carrying Moulleek around on his back calling: "A sack of beans, a sack of hummus peas! Who wants to buy a sack of beans?" "I do! I do! Yallah, bring it here!" Youssra would say and Moussa would unload Moulleek into her open arms. Moulleek laughed and climbed back on Moussa's back for more. He giggled when Youssra played games with his fingers or his toes.

"He has a regular voice, Moussa. He laughs like any other child. So why can't he speak?"

"It's strange, isn't it? We could ask someone, maybe the schoolteacher, Khaled."

"Maybe you should?" Youssra said.

"But do we want to attract attention to Moulleek? Raise questions?"

"You're right, Moussa. Better not. Leave it in Allah's hands."

Moussa couldn't fall asleep that night, the puzzle of the boy's voice kept gnawing at him. In the morning he told Youssra, "I will ask Khaled. We need to know."

"We need to know?" Youssra echoed, a quiver in her voice.

"Yes. Maybe we should be doing something to help him talk."

"You think?" Youssra said, now letting a wisp of hope mark her words.

"Yes. Maybe." Moussa said, then shrugged his shoulders. "I'll find Khaled after I come back from fishing."

He went for a stroll near the school in the late afternoon, the time he had often seen Khaled come out of the squat classroom building and head down to a *nargeellah* shop. Sure enough, he soon saw Khaled coming towards him. Even from thirty steps away, Moussa could see the perfectly ironed crease in Khaled's dark gabardine pants, the precisely aligned corners of the starched collar of his white shirt, tucked firmly into his pants, and the polished brass buttons of a jacket, jauntily slung over the left shoulder.

He always felt awkward around Khaled. Was it because he'd never gone to school? Or was it Khaled's good looks and stylish dress? He was tall and slim, and walked with an elegance —or swagger —that Moussa envied. A deep cleft in his clean-shaven chin and a thin, silky moustache divided his face into perfectly symmetrical halves. His hair was slicked down from an absolutely straight part on the left. Every single hair stayed in its proper place, like extremely obedient pupils at their desks, surely unlike the ones Moussa assumed Khaled had to discipline in his classroom.

"Marhabah, Khaled," Moussa called out. "*Kiff halek*?" he added the obligatory "How are you?"

"Very well. Good to see you," Khaled stopped and took a cigarette box out of his pocket, offering one to Moussa.

"*Players*?" Moussa said, whistling appreciation. "You can still get these?"

"Nah... Not for a reasonable price. But I was clever, I saved a few boxes from before the war. Most of them in here are *Victory*, which I smoke now, but I keep two *Players* —see these on the end? —for the right person or occasion."

"I'm honored!" Moussa said but waved off the cigarette with a small bow and "Shukran." He coughed to clear his throat.

"I see, not good for your lungs, eh?"

Moussa smiled diffidently. He thought it was a good sign that Khaled was going to smoke one of the *Players*, even if it were alone. Khaled lit the cigarette and took a long drag. He seemed in the mood for a conversation.

"Let's walk together. There's something I've been meaning to talk to you about," Khaled said. "A very unusual case, your boy. I've noticed of him playing with the other kids. He seems very clever, like he grasps things quickly."

"Yes, he is," Moussa said emphatically, surprised that Khaled seemed to know why he had sought him out.

"But he never speaks? Maybe at home he does —just with you and Youssra?"

"Never," Moussa shook his head, "but yes, you're right, he is very clever. That's what I wanted..."

"A clever boy," Khaled repeated, walking on seeming engrossed in thought. Moussa kept quiet.

"There are such boys, Moussa, mute or deaf, even blind, but very smart. Better students than the regular boys. I myself have never taught such a pupil, but I've heard and read stories."

"Really?"

"Yes, it is so!" Khaled touched Moussa's shoulder for a brief moment. "So, I hope you wish to ask me about sending the boy to school? He's the right age, no?"

"Yes, around six."

"*Mabrouk!* It's time. Of course, not all the boys his age go to school, but if he has any talent for studying, he should start."

"You think?"

"He should've been in school already. Better to start them young. Sure, a lot of boys his age only go a few years before they have to join their fathers or older brothers to learn their trade. But I think this boy of yours is different. Special, I think."

Moussa nodded but couldn't loosen his tongue. *If only Khaled knew the half of it..* He shuddered.

"I understand," Khaled said, "you are worried, of course. That the other children will tease him. Maybe worse —torment and beat him, right?"

"Yes, we do worry about him." Moussa managed to respond.

"I will keep a special eye out for him," Khaled touched Moussa's shoulder again.

"You'll see, maybe precisely because of his handicap, he would do very well in school."

"How's that?"

"Sometimes when a person is missing one ability," Khaled explained, very much the teacher now, "they make up for it in another. You know how blind people can hear so much better than most people and, sometimes, can understand people better than the rest of us?"

"Yes, that's true. There was a blind man like that in our village."

"That's it, Moussa. If he can't talk, maybe he will be especially good at reading and writing. The world of books will give him an advantage over other boys."

"An advantage?"

"Yes. He could go on in school —to high school, maybe even university. Think about it, Moussa. Your boy could be a scholar . . . maybe a writer. Or, better, a poet!"

"A writer? Even if he never talks?"

"That's the point. He would be eager to learn to write—instead of talking. That will be his way to be a man; maybe even an important man!"

"I see," Moussa said, "he could read and write, that way he wouldn't be mute anymore."

"Exactly!" Khaled looked like he was going to clap. "Reading is the door to the bigger world, and writing is the path inside it."

Moussa winced and curled his shoulders into his chest, as if Khaled had slammed his fist into his chest.

"I didn't mean. Sorry! I insulted you, Moussa," Khaled rushed to apologize. "I know you didn't have the benefit, the luxury, of an education."

"It's alright," Moussa whispered.

"Look, Moussa," Khaled slowed his steps, "all the children in my classes love the stories. They listen, all ears, when I read to them from my books. But so few will go far enough to read books on their own. Your boy —he could!"

Moussa could do nothing more than nod. Khaled took a long drag on his shrinking cigarette and let out a thin stream of smoke. "Most of my pupils, the good ones, will master writing a simple letter, adding up sales receipts or their wages, reading a newspaper. But they'll all end up laborers, fishermen, and small merchants. None will ever read an actual book or a poem."

"It's sad for you," Moussa said and looked into Khaled's eyes. He'd never thought of it this way.

"For a long time, I've been dreaming of a student who will become a 'man of letters.' My special pupil to whom I can lend books from my library."

"You have a library?"

"A small one. But with very good books, on many subjects. And our great poets! Don't worry, Moussa. Even though you are not educated yourself, your boy could be. Better than just a fisherman, no?"

"You mean --" Moussa halted, not sure what he actually wanted to say.

"I've seen it," Khaled cut off Moussa's hesitant voice, "how you and Youssra devote yourselves to the boy. I know you would do anything for him."

Moussa swelled with pride at Khaled's words.

Khaled gestured towards the small Nargeellah shop he favored.

"Let's go in —we can sit quietly, smoke and talk. I'll explain everything to you. I know you have questions: the uniform, money for books . . . "

"Thank you, Khaled. It would be an honor for me."

Chapter 12

"Wake up, Liebling," Gertie whispered into Alfred's ear. He opened his eyes and stared at her, then looked at the clock.

"It's midnight, Gertie," he protested.

"I know, but it's snowing!"

"Snowing, here?" Alfred popped up, pulling the blanket around him like a small tent.

They brought their faces close up to the window glass, their breaths making twin circles on it.

"Yes, it's definitely snow. Not like back home but . . ."

"Not like back home," Gertie sighed, "nothing here is."

"It's still beautiful."

"Yes, that's why I woke you. By morning it may be gone."

"Sure, once the Asiatic sun gets its hands on it," Alfred said.

They stared at the snowflakes flitting in the air. An awkward silence hovered between them. Finally, Gertie blurted it out: "Remember when Emil first saw snow?"

"I was thinking the same thing," Alfred said and extended his arm, encircling Gertie with the blanket. "I didn't want to upset you."

"Silence would upset me more," she said and let Alfred wipe the tears rolling down her cheeks with the edge of his sleeve.

"Wake up, Habibi," Youssra nudged Moussa who was cocooned in his wool blankets.

"What?" Moussa said in alarm, "Not blood again?"

"No, no. Outside—it's snowing." She'd discovered the dusting of snow going to the outhouse. The white sheen of the ground and the flakes floating in the air were so breathtaking she didn't mind the bitter cold.

"Snowing? Youssra, are you dreaming?"

"No, really. Get up Moussa, come see it!"

Moussa loosened his cocoon and got up. The room was frigid, so he picked up the blanket and wrapped himself in it,

"You take a blanket, too, Youssra, it's so cold! Look how you are shivering."

He handed her the thick camel hair bedspread. Moussa opened the door a crack and a gust of freezing air hit them. They didn't mind; their eyes were fixed on the white blanket covering the courtyard.

"How beautiful!" Moussa exclaimed.

"Yes," Youssra whispered in reverence. "And look at the pieces coming down so slowly. They must be so light."

"Like the tiniest feathers. But it's so cold. We better go back in."

They shut the door and got into bed pulling the blankets up to their noses.

"Should we wake Moulleek to show him?" Moussa asked.

"Mmm . . ." Youssra said, "I don't know. I am worried he would be frightened. Waking him in the dark may scare him too much."

"You're right," Moussa said, "the whiteness too. He wouldn't understand and how could we explain it? I remember my first time: I thought the world was going to disappear."

"Oh, you mean that long time ago, when we were kids?"

"Yes, Youssra. I was . . . maybe eleven. I'd never even heard of snow before that."

"Me, too, Moussa. I remember vaguely. I was probably eight.

But then later on—when was it? We were already married but still in the village."

"Of course! The big one —the year before we came here."

"I remember," Youssra said, "It was during Ramadan."

"You are right. That year was a winter Ramadan."

"Ramadan back home," Youssra said wistfully, "how I miss that . . ."

"Back home . . . I miss all of it. It's not the same here."

"But here we have Moulleek!" Youssra retorted.

"Of course. I'll take him over anything back home," Moussa said and wiped the tears on Youssra's face with his cold finger.

CHAPTER 13

At Stella Maris the New Year's Eve prayer service was held in the large chapel. Lucas was relieved that Dondieu was no longer afraid of the crucifix. Father Pierre sermonized about praying for peace —back home in Europe and here in the Holy Land. For once, all the monks and boys listened attentively and nodded in assent. After the service they all went into the courtyard holding long, tapered candles for their customary blessing under the stars and ringing of the bells.

Dondieu found Lucas and took his hand. The boy's face shone in the moonlight that penetrated the passage through arched windows. They stepped outside and both gasped. The courtyard was covered in a white blanket.

"*Niège!*" Lucas called out. "Look, Dondieu, snow!"

The boy's mouth dropped. He squeezed Lucas' hand so hard Lucas looked asked what was wrong. Dondieu seemed in a daze.

Niège?
I have seen this, but a different word.
What word?
Sch...
Sch...
Schnee... Yes, that's what it is!
But much more than this.

Up to my knees.

So cold.

Where is my wool coat? My rubber boots with the fur lining?

Walk on it in the boots. It creaks.

"Careful! Hold my hand so you don't slip."

Who said?

Papa. Papa said.

Dondieu looked up at Lucas.

Not this one.

Different Papa.

Where is he?

Where's Mama?

"*Mon Dieu!*" Lucas yelled as Dondieu crumpled to the ground and rolled himself into a tight ball. He was shaking so violently his elbows thumped the stone floor. Lucas scooped him into his arms and wrapped him in his robe. What happened? It's the older boys! Must have urged him to drink wine. Thought it'd be funny to see him drunk. The rascals!

Lucas rushed Dondieu to the dormitory and settled him in his bed. He brought over extra blankets and wrapped Dondieu tightly, till he looked like an infant in a papoose. Perched on the edge of the bed, Lucas began a lullaby he remembered his mother singing to him whenever he had a fever. Dondieu shook as if chills were ravaging his body. He stared at Lucas with eyes torn wide. Lucas sang and shushed. Finally, Dondieu began to relax and closed his eyes. Lucas held his hand until he was asleep.

"Keep an eye on Dondieu," Lucas said to Brother Michel as he shepherded the boys into the room. "I hope it's just the wine and excitement, but he may be coming down with something."

"You worry too much about him," Brother Michel said.

Lucas gulped. *Was it that obvious? He'd better be more careful.*

"I'll just check on him several times during the night," Brother Michel said as if his comment had meant nothing.

The next day Dondieu had a fever and stayed in bed. Brother Michel tended to him and asked Lucas to come in the afternoon. In the evening the fever spiked and the next day it got worse. Dondieu began to moan and held his hand over his right ear. Lucas put warm compresses on it and gave Dondieu medicine to lower the fever. When the boy got even sicker the following morning Father Pierre summoned Lucas and instructed him to take Dondieu to a doctor. He gave him the name of a Jewish pediatrician in the Hadar Elyon neighborhood. "This doctor has a reputation for his rapport with very young children. Since our Dondieu doesn't speak, he would be best; hopefully understanding him without words."

"And," Father Pierre said while scribbling on a piece of paper, "since the boy is so sick, take one of the Arab donkey carts right to the door and back. Here's the address." Father Pierre handed him the note.

Lucas wrapped Dondieu up in two thick wool blankets and carried him past the monastery's gate, where he was relieved to find a donkey cart waiting. He climbed in and sat down with the blanket bundle that was Dondieu. It was very chilly, and Lucas was thankful he was wearing his thick wool cassock.

"Number fifteen, Herzl Street," he called out.

"Yallah!," the driver shouted at the donkey, then turned to Lucas: "I go fast, but I go careful."

CHAPTER 14

At Dr. Klein's office there were three people in the waiting room but when the receptionist saw Lucas, she asked their permission to let the sick boy go first. They all nodded, and Lucas entered. He sat Dondieu on the examination table and peeled off the blankets. The boy's cheeks were flushed, his eyes were droopy, his hand clamped over his ear. He was shivering violently. Lucas put his arm around him to try to keep him warm while giving the doctor a brief accounting of the illness.

"*Also, wir beginnen,*" the doctor addressed his nurse in German, "raise up the boy's shirt and lay him down on his left side."

Before the nurse had a chance to move, Dondieu grabbed the edge of his short tunic and pulled it up to his armpits, then lay down on the table.

"What?" Klein threw Lucas a puzzled look, "the boy knows German?"

"No!" Lucas exclaimed, as surprised as the doctor. "B-b-but, he is very bright. He notices everything and he was examined by a doctor once before."

"Very bright, indeed!" the doctor said and turned to Dondieu. "So, tell us, little fellow, what hurts?"

"Sorry, Herr Doktor," Lucas jumped in, "he doesn't talk."

"He doesn't talk?"

"I m-m-mean," Lucas stammered, "he's mute."

"Mute? From birth?" Klein tilted his head, eyeing the boy, "that might explain being so perceptive."

"I don't know if from birth. He's only been with us in the monastery for a little over one year."

"And before?"

"We don't know. He was mute when he came to us. An Arab boy, abandoned or an orphan—we think."

"Very strange... very strange," the doctor frowned but proceeded to examine the boy, from head to toe.

"An Arab boy not circumcised?" he asked Lucas when he took Dondieu's pants down. "I thought they circumcise here in infancy."

"Usually," Lucas said, "but from what I've learned, with a sick or weak or ... defective baby," he winced as he said the word, "they postpone."

"Aha, good to know that," the doctor said and completed the examination. He diagnosed strep throat and a raging ear infection and gave Lucas a prescription to be filled in the pharmacy around the corner. "And when he's all better, do bring him back so I can do a more thorough examination of his hearing and vocal cords."

Lucas bowed and thanked the doctor and the nurse. He bundled Dondieu in the blanket and lifted him into his arms, then wrapped the wide hem of his sleeve around him for extra warmth. Dondieu pressed his face into Lucas' chest, still shivering. Only his curls showed above the rim of his cocoon.

Rushing out the door of the infirmary, Lucas almost bumped into a man carrying a baby, this one also well wrapped, in a blue wool shawl. The man stepped aside and held the door open for Lucas.

"From the monastery?" he asked in halting Hebrew.

Lucas nodded, and answered in his Biblical Hebrew "An ailing boy, from our Stella Maris. I get remedy now."

"Dr. Klein is very good. We know him from Vienna." the man said in a reassuring tone.

"From Vienna?"

"Yes."

"Vienna . . . so far away," Lucas said wistfully.

"Yes, so far away. You, too, far away from home, yes?"

"Yes," Lucas said and looked down. The empathic voice made him tear up.

"You go now, get the medicine."

Lucas squeezed out the door and the man approached the secretary's desk.

"I am here for Benyamin's one-year well-baby check. Just a few weeks late."

"No matter," the nurse smiled, "I'll tell Dr. Klein you are here. He'll be happy to see a healthy baby after that poor, sick boy."

"Come in, come in!" Dr. Klein called out though the half-opened door. "Nice to see you Herr Schiff. And Frau Schiff?"

"She's down with a cold, so sorry. That's why I've brought Benyamin."

"There's a nasty one going around. Try to keep her away from the baby."

"Cannot be done . . . " Alfred said, shrugging his shoulders.

"All right, let us have a look at the little fellow," Dr. Klein said and motioned to Alfred to seat Benyamin on the examination table. Alfred unwrapped the shawl and tickled Benyamin to make him laugh.

"*Mein Gott!*" Dr. Klein exclaimed and his hand flew to his face. "He . . . he looks so much like Em . . . Emil, back when I saw him as a baby . . . in Vienna."

Alfred blanched and pressed his lips together. He grabbed onto the edge of the table to steady himself.

"I, a-a-m sorry. I didn't mean to . . . "

"He does," Alfred finally pushed the words out, "it's our greatest joy. And our greatest sorrow."

"And you never . . . ?" Dr. Klein touched Alfred's arm.

"Never. No information, not a clue."

Part VII: November 1944

Chapter 1

Gertie lingered in the apartment, surveying the furniture and boxes lined up for the move. The empty rooms looked so small now. She ran her fingers along the rough edge of the stripped mattress and then soothed them on the cold metal frame. The bed was their most precious possession, with its wrought-iron frame and actual springs supporting the seaweed-filled mattress—a great splurge, much superior to the more common straw-filled ones. The bed and the tall wardrobe were the only "luxury" items they had allowed themselves. Since their arrival in this room and a half apartment, they had painstakingly accumulated the basics of a household. On rare occasions they went to a used furniture store. Mostly, they bought from families who were fortunate enough to be able to afford new furniture or, in some sad cases, too poor to hold onto what they owned, and who sold things by word of mouth.

Their clothes were packed into three jute sacks, lined up against the wall. In the alcove kitchen everything was in order as well. A small wooden box held their dishes, utensils, three pots and a teakettle, and a canvas bag held the staples they were taking with them. Their four chairs were stacked one on top of the other in two pairs and tied together with twine. They had decided not to take the dining table since it was just two wide boards on top of a crate, and not worth paying the porters to haul. If they had any money left after paying the movers, they'd buy a real table, used, of course. Gertie chuckled—she might actually miss this one. But she was ready.

It all happened faster than she had anticipated. Alfred had brought up moving a few times in the course of the past two years, but she always resisted.

"It's not the right time," she'd said in August when he brought it up again.

"Too hot?" he asked innocently.

"Too hot? That would cover half the year here!"

"What, then?

"The war, Alfred. The war . . . "

He said nothing but gave her a puzzled look.

"It just seems wrong, disloyal," she shrugged.

"Disloyal?"

"Disloyal to them . . . back home. Who knows where they are now? Do they even have a place to live?"

Alfred didn't answer.

After a tense silence Gertie said, "And here too. No one knows what will happen, how long the war will go on."

"Indeed. Everyone is worried, if not outright afraid. That's why . . . don't take this the wrong way Gertie, but prices are low."

She shook her head and didn't answer. But to her own surprise she soon changed her mind. It was the day Alfred came back from his appointment to volunteer for the Jewish Brigade, near the end of September.

"They wouldn't take me!" he blurted out the moment he stepped into the apartment. She'd been reading to Benyamin, snuggled on her lap. She stood up and set him on the floor and handed him the book. She hoped the animal pictures would keep him busy.

"Really?"

She had to sit down, nearly tottering over from the wave of relief that swept through her.

"Over thirty, a father, and short-sighted," Alfred quoted the

British officer, with a mock English accent. "Rather arrogant, if I may say so," he added.

"Well . . . " Gertie stopped short. Good girl, she told herself, getting better at keeping that sharp tongue locked up.

"I told him I was an experienced engineer! That I was sure I could be very helpful with support operations."

"And?"

"The Jewish Brigade won't be needing that level of 'helpfulness with support operations.' He quoted me precisely! I know he was mocking me."

"Maybe the people who said the whole thing was a token were right, after all?" Gertie said.

"I sure hope not."

She left it at that, seeing he was fuming.

But after they finished dinner and Benyamin fell asleep, she said, "So now that this option is out, maybe we should move."

"Really? Now you're ready?"

"Now I'm ready. As long as we stay in Haifa."

"Even without a view of the port?"

Gertie closed her eyes for a moment. "Even so . . . " she finally whispered, "so long as on November 25th we go down there." She let two tears roll down silently, then wiped them with the back of her hand.

"Of course," Alfred said and laced his fingers together, pressing hard to stop his own tears. "I know it's hard, Liebling."

Gertie softened towards him and caressed his knuckles.

"I have a list," Alfred said, "it's not up to date, but I'll start on it tomorrow."

Gertie walked to the front of the room where they had piled the packages to carry by hand. If she took their two medium-sized suitcases and Alfred took a couple of boxes, they could make the move in one trip. As long as that man, Shmeel, brought the two promised Arab porters who, he said, could carry anything.

"Big, bulky, heavy or delicate; they have a way with it. A talent for balancing and maneuvering. Wait till you see," Shmeel had promised. "Between the two of them they can easily carry down the bed and the heavy wardrobe."

Shmeel, or as he'd asked Gertie and Alfred to address him in front of the Arab men he hired, "Adon Shmu'el," had a donkey and a cart. "The heavy furniture, the boxes and chairs, will fit into the cart. You will have to walk behind it and carry what you can—the smaller things."

Earlier that morning Benyamin kept bouncing around the pile of luggage and boxes.

"It will be like our own parade in the street, Mama! Let me carry something big."

"Sure, *Benyaminlein*." She looked at the pile. "But everything here is too big for you, Liebling."

"No, it's not," he said, his mouth in a pout she recognized as a precursor to crying.

"It's not about how big, mein Kind. It's about how important. I will give some very important things to carry."

"Goodie, Mama!"

She opened the bag that held his toys; a ball, a bag of marbles, a teddy bear, a small tractor Alfred had built from wood scraps and, of course, his cherished donkey.

"Now we'll put in Papa's pens and pencils. Even his ruler and compass. Those are also the most important."

She opened the hard case that held Alfred's drafting tools, nestled in an indigo velvet lining. Benyamin held his breath as she carefully closed the case and slid it into his bag.

CHAPTER 2

"Everything is in order," she told herself again. Alfred was downstairs with Benyamin waiting for Shmeel at the entrance to the building. Gertie let herself feel a wisp of melancholy about leaving this apartment—their first home in Eretz Yisrael. Their first home since... their beautiful Vienna apartment in what now seemed like a different century.

"*So schön . . .*" she murmured to herself; "that beautiful apartment." They'd bought it towards the end of Alfred's schooling, intending to move in soon. Then everything changed. I know, she chided herself, we had to leave! Still, giving it up was such a shame! Maybe her parents managed to sell it in time—on the black market—before it got too late. Well before she and Alfred had left Vienna, Jews couldn't get decent prices on the open market.

And her parents' apartment? Gone, too, she was quite sure, soon after the Nazi decrees forbidding Jews to own property. Such a gem ... in the heart of town, right off the Ringstrasse. Her favorite room, the parlor, now seemed palatial, lined with carved oak bookshelves, a walnut bureau, armchairs upholstered in deep maroon velvet and delicate brocade, and a credenza with a marble top. When she was little, her mother would seat her on the marble top while she prepared for guests, setting out china plates with candied fruit and cookies, silver-plated ashtrays, a vase with roses. The cold marble under Gertie's thighs made her shiver.

She could feel that Vienna shiver now. Or was it the chill from the open window? Her mind meandered back to the apartment she and Alfred had found. A spacious living room, though, unlike her parents, she planned to furnish it in modern Bauhaus style. She favored its clean minimalism over the ornate late 19th century designs which always made her feel the way you do after one spoonful too many of over-sweetened whipped cream. She thought back to their original plans for the two large bedrooms in Vienna; one for her and Alfred and another for the babies they hoped would come soon. Their room opened onto a small balcony with a wrought-iron balustrade, where you could sit on summer evenings on two matching wrought iron chairs at a stylish coffee table.

The new apartment in Haifa would have a little balcony too. Nothing like in Vienna but still, with a view, too, of the slopes of Mount Carmel, not the port. Her breath caught. But trees, she told herself, green, soothing, peaceful. She wrapped herself in her own arms. Trees, but nothing like . . . she couldn't stop the train of thoughts: the forests, Vienna, Europe . . . her parents, Oma and Opa, Alfred's family. Did his brother, Hans, manage to protect them or were they also sent to . . . She opened her eyes wide and made herself stop. No use. No one talked about what they were reading in the newspapers.

They had not received any mail from their families in a long time. The only connection they had was the heavy wooden trunk they'd retrieved from the Lost and Found office at the Haifa Port after settling down in this apartment. She and her mother had filled it with whatever they had imagined would be useful in Palestine. They had shopped carefully, a list in hand. Her mother had heard that tailored leather coats with wool lining were the most valuable item to pack. You couldn't get them in Palestine and they would keep them warm in the winter. Gertie's came to below the knees, Alfred's to just above. There was an oversized one for Emil, so he'd grow into it and use it for several years. But the coats hung forlorn their first two winters in

Haifa. It never got cold enough to wear them. After two years Gertie sold them to a family leaving Palestine for America. The money was enough to buy the wardrobe, pots and pans, and winter clothes for Benyamin.

They had also packed good leather shoes, wool socks, sheets, tablecloths and silverware. All gone when Gertie and Alfred opened the trunk at the Lost and Found. She pursed her lips remembering how, when they finally retrieved the trunk, they were presented with a huge bill for storage fees. Over seven months of storage at twenty pence a day. It was a fortune! But when the British customs official saw that during the months in storage someone had picked the locks and taken out almost all the valuables, he waived the fee. "It was, after all, this office that was charged with the safe-keeping of your possessions, and we have evidently failed to discharge this duty in full."

All that remained in the trunk were the leather coats, clearly the thieves already knew they were useless, wool underwear, a few pairs of socks, their cherished copy of *Emil and the Detectives*, and their photographs. One each of their parents and grandparents, two from their wedding, Emil's baby picture, taken at the photo studio once he could lift his head up, and his portrait just before they left. The silver frames had been stolen and the photos were scatted throughout the trunk. They replaced the frames with plain wood ones. They had hung their parents' photos and the wedding portrait. But the ones of Emil they'd placed on top of the wardrobe, pushed back from the edge. They were not ready to tell Benyamin who the smiling boy was.

Gertie waved her hand to brush away the memories. No time for this now; she must rally herself. The new apartment would be so much better. It had a real bedroom with a corner for a desk for Alfred's work. The unusually large entry hall could double as living room and Benyamin's room. He'd be so happy to be able to set up his block structures in the corner and keep them for days. He often cried when she made him put them away, his "army castles" destroyed. And the balcony, she reminded herself. She could string a line for drying laundry. She could relish the fresh air and, if she leaned over as far as she could, she'd glimpse a handbreadth of the port's waves.

Much earlier that morning winter was bearing down on the Haifa docks, the low clouds shutting out the horizon. The cold air had turned from swift knife jabs when Moussa opened his jacket, to a vapor that permeated his clothes and seeped into his veins. Despite the four layers he had on, he shivered. His fingertips and toes were icicles. He tried to get his circulation going by rubbing his hands together and jumping up and down. It didn't help. You take your boat out to sea this morning, he laughed to himself, it's like you're a fish set on a block of ice.

Even the fish would be reluctant to come out on a day like this. Better, perhaps, to stay on land and see if Ali had any jobs today. Ali had his quirks and his detractors, but he'd been a good source of supplementary work. The endless war had depleted almost everyone's wallet. Then again, some people were making a nice profit from it, supplying the British troops or serving the officer corps in cafes and clubs. But they were not the people he mingled with.

Moussa checked the knots securing his boat to the dock. Good knots, beautiful knots! He mused: it was thanks to Uncle Abu Zbeid, a master knots-man. He owed him so much! He should thank him again. Maybe Youssra could prepare some sweets, *basbousa*, *ma'amoul* -—filled with dates or pistachio—or maybe her fig-paste cookies? His mouth began to water. Forget about that now, he chided himself. It's cold, you need work, and the pastries are far away.

He left the port and headed to Ali's, not in a hurry, just trying to warm up. He arrived slightly out of breath, each exhalation a tiny cloud hanging in the air for a moment.

"A cold morning, my friend," Ali greeted Moussa. His cigarette, as always, hung from the corner of his mouth making him look like he was sneering. The pockmarked skin and pencil-thin moustache did not help either. But Moussa knew that under that veneer was a decent man, willing to lend a hand and keep confidences.

Ali bent over a tray with a teapot and four glasses and filled one, lengthening the thread of amber liquid as he pulled the pot up and up. He handed Moussa the steaming glass. Moussa flashed him a thankful grin and slurped the mint tea slowly. The sweet and pungent drink slid down his throat and warmed his insides. Soon he began to thaw out. What a joy to feel his toes! He had not had any communication with them since early morning.

Before Moussa opened his mouth Ali said: "A small job to keep you warmer than fishing at sea today, eh?"

Moussa nodded.

"You're in luck. I have a moving job - I could use an extra man. A Jewish family is moving in Hadar Elyon, not far."

Moussa frowned at the mention of the Jewish neighborhood. "Isn't it dangerous for us to go there?"

"Not the way I work. Shmeel—my partner over there—will cover for us. Just don't be too obvious."

"How do you mean?"

"Don't talk when we are in the street and no kaffiyeh on your head."

"Nothing on my head, Ali?"

"A hat is fine. I have one, like they wear, a 'fisherman's cap' they call it, so it suits you. I'll find it in a minute."

"Shukran!"

"Anyway," Ali continued, "we'll do it fast. They are moving only two streets over from where they are now. But . . . " Ali stretched the word a little too long. Moussa frowned: "But?"

"They're in a second-floor apartment, moving to a third floor."

"A lot of stairs then," Moussa tried to suppress the grumble in his voice.

But he sure needed the job, so let there be stairs.

"And you're sure it's safe, Ali? There are rumors that the Jews are arming themselves more and more."

"As are we," Ali said.

"Yes, but I heard they don't let Arabs pass through their neighborhood."

"Don't worry, Moussa. Shmeel will be waiting for us. I've done it before."

"I see." Moussa slowly unwrapped his kaffiyeh and stuffed it in his satchel. "Then let's get some ropes."

Chapter 3

Shmeel arrived at the apartment with his two Arab workers and greeted Gertie. "*Guten Morgen*, Madam. Alles ist bereit? Everything ready?"

"Yes. *Muchanim*," Gertie showed him that her Hebrew was perfectly adequate for the task. Shmeel surveyed the apartment and counted the pieces of furniture, sacks and boxes. She noted that the two Arab men were shorter than her and very slim. Neither looked particularly muscular. Could they handle the heavier pieces?

"Yallah! Ali, Moussa," Shmeel said, "you start. Do the bed together, Then, Moussa, you do the rest of the bedroom. Ali, you do the kitchen."

The two men first lifted the mattress off the bed and set it against the wall. Gertie was not surprised it looked easy. The mattresses here in Palestine were nothing like the heavy overstuffed ones back home. Even she could have lifted it. Next, they turned the bed on its side and, with impressive agility, maneuvered it through the narrow doorway, down the hall to the top of the stairs. Coordinating their steps with "*Ouahad, Tnen; Ouahad, Tnen*," they negotiated the stairs. They placed the bed on its side in the cart. Step one was done.

Moussa saw the man standing by the cart, he assumed the husband, eyeing him approvingly. He waved to the little boy hiding behind the man, though he couldn't see his face, as it was buried in his father's pant leg. Ali got onto the cart to rope the bed into place and Moussa hurried up for the next item.

Back in the apartment, with the bed frame gone, the room already looked smaller. Moussa eyed the tall wardrobe. Gertie did too, lovingly. Made of oak back in Europe, it gave off a whiff of home. Another immigrant had shipped it here in better times and they'd bought it third hand, a bit battered by time and use, but still as solid as could be—and very heavy.

Moussa first lifted the wardrobe's corner an inch to estimate its weight. Substantial, he told himself and looked at the lady —yes, she knew. He circled it, measuring its girth with the rope he had coiled around his forearm. He stepped into the doorframe and measured its dimensions. He noticed the puzzled look on the lady's face. She must be wondering how in the world he would maneuver the wardrobe out by himself. *Well, wait and see, lady, I have hauled even larger ones, all on my own.*

He'd have to put it on his back, lying on its narrow side, harness it and support the weight by placing the rope across his forehead. An old trick of the trade. The head bent forward shifts the weight, so even a very heavy piece feels as if it almost floats on your back. He wrapped his rope around the wardrobe twice, then made a double knot. Next, he pushed up on his tiptoes to stretch the rope across the top.

There was something on top of the wardrobe. He stepped back and looked up. It was pushed in from the edge so only a tall adult - taller than him, as so many of the Yahoud were, could see it. He rose on tiptoes. A framed picture of a boy. He stretched out his hand and picked it up, casting a glance just before handing it to the lady. His eyes froze on the boy's face.

He looked away, trying to bring together what his eyes saw and what his mind perceived. He looked at the photo again: how could this child look so much like him, like he looked back then? Is it true that every person has a twin somewhere in the world about whom they know nothing, only the lucky ones meeting each other? He willed the hand holding the picture towards the lady. His arm was shaking. He leaned into the wardrobe to steady himself.

"Lady, w-w-what this?" Moussa drew on his modest Hebrew vocabulary.

Gertie took the picture and clasped it to her heart. A muffled cry escaped her tight lips. *How could I have forgotten it?* she shook her head. She looked back at Moussa, but he was elsewhere. She waited until he looked up.

"We have before had another boy," she finally said in stilted Hebrew. In a strange way, it was easier to say it in a foreign language, though she wasn't sure of the correct form for the past tense. "Emil. Four years old. Four years before now, a terrible . . . "

Moussa gripped the rope and looked right into her face, something he'd never done before with a woman other than Youssra, let alone a Jewish woman.

"Our ship . . . " she stopped and ran her finger around the picture frame. "On our ship is bomb. Here in port of Haifa. Emil, our boy, he disappear. Also, many other people —they drown."

Moussa stepped back and looked away from her anguished face. He repeated to himself in silence: "Four years ago. A ship, a bomb. Haifa port. Boy drowned. Four years old. Emil." If only he could shut his eyes to focus on the fragmented thoughts ricocheting inside his head. But he must respond now.

"I look the picture, lady?"

She opened her stiffened fingers and let the photograph lie on her palms face up, as if it were an offering. Moussa leaned in. *Here is his picture!*

"Very nice boy," he managed to say after a long moment. "He look sweet."

"Very sweet. He was . . . our Emil."

Chapter 4

What now? Moussa gulped hard. If only he could swallow his thoughts and make them disappear. The wardrobe! Move the wardrobe! He ran the rope over the top and made three knots close together. He crouched down and hoisted the wardrobe onto his back, thankful that its weight forced his head down so all he could see was the floor. He counted his steps. Eight to cross the room, ten out the door to the top of the stairs, where he rested momentarily to steady his breathing. He took each stair in slow motion, feeling as if a gong banged in his head with each step: One—Emil; two—Moulleek; Three—Emil; four—Moulleek.

He bent his head further down to balance the heavy weight, his eyes glued to his worn shoes and the width of each stair. Counting was the only way to try to slow his racing thoughts and keep his footing.

The lady followed right behind him, slowed by the weight of a suitcase in each hand. Outside she joined her husband who lifted the suitcase onto the cart. At his side was the little boy. Moussa tilted his head just enough to get a glimpse of the boy's face, shining with pride, as he held onto a green burlap bag. He looks so much like the one in the photo! Only darker hair and eyes. A little darker than Moulleek's. Moussa wasn't fast enough to stop the thought from exploding in his head. He bit down hard to squeeze it out. Not now! He can't think about it now. He must finish and go, fast!

Moussa slid the wardrobe onto the cart and Ali tied it down. Together they went upstairs twice more, one time hauling the mattress and the next carrying everything else. Shmeel got on the cart, yanked the battered leather harness and called out: "Yallah, yallah!" The donkey pulled forward, straining against the straps. Ali and Moussa pushed the cart from behind to get it going. Then they drifted back to walk behind the family. Moussa tried to shut down his mind by counting his steps, but the boy's excited chatter pounded his ears. "Yallah!" he chided himself, "yallah, yallah, Moussa, keep walking and stop thinking!"

It was not far - only a few minutes' stroll for an average person, but with everything they were carrying, they all moved slowly. Except the boy who held his bag with great care yet kept running ahead of the donkey and then back to his mother, then around to the front again.

"I'll have my own room, right, Mama?"

"Yes," she said and tried to take hold of him. "Don't run like that, Benyamin, it's dangerous. But yes, most of the time it be will your room. Only sometimes we will have guests and you'll let us use your room, right? You'll keep everything clean and neat, alright, Liebling?"

"Yes, yes!"

He beamed when she said he could have friends come to play together in his new room.

"Good, Mama. Sometimes I do want friends, because the other children in kindergarten have brothers and sisters to play with, and I don't."

Gertie made herself stay erect and march on.

Moussa was the first to climb the stairs with a large load when they arrived at the new apartment. He ran right back down for the wardrobe, hauling it up the three flights of stairs. He lowered it to the floor in the bedroom and slid it flush against the side wall so there would be room for the bed under the window. From other moving jobs he was familiar with, these kinds of Jews who'd come from Europe, they liked a lot of light and a breeze. It was almost a religion with them - fresh air and sunshine, regardless of the blazing heat of summer.

"Here is good, Lady?" he asked Gertie when she entered the bedroom.

"Good," she smiled at him. *Something endearing about him,* she thought, *maybe his seeming vulnerability?*

Moussa ran downstairs again and, with Ali, brought the bed and mattress and set it under the window. The lady was clearly happy with that, too. He told Ali he had to rush home now to take care of something urgent. Ali could pay him tomorrow or the day after. Ali raised an eyebrow. His workers always wanted to get paid on the spot, but he shrugged and waved to Moussa, already down a flight of stairs.

―――――――

Once all the furniture was placed in the apartment, Gertie and Alfred took a little tour of their new place. Benyamin was on his hands and knees unpacking his bag and lining everything up against the wall.

"This could feel like a home, Gertie."

They entered their bedroom and walked over to the window.

"Look at our view," Alfred stretched his hand out.

"We have a view!" Gertie announced, mocking Alfred's proud tone.

"Don't Gertie! It's a very nice view of the Carmel. Beautiful trees. In the spring there will be wildflowers. You said you were ready."

"I know, Liebling. I did, and I am happy about it. I am," she leaned her forehead against the window. "I'll sew some pretty curtains," she added after a moment.

"Papa," Benyamin called, "here's your special box for special things."

Alfred knelt by the boy and took the drafting tools case and slid the top open.

"You did a very good job, Benyamin. Everything is exactly where it belongs."

"I know, Papa. I was very careful," Benyamin puffed out his chest.

"So much space!" Gertie said.

"Yes. As a matter of fact, it's almost twice the square meters."

"Well," she surveyed their belongings, "we'll have to find some decent furniture, one piece at a time, to make it a real home."

"Yes. Bit by bit."

"And it's time to buy Benyamin a real bed."

"You're right, Gertie. He's outgrown the little one we had in our room. And it will be so nice to finally have our bedroom to ourselves."

"Ja . . . " Gertie gave Alfred a sly smile.

"A real bed, Papa? Where is it?"

"We'll find one tomorrow," Gertie said.

"And I'll make you a shelf for your books and treasures," Alfred bent down to kiss Benyamin's head.

"Thank you, Papa! But for now, everything by the wall?"

"Perfect, mein Kind."

Gertie called Alfred into the bedroom and showed him the picture Moussa had found. "Same place as before?" Alfred nodded. She could see he was holding back tears and couldn't speak. She propped the picture up on top of the wardrobe and pushed it back from the edge. Will they ever be ready to tell Benyamin about Emil? At what age would he understand?

She sat down on the bed, her hands folded in her lap. Alfred started to unpack and arrange things. She lingered on the bed for another moment but then got up and joined Alfred, hanging clothes, taking out sheets and towels. It's better this way, she told herself, moving forward, not getting yanked down into the vortex. Her busy hands would soothe her, at least for a while.

Chapter 5

Moussa rushed home, trying to outrun his thoughts. Turning the last corner, he saw Moulleek with his friends climbing the old mulberry tree in the back alley. How they could keep themselves entertained for hours climbing that puny tree, he couldn't fathom. But now it was a godsend. It will give him time with Youssra. By the door, he heard himself appealing in his heart to someone—Allah? Help me! How do I tell her?

He steadied his breath, closing and opening his fists in slow motion. Should he have her sit down before he starts? Maybe a walk would be better? No, someone might see them, try to eavesdrop. Just go slow and give her time to digest every piece of the story. Give it to her in small bits, as you would feed a gosling.

He entered. Youssra had her hands deep in a warm lump of dough she was kneading for their evening pita. "Habibi, back already?" she called out but hushed upon seeing his face. She let go of the sticky dough and rubbed her hands together to roll off the little pieces stuck to her fingers. She followed Moussa where he'd dropped down on the rolled mattresses and blankets stacked against the wall.

The floor was gleaming from her morning cleaning and the scent of the pine extract she'd dribbled into the water bucket hung in the air. Moussa usually commented on the shiny tiles and the fresh smell, but not now. His shoulders were collapsed and he held his head in his hands. Youssra lowered herself onto a low stool near him. He saw her eyes searching his face for clues. He coughed to clear his throat but could not get started. He was thankful for her patience. She must know from experience that prodding him wouldn't help. But he could practically see the tight knots already twisting her gut.

"He . . . is not ours," Moussa blurted out.

She can see the tears welling up in my eyes. She must be shocked; she has never seen me cry.

But she merely looked confused.

"Of course, Moussa, we knew he wasn't ours. He was a gift from Allah. Haven't we done a very good job keeping him for the Merciful One?"

"Yes . . . but no. Not anymore. He has parents. They want him."

"Parents? Want him?"

"I . . . I met them. Today."

Youssra stared at him wide-eyed, her mouth open. Moussa felt his face looked like a broken pot. Youssra sat frozen, wrapping and unwrapping the end of her braid around her fingers.

He waited for her as she had for him. She swallowed hard, looking as though she had just ingested a whole plum - everything he had said in one huge lump.

"No. No!" Youssra cried out, trembling.

"Moussa, my heart is in your hands!" she cried out. He'd never heard her like that.

"Tell me everything, and only what you actually saw! Where did you go this morning? How could this story . . . ?" She grasped her chest as if trying to keep in place what had been sliced clean off with a sharp cleaver.

Moussa opened his mouth, but no words came out. Youssra brought him a glass of water.

"You must tell me," she said, gently cajoling now, "exactly what happened, from the very beginning to the very end. Don't skip any details."

Moussa took a sip of water and licked his cracked lips. He began: the frigid morning, the moving job, the picture on top of the wardrobe and the Jewish lady's words. He described the younger boy too, a copy of Moulleek when he found him on the dock, just darker hair and eyes, as if some black ink had spilled into the brown. Youssra sat staring at him, her mouth open, as though she were drinking his words. Moussa couldn't look directly at her, but he felt her take his hand and squeeze it.

"Tell me . . . again, the exact w-w-words the lady said."

"They'd had another boy," Moussa recited, "four years old. They were on a ship in the Haifa harbor that exploded. Many people drowned. Four years ago. They never found the boy." He bit the insides of his cheeks and said no more. They sat listening to their own breathing. Moussa only realized how cold the room was when Youssra shivered and gathered her feet under her thighs to give them some warmth from her body. He slid his shoes off and wedged his icy feet between the mattresses while tucking his palms, cold yet sweaty, in his armpits.

He got up and took out the Primus stove they reserved for frosty days and cooking holiday meals and lit it. He glanced at Youssra. Her eyes were shut, her face contorted, her body swaying. After a very long silence she spoke: "Do you remember anything about the harbor that morning?"

Moussa closed his eyes, straining to capture even a wisp of memory. At first it was like trying to recall a dream when you've woken up —an image fleeting; the more your try to grab hold of it the faster it vanishes. Four years ago . . . the port. He visualized his small boat, but was it a memory from that day or from yesterday? And a big ship . . . did he see a big ship, the day he found the boy?

The first tangible memory to surface was the stench of the boy, then the eerie quiet of the dock that morning. Next, the brown wool robe of the monk. It had looked so warm; Moussa remembered recalling how cold he'd been that morning. Now the memories unrolled themselves like a bolt of fabric. His icy, stiff fingers untying the hard knots around the wood post, his hand slipping through a hole in the fishing net, searching in the clutter of debris for some yarn, the boy rolled up into a ball in the wooden crate.

"Yes, I remember now how I found him and how strange it was that there were no other fishermen and no customers for fish."

"What else?"

He laid out the memories like they were stepping-stones: the frigid morning, thick grey fog blanketing the docks, his guess that people were lingering in their warm beds a bit longer than usual on account of it. The search for some twine, the boy in the crate, the bruises, and the monk. Then the walk home and the baklava.

But where was he the day before? Why didn't he remember the explosion?

He ran his mind backwards.

"Do you remember, Youssra —we had come home from the village the night before. Arrived back here very late."

"I remember the long journey. Yes, and the beautiful sunset and you were suddenly a poet . . . "

"You remember that?" Moussa couldn't hide the touch of pride in his surprise.

"I do." Finally she could look at him. "Moussa! You are blushing," she blurted out before thinking the better of it.

"No. It's just getting hot in here."

"Hot?" she said and gathered her icy hands into her sleeves.

"Here by the stove," he made a show of turning down the knob to lower the flame.

"All and all," Youssra navigated out of the awkward moment, "I just remember being terribly tired."

"Yes, we were so tired. We didn't speak to anyone."

"I suppose we just went to sleep. Maybe we ate something?"

"I don't remember that, Youssra. But that's why we did not hear the explosion."

"Wait! Moussa. Now I do remember: the neighbors talking the next day, the curfew. I was so worried until you came back."

"Yes, I imagine so, but I am not sure I actually remember that part. That curfew would be one among many."

"Yes, the explosion, too. But you better find out now —everything you can —about that one."

She slumped down and squeezed her hands between her thighs, pressing them into the fabric of her dress. Her gaze disappeared.

Chapter 6

"I'll go ask the Qadi," Moussa said after they finished their midday meal with Moulleek, pretending all was well, and sending the boy back outside to find his friends.

"Are you sure the Qadi is best?"

"Why not, Youssra?"

"I've heard that his nose is buried in the Quran. Does he really know what's going on around us?"

"Oh, he knows. He makes sure to know."

"If you say so."

"Also, it's a matter of showing him the respect he is due, as the judge."

"You must be right," said Youssra, resigned to it.

"And speaking of respect," Moussa said sheepishly, "I am sorry that you can't come along. Women don't . . . "

Youssra turned the corners of her mouth down just enough to let Moussa know she knew but did not appreciate it.

"Be careful how you ask him about it," she warned.

Moussa promised to ask only simple questions, not revealing what was really on his mind. He pulled his feet out of their mattress pocket and massaged them, then shoved them back into the cold caves of his shoes. He splashed some cold water on his face. He couldn't fathom how Youssra would be able to stay home and wait. He knew he wouldn't have been able to bear it.

Go! he ordered his feet. He shuffled out of the house and into the street. Somehow the walk, only about a hundred meters, seemed both interminable long and incredibly short. Rehearsing his questions was of no use. His stomach was in knots and he was sweating. At the Qadi's house, only his wife was home. All she could tell Moussa was: "He'll be back when he comes back. That's how it is with him. But you can count on him coming home in time for his dinner."

Moussa thanked her and headed back, his eyes trained on his feet. Despite feeling frozen inside, he let the warm rays of the midday sun thaw his neck and back, softening his muscles. Breathe in deeply, he instructed his lungs, that will help, too. He was amazed to notice a sweet fragrance in the air, perhaps the last citrus flowers. He hadn't noticed anything around him until now.

Chapter 7

Moussa was not ready to go home. He had to steady his breath and make some order in his scattered thoughts. And he knew he really needed advice. But he must get it without revealing why. So . . . not the Qadi. Who else? Who would know? Khaled, the teacher, why not? With his education and reading the newspapers, he would know. Moussa looked up at the sun in the west: yes, and it's just about the time Khaled is done at the school and goes to his favorite nargeellah shop.

Moussa loitered on the street, pretending to look at the shops' windows. When Khaled emerged down the street Moussa greeted him with "Marhaba, honored teacher!" He shuddered a bit: perhaps he'd greeted Khaled a bit too eagerly, he thought to himself. But Khaled gave him a huge smile and called out, "Moussa, my friend, kiff hallek?"

"Good, good," Moussa mumbled.

"The fishing is good?" Khaled continued to seem truly delighted to see him, "the prices good?"

"Yes, good. And you?" Moussa dared speak as if he were Khaled's equal. "How are the boys in school? They're behaving? Learning to read?"

"Behaving . . . " Khaled sighed, "they behave like boys do. You know how they are."

Moussa nodded. Khaled noticed the tightening in Moussa's shoulders. *Of course, he finds it hard to talk about "regular boys."* Khaled didn't say anything as they walked down the street in silence, hoping the tension will dissipate.

"And your boy, Moussa?" Khaled finally spoke up. Now turning serious, he added: "You still don't send him to school. Why? Is it money? I can help, make arrangements."

Moussa couldn't think of anything to say.

"I understand, Moussa," Khaled said, "it's hard. Let's go sit down, take some coffee and really talk. Right here," he pointed to the nargeellah shop.

They ordered two nargeellahs and sat in silence, eyes nearly closed, as they sucked on the pipes. Moussa counted in his head to fifty, a respectable time to wait before talking. He tried to compose his face into a nonchalant expression, then cleared his throat again.

"Thank you for what you said about helping Moulleek going to school. It's a great honor for us. I will think about it, for sure. But . . . actually, I wanted to ask you something. About something else that happened a few years ago."

Khaled looked at Moussa with great surprise and then peered closely at his face.

"What?"

"Do you know anything about a ship that exploded in the Haifa harbor this time of year, four years ago? Something to do with the Yahoud."

"The Yahoud?" Khaled frowned.

"Yes, on the ship that exploded. Many drowned. That's what I heard"

Khaled drew his eyebrows towards the bridge of his nose where his thick black glasses rested. He ran his index finger and thumb along his moustache, from the middle to the fine-point edges and back.

"Let me think . . . four years ago? I'm twenty-eight now, so I would've been twenty-four. So just a few months after my marriage."

"What a wedding it was!" Moussa said.

"Ameena . . . " a smile spread on Khaled's face. "Such a beauty she was."

"A real beauty! Still is, if I may be permitted to say that," Moussa bowed slightly.

Khaled put his fingertips to his lips and kissed them. "So many years I dreamed of her until our wedding," he seemed to sail somewhere far away. "You know what I mean, Moussa, right? You dreamed about your Youssra?"

"Five years," Moussa said and couldn't help a shy smile spread across his face.

"Five years!" Khaled exclaimed.

"And still."

"Even though she can't . . . " Khaled coughed awkwardly.

"Even though. She is my Aisha," Moussa looked down to hide his blushing. "N-N-Not that I dare compare myself to the Prophet . . . I mean the feeling, not the age. Certainly not the importance and holiness."

"Of course, my friend," Khaled said warmly, trying to help Moussa out of his discomfort. "And you have Moulleek. It doesn't matter where he came from, only where he is going. And that's why I said what I did about sending him to school."

"Yes, yes. I understand, of course. Thank you. I will speak with Youssra and come back to you."

"Good," Khaled said and started to rise.

"But wait, please" Moussa pleaded, "what can you remember from that time?"

"That time?"

"What we were talking about before. Four years ago. The ship that exploded."

"Ah, the Yahoud and the ship exploding in the port," Khaled repeated, pressing into the back of his chair. "You know, there have been so many shootings, bombings, explosions. Us and the Jews against each other, the Italians and the Germans against the British. The British against us. Who can recall the details? I do remember that not long ago, this summer, the port was bombed by airplanes."

"I remember that one."

"So many people killed. Many injured, too. And so much damage . . . But let me see," Khaled scratched his chin, "four years ago: that was different. People were still talking then about whether the Germans would take Palestine."

"I remember —until the British won in Egypt, right?"

"Exactly. You know, at that time some of my friends thought it would be good for us, Arabs; help us against the Jews."

"What would be good?"

"If the Germans conquered Palestine."

"Really? Did you think so?"

"Not at all. To me, Moussa, and I wasn't the only one, there was plenty to worry about: what the Germans would do to us too, not just to the Jews."

"They don't like us much either, ha?"

"I don't think so, despite what the Mufti tells us. Now, about that ship: as far as I remember, the British controlled the Mediterranean coast near Palestine, so who could've bombed a ship that inside the Haifa harbor? It was already in the port, you said, right?"

"Yes."

Khaled inhaled slowly from the *nargeellah*. Moussa stared at his face as if hoping to see the thoughts unfold in his mind.

"Oh, yes! Now I remember."

"You do? What?" Moussa sat up, straight as a plank.

"There was a ship full of Jews; trying to infiltrate into Palestine. They had no papers but thought they could sneak in under the British' noses. Several ships like that came."

"Several ships?" Moussa asked just as a long-sealed memory of rowing towards a dilapidated boat began to unfold.

"Yes, from Europe—running from the Germans. The British

were going to deport them. The Arab leadership was pleased to see them enforcing the White Paper."

"White Paper?"

"Don't you know it, Moussa? It was a British declaration restricting Jewish immigration to Palestine. There are too many Jews here already."

"Yes, Khaled, I know the White Paper you mean."

"Well, here in Haifa they are taking over, soon they will be more than us."

"You think so, Khaled?"

"Well, maybe I'm exaggerating. But you see how they get all the good jobs from the British? All we get are the manual jobs. Hard work and very little pay."

"You're right. And I heard in the village that they are buying our lands, too. Still," Moussa went on, surprising himself, "people say that many of them are doctors, engineers, rich businessmen, from the best universities in the world, from the big cities back in their countries. They can help build things up here."

"Yes. That's why I say education, Moussa! That's why you should send your boy to school," Khaled said, pleased with the triumph of his point.

"Yes, yes. But that ship, Khaled. What else?" Moussa maneuvered the conversation back.

"Ah, yes, your ship . . . " Khaled took another long inhalation from his nargeellah. "As I remember, the ship was standing in the harbor full of passengers. The British were going to send them away, somewhere far from here, but it exploded with all of them on board. People said the Yahoud did it, but why bomb their own people?"

"Wait! Now I remember something about it, too!" Moussa exclaimed. "I overhead some guys . . . the *Shabbab* types. One of them said the Arab Resistance did it. But the others laughed at him."

"Who knows? In truth, nobody knows much of anything about what was really going on then; and these days, too."

Khaled shook his head and slowly exhaled a long train of pungent vapor.

"What about the passengers on the ship. They drowned?"

"Many did. Hundreds."

"So many?" Moussa was shocked.

"So people said. Women, children, old people. Terrible. They were refugees, those poor people. Running away from Hitler," Khaled's empathic tone surprised Moussa.

"Not soldiers?" Moussa asked, though he already knew.

"Some soldiers —British ones. They were on the boat to control the Jews. Some of them drowned, too."

"Were any people saved?"

"Yes, most of them—there were over two thousand on the ship —pulled out of the water and from the ship. It sank slowly. I heard a lot of our Arab fishermen helped save people," Khaled said, a hint of pride in his voice.

"Really? Nobody said anything to me. None of my friends."

"Maybe they did not want . . . you know, people to know they saved Jews."

"What happened to them after they were saved?" Moussa continued after a quiet moment between them.

"The Jews?" Khaled looked puzzled.

"Yes."

"The British took them somewhere. I don't know what happened to them then."

"I see."

"Sorry, I don't really know more. But I could find out if you explain to me what you need the information for."

Moussa froze, frantic for an explanation that would not lead the conversation any further.

"Don't worry about it, Khaled. It's not that important. Just something a Jew had thrown at me, accusing me. As if I —we Arabs —were somehow responsible."

"A Jew said that to you? Where? How?"

Moussa froze. "P-p-please, Kh-khaled - "

"What's the matter?"

"Please! My hand is on your belt. Don't tell anyone. Don't spread the word."

"What word?"

"Once in a while, when I really need money, I do some moving jobs for the Jews," Moussa blurted out. Khaled raised an eyebrow.

"Not very often," Moussa hastened to add. "And I charge them higher prices."

"What's it to me?" Khaled said. "My one ear is of clay and the other of dough."

"Thank you," Moussa let out the breath trapped in his windpipe.

"I understand," Khaled said "don't worry."

Before he could calm his breath Moussa rushed to change the subject. "How are your two girls?"

"Oh, wonderful! Wonderful girls," Khaled grinned broadly. "And," he bent closer to Moussa's ear, "another one is on the way."

"May it please Allah that this one will be a boy," Moussa said.

"Kullu min Allah," Khaled answered, as he was obliged to, but then a smile spread across his face. "Inshallah! If it's a boy he would be the last grape in the bunch."

"Really, the last?"

"Three is enough," Khaled said definitively. His face suddenly clouded.

He must have realized it was painful for me to hear this, Moussa thought, *he's a good man* . . . He smiled at Khaled to show him it was fine and put a handful of coins on the brass-plate table. Getting up to leave, he told Khaled again that he would talk to Youssra right away about Moulleek starting school.

"You do us a great honor, Khaled!"

Chapter 8

Moussa walked home feeling unsteady on his feet. *I must look like I need a cane, or like I've been drinking, may Allah forgive me! If anyone sees me like this, rumors will fly.* He forced himself to straighten his back and step more confidently. It was hard, as the threads he'd pieced together now twined into a rope around his neck. Their Moulleek had been on that ship, had survived but never found his parents and baby brother. Instead, he had found him the next day in the wooden crate. He'd thought he saved the boy, but now he knew: he'd actually stolen him from his parents.

Did they come back to the dock the next day to look for him? And the next day, and the next? How had he convinced himself so easily that he knew that the boy had been abused and abandoned? Was it just a little bit, just a hint, because he was so eager to have him as his own? Was that the real reason he and Youssra never did much to find the boy's family?

Moussa, Moussa . . . where's your mind running to? he chided himself. But then it hit him and knocked the wind out of him: the boy doesn't know his parents are alive! Surely, even though mute, he would have shown somehow that he wanted to go back to his parents if he thought they were alive. Or maybe a four-year-old child could not think this through? Was he just utterly baffled and gradually nestled into his new life, the memory of his parents fading likes wisps of vapor? And the parents —did they believe he'd drowned that day?

Moussa felt a rip inside his chest and his knees nearly buckled. Slow down, he told himself and fastened his eyes on his feet to steady his steps. He took a long, winding way home, trying to manufacture a plan. His eyes were wide open all along his way but saw nothing. The lady holding the picture to her chest kept flashing before them.

At home he found Youssra in the very same spot where she had sunk onto the mattresses, gathered into a ball. She barely lifted her head when he entered. He called her name softly. She looked at him with a question in her eyes.

"Yes. It seems so . . . "

She shook her head and looked away. Clearly now was not the time to go into any details.

Moussa went to the kitchen and cut up some onions, radishes, and parsley. The lump of dough was sitting where Youssra had left it. It had risen all this time and was now quite plump, its skin stretched like that of a very pregnant belly. He didn't even ask Youssra about taking it out to bake in the taboun. They'll make do with stale pita left from yesterday. He prepared two plates, each with vegetables, a handful of olives, hummus, and the dry pita. He handed Youssra a plate, but she averted her eyes and shook her head, as he had known she would. He put it by her and sat next down and ate slowly. It was so quiet he thought she could hear his teeth grinding the food and his throat closing when he swallowed.

"Moulleek will probably be coming home soon. What are we going to say?"

"Nothing," she shouted.

He recoiled. "Nothing?"

"Nothing now," she lowered her voice, "we must think first. And nothing until after we celebrate his birthday."

They had celebrated his birthday on the day Moussa had found him. The fourth one was coming up in a week. Moussa agreed and lightly touched Youssra's arm. His eyes sought hers, but she stared into the corner. She sank her face into her hands. Tears trickled down between her fingers.

At sunset, Moulleek came in. His face was flushed from playing outside in the chilly wind and his curls flew every which way. Youssra handed him her untouched plate, and he plunged into the food, oblivious to the way they embraced him with their eyes. Moulleek cleaned the last of the hummus, circling the rim of his plate with his index finger. Moussa and Youssra exchanged glances, confirming they would carry on as if nothing had happened.

Youssra rose in awkward jolts, as if her body were a half-broken apparatus. She shuffled to the kitchen and pounded the dough down into eight rounds. She went out to the taboun and raked the coals, rekindling the fire with some dry twigs. Moussa asked Moulleek about his friends, the games they'd played and trees he climbed. Every word was like a slash in is flesh, every nod Moulleek offered in response, like salt on in.

Finally, Youssra came back with fresh pitas. Moulleek ate most of them. The evening passed so slowly that Moussa felt the time as an ache in his bones. One glance told him Youssra did too. Thankfully, it being November, nightfall came early. Moulleek had played hard all day, so he fell asleep curled in the corner of the mattress they had spread out after dinner.

They prepared for bed in silence, praying they'd sink into the oblivion of sleep quickly. Let a little time pass, Moussa thought, it will help. Maybe an understanding of what they should do will emerge on its own. Maybe Allah will send a signal. They lay side by side, each making their own blanket into a cocoon, a lone traveler down the mind's paths.

Chapter 9

Moussa rose earlier than usual the next morning, hoping to make his exit before Youssra awoke. It would be easier that way. Just for now, he told himself. He bundled up and stuffed the leftover pita, hardened and dry, into his satchel. He tiptoed to the door and opened it with great care so it wouldn't squeak.

He entered the port, hanging onto hope that a day at sea would help him reach a decision. He launched his boat quickly and outside of the harbor let it float of its own accord. He cast his net, offering a perfunctory prayer for Allah's benevolence.

It was almost as if the fish were tired of the frigid water and wanted to be caught. In an hour, his buckets brimmed with fish. He did not want to waste this stroke of luck, so he continued fishing past his usual late morning hour, dragging additional fish in a small net cinched with rope and tied to the back of the boat. As soon as he docked, he found several of his usual buyers waiting. Evidently other fishermen hadn't been as lucky. He sold his catch at excellent prices, doing so well that he decided to bring home two beautiful fish. One for them, the other for Khaled, to thank him for his help and encourage him to keep the conversation in confidence.

At home Youssra was kneading new dough. Her hands were fully immersed in the task, but her eyes were elsewhere. Moussa put the fish in a pan with water.

"Good fishing this morning. I was lucky today, Youssra."
"I have to see her."
"What?"
"I have to see her first," Youssra repeated.
"Who?"
"The mother."
"The mother? Why?"
"Because . . . I have to, Moussa.

Moussa shook his head. How could that possibly happen? They'd have to go into the Jewish neighborhood, which was dangerous enough, and then . . . what? Though he was fairly certain he could find the apartment, he demanded: "How? On what pretext would I come to the door? Disguised as fruit peddler? Buying old clothes? These tricks might have worked in calmer times, but not now!"

Youssra held her hand up.

"I've already thought of all these questions."

"Really?"

"Yes, I have a plan," she said with a confidence Moussa had never seen.

"A plan?"

"Yes, disguised as Jews."

"As Jews! Are you —"

"Yes!" Youssra shot back so fast and loud, Moussa shrank back. He swallowed his pride and asked incredulously: "Jews looking for a job?"

"Yes. It won't be that hard. We . . . "

"We?" Moussa registered only now that she was speaking in the plural.

"Yes, we! We put on some old clothes like they wear."

"How?" Moussa tried to catch up.

"You can buy them in the street by the port. Then all you just take off your kaffiyeh and put on an old hat."

"Maybe I could do that . . . But you?"

"I, too. I'll put my hair up under a hat and wear men's clothes. We'll get through the Jewish streets and come to the lady's apartment. You can find it, right?"

"Yes, but . . . "

"But what, Moussa?"

"She will recognize me as soon as I speak."

"You'll say you came back for a job; anything she needs help with. She is a kind person, don't you think?" Youssra's voice wavered a bit.

"I think so . . . "

"She won't harm us, right?" Youssra pressed him.

"Youssra! This is such a risky plan!"

"Yes, but Allah will help us."

"And what would Allah think of you disguising yourself as a man? That's blasphemous!"

"Not in His eyes."

Moussa shook his head but had to admit: with her slender figure and small breasts, she could pull it off.

"I don't think so . . . I don't know," he mumbled, but already knew he wouldn't be able to budge her. She was generally very accommodating, never complained and never nagged. She bore the pain of their infertility with a quiet, plaintive sadness. But when she felt she had to have her way, usually about Moulleek's welfare, she was as tenacious as that old mulberry tree behind the house. "Small and scraggly, but totally unmovable," Moussa said under his breath.

"What?" Youssra asked.

"Nothing," Moussa said, hearing his father's oft repeated words when he dealt stubborn customers: "Keep the donkey where its owner wants it." He saw no alternative but told Youssra he would have to think about it and consult with Ali, who frequented the Jewish neighborhoods.

"Don't worry," Moussa said, "I won't give him a hint about why."

"Be careful. Think what you'll say in advance. Word for word."

"Exactly. Fortunately, he is no Ali Baba, not a thimbleful of cunning in the man."

"Thank Allah for that."

Youssra prepared Moussa a snack while he sat on the low stool mulling over his next steps. "While I plan this, Youssra, you decide on a special birthday celebration for Moulleek. Maybe we can even splurge and buy pastries from *Al-Tamira*."

"Really? Al-Tamira? That's the fanciest bakery!" Youssra looked at Moussa, amazed to hear him suggest such a luxury.

"Yes," he said, gulping down the words on the tip of his tongue, *it will be his last birthday with us.* He counted out the largest coins he'd earned that day and Youssra slipped them into the leather pouch tucked under her dress.

Chapter 10

Three days later they were ready to set out. Neither of them could get down more than a few bites of pita and half a glass of weak tea with two sprigs of mint. "Good to calm the stomach," Youssra urged Moussa to drain the glass. After they pecked at the pita, she packed the rest in her satchel for later. They will get hungry and she knew they would not dare buy food in the Jewish neighborhood. She made Moulleek put his sleeveless sweater on over his shirt before going out to play with his friends.

"Baba and I have to go to town. Stay near the house. We'll be back by lunchtime." She cringed when she realized she was thankful that he couldn't ask where they were going.

They went to the main street where Ali was waiting with his cart and donkey at the end of the block.

"Since Ali doesn't want me to ask too many questions about his business in the Jewish neighborhood, he didn't ask any about ours," Moussa reassured Youssra. As they reached Ali, Youssra caught him raise an eyebrow when he saw she was coming too. But he said nothing.

"You know where we did the moving job last week?" Moussa said in a hushed voice, "that's where we need to go."

"So that's where I take you!" Ali said, keeping a blank face that made it clear he wasn't going to ask any questions.

The cart climbed up, weaving back and forth along streets leading diagonally up the mountainside. On Herzl Street, the main thoroughfare, Ali skillfully maneuvered between cars, buses and carts much larger and fancier than his.

"Here," Moussa told Ali.

"I know," he said and stopped the cart. Youssra flashed Moussa a smile, impressed that he knew his way around the Jewish part of town where she had never been.

She removed the large dark shawl she was wrapped in. Ali frowned, then quickly looked away, when he saw she was wearing pants, a man's shirt and hat. Moussa gave him a wink. Good, he was letting Ali know they appreciated his discretion, now and later, when they all got back to their neighborhood. She rolled up the shawl and stuffed it into the canvas satchel, quickly hooking the bag over her shoulder. She ran her fingers around the rim of her cap to make sure no strands of hair showed. "Ready, Moussa," she whispered. She took Moussa's offered hand to climb down from the cart. He gestured to the right and started walking.

A jolt of panic—she almost lost her footing. She was in totally foreign territory! Not just the neighborhood and its potential dangers; she'd never walked side by side with her husband, nor any man, for that matter. Back in her village, women walked in deference a few steps behind any male relative. How many times had her mother chastised her when she was little and ran ahead of the family as they walked through the village? True, some of the women in the Haifa neighborhood didn't follow this custom, but she had clung to her village ways.

Now, to pass as a man, she must appear as Moussa's equal. It was a strange feeling, frightening but also exciting. The world looks different without a man's back in front of your nose. And not just the world... she looked nothing like herself to the world around her and to whomever may be watching over it. She apologized to Allah in her heart. It is for a worthy cause, she explained to the Merciful One.

Before she could get the full measure of this new experience, the sights around her overwhelmed Youssra. So many shops, so many people who looked and dressed so differently! Everyone walking swiftly, going in and out of stores, carrying their purchases in bags of all sizes. Some women walked arm in arm with men, others strutted on their own like confident queens.

"The shops look completely different than ours," she exclaimed.

"Shah! Don't speak so loudly."

"Sorry," she lowered her voice, "but, look, such big windows! And see the high ceilings and beautiful lighting?"

"Youssra! Are we looking at the shops or doing what we came for?"

"I know, Moussa. Of course, but we can walk just a little slower and look quickly. I am never going to be here again . . . "

"Alright," Moussa slowed his pace; she was right. "You can look. But let's not talk."

Youssra's eyes devoured the merchandise in the shops. She'd never seen such elegant displays, arranged in glass windows instead of stacked on the sidewalk. She longed to feel between her fingers the fine wool suits for women, touch the velvet hats, each with a feather or artificial flower tucked into a silk ribbon. Another store had clocks and watches in gold, silver and elaborately carved wood. She turned her head back to hold them in her sight as long as she could, but then forced herself to look forward. She must keep her eyes on the pavement and step carefully; it wouldn't do to fall now.

Another storefront startled her —a bookshop. Shelves and shelves of books in all sizes, bound in colorful paper or rich brown leather.

"Look," she tugged on Moussa's arm, whispering, "can you believe how many books they have? I had no idea there were so many books in the world!"

"Sh . . . sh, don't attract any attention to us," Moussa hushed her, but she could tell he, too, was stunned by the display. She felt dizzy and wished she could hold Moussa's hand but, remembering she was passing as a man, thought it might look odd here.

Moussa sensed her agitation. He slowed down and brushed his upper arm against hers. She took a deep breath and matched her stride to his. Soon he turned into an alley off the main street. They passed three large houses on the right, and Moussa stopped: "Here, this one."

She scanned the three-story apartment building's walls, originally whitewashed, now a tired beige, discolored where water had run down the sides.

"What floor?"

"Third."

They waited to see if anyone would come out of the building. Three people did and, without noticing them, rushed away.

"Must be hurrying to their jobs," Youssra whispered to Moussa.

Several people crossed the alley but took no notice of them beyond a vague nod. Youssra saw the relief in Moussa's eyes.

"It seems we don't stand out, Youssra. No one can tell we are Arabs." They took a deep breath simultaneously and she knew they were in agreement - now was the time. They entered the building and climbed to the third floor.

"Let me to do all the talking," Moussa whispered.

"Like I would dare to open my mouth . . ."

They rested at every landing, so as not to get winded. At the top they stopped for a moment to get ready. Youssra smiled at Moussa in encouragement. He looked into her eyes to screw up his courage.

He knocked on the door, first very softly, then a little louder. A woman called out, something Youssra didn't understand. They heard steps coming to the door. Youssra saw how Moussa's body tightened. He hunched his shoulders. She stopped breathing altogether.

The door opened and there she stood. Youssra's first thought was that she was too tall for a woman: frightening. But the blond, wavy hair that grazed the woman's shoulders and her flower-print blouse softened her. Moussa nodded almost imperceptibly, letting Youssra know it was the same lady. The woman glanced at both of them, and then focused on Moussa's face, a frown on her forehead. Youssra's stomach spasmed. Just then the woman's face seemed to relax.

"The moving man, yes? Why you come back?"

Moussa tripped on the English phrase he'd rehearsed earlier with Youssra.

"G-G-Good job . . . no? Good Lady, m-m-more job for me, please. Is possible?"

Youssra felt a swell of pride. He can speak the language! The only words she had known were "Lady" and "job," but as Moussa had earlier practiced the words over and over at home, she understood the whole sentence.

Chapter 11

What does he want? Gertie wondered. They were hemmed in at the apartment door. She worried for an instant: was she putting Benyamin and herself in danger? But she dismissed it. Something had passed between her and this man when she told him about her Emil. Surely, he meant no harm. The younger man next to him - perhaps his brother? - seemed innocuous too. So slender and delicate —probably just a boy —but already must work to help support his family. She opened the door wide and invited them in.

"Mama, who is this?" Benyamin dropped his book and looked startled, maybe even afraid.

"Nice people. Don't worry."

The boy approached, eyeing them warily, and snuggled into her skirt. She put her hand on his head and played with his bouncy curls.

"Who are they, Mama?"

"They're workers. It's all right, Liebling. Don't be afraid. Go look at your book. Mama is a little busy."

He ran off and she turned to them and with an apologetic smile: she was sorry, she had no job for them. But something made her keep the door open; she did want to do something to help them. She looked around.

"One moment," she said and used the gesture she had often seen in the street, her thumb joined with the first two fingers, dancing up and down. She walked to the kitchen and came back with a half a loaf of yesterday's bread.

"Here, you take. Bread. Is good."

Youssra could see that Moussa hesitated. She knew he didn't want a handout but wasn't sure if it would be an insult not to accept the bread. He bowed his head and took it, dropping it into his bag.

"Thank you, Lady. I come back for job tomorrow?"

"No," she said, "no come back. No job here."

Gertie wanted to say more. To warn him: it was dangerous for them to come to this neighborhood. True, they had disguised themselves well and could pass as Jews in these clothes, but the moment they opened their mouths people would spot them as Arabs. And who knows what would happen then. Each side was terrified of the other. How many rumors of knifings had she heard already? She was about to shut the door, but something stopped her. The porter's gentle gaze when he looked at Emil's picture flashed before her, the way he'd said: "He look sweet."

"Wait," she said, "one minute, please." She felt compelled to do more, find some kind of job she could give the man and his brother; a gesture of kindness. She went into the bedroom for a burlap bag filled with clothes Benyamin had outgrown. She'd planned to give them to the kindergarten teacher to pass on to poor families. Hanukkah was next week, and people would be thankful for anything to give their children as holiday gifts.

But she needed a second package for the younger man. The box with cans of food she had put aside for charity would do. It was about time to take Benyamin to kindergarten anyway, so all the pieces of this sudden puzzle were fitting together.

She dragged the bag across the floor to the living room.

"This," she said, "this I need your help to carry."

"Yes, Madam," Moussa said eagerly. "I do. I carry. And for boy to carry?"

"For the boy, I know," Gertie said and signaled Moussa to follow her to the balcony and pick up the food box. "The boy to take this one, yes?"

"Yes, he take!" Moussa bowed.

"Good," she said, "you just to wait one, two minutes."

Moussa bowed again. "Thank you, good lady."

"Time to go to kindergarten, Benyamin," Gertie called out. The boy put his book on the small bookshelf and put his hand in hers. She licked her palm and tried to flatten his hair, but the curls bounced right back up. She put a jacket on him and kissed his cheek, then pulled a shawl around her shoulders.

"Yallah," she called out, proud she knew the Arabic word.

"Yallah, Yallah," Moussa answered. He picked up the bag and flipped it over his back. He nudged Youssra to pick up the box. She lifted it and found it was heavier than she'd expected. She raised it up, ready to put it on her head but Moussa nudged her, his eyes wide in alarm. *Of course! Only women carry things on their heads!* She glanced at Moussa, who nodded and handed her the bag he was holding, then picked up the box.

"Shukran," she mouthed and slung the bag over her shoulder.

They stepped out and walked down the stairs, following the woman and her boy. They knew to stay a few paces behind. Youssra was thankful: this way, she could freely observe mother and child. The boy addressed his mother with great excitement. Youssra leaned forward slightly to capture every nuance in the mother's voice. It was soft, enveloping, warm. Youssra's heart softened despite herself. She couldn't deny the recognition: a good mother. Nor could she ignore the striking similarity between this boy and hers. Not, of course, in his speech. Moulleek still did not talk. But in the way he moved, the way he titled his head up towards his mother's face, the way he held her hand.

The walk seemed to Youssra as if it were nearly as long as the walk from the village to Haifa. And yet, once they entered a small yard through a creaky metal gate, it seemed as though it had passed in a heartbeat. The woman gestured for them to put the things down on the front porch. She pulled a purse out of her handbag and handed Moussa a large handful of coins. Youssra saw that he was too nervous to look at the amount.

"Thank you, Lady. You very good," Moussa said and Youssra joined by bowing her head and clasping her hands together.

"Goodbye," the woman said and waved. The little boy did too.

Youssra wanted to turn around and run. She knew Moussa did too. She was at the end of her capacity to reign in her anxiety. Moussa's straining neck muscles told her he was too.

"Be careful!" the woman called after them, took the boy's hand and entered the house. As soon as she closed the door behind her, Moussa and Youssra bolted out of the yard, then down the street. Moussa sought the narrowest lanes to lead them down the slope towards the port and the safety of their neighborhood.

They maneuvered through mostly deserted alleys. Youssra drifted back to her customary place, a few paces behind her husband. He slowed down each time and let her catch up. Once out of the Jewish neighborhood Youssra pulled her shawl out of her bag and re-wrapped herself up, partially veiling her face. She sank into the comfort of her familiar dress and body habits, safely trailing Moussa. The shaking in her knees took a long time to subside. They walked in a silence she was grateful for. So many thoughts were pent up inside her that, were she to open her mouth, they would tumble out as marbles spill from a pouch filled to bursting.

At home Youssra collapsed on the mattresses. Moussa sat by her and took her hand.

"So?"

She shook her head, her eyes filling. "Tomorrow," she whispered, "we'll talk tomorrow." She pulled her hand out of Moussa's grasp and covered her eyes. He tiptoed to the kitchen and took the bread out of his bag. He couldn't tell who looked at whom more accusingly: he at the bread or the bread at him. He was right to do it at that moment, but he hated taking alms. He picked up the bread to gauge its weight. Heavy! A much denser bread than what they were used to. He brought it up to his nose. Not bad —dense and a little sour and yeasty. Throw it out? No, they were not that well off; he was not that proud.

    He sliced two thick pieces. He chewed one slowly and put the other on a plate he laid next to Youssra. She glanced at him. He hoped it was thanks that he saw in her drawn face.

Chapter 12

Moussa stayed home the next morning, waiting to talk with Youssra. She slept and slept. When Moulleek got up, Moussa made him breakfast: a slice of bread with olive oil drizzled on it and a handful of olives. Moulleek looked at the plate, puzzled. "Yumma is still asleep," Moussa said. Moulleek glanced towards the mattresses, shrugged and turned to the plate.

What's this? Is this pita burnt?
Smell it.
No, not burnt. Just strange.
Better eat it anyway, so I can go play. I see the sun. No rain today.
This pita . . . it tastes like something else.
What?
Something I've eaten before.
So chewy! It's good.
What is it?
Not pita.
What?
Brot. That's what it is!
Bread! I used to eat it.
With butter and Konfitüre. Strawberry jam.
Not olives!
Brot und Butter.

Mama, can I have more?
I wanted more.
More butter, more Konfitüre.
Mama . . . Mama?
Where is Mama?

Moulleek pushed the plate away.

He looks angry, Moussa thought, doesn't like this bread. No wonder, he's used to Youssra's fresh baked pita every day. This is so different . . .

"All right, Moulleek, you don't have to eat it. Go play outside and come back when you're hungry. Yumma will make pita soon."

Moulleek cleared his plate and opened the door.

"Wait! Take your sweater," Moussa called out. He laughed —Youssra's words sounded funny coming out of his own mouth. Moulleek scooted to the shelf where his neatly folded clothes sat in a small pile. The sweater was on top. Moulleek pulled it over his head and rushed outside.

When the door banged shut, Youssra opened her eyes and scanned the room. Moulleek must have just gone out. Moussa was still there. The room is warm . . . and the light so bright. Must be terribly late. *The baking!* She rose slowly. Every movement registered another part of her body that ached; shoulders, neck, pelvis. She looked at her arms and legs: where were the bruises she felt? She laid her palms against her chest; it felt as if it had been ripped open, then hastily sewn shut.

She pulled her dress over her nightclothes in jagged movements, as if her limbs were wooden planks. She made herself rinse her face with cold water. It did not wash away what felt like a heavy mask clamped onto her skin. She rolled up the mattress and sank down on it. Moussa slunk towards her, as if he were a thief entering a strange house.

"She has another child." Youssra's voice was so raspy Moussa got up and brought her a glass of water.

"She does, but..."

"Moussa! We will have nothing!"

"We have each other..."

"You don't make a jug of oil from two olives."

Moussa gritted his teeth, "But Youss..."

"She has one and we have one. Isn't that justice?"

"I... I don't know."

"Why would The Merciful One bring him to us and then take him away?"

"I don't know," Moussa laced his fingers together and rolled his thumbs around each other.

Youssra wrapped her palms around Moussa's hands to stop the twirling.

"Moussa, I can't."

He didn't answer. He clasped his hands tightly but then released them and started turning one thumb around the other again.

"What?" Youssra said. "I know you have something to say when you do that."

Moussa forced himself to separate his hands and look into Youssra's eyes.

"It's like in the Holy Quran, Youssra. Don't you see? Like Yussuf."

"Like Yussuf?"

"His family... his brothers, they throw him in the well. Like we thought about Moulleek's family—that they threw him out."

"We did."

"But now we know they didn't. And even Yussuf, in the end, he forgives them and the family is back together."

Youssra shook her head and shivered. She pulled a blanket over her shoulders. If only she could just pull it over her head and disappear.

"Youssra..." Moussa said softly and touched her knee.

"So maybe when he's grown, we'll tell him," she said. "Then he can decide, like Yussuf did."

Moussa looked down at the floor, silent for a long time. Youssra could tell he was searching for another answer.

"Maybe it's more like what happened with Moussa," he finally said.

"You, Moussa?"

"No, also in the Holy Quran."

"How?"

"With Moussa, his mother put him into the river to save him. Then the daughter of Pharaoh found him and took him and raised him in the palace and . . ."

"I know that story, Moussa, as well as you."

"But don't you see, Youssra? In the end he has to go back to his people. He must. His real family comes first."

Youssra didn't answer.

"I have to go fishing, Youssra. We can't go two days without it," Moussa blurted out and rose to go.

Chapter 13

Youssra spent the day hunched over, embroidering a dress. Three times she pricked her finger. "Thank you," she whispered to the drop of blood rising on her thumb. She checked the dress: no stain. "Thank you for this, too." It was a dress for Ameena, Khaled's wife. She had come the week before to get measured and consult on the design.

"I am pregnant, Youssra. It's still a secret, but the dress is Khaled's gift, to celebrate and . . . "

"And?"

"Maybe it will help? He prays for a son this time, a boy, please Allah, every morning. I am sorry, Youssra. I shouldn't . . . "

"I'll pray for a boy for you, too. It's in the Merciful One's hands. Kullu min Allah."

"Kullu min Allah," Ameena echoed and nodded. "Thank you, but it's only for Khaled. For me it doesn't matter. Each child is a treasure, boy or girl, no matter how many you have." She placed her hands on her belly. "You would understand, Youssra, as a woman —even if you only have one . . . " Ameena slapped her hand across her mouth. Youssra lowered her head.

"I am sorry, Youssra! Inshallah you'll get pregnant too. You're not so old. Such things have happened."

"Thank you for your blessing. Come back next week. You'll be able to see how the pattern looks and still make changes if you wish."

The door had hardly shut behind Ameena when Youssra squeezed her eyes hard, trying to press the tears back up their ducts. Her mother's voice rang in her ears: "Envy is your biggest enemy."

Youssra began working on the dress immediately. Concentrating on the pattern would help keep her mind from going to that dark place. The Cypress trees Ameena had chosen seemed to be growing out of her fingers. She always felt a slight fluttering of her fingers when she thought about a new embroidery. She would stroke her fingertips along the pad of her thumb, the way her father ran his fingers along the amber beads of his *mishbaha* reciting the names of Allah ninety-nine times each day. Prayer beads were not for women, but to her, that sensation in her fingers before picking up the needle and thread was a kind of private supplication. Even now, with her state of mind —as if a huge crater had been dug in her brain —that sensation was there, a reassurance of something alive inside her.

Chapter *14*

When Moussa came home, Youssra was at work on a long row of Cypress trees, punctuated by the red, eight-pointed "Star of Bethlehem," an omen for fertility. He leaned in, eyes tracing the tiny stitches.

"Beautiful! How do you do it? The thread is so fine."

"That's why I'm bent over it like this." Youssra straightened her back.

"It's so delicate. Look at the little trees —Cypresses, right? And the Stars of Bethlehem are perfect —all the sides identical."

"You can see that," Youssra said, thankful. She cherished Moussa's eye for beauty, for her work. Her mother never got such appreciation from her husband. Her husband? Youssra chastised herself for the thought. He's your father! Yes, my father, she swallowed the lump in her throat.

When was it that she'd first realized how it was between her parents? How arid and harsh? Her father was not much more delicate than the donkeys he tended and sold. When did she first see how her mother suffered in silence? Was it that day she discovered her in tears by the taboun behind the house?

"From the smoke," her mother had said, but it was afternoon and the taboun's embers had died down long ago.

"Of course, I can see it," Moussa didn't hide the pride in his voice. He brought his nose to nearly touching the thread: "Such tiny stitches - all exactly the same length!"

"Thank Allah, I inherited my mother's hands and eyes."

"You sure did," Moussa swallowed, burying the words that lay on his tongue —"Too bad you didn't inherit her womb."

Youssra had bent back down quickly to squelch the very same words in her own head.

"Who is it for?" Moussa broke the awkward silence suddenly hanging between them.

"Ameena."

"Ameena? Khaled can afford another dress on his teacher's salary?"

"It's special. She is pregnant. But don't tell anyone. She told me in confidence."

"Khaled already told me."

"She made it seem like it was a big secret! I guess he doesn't keep them that well." She gave Moussa a sharp look. He understood —better not spill ours.

"When did he tell you?" Youssra asked softly, realizing Moussa had taken her glance as an accusation.

"When I asked him about the *Patria*."

"You asked Khaled?"

"The Qadi wasn't home. I ran into Khaled on the street. You didn't seem to want to hear details that day."

Youssra nodded. He was right.

"He won't say a word about what we discussed, he promised."

"What did you tell him?" Youssra gasped. "Did you put Moulleek together with the *Patria*?"

"No. But I had to say that I heard about the *Patria* from a Jew. How else could I explain it?"

"I see," she said but shook her head.

"I hope you do, Youssra. Then I had to explain talking to a Jew, so I told him about Ali's jobs and asked him to keep it in confidence."

"Hopefully he doesn't have any suspicions about Moulleek."

"Not at all. In fact, we talked a lot about Moulleek. I didn't sense any suspicion."

"You talked a lot about Moulleek?" Youssra stuck the needle into the cloth. She couldn't concentrate on the stitches.

"Yes. Khaled thinks Moulleek should start school."

"But, he doesn't . . . "

"That's exactly it. Khaled thinks that because he doesn't talk, he would do well reading and writing. He said this happens often. If you can't do one thing you are better at another; like blind people with hearing."

"I see," Youssra said.

"Khaled thinks Moulleek could read and write very well. He thinks Moulleek is clever. I said definitely, yes."

"Definitely!"

"So, he said: Moulleek could be an excellent student, go to high school, even university."

"University?"

What are you doing? Moussa yelled at himself in his head. *You know it can't happen. He must go back to them. Don't lead her on! It's utter foolishness. And cruel!* But his tongue moved much faster than his mind and the words tumbled out: "Yes, that's what he said. University —in Beirut or Cairo. Just imagine, our boy a real scholar."

"Our boy a scholar," Youssra let the words tickle her tongue. "Khaled said so?"

"He did. He said, 'Your boy could be a scholar or a writer; maybe even a poet.'"

"Our boy, a poet . . . " Youssra mouthed the words, but a strange look came over her. "But . . . "

Stop! Moussa warned himself, but he couldn't. "Our boy a famous man, ah? Moulleek Ibn Moussa. Moulleek Ibn Youssra."

"Stop, Moussa!" Youssra covered her ears.

"Stop?"

"Stop!"

Youssra clutched the embroidery to her chest and crumpled to the floor. Moussa rushed to help her.

"No!" she put her hand up to stop him.

He stared at her in incomprehension, then took a step forward. She waved him away. He shook his head and turned around, heading to the sink. He cupped his hands and drew water from the enamel basin and let it cool his face and run down his arms.

Chapter 15

Moussa left early the next morning without speaking to Youssra. He came home in the mid-afternoon. The fishing had been good; he'd made up for the missed days. He waved to Moulleek, up in the mulberry tree with a friend. Good, he would be able to talk to Youssra. The day before she had shut down completely after the conversation about Moulleek going to school. Now he must broach the question of taking him back to his parents, but how?

He entered the house and emptied his pockets, placing a big pile of coins on the table, right in front of Youssra's eyes.

"Not bad, eh?"

"We have to take him home, Moussa."

"What?"

"We have to take him up there. To his moth . . ." she gripped his hand, almost losing her balance. Moussa held onto her elbow. "Sit down, Youssra. You'll fall."

She let him support her as she took slow steps and lowered herself on top of the mattresses. He brought a stool and sat facing her.

"What are you saying, Youssra?"

"Back there. He has a mother."

"Yes," Moussa murmured, "I know. And a father and a brother. That's what I said." He cupped his hands over hers.

"You did. I couldn't before, but now I see it. We can't keep him away from his real family, now that we know."

Moussa nodded. His throat was too tight to speak.

"Even if it means we have nothing from now on," Youssra hammered it in.

CHAPTER 16

Moussa held his head in his hands, his elbows digging into his thighs. Youssra curled herself into a ball on top of the mattresses. After what seemed like a wordless eternity, she sat up and touched Moussa's shoulder and spoke, chiseling each word as if it were granite. They had to return him. They'll have to work out how. She only asks one thing: for Moussa to take Moulleek to a photographer, so she could keep a picture.

"Good idea," Moussa corralled his voice from where it had vanished. They both scanned the walls, flitting from the prayer rug to the mother-of-pearl mirror.

"Plenty of space," Moussa whispered.

"Maybe by the mirror, so it's next to something beautiful," Youssra said, but then gasped and clutched her breast, "We'll never see him again!"

"Most probably not."

Moussa squeezed his eyes shut, ordering the tears to dry up.

"I will no longer be a father," he blurted out.

"And I a... "

"How will we go on, Youssra?"

She shook her head and lay back down on the mattress, then turned towards the wall and gathered her knees up into her belly. She slung her arm over her face, covering her eyes. Moussa got up, pulled a shawl from the shelf and spread it over her.

He couldn't sit. He paced the length of the room and dug his fingers into his palms. His mind spun out thoughts as fast as a ball of yarn rolling down a steep slope; unraveling so fast you can't stop it. They would have to move out of the neighborhood. How could they tell people what happened? They'll go to a village where people didn't know about Moulleek, say they left because of the bombings in Haifa. People these days didn't ask much about such things. Everyone was afraid, whether they admitted it or not.

He would work for Youssra's family, tending their more distant olive groves and taking their sheep to the farthest pastures. They would not need much to live on. Youssra could still get work sewing, though not for the prices she got in Haifa. She could be with her family and help raise her nephews and nieces. Would that give her at least some succor?

Maybe Allah would reward them for this sacrifice with their own child? Youssra was still young enough. Didn't Allah reward Ibrahim for his almost sacrifice of Ishmael with the birth of Ishaq? Yes, the Quran says so. First, Allah stops Ibrahim's hand holding the knife over Ismael (how he'd trembled when he first heard the village storyteller recount this part!) and calls him "our believing servant." The very next verse says Allah rewards those who do what is right and announces the birth of Ishaq.

But he and Youssra have to go all the way through with their sacrifice. Wouldn't Allah see that and reward them? He can't speak to Youssra about it yet; she's not ready. After the photograph. Meanwhile, he must talk to the boy. Explain it slowly and patiently. Lay each step out while reassuring him of their love.

Youssra will help him find the right words. Tomorrow. And they'll make a plan for returning the boy to his parents. He cannot simply go there with Moulleek and tell them the story. Much too dangerous. What if they accuse him of kidnapping? Turn him in to the police? That would be the end of him.

Youssra made herself swim up from the black pit. She rose to knead the pita dough. She'd started it rising the night before; by now its outer crust was so distended it seemed it would burst at the touch of her finger. "Me, too," she said to the mound and, instead of the usual punching, gently nudged it flat. Moussa watched her form the rounds and go out to the courtyard to fire up the taboun.

She stayed outside for so long, Moussa came out to check on her.

"Almost done," Youssra said and picked up the conversation as if there'd been no pause. "We'll have to concoct a scheme for returning him."

"Yes."

"But not yet. Tomorrow, when our heads are fresh."

"Yes. It's very tricky. Maybe I should ask . . . "

"No! We can't consult anyone. Much too risky."

"Of course, I didn't mean . . . "

"Not a word to anyone," Youssra warned. "You know what my father always says: 'If you let a word out of your mouth, you can find it in the gutter of the marketplace the next day.'"

"My father said the same thing."

The pitas puffed up and Youssra stacked them in a basket. Moussa followed her back inside.

"Let them cool a little," she said and got her embroidery. But it sat in her lap as if it were a dead bird.

"How to explain it to Moulleek . . . ?" Youssra said almost to herself.

"Yes, how? You would know how," Moussa pleaded.

"I would know how . . . " she buried her face in her hands. "I would, but I can't. Not now. Let's just talk about the photo —how to explain that."

"That even I can do," Moussa said. "I'll tell him it's a birthday present. Something very special for him and for us."

"Good plan, Moussa."

"A photo, Youssra! We didn't even have a wedding picture taken."

"Well, in the village, who did? And in town, surely, we couldn't afford it."

She got up and dragged her feet, one small pace after the other, to the kitchen. She placed four pitas on a small tray, piling next to them green onion stalks, a patty of labane, and a handful of olives.

"We should eat something, Moussa. Calm our stomachs. I know mine is in knots."

They ate in silence. His second pita nearly finished, Moussa looked towards the door.

"Shall I go get Moulleek now? Are you ready?"

"Now. Do it now. I can't bear this much longer."

Moussa pushed the last bite of pita into his mouth and stood up. The instant he went out Youssra collapsed on the floor, but then made herself get up. You must hold yourself in one piece for Moulleek, she commanded.

In a minute Moussa was back with Moulleek, face flushed and hands muddy.

"I told him about the special treat, going to the photographer! I also promised a stop at the bakery afterwards," Moussa said with an apologetic smile.

"You are in the mood to splurge," Youssra chided him jokingly, letting him know with a glance: they must keep up the cheery appearance for Moulleek's sake.

"I'll bring you a piece, too," Moussa said, signaling agreement with a flutter of his eyelids.

"That would be really nice. But don't pay too much."

Chapter 17

Youssra poured some water from the kettle into a shallow basin. "Now I must wash his hair," she announced.

"Wouldn't that take too long? Can't you make do with washing his face and combing his hair?"

She agreed reluctantly. "His curls fly in all directions anyway, even after I wash his hair. But take a comb with you, Moussa. Wait a minute!" Youssra went to the small chest against the wall and opened a top drawer. "Here you go," she fished out a small comb. Moussa put it in his shirt pocket. "Now you stay there until it's your time," he told the comb and patted it.

Moulleek was so excited he didn't squirm one bit when Youssra cleaned his face with a wet rag. He gladly put his hands out for her to wipe as well. Wrapping each finger with the damp washcloth, Youssra made herself speak buoyantly: "So, where are you taking our beautiful boy for his photo, Moussa?"

"To Fadeel Sabba's, of course," Moussa said, mimicking Youssra's bright tone. "Fadeel is the best. Everybody says so."

"I've heard that," Youssra said. *Keep going,* she urged herself as she noticed Moulleek's grin get even bigger, *you are doing this well.* "He's the one that worked with that lady photographer in Nazareth, right?"

"Yes, Youssra. Fadeel even has her photographs in his shop

window. When I was in Nazareth once I saw them displayed in her shop."

"She has her own shop?"

"With another photographer. There's a big sign: 'Karimeh Abbud - Lady Photographer.' She takes pictures of places in the Galilee; the holy places for the Christians. She sells to them."

"They buy from her?" Youssra raised an eyebrow.

"Yes, she's very popular. She paints the photographs with colors after she makes them."

"Really?" Youssra marveled. Then she puckered her lips and frowned. "Wait a minute, Moussa, the camera takes pictures of things exactly as they really are in real life, no?"

"Yes, exactly."

"So how does it take the colors out?"

"Well, Youssra, don't you see? Mmm . . . I don't know," Moussa shrugged.

"But she puts the colors back in?"

"Yes. How, is her special secret."

"Well, I'd like to see her photographs someday, Moussa. Especially now that we will have one of our own."

Every finger had been scrubbed, Youssra realized, at least twice. She put the washcloth down and tried to straighten Moulleek's shirt collar, but there was not much point. It was too worn and misshapen. She wet her palms and smoothed down his curls. "Hopeless," she muttered as they bounced right back.

"Ready for the photographer!" she announced and Moulleek rushed to the door.

Moussa joined him, his steps much heavier.

The moment they were out the door Youssra let her body take over. A violent abdominal convulsion and wave of vertigo sucked her into a swirling undertow. She had to crawl on her hands and knees to the back door. She pulled herself along the side of the house to the far corner and vomited. The first surge brought up the pita, the second only sour fluids.

When the heaves subsided, Youssra wiped her sweaty forehead with the edge of her sleeve and shuffled back inside on wobbly legs. She fell onto the mattress and pulled a blanket over herself. She burrowed under it and curled in a fetal position. Moussa and Moulleek should be far enough by now, she told herself, and let the wails out of the cage where she'd held them so long.

Moussa put his hand on Moulleek's shoulder as they walked into the street, wistful for the days when Moulleek held his hand. They passed many shops on the main street but Moulleek paid no attention. At the photographer's studio he sat up on the stool, straight back, hands on his knees. Behind him was a backdrop with a mountain, palm trees and camel. He pointed to the camel, rocked back and forth as if he were riding on its hump, and flashed Moussa a big smile.

Fadeel took several shots and congratulated Moulleek: "Very nice pose, young man. As if you've done it a hundred times. You know, young man, rich and important people have their pictures taken here."

Moulleek smiled but shot Moussa a puzzled look.

"Inshallah, one day you will be important too, maybe even rich," Moussa said.

"Inshallah," Fadeel echoed with a friendly slap on Moulleek's back.

"And now," Moussa announced as Moulleek slid off the stool, "to the pastry shop, Al-Tamira! The fanciest in town, just as I promised."

Moulleek danced more than walked to the pastry shop. Inside, the fragrant pastry made Moussa's mouth water.

"Choose whatever you want, Moulleek."

Moulleek took his time running his eyes back and forth across the display case. Finally, he pointed to the baklava.

"Baklava! The best, isn't it?" Moussa grinned.

"Please, Hassan," he said to the heavy-set shopkeeper, "a double piece of baklava, for the boy." Hassan bent down and slid a large piece unto a square of cardboard. Moulleek's eyes followed his every movement.

"There you go, walad," Hassan handed Moulleek the cardboard tray as if it were a jewel-encrusted crown on a velvet pillow. Moulleek brought it close to his face. He squinted, trying to look through the paper-thin flakes, then sniffed the honey-soaked chopped nuts. He took his first bite with his eyes closed. He chewed slowly and swallowed, and his mouth turned up in a moon-shaped grin. He lifted the baklava towards Moussa, offering him a taste. "Just a tiny one," Moussa said and bit off the corner.

"And a piece for my wife," Moussa turned to the shopkeeper. He pulled a handful of coins out of his pocket and put them down on the glass counter. The shopkeeper picked out a few coins. "Shukran, that will cover it." He placed a piece on a cardboard tray which he set on a sheet of butcher paper, making a small tent by tightly twisting the corners at the top.

"Hold it by the tip so the paper doesn't stick to the pastry," he instructed Moussa and passed him the small package, to be carried between two fingers and thumb.

They took their time on the way home. Moulleek stopped every few steps to take another small bite. "Keep the last bite for when you go to sleep," Moussa said, "that way, you'll have sweet dreams." Moulleek smiled and took Moussa's hand. They walked for a few moments like that, each holding a baklava in one hand and a warm palm in the other.

"There is something I have to tell you," Moussa began when

they'd finished their baklava and turned into their alley. He stopped and stood still.

"Something very important. Listen," Moussa kneeled down until their eyes met, at level. Moulleek looked at Moussa, drawing his eyebrows together. Moussa withdrew his hand from Emil's grasp and opened the sticky fingers one by one, until Moulleek's palm was open. The flesh glistened from the baklava's honey. Moussa kissed the softest part, right in the middle, then withdrew something from his pocket and placed it on that wet spot.

"This is yours," Moussa whispered, touching the gold-plated anchor button with his fingertip, "and your real name is Emil."

Part VIII: November 1944

"Doubt everything. Find your own light." Buddha

Chapter 1

Lucas dressed in ordinary clothes and placed his neatly folded robe in a canvas bag. He was going into the Jewish part of town and it would be better to blend in. The atmosphere in Haifa had been tense for years by now. Before the war it was even worse: repeated attacks by Arabs against Jews and retaliations by Jews against Arabs. Since the war started those abated but the air raids and bombings had everyone on edge.

Father Pierre had repeatedly admonished the monks: "Each side suspects us of secretly siding with the other. Surely, each side has reasons to imagine we oppose them. The Jews, for the oldest accusation we've laid at their feet, while the Arabs suspect us of harboring resentment, even desire for revenge, for destroying our monastery. Even though that was over seven hundred years ago, they may think our memory is as long as theirs. And maybe it is. Enough subsequent attacks have kept it going, though we must forgive, of course, and pray for peace. And for our safety. Navigating this requires utmost discretion."

Lucas hurried to Herzl Street in Hadar Ha-Carmel. The idea had come to him in a flash. His parents hadn't seen him for seven years. The promise that he would return after he reached maturity at twenty could not be kept because of the war. Two Sundays ago, when he undertook his permanent vows, he was heartbroken that his parents could not witness the day. How different it would've been had he been permitted to go back to Pamiers to celebrate these Final Vows.

His parents would have stood behind the grillwork in the church wing, straining to hear every word. His mother, he was sure, would've peeked through the hexagonal openings. Marie, now nearly grown, would've kept her hand on Philippe's back, beaming in pride but terribly itchy in his new suit. Lucas prayed that Jacques, three years older than Philippe, had not yet left home, but suspected he might have, perhaps to join the Resistance. The older brothers, Martin and André had enlisted early on. Lucas expected that they had not yet returned.

In the midst of the ceremony at Stella Maris, as this sadness trickled into his joy, it had suddenly come to him. He would get his picture taken in his new robes to send to his family. Given the war, it could take months to arrive, but he would send it to the Abbot in Pamiers. Surely, the Post Office would treat a clerical letter with special care now, after the liberation. How he and the rest of the French-born monks had rejoiced when the news had reached them that Paris was freed on August 25!

The day after he took his vows Lucas had asked Father Pierre for an audience. It was certainly a novel request as photography was generally frowned upon, certainly individual portraits. He had gone into the library in trepidation, sweat itching in his armpits. But Father Pierre seemed softer than usual; his eyes were not the narrow slits of skeptical assessment he reserved for "special requests." He listened to Lucas' whole statement without one interruption and did not hurry him with his usual "come to the point, my son." Rather, he said: "I understand and will make an exception. We don't want your parents to think we have forgotten the promise we made to them. I'll even add a letter."

"Thank you, Father. It's more than I could have asked for," Lucas bowed.

"Do it, but let's keep this just between us."

Getting ready that morning, Lucas had studied himself in the small mirror above the sink in the communal washroom. It was a rare thing, looking at himself with such care. He stroked his beard and combed it out, pleased to note it had finally come into its fullness. Made him look the part, didn't it? He ran the comb through his hair though that hardly mattered - he planned to pose in his hooded vestment. He folded Father Pierre's letter and inserted it into the stiff cardboard envelope. He had allowed himself a peek, for his parents" sake, to make sure it wouldn't upset them. He blushed to read Father Pierre's praising him and smiled, knowing how much his consecrated blessings would mean to his parents.

On Herzl Street he tried to ignore the enticing stores he was passing. Enjoy the warm sun, *sine peccatis* and the fresh air is also sin-free, though here, in town, not as pristine as at Stella Maris. Passing one store after another, he noted the usual tug was absent. "I guess there's no need to worry about temptations today, Holy Father," he whispered. His mind was only on his parents' astonishment when a monk from Pamiers would knock on their door and deliver the letter. And when they opened the envelope! They'd call out in astonishment: "Come! Marie, Jacques, Philippe!" and sit in a circle to behold the photograph, passing it from hand to hand as if it were a fragile gilded leaf.

He could hear the conversation in his mind.

"Look at him!" Mama would say, "a man! A full-grown man!"

"Look at the robe," Papa would jump in. "Not just a man, but a man of God. Look how dignified. No tattered-clothes farmer, our boy!"

Philippe would beg: "Can I take it to bed with me tonight?" The others would clamor for the same privilege. Father would shush them, then find a spot to display the photograph for everyone to see all the time. Where would that be? Lucas thought for a moment, visualizing their modest home. Yes, in the alcove under the crucifix, next to the fireplace, where every single person in the village would be invited in to admire it.

If he's lucky, really lucky, it would get to them by Christmas. What a gift that would be! He could already see himself, looking at his family eating their Christmas dinner and every meal thereafter. Would they turn towards the photo to include him when reciting Grace? Knowing Philippe, he would raise a chicken wing or a potato to show his big brother what he was eating. Look at me, I haven't even found the photographer's studio and I already see my family admiring my picture. Better find the studio first.

Now that he had to check each storefront he passed, it was harder to resist the allure of their merchandise --unfathomable luxuries to someone steeped in the Order's vow of poverty. He averted his gaze from elegant clothes but allowed himself to look at housewares. He passed a shoe store with finely-tooled leather boots. He lowered his eyes to his bare feet, clad in coarse leather sandals. He couldn't stop a small sigh.

The bakery was going to be the toughest test. As soon as he smelled the fresh pastries he hurried to the opposite side of the street. Just then he saw a brass sign above a window filled with portraits: *Korngold Photography Studio: Viennese Trained - Highest Quality Guaranteed.* He took a deep breath and clasped the cold metal door handle. My first photograph, he congratulated himself: like a man of the world! What? he almost slapped his own wrist. Man of the world? Since when is that my aspiration? But he forgave himself for getting carried away with excitement. He was not much past a novice, after all. Another, still very needed, lesson in humility. He pulled the door open.

Inside the well-lit shop, a smartly dressed woman stood at the counter. She was holding a boy by the hand and talking to a beanstalk of a man, presumably Mr. Korngold. The boy was on tiptoes, lifting himself so his chin to almost reach the glass countertop. Lucas sat on a bench by the wall to wait his turn. He inhaled the smell of chemicals, acid-sharp, but didn't find it unpleasant at all. The real thing! I, Lucas, a mere week past novice, getting a professional portrait. It's almost a miracle; certainly, only Divine intercession can explain Father Pierre's benevolence.

The woman and the photographer were speaking in German. Lucas chastised himself for it, but couldn't help eavesdropping, trying to piece together from his modest German vocabulary what they were saying. Meanwhile the boy, probably bored standing pressed into his mother's side, scanned the room. His curls bounced with each small movement of his head. He turned towards Lucas. Lucas felt a hard tug; the boy's sweet smile and sparkling eyes seized his heart. Something mesmerizing about this child . . . He looks somehow familiar; have I seen him before? That seemed ludicrous, so Lucas refocused on the adults' conversation.

There was something intimate about the way they spoke, but that, he knew, shouldn't be a surprise. So many of the Jews who had settled in Haifa in the past two decades were German speakers and, despite their hatred of the Germans, they loved the language and mourned the grandeur of the lost culture.

CHAPTER 2

"So, to our business today, Herr Korngold," Lucas listened more carefully after the exchange of pleasantries and complaints about the weather, "we've come in for Benyamin's fourth-birthday photo."

"Already, Frau Schiff! Who can believe he's already four? Remember the picture I took of him right after he was born?"

"Ja, of course," she sighed.

"Which backdrop would you like?" Mr. Korngold asked, directing himself to mother and child simultaneously. "I have one with palm trees and a camel, and one of the Carmel Mountain."

Why didn't he mention the backdrop, hanging on the far right, Lucas wondered. It showed the Haifa harbor with several large boats, including a battleship. Wouldn't a boy this age prefer the ships?

"Und so," Mr. Korngold beckoned the boy to come around the counter, "the *Atlantic* baby is four years old! Let's see how tall you are, kleiner Junge!"

"*Ani lo katan! Ani gadol!*" the boy protested.

"He prefers to speak in Hebrew," the mother said with an apologetic smile.

"Of course, they all do. He's almost a *sabra*, after all"

"Ja, a week shy of it."

Korngold bent toward the boy, declaring: "Of course you are not small. You are really a big boy now. It's just that . . . I took your picture when you were born. You were this small," Korngold held his hands less than a foot apart.

"You came to my house?"

"No, my friend. You were born on a ship. In the middle of the sea. I was there."

"Mama said I was born on a ship, but she didn't tell me about you."

"I wasn't as important as you," Korngold chuckled and pinched the boy's cheek. Benyamin looked at his mother and she tussled his curls. Lucas could feel the curls in his own palm, soft and bouncy at the same time.

"Just a moment," Korngold said and leaned under to the counter. He rummaged through some cardboard boxes, muttering "I know it's here somewhere."

"There!" he straightened his back and propped up a photograph of a smiling boy standing next to an infant in a man's arms, cut off at the elbows.

"I made an enlargement and cropped it, to better effect, I think," Korngold said.

The woman blanched and clutched the edge of the counter. "Ah, that's the picture that's been waiting for me for four years."

Lucas' mouth dropped open, and he pressed hard into the wall to keep his balance.

Korngold didn't notice. "I was just an amateur photographer then," he barreled forward, "but don't worry, now I really know how to do portraits."

"Of course," the woman's voice trembled, "e-everyone knows you are one of the best in Haifa."

"Danke. That's kind of you to say," Korngold beamed and turned to position his camera, still muttering, "and to think I got my start on the *Atlantic*."

"Really, Herr Korngold?"

"I took some pictures before, of course. In Vienna. But they meant nothing to me. Just learning the trade. On the *Atlantic*, those were important pictures. I felt like a professional photojournalist."

"What do you mean?"

"I took those pictures to document the horrid conditions on the boat."

"I see. Well, horrid is right. Did you ever publish them? In the newspaper?"

"I printed them after we arrived, went around with them, but no one was interested . . . with the war going on."

"Ja, our story was no headline grabber."

"Maybe after the war. When people write the history," Korngold offered.

"After the war . . . what will the world look like?"

"You are right, Frau Schiff. And what will remain back home?"

"Surely less than we hope," she said and looked away.

"Surely."

Mr. Korngold cleared his throat as if to say one more thing, but then said: "Let's take the picture. At least that we have control over." He turned to his camera and adjusted the lens.

"But how, actually, Herr Korngold, did you get your camera past all the inspections we faced? Ach, what we went through," she took a deep breath. "I remember each one, unfortunately in vivid detail. First, the Germans when we boarded the riverboat in Vienna, then the Romanian Port Police when we disembarked in Tulcea. Then, again, when got on the *Atlantic*. Remember?"

"Who could forget?"

"Of course, if you had a bottle of schnapps to hand out you could get past them," she said in a sarcastic tone.

"I remember that too. But who had anything?"

"Some people always manage."

"Some people do."

"And the British on the *Atlantic* and then at Atlit," she continued, "How did you get past them?"

"That was the most highly guarded secret at the time," Mr. Korngold gave her a sly wink. "But I suppose I can tell you now."

"So?"

"I put it in my underpants. Down there - you know, with *meinem kleinen Schmuckstück,* the little precious jewels. No one wanted to search down there."

"That I can see!"

Gertie turned her gaze to the wall to look at the backdrops. She picked the Carmel Mountain backdrop. As Korngold helped the boy up to the tall stool in front of it, his eyes rested on the round face and crown of curls. In a near whisper, he said: "He looks so much like your Emil, only darker hair. Everything else is the same." She nodded and squeezed her lips together. With the end of the blue shawl draped across her shoulders, she touched the corners of her eyes.

"*Entschuldigen Sie.* Forgive me," Korngold apologized.

"No, no," she said, "it's good to see that someone remembers our Emil. Since that *Patria* horror, no one wants to mention him. He was such a wonderful boy, our Emil."

"Ja, he was a sweet one. The charming smile, the intelligent eyes, so outgoing. Everyone on the boat was his friend. And how he climbed on everything, like a little monkey. Once I saw him on top of the *Panama Room*."

"That room . . . " she let a heavy sigh out.

Korngold's fleeting smile turned into a grimace. "The *Patria - schrecklich*! What a horror . . . a catastrophe." He stopped himself with a shallow cough. "I am sorry. I got carried away. I shouldn't have."

"It's alright," she assured him. "We never see anyone who knew him anymore."

"He was so bright, your Emil," Korngold was emboldened now, "a little *Wunderkind*. Once I showed him how the camera works. He got it like—1,2,3!"

"He loved mechanical things. His father is an engineer, you know."

"That's right. And how he loved those ropes! Remember?"

"Of course," she winced.

"You and your husband . . . had a few little heart attacks from his climbing."

She tried to smile but her tears now overflowed their banks. She pressed her face into her shawl.

Suddenly aware of her quiet boy, she asked Korngold to take the picture now.

"Smile my boy," he said in a perfunctory manner and slid under the camera's black cloth and took several shots.

When he emerged from behind the camera, he asked her if the photos were needed urgently.

"No, no rush."

"In that case, I'll take a little extra time and care in printing them. Make sure they're perfect. Could you, Frau Schiff, come back on Thursday?"

"I think so."

"Right at 4 o'clock in the afternoon. I am in the shop then, getting ready to open but it won't be crowded yet. We can look at the photos together and you'll choose the best ones."

"That would be very nice," she said and took the boy's hand, ready to leave the store.

"Will you want me to make small duplicates to send to . . . relatives?"

"No, thank you. There's no one left."

"All of mine in Europe are gone from their homes too. Nowhere to write to them."

"We had an address in Hungary," she said, "good for a while even though it took months to get an answer. But nothing this year. Who knows what exactly has happened to them? Nothing good, I would think."

"I'm afraid you are right. Maybe after the war? Maybe you'll find . . . some of them?"

Korngold took the boy off the stool and shook his hand. "You were a very good boy, Benyamin. He's very polite, Frau Schiff," he turned to her with a big smile.

"He is," she said and kissed Benyamin on the cheek, whispering in his ear, "and now we're going to get you the lollipop I promised."

Chapter 3

Lucas had waited quietly all this time, but in his head raged a tornado. Who was this Emil? What exactly happened to him? What was "the *Patria* catastrophe?" Should he ask Mr. Korngold directly? Why did this sweet boy, Benyamin she called him, touch him so deeply? Why was he so agitated? Somehow, he must pull all these bits and pieces into a coherent picture. But right now, better ignore the turmoil and get on with his business.

He stepped up to the counter, introduced himself and explained the circumstances of his desire for a formal portrait. It was laborious, as he spoke to Mr. Korngold in German. But he was proud of himself and Korngold seemed to understand. Lucas took out his robe and slipped it on, fished a comb out and ran it through his beard. Korngold smiled appreciatively and gestured towards the Carmel Mountain backdrop. He pointed to a small dark shape: "This may be your Stella Maris, right there." Lucas leaned in and peered closely. "It is a possible . . . too small to be completely surely. But this location on the mountainside is right."

"Why don't you stand just to the left of it," Korngold suggested, "you can write a note to point it out."

"Danke," Lucas said, surer of his German now, "a wonderful idea. I will write this to my parents."

Korngold took three photos, explaining, "We want the best possible expression."

Lucas' stomach was so cramped by now he was afraid he would have to find a public toilet the moment he left the studio. Where would that be? And how clean? No! just calm yourself down. Leave it for now. First gather information: what was the explosion they talked about? And the *Patria?* He remembered something vaguely, but it had been four years. He kept his lips tightly sealed to make sure the words racing through his head couldn't spill out.

"Is this possible for the photographs to be ready on Thursday?" Lucas measured out the words. Korngold opened his leather-bound appointment book and leafed through it.

"Yes, indeed. They'll be ready by then."

"I will come in the afternoon," Lucas blurted out before he fully understood why he knew he had to come back at the very same time as that lady.

By the time he reached the monastery, Lucas realized he would have to ask Father Pierre. There wasn't anyone else he could consult to find out what exactly the words ringing in his ears meant: "Horror, Katastrophe." He marshaled his courage and asked Father Pierre for an audience. The Abbot raised one eyebrow, but said "Come to the library after Vespers."

He's probably wondering what kind of trouble I got into today, Lucas thought. He knew Father Pierre frowned on monks going to town too often, especially to Hadar Ha-Carmel where they would encounter beautiful shops, elegantly dressed women and mouth-watering pastries.

At Vespers Lucas struggled to empty his mind, focus only on the words he was chanting. But to no avail. "*Gloria Patri et Filio* . . . " kept colliding with "*Patria* horror," and "your boy." He lifted up his eyes and stared at the mosaic icon of Jesus crowning the copula. The Lord's well-coiffed hair morphed into the boy's bouncy curls, his somber face into Korngold's pained expression when he spoke of "the catastrophe." The cobalt robe on Jesus' shoulders turned into the blue shawl wrapped around Frau Schiff's shoulders. Lucas bit the inside of his cheek. It helped momentarily. By the end of the service the taste of blood permeated his mouth.

Father Pierre was reading from a large volume when Lucas entered. He motioned to a straight-backed chair tucked against the side of the desk. Lucas sat down, surprised he was invited to sit. Usually, these audiences were kept very brief, the novice or monk kept standing. He squeezed his hands between his thighs to stop the tremors. He bowed and waited.

"What is it, my son? Any trouble in town?"

"No, Father. I found the photography shop quickly. Everything went fine."

"Very good. I worried that . . ."

"No need to worry. I m-m-must return next Thursday to get the prints and mail them."

"That should be no problem, as long as you go directly from the studio to the Post Office and come right back."

"Exactly my plan," Lucas assured Father Pierre, who nodded and signaled that he may leave.

"There's something . . . something else."

Father Pierre frowned but motioned to Lucas to continue.

"Father, do you remember the *Patria* catastrophe?"

"*Patria* catastrophe?" Father Pierre looked surprised. He thought for a moment, a slight frown on his brow. "Yes, but why do you ask? Are you mixed up in some kind of trouble?"

"No, no trouble."

"Then why do you need to know this?" the Abbot shot him a suspicious look.

Lucas stiffened at Father Pierre's famous "penetrating gaze," and tried to force his mouth into a nonchalant smile. Father Pierre rested his hands on the open book, remaining silent.

He's trying to force me to reveal the secret, I need to win this struggle. Lucas bowed obediently.

"A lot of people drowned, right?" Lucas pushed on.

"Indeed, over two hundred."

"*Mon Dieu*! More than two hundred, Father? And the ship?" Lucas pressed, hoping Father Pierre will get carried away by the conversation, not questioning his motives.

"It's lying on the floor of the harbor; like a rotting carcass."

"W-what happened to the rest of the refugees?"

"The British detained them at Atlit for a while but eventually let them stay here. Churchill intervened, as I recall, because of the tragedy."

"I see."

"One of many," Father Pierre said shaking his head, and looked back at his book.

Lucas got up to leave. At the door he heard the Abbot mutter under his breath: "How is all this going to end?"

Chapter 4

Lucas rushed to his cell, a cacophony of conclusions already screaming in his head. Better write them down, one by one, and put them in a logical order. Then, with God's help, try to make sense of all this. He fished out the small notebook hidden under his mattress and took up the slim pencil, tied to the spine with a blue ribbon. He chewed on the pencil's end, eyes closed, then started writing. He marked the beginning of each line with a small cross: †

† The boy she spoke about with Korngold must have drowned in the *Patria* explosion.

† His name was Emil.

† The boy, Benyamin, is his younger brother.

† He was born on a different ship (before the explosion) —the *Atlantic*. What happened to that one?

† Benyamin looked so familiar, as if I already knew him.

Lucas drew a line as if it were a math problem, but he wasn't ready to do the sum. He put his pencil down and clasped his hands in prayer for mercy. He picked up the pencil again, then pressed down so hard the paper began to tear.

† I found Dondieu with that Arab fisherman at the same time of year.

† It must have been the day after the explosion.

† We thought he was an abandoned Arab boy. But he didn't respond when the fisherman spoke to him in Arabic.

He also didn't seem to understand Hebrew or English.

He appeared to understand German that time at Doctor Klein's.

He drew a thicker line now and scanned the points from top to bottom. "Mon Dieu!" he cried out.

He had to sit on his hands to stop them from shaking. He fixed his eyes on the small bronze crucifix high above the narrow lancet window. The prayer came before he had a chance to wish for it:

"I raise my eye to the mountain tops; whence cometh my salvation?"

He got down on his knees, welcoming the cold hard floor lacerating his flesh. He chanted the psalm over and over, swaying back and forth. Finally, his knees hurt so much he pulled the blanket off his bed and tucked it under them.

"Help me," he prayed "help me find my way to You." He mouthed softly, "Dondieu, Emil; Dondieu, Emil," like the childhood game he remembered his sister playing, tearing petals off a daisy with a singsong: "I love him; I love him not."

But there is no "love him not for me!" a shout burnt his throat. Slow down! he admonished himself. First make sure of the facts. Maybe it's not... He got up and sat on his bed, wrapping himself in his own embrace.

Alone in his room, Lucas prayed into the evening. At dinner he moved through the meal as if his own body were a mechanical apparatus, pressing a lever for each action: fork to mouth, chew, swallow, repeat. Immediately following Grace, he hurried back and prayed and meditated, hoping for an answer. The silence hurt more than the cold floor. Finally, an answer did come. He thanked God for His gift and headed to the boys' dormitory.

Brother Donatien was at the door, shushing each boy who fidgeted in his bed with a stern look.

"I can help Brother Michel get the boys to sleep tonight," Lucas said.

"Why? What's this about?"

"Don't you remember? I owe you a favor."

"You do?" Donatien frowned, but a smile began to raise the corners of his mouth.

"From two weeks ago, I am sure you recall," Lucas recited the lines he'd prepared, "you helped me with morning chores."

Brother Donatien shrugged, but now a full smile spread across his face. Lucas had known that any excuse to get off duty would work. Donatien had confided not long before how worn out he was from attending to the boys every night. He pined for one evening in silence, an hour with no obligations. "Some of the boys still need so much, you know . . . parental tenderness at bedtime. It whittles you down."

Donatien named the most vulnerable boys and pointed to their beds, then slipped out of the room. Lucas walked between the two rows of narrow beds, stopping by each boy to tuck in his blankets and wish him good sleep. He recited the first stanza of the *Pater Noster* with the boys Donatien had pointed out. Others only needed a hand on their shoulder and a brief blessing for pleasant dreams.

The boys fell asleep quickly, exhausted from their day. Of course, Lucas thought, they don't get up at 4:00 am like us, monks, but they're up by 5:30 —plenty early. Some boys curled up into balls, others had thumbs nesting between their lips. He came to Dondieu last, making sure the boys in the neighboring beds were already asleep. Dondieu was awake. Lucas was certain he'd been waiting for him. He perched on the edge of the bed and recited the prayer. Dondieu's lips moved without making a sound. The prayer done, Lucas tucked Dondieu in, put his hand on his shoulder and whispered, "Good night, Emil."

The boy did not react. Lucas repeated it, a little louder, stressing "Emil." Even in the dark, Lucas could see the boy's eyes open wide. His body trembled.

"Is your name Emil?" Lucas asked softly. The boy grasped Lucas' hand as if he were drowning. He heaved with sobs.

Lucas held Dondieu for a long time, until the boy finally drifted off to sleep in his arms. He lowered him to the bed and loosened his fingers, sliding his own hand out of the tight grip. "Good night, Emil," Lucas whispered one more time, and walked out of the room.

He stepped into the dark courtyard and began to pace around its perimeter, taking no note of the biting cold and penetrating dampness. Everything had shattered; a magnificent setting of fine china and crystal had crashed to the floor. There had been clues — now he understood them. They rushed in like rocks tumbling down a steep slope. Coming back from the port: how surprised he'd been that the boy seemed familiar with riding a bus. How well he used his cutlery. Later, at Dr. Klein's —of course! Lucas nearly smacked his own forehead, they spoke German! How could he have been so blind?

He circled the courtyard another time. It felt reassuring to be hemmed in by the walls, as if they would corral his thoughts into some kind of order. Blinded! Blinded by his desire to love the boy, assuaging his longing for Philippe by playing older brother to Dondieu. No, more than a brother —a father! Lucas looked up at the dark sky and glittering stars. *"De tribulatione invocati,"* he began to chant.

He returned to his cell reciting the psalm, until finally his mind stilled. Now he hoped he could sleep. He slid under the blanket, but the moment he closed his eyes the tranquility evaporated. A father? Really? Had he made a terrible mistake taking his vows?

Chapter 5

Lucas startled awake. By the sliver of moonlight through the window, he sought the crucifix on the wall. "In the dark —both of us," he whispered. He retraced his thoughts to the precise point when his conclusion seemed inevitable. But, if his deductions were right, why hadn't Dondieu protested? Why hadn't he cried or called for his parents? He has a normal voice; he sings. What had Father Pierre said the Abbess told him? "A psychological condition, maybe a reaction to traumatic events." A reaction to the explosion and losing his parents? And to landing in a totally strange place, surrounded by people he didn't understand, practicing a religion he didn't know. Lucas shuddered, remembering Dondieu terrified when he first saw the crucified Jesus in the chapel. What on earth had the poor boy made of that? Of the past four years?

Lucas moved through the next day as if wading through a tar pit. Don't think, he kept telling himself; later, when you're alone. He spent the *Angelus* meditation in the farthest corner of the chapel. He declaimed the psalms as if his mind were severed from his lips, sleepwalking through the Scriptures. But the 68th Psalm awakened him with a jolt:

"The Lord said: I shall bring them back from Bashan,

I shall bring them back from the depth of the sea."

Lucas gripped his Psalter, his nails digging into the leather cover. "Bring them back from the depth of the sea. Bring them back from the depths of the sea," he recited out loud.

"We will bring him back to you," Abbé Jacques André had pledged to his parents years ago in Pamiers. It rang in Lucas' ears as if just spoken. The promise had not been fulfilled and there was no chance of returning to France in the foreseeable future. Soon he was to follow his "Final Vows" with the "Stability Vows" which would commit him to remaining here, in Stella Maris of the Carmel, for the rest of his life.

His parents' faces flashed before his eyes, sculpted by sorrow. Up until now all he could do for them was recite the words of the Psalmist assuring his people a merciful God "will heal the broken hearts and bind up the wounds." But now there was a way he himself could mend what had been shattered. He would transfer the promise made to his parents to this boy's mother and father. One act will be woven into the other through the unity of the universe, just as Father Pierre had explained about the doctrine of the *Mysticum Corporis Christi*.

The Abbot had read out loud from the new Papal Encyclical of Pope Pius XII --about a year ago —and then expounded: "It is hard to grasp precisely because it is so simple. All people and their actions are part of the gradual perfection of the body of Christ, which is the world in its fullness. All people and all actions are part of one endless tapestry, the *Corpus Dei*." All the Brothers nodded but Lucas overheard several conversations afterwards that revealed he wasn't the only one still grappling to understand it.

Now it made sense. The boy and his parents who mourn him, he, Lucas, and his mother and father, are all part of the Corpus Dei. The promise made there will be fulfilled here. Surely the Abbot would agree, since he'd been so thrilled with this new doctrine.

Lucas went to the library, propelled by this certainty. But at the door it vanished. He stood there for a long moment, lacing his fingers this way and that. Finally, he knocked.

"Enter," Father Pierre called out.

Lucas walked in, the deep silence of the room made each footstep echo in his ears, as if a warning bell. Though he was shivering inside, Lucas couldn't help note how much warmer the library was than the Brothers' cells. The smell of the leather-bound volumes made it feel even more cozy. Father Pierre was reading by a large candle. It illuminated his face at an oblique angle, the brow and nose casting long disquieting shadows.

"What is it, my son?"

Lucas opened his mouth but nothing came out. He cleared his throat and coughed, but still no words.

"Let us walk together," Father Pierre gestured towards the door.

"No, thank you, Father. We must speak here, where no one will hear us."

Father Pierre frowned, but said, "Then we might as well sit."

He picked up the candle and put it on the edge of his desk. Fully lit, his face was less frightening.

"It's about Dondieu."

"Dondieu? But he seems like such a good boy. Has he been making trouble?"

"No, not at all."

"What, then?"

Lucas' stomach heaved. He had lost his nerve. Father Pierre leaned towards him. Lucas shrank back; the words tumbled out:

"I know who his family is. I mean, his mother."

"His mother?"

"I met her."

"You met her? How is that possible?"

"I mean, not e-e-exactly. I saw her and I overheard her talking at the photographer's studio when I went for my photo."

"A few days ago, you mean? The photograph for your parents?"

"Yes. There was a woman there, talking with the photographer. In German, but I could follow."

Lucas stopped and imprisoned his hands between his knees to stop their trembling.

"Continue, my son."

"She and her husband lost their child four years old. In the explosion of the *Patria*."

"The *Patria*. I see."

Lucas recoiled from the infamous piercing look the novice monks feared so much.

"You came to speak to me about that just two days ago. I couldn't understand why you were interested in that."

"Now I have put it all together."

"So, tell me," Father Pierre said and leaned his chin on his clasped hands. His face softened. Lucas enumerated the details he'd pieced together. He hesitated for a moment. Courage, he told himself, it's God's will.

"His parents think he drowned in the explosion. But he didn't — we have him here. I-I-I . . . w-w-we must return him to his parents."

Father Pierre remained silent for a very long time. Lucas kept his head bowed down. Finally, the Abbot spoke in the grave voice he reserved for chastisements.

"No, son. That would be wrong."

"Wrong?"

"Wrong. You saved the boy, body *and* soul. An act of faith and charity in Divine Grace. Now you want us to doom him to the eternal cursed fate of the Jews? How could we?"

Lucas tried to muster an obedient expression on his face.

"I can see how you'd come to feel this way," Father Pierre continued, "it's certainly likely that the parents—if indeed they are Dondieu's parents —after all, your whole theory could be false

... yes, they surely loved their boy. It seems he was not abused, as we had all thought when you found him. But let us think about the boy, Lucas, about what's good for him."

"Yes, Father."

"The boy doesn't seem to miss his parents, not now and not when he first came here. No sign of it, was there? And even if he did, he must've forgotten them by now."

"He was only four," Lucas began but stopped, not sure where this point would lead.

"He should not be ripped from our embrace!" Father Pierre became adamant. "It would be another trauma for him. And the Church and our Order would lose a soul."

"Lose a soul?"

"Indeed!"

"B-B-But - "

"And people would misinterpret this and say we just got rid of the boy, no longer wishing to care for him. We must protect our reputation."

Father Pierre pursed his lips and seemed to go somewhere far away in his mind. Lucas waited; he knew there was more coming.

"In fact," the Abbot lowered his voice, "we face an even greater danger: we could be accused of kidnapping him."

"Why?" Lucas couldn't follow.

"There are rumors. They circulate all over the world. They go back a century—the case of Edgardo Mortara."

"Who?"

"Edgardo Mortara. A Jewish boy in Bologna. The Papal Police seized him when he was six-years old. They had been informed that the maid had baptized him as an infant."

"I don't understand, Father."

"He'd been very ill. She was trying to protect him."

"But why did they take him? It sounds like it was by force."

"It's the law. A baptized child cannot be raised by non-Catholics," the Abbot thundered, implying Lucas should know. "They took him to Rome and Pope Pius IX adopted him."

"I... I've never heard of it," Lucas lowered his eyes apologetically.

"It was an international scandal. Tarnished the image of the Church and the Pope. There were protests everywhere and not just from Jews. All over the world: Britain, France, Germany, the United States. Even Napoleon —the Third, that is."

"So, we have to worry about this even though it happened almost a century ago?" Lucas said, shaking his head.

"These things don't go away, my son. They lie in wait in their lair until a vulnerable moment arises. There is so much tension in this country, this could ignite the tinder box."

"But in the end," the Abbot summed up, "it's for the boy's sake. He would forfeit his chance of eternal salvation."

CHAPTER 6

Lucas saw how Father Pierre's arguments lined up like soldiers in battle formation. They pounded his ears like mallets hitting a tin drum. He must obey Father Pierre; the rule of St. Albert was very clear on this. He had recited it many times: "Hold your prior in humble reverence, your minds not on him but on Christ who has placed him over you." Defying the Abbot is defying Christ. Impossible.

"But . . . " a voice said in his head. He shut it down. He bowed and rose, heading to the door.

"One more thing before you leave," Father Pierre called after him.

"Yes?"

"I know how painful this is for you but, for your sake, you are to have no further contact with the boy."

"No contact?"

"None. I will inform Donatien and Michel."

"But . . . "

"Don't be afraid, son. I will do it so they suspect nothing, nothing about the boy and nothing about you. Trust me."

Lucas wrestled back the words clamoring to leap from his lips. He bowed and rushed out. The heavy door swung shut and he yanked his arms into his body, as if the door had smashed them. With each step forward he felt another rip tearing him in two halves, pulled apart by warring sides: one his Father in Heaven, who wants him to return the boy; the other, Father Pierre, God's emissary here at Stella Maris.

Lucas dropped to the floor in his cell and scooted the blanket under his knees. He held his hands in supplication: could he accept that the Lord had spoken through his vicar? If he doubted Father Pierre, could he remain the obedient monk he had vowed to be? A Carmelite Brother? A Christian? "I raise my eyes to the mountains; whence cometh my salvation?" he cried out, but felt no comforting hand on his heart. He prayed and prayed, but nothing came.

Finally, his mind stood still, emptied by fatigue. He rose slowly, removed his sandals and twisted each numb foot this way and that. He rubbed his palms together and cupped them over his frozen toes. "Help me," Lucas mouthed towards the crucifix and crossed himself. He lay down on is bed and pulled the blanket up to his chin. He thrust his icy hands into his armpits. He wished for sleep, but it did not come.

He pulled his notebook from under his mattress and began writing. He wrote about himself in the third person, as if reporting a Church Investigation. It might help him see things more clearly: an inquest or an Inquisition?

He says he thought he found a lost, abused child.

Now he says he stole the boy from his parents.

He says he should have known; there had been clues.

He says he didn't understand them at the time.

He believes that was because he wanted the boy —to raise as a father.

He now believes that he desires love on this earth; it's not enough for him to love his Father in Heaven.

He now wishes to have a son.

With all due humility, he likens himself to the Virgin Mary. He did not ask for a son, but a son was given to him. Mary was too, and she accepted. So had he.

Jesus had a mother, and this child does too.

He says he must return him to her.

Father Pierre says that he and the Church were the boy's saviors.

Father Pierre insists the boy must stay; his salvation vouchsafed at Stella Maris.

He disagrees.

Lucas put his pencil down and wrapped the blue ribbon around his finger. He read the list. *Ergo*, he wanted to write at the bottom. But he couldn't. He left the pencil dangling in the air.

CHAPTER 7

He must pray, and this time in the chapel. Alone in his room he's going in circles. He dressed in his warm robe and headed out with the hood pulled low, shading his downcast face. He hoped to evade Father Pierre. Inside the chapel he leaned into the back wall, waiting for his eyes to adjust to the dim light. His legs were trembling. He lowered himself onto the bench in the last row and pressed his forehead into the edge of the seat in the row ahead until it hurt. He welcomed the pain.

He began the *Pater Noster*, hoping that "Thy will be done" would help him arrive at a congruence of his will and the Lord's. But the words limped out with no life in them. New words, the right ones, would have to be bestowed on him, not fished out from his own tired reservoir. He waited for the words to come.

They did. "I raise my eyes to you," Lucas called to the Madonna, knowingly subverting the psalm, "from *you* shall come my salvation." He mouthed it again and again. A warm spot began to glow in his belly; calmness spread like nectar through his body, reaching even his stiff, cold toes. His answer had come not in words but in a visage: The Holy Mother holding her Son. Mother and child is how it should be. He must return Dondieu to his parents. In Mary's presence, he was completely certain. He began the Hail Mary in gratitude.

But when he uttered the words "pray for us sinners," a new doubt slithered out like a snake emerging from under a rock. Not about the boy; about his own soul. His fatherly love for the boy had grown so big it was a realm onto itself, vying with his love of God. What of his monastic vows? True, he'd had his doubts early on and some lingered until close to his Final Vows. But they were always about his ability: memorizing, mastering the theological nuances, the discipline, the silence, even —he had to be honest with himself—the freezing toes mandated by the order's insistence on sock-less sandals year-round. But never about his desire. He had taken his vows as Scripture required, "with all your heart, all your soul, and all your might."

And now?

"Show me the way," Lucas beseeched the Madonna. He fixed his gaze on the statue, noticing for the first time that Mary had hairline wrinkles at the corners of her eyes. Grief, she already knows the end of the story. "Our story --" Lucas silently spoke to the Madonna, "losing our sons."

Rising up, he clasped his hands and touched each knuckle to his lips. He felt a delicate breeze pass over him: Grace. He bowed his head; his eyes welled with tears. The pain in his shins and strained knees now spread through his body like a sweet ambrosia.

All that was left to do was work out a plan.

Chapter 8

Thursday finally came. Lucas set out for town after the midday meal. He walked part-way down the hill and caught a bus to Hadar Ha-Carmel, arriving at the photographer's studio much too early. He tried to pass the time looking at the shops nearby, mostly closed for the afternoon nap. He'd heard about the German Jews' beloved *"Schlafstunde,"* coinciding with the Brothers' afternoon rest and recitation of psalms at the None prayer.

There were very few people in the street, each hurrying somewhere and paying Lucas no heed. He held the envelope with his and Father Pierre's letters pressed into his chest. He caught himself reciting each letter from memory. He checked the address once again: his parents' names, care of Abbé Jacques André, Monastère du Carmel, Pamiers, France, with *Par Avion* across both top and bottom.

He spent most of his time in front of the Carmel Hats shop. Hats, he reasoned would be the least of all temptations, as long as the shop didn't happen to carry socks, too. He scanned the men's fedoras, then the berets —wool, felt and leather, which reminded him of his father's, always sloping down to the left. "Soon, Papa," he whispered and caressed the envelope, "at least you'll see me."

Every few minutes he glanced up at the large clock up on the second floor of a large office building at the intersection of Herzl and Balfour streets. He remembered first seeing it soon after arriving at

Stella Maris when it was brand new and how surprised he'd been to find so many modern, European-style houses in Haifa. How different she was from what he'd expected based on the few David Roberts lithographs of the Holy Land displayed at the Pamiers Cathedral. He knew now they were merely sentimental versions of Arab villages.

Lucas set his eyes on the clock's hands and ordered them silently: "Move!" He looked up again, two minutes had passed. Soon his neck began to stiffen and his shoulders ached. Finally, it was almost time. He approached the photography studio and tucked himself into the entryway of the neighboring shop, flat against the wall.

At 15:59 he heard the staccato of a woman's determined steps. One minute later Korngold opened his door, welcoming Frau Schiff with "Guten Tag." Lucas' eyes were fixed, as if pinned by a thumbtack to the studio's door. It seemed to take forever, yet when Frau Schiff stepped out Lucas started. The clock read 16:06. She stepped into the street clasping a slim package like it was an elegant pocketbook, and turned right. Lucas followed about twenty paces behind her, praying she wouldn't look back.

At the corner she turned right again and walked two blocks on a narrower street, then into a small alley, slowing down on the uneven pavement. Lucas matched his pace to hers. She entered a three-story building and Lucas rushed to its side. He listened to her climbing the steps, counting the clicks of her heels on the tiles in the hope of determining what floor she lived on. As carefully as he counted, he wasn't sure if she had she gone up two flights, or three.

He slipped into the building's entry-way, thankful it was deserted. Despite the shabby exterior, the hallway and stairs were sparkling clean. On the right wall he saw a bulletin board filled with notices, shiny thumbtacks holding the corners of the perfectly aligned edges. Right underneath, a Godsend! A list of residents. He scanned it slowly. There it was: Alfred and Gertrude Schiff: 3rd Floor, Apartment #2. He read it twice more to be sure he had it memorized, then rushed out.

Heading back to the photographer's studio, Lucas repeated slowly "Third floor, Apartment two," to cement the memory and steady his breath.

Returning to Korngold's studio, it was only once he was inside and the door shut behind him that Lucas allowed himself a sigh of relief. Korngold greeted him warmly, bent down and pulled out an envelope. He opened its clasp with a smile and laid three photos on the counter.

"I think you'll be pleased. It may be hard to choose the best, but you have a slightly different expression in each one."

Lucas was taken aback: he looked so impressive and devout with his full beard, deep-set brown eyes, and the hood hovering over his head like a halo! He realized how little time he spent looking at himself in the mirror. When he did, it was for a quick combing or adjustment of his habit. He never really saw himself.

"I am not used to staring at myself," he smiled awkwardly at Mr. Korngold.

"I understand. But they are good photos, no?"

"Yes. Very, very good!"

Lucas leaned in and examined each photograph closely, and then chose the one in which he thought he looked the most convincing as "a man of God."

"Good choice! I agree it's the best one."

"Thank you, Mr. Korngold. You did a wonderful job."

"Here," Korngold handed Lucas a piece of tissue paper, "cover the photo to protect it."

"Of course," Lucas laid the onion skin paper over the photo, then carefully slid it into the envelope behind the letters. He licked the tab and folded it meticulously at the perforated line, running his thumb along the flap to make sure it was well sealed. He took the small purse Father Pierre had given him out of his pocket and laid out the coins. He let Korngold pick out the ones needed for the payment, embarrassed to admit he had no clue how much it cost.

"Let's hope it gets there," Lucas said as he thanked Korngold and prepared to leave.

"I hope you'll be lucky. You, your parents. At least you have your parents; your family," Korngold said somberly.

"But my brothers . . . " Lucas grimaced, "they're caught up in the war. We don't know where or how. We pray for them."

Korngold nodded and Lucas flattened the crease with his thumbnail again, then held the envelope upside down to test the seal. Out of the corner of his eye, he noticed Korngold nodding approvingly.

Outside, Lucas let out a long exhalation. He loosened his jaw, realizing only now it'd been clenched the whole time. He headed down the street to the Post Office. After a short wait in line, he handed the envelope to the clerk, who looked at the address and shook his head.

"You know we cannot guarantee if and when this will arrive. Now that France is liberated, we believe there is regular mail service, but we don't have any actual information. The package will be in the hands of the local Post Office. They'll try, I'm sure, but who knows if they have any staff these days?"

"Of course. I understand."

"It's good that it's going to a monastery," the clerk said after copying the address onto a receipt. "They will be respectful of this address."

"I thought so. I'd hoped it would arrive in time for Christmas . . . but I know you cannot make any promises."

"Indeed, no promises."

"Maybe I'll have some help," Lucas lifted his eyes upwards.

"We could all use that," the clerk said, and placed the envelope in the bin for overseas mail.

Chapter 9

Lucas waited nearly three weeks before what he had been calling "the fateful day." He found times to be alone with Dondieu, even though the Abbot had forbidden it. He unfolded the story for Dondieu step by step, as though opening a delicate origami box, one corner at a time. Lucas found himself relieved that Dondieu was mute. What a terrible thing to be thankful for, he chastised himself. He wondered whether once Dondieu-Emil was back with his parents and the trauma healed, he would speak again. If so, what would he relate about his four years here? Were they, in fact, in danger at the monastery as Father Pierre had said? Was he, Lucas, in particular?

He told Dondieu children's stories he remembered about lost children, at long last reunited with their parents. He taught him words from his modest German vocabulary: "*Mama, Papa, Bruder, Liebe, Auf Wiedersehen.*" When they prayed at the chapel of the Virgin Mary, he whispered: "You'll go back to your real Mama, but don't forget the Madonna. She will always love you." Dondieu looked at Lucas with dewy eyes.

"And I . . . " Lucas choked up, "I will, too. Forever."

"Very soon," Lucas told Dondieu one morning, "I will take you back to your parents. But it's a secret." The boy nodded.

"I will tell you the day before we go," Lucas enunciated every word as if he were giving dictation. "You will do exactly as I say, right?"

Dondieu nodded again and wrapped his arms around Lucas' neck.

Chapter 10

"Thank you, Madonna," Lucas whispered under his breath when he heard at Tuesday's dinner that Brother Michel had taken ill. Father Pierre asked for a volunteer to take his place at the children's dorm. Lucas raised his hand and Father Pierre nodded. After Grace, Lucas went to the dormitory where the boys were still roughhousing and jumping from one bed to another.

"I came to help you, Donatien. Just tell me what to do."

"But Father Pierre said . . . "

"I know," Lucas sucked in his breath to keep his voice even, "but Brother Michel is sick. I thought it would be hard for you, by yourself. I thought I should help"

"That's good of you. Brother Michel has them well trained. He calls out loudly, '*Silencio*,' and they scamper to their beds. Then we walk between the beds. Just passing by them calms them down."

"Sounds easy enough."

"Some boys need a little more, like I told you last time," Donatien added. "I sit on the edge of their bed and whisper to them. I think that works better than yelling at them when they fidget."

"I am sure."

"Good, then," Donatien summed up. "I'll start from the far end and you from here."

"*Silencio!*" Brother Donatien bellowed and, sure enough, the boys hushed and slid into their beds. It was cold, so most of them burrowed under their wool blankets. Lucas started at the far end, stopping by each bed, sitting down with several boys before he reached Dondieu. He perched on Dondieu's bed and whispered: "Tomorrow morning I'll come to take you. When it's time to get up, stay in bed and act like you are sick. Hold your tummy and your head. Even pretend you are about to throw up."

Dondieu looked at him quizzically.

"Yes, do exactly that. And then wait until I come."

Dondieu nodded and closed his eyes. Lucas went to another boy's bed and made sure to stay with him for the same length of time, murmuring softly.

Wednesday was laundry day; that was the crux of the plan. Lucas lay in bed reviewing it —the best option under the circumstances. He knew he needed a good night's rest, but he couldn't even keep his eyes closed, let alone fall asleep. He recited psalms to calm his mind.

Somehow, imperceptibly, it became dawn. After hurrying through prayers in the chapel, Lucas slipped into the dormitory. Most of the boys were already dressed and lined up near the door to go to breakfast. He glanced towards Dondieu. Yes, still lying in his bed with his right arm slung over his eyes, emitting little groans.

Brother Roland was assisting Donatien. As Lucas approached them, Donatien gave him a questioning look. Before he had a chance to bring up Father Pierre's instructions, Lucas hurried to say: "I came to help you because it's laundry day. So much work, and Brother Michel is still ill."

"That it is," Donatien said, "a lot of work ahead of us."

"I thought I should help, you know . . . " Lucas tightened every muscle to maintain a calm appearance, "Brother Roland and I will get done what Brother Michel normally does by himself. You just tell us what to do."

"That's very kind," Donatien said and instructed them: "Stretch out a blanket on the floor and pile all the sheets on it, then tie the blanket into a big bundle. You understand?"

"Of course!" Lucas said, "how do you think we did it at home with six children?"

"Good. So, I'll go to the kitchen and start the water boiling. Brother Roland can lead the children to the chapel and you'll start with the sheets. Then he'll come back and help you."

"Good idea," Lucas said, trying to sound nonchalant as his heart brimmed with thanks to the Madonna.

"And one more thing," Brother Donatien said "that boy of yours, Dondieu, is sick. Just leave him be in his bed. I think he might throw up, so why wash his bedding twice?"

Donatien headed to the kitchen and Roland led the boys out in an orderly procession. Lucas rushed to Dondieu's bed.

"Now! As fast as possible!"

The boy got out from under his blanket and immediately began shivering in the frigid room. Lucas pulled a wool robe over Dondieu's head and down to below his knees.

"Sit down. I'll help you get these on," Lucas bent down to pull the socks and sandals onto his feet. Dondieu put his hand on Lucas' shoulder.

"Now lie on top of your blanket and curl yourself into the smallest ball you can make. That's right," he added, seeing the puzzled frown on Dondieu's face, "you'll see."

Dondieu lay down on his side, pulled his knees into his chest and wrapped his arms around them. He rounded his shoulders and looked up at Lucas.

"Yes. Very good."

"Now hold onto the ends of the blanket as tightly as you can," Lucas handed Dondieu two opposite corners. Dondieu clamped his fists around them and pulled into his chest.

"Don't be afraid," Lucas whispered and grabbed the two other tips and tied them in a double knot on top of the boy. He crouched down and called: "Now I'm going to pick you up."

Lucas hoisted the blanket bundle up on his back, pulling the knotted ends over his shoulder. Heavy! Much heavier than he'd imagined. More than a full sack of flour, for sure. How far can he carry it? He maneuvered between the beds and slid out of the room, careful not to bang the blanket against the doorposts. He traversed the corridor with lumbering steps, scanning the passage ahead, and craning his neck to glance back. Thank God, no one there. Everyone should be at Lauds. "Please, Holy Father, keep them away until I get out," Lucas mouthed.

Chapter 11

Father Pierre! Lucas froze. Down the hallway: standing in silent meditation, or looking for wayward novices? Keep calm, Lucas instructed himself. Put a smile on your face, however you manage it.

"Good morning, Father," Lucas forced the appropriate words out.

Father Pierre raised an eyebrow. Lucas felt his gaze bore a hole in his forehead, ready to extract his thoughts.

"Why aren't you in the chapel?"

"I am helping Brother Roland and Donatien. It's laundry day; Wednesday always is."

"I see. Nice of you to help, but why this blanket? Isn't it enough to wash the sheets?"

"Well —"Lucas' mind raced. To buy time, he gently lowered the blanket to the floor. "The blankets . . . Father Pierre. Umm, we don't want to bother you with this detail, but some of the boys . . . they still wet the bed."

"Really?"

"Yes, the little ones."

Father Pierre sniffed the air. "Yes, I smell something, but it's not too bad."

"That's because we wash them whenever we can, Father. We don't want the other boys to taunt them."

"That's very good. I did not know, but I am glad to hear of it," Father Pierre said and turned around, heading down the hallway.

Lucas leaned against the wall for a moment to let the wave of nausea pass and steady his shaking hands. He picked up the blanket, heaved it up his back and stepped forward again, eyes on his feet. One, two, three, he counted his steps. Only ten more; only nine, eight ... No time to stop to wipe off the sweat dripping from his brow. At the end of the hallway, he pushed open the heavy wooden door. The gate was right in front of him; only a few strides away. He listened for footsteps and looked left and right. Lucky this time: no one nearby. Though his feet wanted to run, his head told them to walk slowly, keeping up the appearance of "nothing special" until the last second.

He put his hand on the gate's heavy lever. The cold metal bit into his palm. He pushed down and slowly swung the gate open, to avoid any creaking. A gulp of air and a long step —we're out! He closed the gate equally carefully and walked along the wall, quickly now, to a large bush he'd selected days before to provide cover. He lowered the blanket to the ground.

"We are out now; safe!" he whispered and untied the knots. He helped Emil unfold his tightly packed limbs and rise to standing, then rolled the blanket up and tucked it under the bush. He'll come back for it later.

"Now we go to town," he said and took the boy's hand. They walked along the goat path that wound down the hillside towards the paved road. Lucas stopped and pointed back at the monastery. "Say goodbye, but don't forget." Emil nodded and put his palms together as in prayer.

"Your name is Emil now. but I will always call you Dondieu — God's Gift —you were ... to me."

They took another turn and reached the road. They both breathed in deeply and straightened their backs, looking out into the distance, towards the port. Down there, under the sea, is the *Patria*. Should he tell that to Emil? No, his parents will, when they are ready.

At the bus stop they stood side by side and waited. Lucas wrapped his hand around the boy's shoulders but couldn't think what to say. Emil smiled when he saw the bus pull up. Lucas wanted to believe he remembered the bus ride from the port, that very first day. Once on the bus, Emil slid into the first open seat and pressed his face to the window. Lucas sat close to him, shut his eyes and ran his tongue on his dry, cracked lips.

The ride seemed much longer than other times. Emil didn't take his eyes off the passing scenery. Lucas stared at Emil's head of curls, etching each one into memory. They got off in Hadar Ha-Carmel and walked down Herzl Street. Emil's eyes opened so wide it looked as if they would pop out. His mouth fell open. He turned his head from left to right, staring at every shop window. Lucas led him swiftly down the street. "We have to hurry now," he apologized. "Mama and Papa will bring you back here and you'll look at all the stores for as long as you like."

Lucas traced back the route from Herzl Street to the smaller lane and then into the alley. At the entrance to the apartment building, they stopped by the residents' list. Lucas put his finger on the roster: "See here, Emil? Alfred and Gertrude Schiff, 3rd Floor, Apartment #2." They climbed up, stopping at each landing to catch their breath. Lucas realized he had been holding Emil's hand in too tight a grip. He loosened his fingers. Emil did not withdraw his hand. When they entered the corridor on the third floor Emil's eyes scanned the row of doors, like a flashlight in the dark.

Half way down the hallway they stopped in front of the door to apartment #2. Lucas bent down and embraced the boy. He put his hand into his pocket and slowly pulled it out. "This is yours," he opened his fist. The gold-plated button lay in the middle of his palm. Emil picked the button up, examined it and touched it to his lips. Then he put the button back in Lucas' still open palm and bent the fingers in to enclose it.

"Count to twenty," Lucas said, "then knock on the door."

AFTERWORD

The phone in my mother's kibbutz apartment rang. She lifted her hands from the kitchen sink, and quickly dried them. When she turned eighty-eight, she'd promised me she would no longer run to answer the phone. So, she walked over briskly but carefully. She picked it up on the sixth ring. Fortunately, the caller had been patient.

"Hallo," she said.

"Shalom. My name is Uri Engler. You don't know me."

"No, I don't. So, I am interested to hear: why are you calling me?"

"I am calling because I understand you were on the *Atlantic*."

"The *Atlantic*! Yes, I was, but I don't often get many calls about that. It's been nearly seventy years."

The phone was silent for a moment. She waited.

"Well," the man began again, "do you remember that a baby was born on the *Atlantic*?"

"Yes, I certainly do. One of the only moments of joy on that dreadful journey. My friend and I collected some baby clothes for you from the other mothers. I remember a light blue outfit . . . with a cute little bonnet."

"I am that baby."

"Well, then you must be looking forward to celebrating your seventieth birthday in November."

"Yes. I am calling because of that. My parents... they were from Vienna. And you?"

"From Prague. I came with my friends from the Youth Movement."

"Yes, I heard about the Prague youth—the Leadership."

"Not me. I was just an ordinary citizen."

"My parents died a very long time ago. It's only in the last few years, as I get older, that I'm really curious about the story, about what it was really like on the *Atlantic*."

"Of course, I understand."

"I heard about you from a cousin in London. He plays tennis with the son of one of your friends from Prague and Mauritius. He says he's a friend of yours, too."

"Yes, I know who you mean."

"Well, you are the only person I know of who is still alive and ... hmm, with it. You know what I mean?"

"Yes. And I do remember it all very clearly. I have a few photographs, too."

"Photographs! That would be something. May I come visit you?"

"Of course. But, you know, I live a little far, in Kibbutz Kfar Ruppin, right on the Jordan River. In fact, it's the last place, at the very end of the road."

"Far? But I haven't even told you where I live!"

"It doesn't matter. It's far wherever you come from. But it sounds like you wouldn't mind."

"Not at all."

"So, how about next week? Thursday mid-morning?"

"That will be fine."

"Do you need directions?"

"No, I have a GPS."

"OK, I know about those. Good, then."

"*Le'hitra'ot.*"

"*Le'hitra'ot.*"

Uri Engler spent several hours with my mother. He told her the story of his family: from Vienna to the *Atlantic*, to the *Patria*, to the disappearance of his older brother, Peter (later given the Hebrew name Ze'ev), and the aftermath. After Peter returned to his family—not four years later, as Uri had told my mother, but, in fact, 5 months later at Atlit, as I learned from Ze'ev—he was mute for several months. When he started speaking again, he had no memory of what had happened to him between his disappearance and his return. Despite years of research, to this day Ze'ev still doesn't know what happened to him.

I have also met both Uri and Ze'ev and heard them each retell their story. This novel is inspired by their story, though much of it is fictional.

ADDENDUM

The description of the voyage on the *Atlantic* and all the major events included are factual, based on Uri and Ze'ev Engler's story, my mother's memoir and memories, and her contemporaneous diary (in Czech). The letter from Bronia (from Mauritius) is taken nearly verbatim from my mother's diary with some alterations in tenses and added opening and closing sections, necessary to weave it into the overall narrative.

HISTORICAL FACTS ABOUT EVENTS IN THE NOVEL

1. **The *Patria* explosion** was caused by a bomb smuggled onto the ship by Munya Mardor, a member of the *Haganah*. He gave it to a passenger (recruited by the Leadership) to place by the turbines. The detonator failed on the first attempt and a new one was brought onboard by Mardor the following day. The goal was to disable the engines so the British would not be able to carry out the deportation of the Jews to Mauritius. For reasons never fully understood, much greater damage was caused and the ship sank. Between 253 and 267 people drowned (accounts vary): about 200 Jewish refugees and 50-60 British soldiers and policemen. Only in 1957 was this all publicly revealed by Munya Mardor in a newspaper column.

Following the explosion, the Mandate authorities in Palestine insisted on pursuing the deportation plan, but Winston Churchill intervened. Overruling the plan, he instructed that the survivors of the *Patria* explosion be allowed to remain in Palestine legally (above the annual immigration quota) on humanitarian grounds. International maritime standards hold that survivors of a shipwreck must be given refuge in the country on whose shores they are rescued.

2. **The bombardment of the Haifa port** on June 9, 1941 was, in fact, carried out by the German Luftwaffe. It actually took place before sunrise. In the course of the war, the Haifa port was bombed several times, mostly by the Italians.

3. **Snow in Haifa:** I found no definite information about a dusting of snow on December 31, 1941, but on January 2-3, 1942 a snow storm blanketed most of Palestine, including Haifa and the Galilee. The snowfall Moussa and Youssra remember from their childhoods refers to the storm on February 12, 1920. Snow covered the ground in the Galilee and Haifa for most of a day and Jerusalem was blanketed in 2-3 feet of snow that took two weeks to fully melt. The storm they remember from two years before they moved to Haifa occurred February 7-8, 1932. Again, the heaviest snowfall was in Jerusalem, but in the Galilee, the Carmel, the coast from Haifa to the north and even the Jordan Valley, snow lingered on the ground for a full day.

4. **The refugee boat, *Pentcho*,** which the *Atlantic* passed on the Danube around September 10, 1940, transported approximately 300 members of Beitar (the revisionist Zionist Movement) and 200 other refugees. The boat left Bratislava on May 18, 1940 and had been stuck on the Danube for months. Following a concerted effort by the Jewish communities in Yugoslavia and Bulgaria, the boat was repaired and provided with food, water and coal. It finally sailed down the Danube to Romania and departed from Sulina, Romania (a port in the Danube Delta), on September 21st, making its way

through the Black Sea and into the Mediterranean. But on October 9th the single boiler exploded (it had run out of fresh water, so the crew had mixed in seawater), and caused a shipwreck.

All 505 passengers survived for 10 days on the barren Island of *Camelinissi*, until discovered by an Italian Air Force plane and rescued by the Italian Navy. The refugees were taken to Rhodes where they were housed in a tent camp and guarded by Italian soldiers. In January 1941 the approximately 200 remaining passengers (unclear if there are counting discrepancies or many deaths in the camp in Rhodes) were transferred to the *Ferramonti Di Tarsia Internment Camp* in southern Italy (Consenza Province), thus escaping the subsequent Nazi deportation of all the Jews of Rhodes in July, 1944. They were still in Ferramonti when the Allied Forces liberated the area in September 1943.

In June 1944, Moshe Sharett, then head of the Jewish Agency, visited them while touring Jewish Brigade units in Italy and secured permission from the British for them to enter Palestine. They traveled on the Polish liner *Batory* to Alexandria and then by train to Palestine.

5. **The Mauritius Deportation:** Over 1,500 *Atlantic* passengers, my parents included, who were still awaiting their turn to board the *Patria* when it exploded, were loaded onto two new ships on December 9th and sailed to Mauritius. They arrived on Christmas and were imprisoned in Beau-Bassin, where a prison built under Napoleon for his political enemies housed the men and a hastily constructed barracks camp housed the women. Gradually the prisoners created as normal a communal life as they could including a school for children, a hospital for the detainees (staffed by both local physicians and those among the refugees who were doctors and nurses. My mother worked there as a nurse's aide). After a while, contact between men and women was permitted within restricted times and after about one year, detainees were able to get passes for

short visits to town. About 60 children were born in the camp in the ensuing years while 128 people died, mostly of tropical diseases, and are buried in a Jewish cemetery in St. Martin.

In 1942 the British authorities allowed young men of Czech nationality to volunteers for the "Free Czech Army" unit within the British Army. Many young men, my father included, chose that option and served the remainder of the war with British forces. At the end of the war the British allowed the remaining refugees to return either to the country of origin (few chose that option) or to Palestine, where over 1,300, my mother included, arrived on August 6, 1945.

6. **"Elective Mutism"** (later renamed as "Selective Mutism"), the condition Emil exhibits after the *Patria* explosion, was first diagnosed and defined in 1934 by my paternal great uncle, Moritz Tramer. He was Czech-born and went to Switzerland to study medicine in 1906. He became one of the founders of the field of Child and Adolescent Psychiatry.

Photographs and Illustrations

The Atlantic: drawing by passenger, possibly my parents' friend, Uri Spitzer..

Hanhagah member on deck.

494　Lost and Found

The Panama room.

Patria sunk in Haifa harbor 11-25-1940.

Atlit detainees outside barracks.

Egged bus, circa 1940.

496 Lost and Found

Bombing of Haifa's Port 1941.

Haifa Arab neighborhood near the port, circa 1940.

Haifa—King's Way, circa 1940.

Stella Maris Monastery circa 1900.

Stella Maris Madonna and Child.

Mauritius men's prison interior woodcut by Bada Mayer.

Mauritius men's prison interior.

Mauritius prison entrance.

Mauritius women's quarters.

ACKNOWLEDGMENTS

My first reader—when the novel was only a very long short story—was my husband, David, who encouraged me in more ways than I can recount to keep writing. My mother read the first draft and, when she said "But, Racheli, I was on the *Atlantic*, not you," I knew I had captured her experience and, in an indirect way, her voice. She also corrected all my German phrases.

Early readers were vital for my progress, whether stellar literary scholars, namely, Robert Alter, Chana Kronfeld, and Naomi Seidman, or dear friends who are discerning readers: Carol Cosman z"l, Marcia Freedman z"l, Sara Bolder, Diane Wolf, Sue Fishkoff, and Jill and Martin Dodd. My children, Noam and Tali Biale, managed to combine their love and amused appreciation of their sometimes-quirky mother, with extremely sharp-eyed editorial suggestions.

Noha Radwan, Muhammad Siddiq, and Lena Salaymeh, scholars of Palestinian society and literature, graciously reviewed the work for the accuracy and cultural authenticity of the sections about Youssra and Moussa. Sister Marianne Farina provided insights into monastic life. Wendy Ferris showed me how to trim twenty percent of the text without removing an ounce of essential information.

Joan Von Kaschnitz assisted me by translating documents written in German by the leaders of the detainees in Mauritius.